THE Scent OF Lilacs

THE Scent OF Lilacs

ANN H. GABHART

Revell
Grand Rapids, Michigan

© 2005 by Ann H. Gabhart

Published by Fleming H. Revell
a division of Baker Publishing Group
P.O. Box 6287, Grand Rapids, MI 49516-6287

Second printing, November 2005

Printed in the United States of America

Library of Congress Cataloging-in-Publication Data
Gabhart, Ann.
    The scent of lilacs / Ann H. Gabhart.
        p.   cm.
    ISBN 0-8007-3080-1 (pbk.)
    1. Clergy—Fiction. 2. Children of clergy—Fiction. 3. Fathers and daugh-
ters—Fiction. I. Title.
PS3607.A23S28 2005
813'.6—dc22   2004029366

Scripture is taken from the King James Version of the Bible.

To my mother, who has always believed.

ome days David Brooke didn't know whether to count his blessings or to hide from them.

He'd come home early from the newspaper office, since June was settling into the summer of 1964 like an old hen spreading out her wings and plopping down in a puddle of dust for a good rest. The Hollyhill schools were out till September, so there weren't any PTA open houses or 4-H Club award meetings to cover. The biggest story he'd been able to dig up for this week's issue was Omer Carlton's Holstein cow having twins, and he'd already been out to take pictures of Omer's little girl Cindy bottle-feeding the black-and-white calves. He'd told Wes to blow up the picture and put it on the front page. Baby animals and a freckle-faced kid ought to move a few dozen extra papers off the store counters this week.

Sometimes it might be nice, or at least interesting, to have some real news to fill up the pages of the *Hollyhill Banner*, but real news often as not meant something bad happening. So dull and peaceful could be a blessing. For one thing, not having to put in a full Saturday at the newspaper gave him extra time to work on his sermon for Sunday. And he needed to have a good one tomorrow for the Mt. Pleasant Church if he had any hope of them voting him in as interim pastor.

After all, preaching was his first calling. The paper was just a sideline to put meat on the table. He didn't have to worry about the vegetables this time of the year, when everybody and his brother was anxious to give away beans, zucchini, and cabbage, much to Jocie's distress.

"Why can't they have an overabundance of strawberries or raspberries?" she'd asked last night when faced with yet another bowl of stewed cabbage.

"In everything give thanks," Aunt Love had told Jocie. "Some children don't have enough to eat."

David had held his breath waiting for the explosion, but Jocie had just mumbled, "I could be just as thankful for strawberries."

Jocie was thirteen, barely out of babyhood to David but almost grown to Jocie. Aunt Love was seventy-eight, one foot in the grave to Jocie and of an age to demand respect to David. Jocie and Aunt Love coexisted under a David-negotiated truce most of the time. It didn't help matters that Aunt Love had been misplacing more and more of her mind lately, but she never had any problem pulling out appropriate Bible verses to attempt to whip Jocie into line.

It hadn't changed Jocie's behavior much, but it had improved her Bible study, since she kept trying to prove Aunt Love was making up some of the verses. So far Jocie hadn't caught Aunt Love in anything worse than "Cleanliness is next to godliness," and Aunt Love said she'd never claimed that was in the Bible but that plenty of folks might agree it should be.

But now from the shouts—or, dear God, surely that wasn't howls—beating their way over the sound of the oscillating fan ruffling the papers on the desk in the corner of his bedroom, it sounded as if the truce had ended and active warfare had broken out. David read one more verse from his Bible just in case it might offer a bit of inspirational help before he pushed back from his desk. "Happy is the man that findeth wisdom." Even King Solomon couldn't make Jocie and Aunt Love see eye to eye.

By the time David got to the bottom of the stairs, the war

had escalated. Aunt Love was quoting Scripture in a string. Her cat, Sugar, was screeching. Jocie was shouting over the sound of barking. Great, tremendous barks barreled through the screen door and bounced off the wall behind David.

David's spirits sank lower. They didn't have a dog. Jocie had been throwing in a "Please, Lord, send me a dog" when she said grace before supper, but David had been hoping the Lord would just hear the "Thank you for our food" and skip over the dog part.

Not because he minded having a dog around the place. He liked dogs, but he could still see Jocie's face after their last dog had run out in front of a car. Jocie had stopped eating, stopped talking, stopped smiling for way too long. David knew it wasn't just Stumpy getting killed that had pierced her heart. The dog had died just over a month after Adrienne had taken Tabitha and disappeared into the night.

How long ago was that now? It always amazed him that he had to think about it. Surely he'd know to the day, hour, and minute how long ago his wife had driven away from Hollyhill and him. He shouldn't have been surprised. She'd warned him plenty of times. But he had been surprised. Worse than surprised. Shocked. Devastated. Lost. Injured. All that and more. Some things couldn't be described with words. Those kinds of things clunked you right in the heart and sent you reeling.

And worse, she'd taken Tabitha. Tabitha, who had still been sleeping with a teddy bear by night and begging him to wear lipstick by day. He still didn't know why Adrienne had taken her. A parting shot perhaps. A way to make sure the wound of her destroying their family had no chance of healing. A man might get over losing a wife but never losing a daughter.

How long? Tabitha had been thirteen, and Jocie was thirteen now. Seven years. Tabitha would be turning twenty on her birthday next month. He wondered if she would have a cake. Tabitha used to love to blow out the candles and make wishes. She always said why just one wish? Why not as many wishes as candles? He should have gone after her so he could make sure she had cakes.

David shoved the memories aside and stepped out on the porch. "What in the name of Methuselah is going on out here?"

ocie found the dog over in Johnson Woods. The woods had been owned by Jocie's grandparents before her grandfather died, and Jocie figured that ought to give her walking-on privileges without having to ask anybody's permission. She just hid her bike behind some yellowwood bushes and disappeared into the trees. She'd walked there so much that she felt as if the woods were hers, something her grandfather had passed down to her, even if he had died before she was born.

It was a great place. Huge maple and oak and hickory trees. Ferns and wildflowers. Tarzan grapevines. Devil's puffballs. Wild raspberries and blackberries. Birds and squirrels. She kept a journal of the things she found there. But she'd never found a dog until today.

Or she supposed it was more accurate—and her father said it was always good to strive for accuracy in any story—to say the dog found her. He just appeared behind her as she was heading back to the road to get her bike. She'd heard rustling noises among the trees while she'd been walking, but there were always birds in the bushes or rabbits and chipmunks scurrying for cover. And once she'd scared up a deer. The first one she'd ever seen. Her father had said she should have been carrying her camera, that a picture of a real live deer in Holly County would have been front page news. Even without the picture, he'd published an article about

11

how the wildlife agencies were bringing in deer from out west in an attempt to repopulate the area.

She stopped. The dog stopped. She looked at the dog. The dog sat down and looked at her. He didn't wag his tail. He pulled his tongue in, closed his mouth, and cocked his head to the side as if he needed to listen closely to what she might have to say.

"You need to go on home, dog." She didn't say it real loud, but she did say it. She even shooed him away with her hands. "Now, go on. Get on home."

The dog stood up and walked right up to her. He was some kind of shepherd beagle mix. Not a particularly good combination. One ear poked up straight and the other drooped over. His nose was too long, and his coat was the gray-purple color of watercolor-paint water with a few darker splotches here and there that could be dirt. She smiled at the way just the tip of his tail clicked back and forth in a cocky little wag. He didn't care if he was ugly. He was a dog, and a dog needed a person. His brown-black eyes said Jocie was it.

"I told you to go on home," Jocie said, her voice barely above a whisper.

The dog picked up a paw and held it out toward her. Jocie had been told a thousand times not to pet strange dogs. She had a couple of scars to prove it was good advice, and her Aunt Love was always going on about rabies. But this dog didn't have any foam around his mouth. He just wanted to shake hands.

The hair on his head was spiky and rough, but his ears were silky soft. The rest of his tail joined in with the tip as it flapped back and forth when she scratched him under the chin. "What's your name, dog?" Jocie asked.

The dog didn't have a collar and no sign he'd ever worn a collar. His ribs were poking out on both sides as if it had been a while since his last meal. Maybe he didn't have a home, and hadn't she been praying for a dog for about a year now? Aunt Love was always saying God answered prayers in his own time. Did she dare hope this was God's time? That he'd plucked her dog prayer out of the great sea of prayers offered up to him every day as the one to answer? That thought made Jocie feel a little guilty, since she knew a lot of those prayers were for sick people getting well or lost people getting saved. Still, she'd never read anything in the Bible that said you couldn't pray for a dog.

"It was nice meeting you, dog," Jocie said, determined to make the dog do the deciding about following her home. "But now I've got to go home, and you've got to go home, okay?"

The dog sat down and swept the grass behind him with his tail. He stared straight at her, pulled his tongue inside his mouth, and bared his teeth in a doggy grin.

Jocie couldn't keep from laughing. "You are without a doubt the ugliest dog I've ever seen, but I didn't tell God I wanted a pretty dog or even a cute dog. Just a dog, and you are a dog." Jocie stared at him. "I think."

The dog stood up and trotted ahead of her. For a minute Jocie was afraid he'd just remembered where home was, but then he stopped and sat down beside her bike as if to say, "Let's get on with it. It's going on supper time."

Jocie didn't try to chase him off after that. She didn't try to get him to follow her either. She had that line practiced out for her father. She got on her bike and started pedaling. She didn't look back even once to see if the dog was following. It was a test. Like Gideon and the wool with dew on it or not on it to prove God really was talking to him in the Bible. She decided if she got to the barn this side of the house and looked back and the dog was still there, then he was hers. She really wanted to look back when she passed by the Wilsons' house, but she kept her eyes on the road in front of her. It would be cheating to look back before she got to the barn.

Just in case the dog was still chasing after her bike, she began making up reasons they needed a dog. He could be a watchdog to let them know when people were coming. Maybe in time to lock the gate if the people were carrying sacks of zucchini or cabbage. Her dad could try out his sermons on the dog instead of on Jocie. Taking care of a dog would teach her responsibility, since she'd have to feed him and brush him and stuff. That should please even Aunt Love—the more responsible part. The dog could be somebody she could talk to who wouldn't come up with Bible verses for answers. Aunt Love had to have the whole Bible memorized. No wonder she couldn't remember to turn off the soup anymore. All the Scripture she had stored up there in her head didn't leave any room for anything else.

Jocie didn't come up with a name for the dog until she slid off her bike in front of the porch and the dog started barking at Jezebel. Great tremendous barks. Thunderous barks. Zebedee.

"Zebedee," she yelled. The dog quit barking long enough to look over at her and give her that stupid doggy grin again. More reasons she could add to why they had to keep him. He had a name. And how could you not keep a dog who kept grinning at you?

Jezebel jumped up on the porch railing and yowled. Aunt Love came outside and grabbed the broom they kept by the door to sweep stray leaves off the porch. She waved it menacingly at Zebedee. "Get that mangy excuse for a dog away from Sugar."

Aunt Love called Jezebel Sugar, but in spite of the fact that Jezebel's fur was white like sugar, there was nothing sweet about her. Her cat heart was black. Definitely a Jezebel. She lived to pounce out of the shadows at Jocie's ankles at the top of the stairs. Her bed of choice was Jocie's favorite navy blue shirt. She threw up hairballs in the middle of Jocie's bed. Worst of all, if Jocie ever had a weak moment and tried to make friends, Jezzie would pretend to want Jocie to rub her before swiping at Jocie's hand as soon as it was close enough. The cat never pulled in her claws.

So when Jocie yelled at Zebedee again, it wasn't to save the cat. It was to save the dog. But it was too late. Still barking, Zebedee put his front paws on the railing under the cat and got too close. Jezebel landed a quick swipe across the dog's nose. Beads of blood popped out.

Jocie winced and grabbed for the dog at the same moment that Aunt Love swung the broom. Jocie got a face full of broom straw and landed in the striped grass beside the steps. She tried to pull the dog with her, but Zebedee wriggled free and ran back over to the railing under the cat, who was swishing her tail and licking her paws in victory.

The front door opened, and Jocie's dad stepped out on the porch to join in the fray. He yelled something, and Aunt Love quit swinging the broom and leaned on its handle as she clutched her chest. Jocie wasn't worried. Aunt Love clutched her chest a lot.

Jocie scrambled out of the striped grass and went after Zebedee again. The dog had quit barking. Instead, he was studying Jezebel with the same assessing look he'd given Jocie out in the woods, but his tail was as still as a stone. When Jocie started to grab for the dog, Zebedee turned his bloody nose toward her and slid his lips back in another grin as if to say, "Let me take care of this."

Jocie froze in midgrab.

The dog turned back to the cat, let out one thunderous bark that made the porch windows rattle, leaped straight up like a kangaroo, and popped Jezebel with his nose. Jezebel went flying off the rail and barely had time to get her feet under her before she splattered on the wooden porch.

Aunt Love turned loose of her chest and threw the broom at the dog. The dog jumped nimbly out of the way, then sniffed the broom before he trotted over to Jocie. Jezebel, her belly brushing the porch, slunk to the door, where Aunt Love scooped her up and disappeared inside with a muttered, "That mongrel digs up the first flower, I'll shoot him myself."

Jocie pulled Zebedee out of the flower bed next to the porch and stared him straight in the eye. "Bad dog," she said.

"Try not smiling while you say it," her father said as he sank down on the porch steps. He looked up a moment as if he were checking the sky for some kind of message from God. Then he looked back at the dog and said, "Okay, let's hear it."

"His name's Zebedee."

"He told you that, I guess."

"No, of course not. He can't talk. At least he hasn't yet, but you heard him barking. Definitely thunderous. You know, your sermon about James and John last month."

"Ah, sons of thunder."

"Zebedee. Zeb for short."

"Hold on. Let's not get carried away," her father said as he stared at the dog, who sat in front of him politely listening to every word. "He may belong to somebody else."

Jocie stroked the dog's head. "Does he look like he belongs to anybody?"

"No, he looks like the kind of dog nobody would want."

"He'll look better after I give him a bath and some food." At the word *food*, Zeb wagged his tail. "He may not be very pretty, but he's real smart. You saw how he handled Jezebel."

"The cat's name is Sugar," her father said.

"You call her what you want to, and I'll call her what she is," Jocie said. "I mean, Jezzie's pretty, but who cares about pretty? Smart's better."

Her father laughed, and Jocie knew she had him. But just to be sure, she threw out some of her practiced reasons to keep the dog. Zebedee used some of his brains and held his paw out to her father.

"You're always saying the Bible says to ask, and I've been asking. So maybe God sent him to me," Jocie said.

3

That night at supper, David tried to summon up a thankful heart to add to Jocie's as she said grace. The Bible taught to be thankful in all things, and he supposed that could apply to what was surely the ugliest stray dog in the county, maybe the state. The dog had latched onto Jocie as if she'd raised him from a pup instead of just finding him in the woods a few hours ago. Even now he had his nose up against the screen on the back door, his eyes locked on Jocie and his ears cocked almost as if he knew what she was saying. David wouldn't have been surprised to hear an amen woof.

Jocie asked the usual blessings on the food before saying, "Thank you, Lord, for Zebedee. I'd begun to worry you didn't mean for me to have a dog, but Aunt Love says the Bible says to keep asking, so that's what I did. And I thank you that you let Zebedee find me."

David heard Aunt Love pull in a little puff of breath and knew her heart wasn't feeling a bit thankful. She'd hardly been able to put supper on the table for worrying about her cat. After the confrontation on the porch, Sugar had ensconced herself on the top shelf of the bookcase in the living room and had snarled at anyone who came close, even Aunt Love.

17

Jocie was still praying. "I promise to take good care of him. And, Lord, please give Daddy a good message for the people at Mt. Pleasant in the morning, and watch over Tabitha wherever she is. Amen."

"Amen," David repeated after her.

Aunt Love unfolded her napkin and spread it across her lap. No amen passed her lips. Aunt Love had been living with them ever since his mother had died four years ago—another time Jocie had been on the front lines for heartbreak. One late fall day he'd come home from the paper to find Jocie sitting beside his mother's body in the freshly dug tulip bed. Tears were making dirty tracks down Jocie's cheeks and dropping on her grandmother's hands.

David had dropped down beside them in the dirt and cried like a baby. That had scared Jocie more than finding her grandmother dead among the tulip bulbs, but he couldn't help it. He'd felt as if God had reached down and poked him right in the nose to see if he could get up off the ground one more time. And he'd wanted to stay down.

Jocie had hugged and patted him, but that had made him wail louder. Finally she'd jumped on her bike and pedaled the two miles to town to get Wes out of the pressroom. Wes, who had never darkened the door of a Hollyhill church in the ten years he'd known him, had gotten David back on his feet that night before darkness fell over the farm and his soul.

Wes had listened to his story and then said, "It ain't God knocking you down, son. It's life. God's right here beside us, taking hold of your hand to pull you up." Wes had leaned down close to his face and almost whispered, "You take a look at this child here and tell me that ain't so."

David had listened to Wes, because if anybody knew about life knocking a person flat, it was Wes. David had let Wes and Jocie pull him up and had gone about doing what had to be done. By the time the funeral was over three days later, he'd even been able to tell Jocie God must have needed help with the tulip planting in heaven.

But they'd needed help too. At the time, he'd thought Aunt Love would be able to step in where his mother had stepped out and help him make a home for Jocie. But Aunt Love had never had children, never been married. Sometimes he wondered if she could even remember being a child. She could cook, or at least she had been able to when she first came to live with them. Now she tended to let things burn or to forget whether she'd already added salt to the stew. Still, he didn't regret giving her a home. She'd needed a place, and they'd needed family.

Aunt Love smoothed down the lace collar on her dark purple dress and passed David the new potatoes boiled in their skins, a gift from Matt McDermott, one of the deacons at Mt. Pleasant. He figured he had the McDermott family's vote on the interim job even before they heard his sermon in the morning. Last week they had brought him cabbage and broccoli. He wondered when their tomatoes would start getting ripe. Even Jocie liked tomatoes.

"What are you preaching on tomorrow morning?" Aunt Love asked him.

"The Lord hasn't laid a sure message on my heart as yet."

"Well, don't you think it's high time he did? The vote's tomorrow night."

"I'm not worrying about the vote." David felt guilty as the lie passed his lips, so he added, "Well, not overly much anyway. If the Lord wants me to serve there, he'll give me the vote."

"If they had any sense, they'd offer you the job full-time," Aunt Love said.

Jocie looked up from her potatoes. "Why don't they call you as their regular pastor, Daddy? I hear them telling you they like your sermon on the way out every week. That must mean they like you."

David put his fork down. "Church people think they have to say that to preachers. Even when they sleep through the sermon. But even if they really do like my sermons, there's more to leading a church than preaching, Jocie."

"You mean visiting the sick and keeping folks from fussing? You do all that too." Jocie spooned three or four potatoes out on her plate. "Except, of course, at Brown's Chapel, and nobody could have made those people happy."

"That's God's own truth," Aunt Love muttered. "Those people would fight over what color the pulpit Bible should be."

"They had some issues to deal with," David said with a smile.

"When anybody with any sense knows it should be black," Aunt Love went on. "But why don't you tell the child the truth? The reason they won't ask you full-time is because of Adrienne."

"Mother?" Jocie said. "What's she got to do with Dad preaching? She's been gone forever."

"Baptists like their preachers to be married," Aunt Love said. "Catholics won't let their men of the cloth marry, but Baptists figure they need a preacher's wife to cook for church dinners, teach Sunday school, call people, whatever needs doing that the preacher can't get done."

David stared at the potatoes in the middle of a little pool of butter on his plate. He wished Aunt Love hadn't brought up Adrienne, but that was another thing about Aunt Love. She never sugarcoated anything. He decided to be as honest. "Not having a wife isn't exactly the problem. Once having a wife and then not having her anymore is. I'm lucky any of the churches in the county ever let me stand behind their pulpits."

"Luck has nothing to do with it," Aunt Love said. "You're a fine preacher. The best I ever heard, and I've heard plenty."

"And how many would that be?" David asked, trying to shift the talk away from wives, or the lack of them.

"Way more than I could put a name to."

"I'll bet you could count the Sundays you've missed church on one hand." David began eating his potatoes.

"Actually, it would take quite a few hands," Aunt Love said. "When I was a child, we generally had to share a preacher with another congregation, so sometimes we didn't have services every Sunday, unless my father, who was strong on church attendance, led the services when the preacher couldn't be there." Aunt Love frowned a little as she added, "He was a very religious man."

"Mother always said he should have been a preacher. That maybe that's where I got my calling."

"Nonsense," Aunt Love said sharply. "Your calling came from God. Father never had any kind of calling. He just liked to expound on the Scriptures."

"He knew the Bible well."

"So do I, but that doesn't make me a preacher," Aunt Love said.

Jocie's head came up at that remark, but her father gave her a look that made her clamp her lips shut. She couldn't take a chance on getting in trouble until Zeb was a permanent member of the family. Besides, she wasn't all that interested in how much Aunt Love had gone to church anyway. It was obvious she'd gone way too much. And here Jocie was following right in her footsteps, but most of the time she didn't mind.

Church wasn't so bad. The pews got hard sometimes, but she liked the singing and the Bible stories. Miss McMurtry, who taught the intermediate Sunday school class at Mt. Pleasant, was nice enough. She was always giving them chewing gum to give their mouths something to do besides yawn.

Of course, going off to church tomorrow might be hard, what with having to leave Zeb and not being sure if he'd still be on the porch when they finally got to come home after the night service. They always went to somebody's house for Sunday dinner after the morning service. Jocie hoped they had something besides cabbage ready in their garden. Even peas might taste good after all the cabbage.

Then her father would have to go work the church field in the afternoon. Pastors, even the fill-in kind, had to pray over sick church members. It was expected. She wouldn't have a chance of talking her dad out of doing the visits this week. Not with the vote looming. Maybe she could pretend to be sick in the morning, but she'd have to be really throwing up before Aunt Love would fall for that. Maybe she could lock Zeb in the garage while they were gone.

Jocie dipped a couple more potatoes out of the bowl and wondered if she could smuggle them out to Zeb. Aunt Love would never notice. She was still wandering around in the past as she said, "But I can't claim to having gone to church every time the doors were open. Fact is, there was a time I fell away completely, thought I might never pass through a church door again."

"That's hard to believe," David said. "Are you telling us you were a rebellious teenager?"

"I was well past my teen years." Aunt Love pushed her still full plate of food away from her. "A lot of bad things were happening. The First World War. Mother was sick and then passed on. It was a dry year, and the crops just withered in the field. Our old workhorse went lame. Other things. Just didn't have the heart to go to church."

"Did Grandfather quit going too?" David asked.

"Oh, no. Father went." Aunt Love got up from the table and went into the living room to stand at the shelves full of pictures and books. This time the cat gingerly climbed down low enough for Aunt Love to scoop her up. Aunt Love carried the cat down the hall into her room and shut the door.

Jocie looked at her father. "You think she's still that upset about something that happened fifty years ago?"

"It appears so."

"Then she'll never get over Zeb punching Jezzie."

"I don't think Zeb and Jez—I mean Sugar—fighting can compare to the times she's remembering. Your Mama Mae told me one of their brothers died in World War I. That may have been what she was thinking about."

"I guess people never get over losing somebody in their family." Jocie's eyes strayed to a picture of her mother and Tabitha on top of the old upright piano in the living room, but she didn't let her gaze linger there. She felt disloyal to her father when she let herself think about her mother, so she quickly said, "I still miss Mama Mae."

"Of course you do." David's eyes were steady on Jocie. "The same as you miss your mother and Tabitha."

"But they wanted to leave. That's different than Mama Mae. She would have asked God to let her stay with us a few more years like he did Hezekiah in the Bible if she'd had the chance."

"You could be right," David said.

"She probably would even know how to cheer up Aunt Love."

"You might be able to do that yourself."

"Me?" Jocie said. And then she grinned. "Well, I could let Zeb in so she could yell at me and think up some Bible verses. Do you think there's anything in there about dogs? Oh no." Jocie's eyes got big. "What if she remembers about God telling Jezebel the dogs would lick up her blood?"

David laughed. "I think you're safe there. Her cat's name is

Sugar. Something it might be well for you to remember for a few weeks so that particular passage won't come to mind."

"You don't think God will want you to preach on that tomorrow, do you?"

"No. I'm leaning toward Jesus feeding the five thousand."

"Oh, that's good. That should be a vote getter."

"I'm not running for preacher, Jocie."

"Same thing as. You have to get the votes."

"Well, we can hope for divine guidance rather than politics when the votes are cast."

"I don't get to vote, do I?"

"Of course not. You're not a member of Mt. Pleasant Church."

"But I am a member of the church, and if they call you there, we'll be changing our memberships, won't we? I could change it tomorrow morning and slip in under the wire in time to vote."

"You don't get to vote." David took hold of Jocie's arm as she began gathering up the plates to carry to the sink. "You don't even get to say anything. Is that clear?"

"Yes, Dad. I know. Nobody wants to hear what a kid thinks." Jocie had gotten into trouble at one of the churches where her father had filled in for the regular pastor who'd had the flu. They'd had this meeting and were discussing ways to get young people interested in church. All she'd done was suggest having a dance. And then after the chairman of the deacons had turned beet red and begun sputtering, you'd have thought she'd thrown gasoline on the flames when she pointed out that King David had danced all the way to Jerusalem in front of the ark of the covenant.

Her father pulled her closer and kissed her cheek. "Well, not exactly nobody. I do. You can tell me what you think anytime. If it's good enough I might even put it in the paper. Or who knows? In a sermon."

Jocie leaned her head on her father's shoulder. "How old is Tabitha now, Daddy?"

"She was thirteen when she left."

"My age."

"That's right. Your age. That means she'd be nineteen now. Twenty on her birthday in July."

"Wouldn't it be fun if she came home for her birthday this year?"

Her father's arm tightened around her waist as he said, "Maybe we could have a party for her whether she's here or not, and then you could write her about it. I'll bet she'd like that."

"What was her favorite kind of cake?"

"Chocolate. Your grandmother always made her a chocolate cake with chocolate icing and pink and white candles."

"Uh-oh. The last time I made a chocolate cake it turned out like rubber."

"Practice makes perfect."

"We'd better buy a mix," Jocie said. "Maybe you could write to her and tell her about the party. Maybe send her some money. I mean, when you get this preaching job at Mt. Pleasant, we'll have some extra coming in, and we won't have to buy hardly any groceries all summer with the way the people out there like to grow vegetables. She sometimes asks you for money to come home to visit when she writes, doesn't she?"

"But she never comes," her father pointed out. "I think it's just their way of getting a little extra money."

"But you always send the money just in case." Jocie watched her father nod his head. "Has she written lately?"

"Not for months. My last letter came back, so they must have moved again."

"Where was she?"

"Los Angeles the last time she wrote. She had a boyfriend."

"Like Mama."

25

"I don't want to talk about your mother's boyfriend."

"Sorry." Jocie straightened up and began to stack the dishes again. "What's it like in California? Were you ever there?"

"Once, when I was in the navy headed toward the Philippines. It rained the whole time I was there, but it was warm. They said it was really sunny and nice to the south. The whole place was sort of crazy then with the war and everything. Everybody was in a frenzy thinking the Japanese might invade any day. It was a lot different from here."

"Did you wish you could stay?"

"Never. From the day I went into the navy all I wanted was to get back home. I joined the navy to see the world, but I never saw a place I liked better than here. Of course, most of the time I was down below in a submarine and not seeing much of anything."

"Do you think Tabitha likes it out there?"

"She said she did when she wrote last time."

"Wes says it's still sort of crazy out there. With hippies and everything. Do you think Tabitha's a hippie?"

"I hope not."

Her father frowned, and Jocie remembered Wes saying no father would want his daughter to be a hippie. "Still, no matter if she did like it there, she might come for a visit." Jocie scraped the leftovers out into an old pan. She could see Zeb at the door, his tongue hanging out at the smell of the food. "I mean, I've been praying about Tabitha coming home even longer than I've been praying for a dog, and the Lord sent Zebedee."

"We're not all that sure that Zebedee doesn't belong to somebody else."

"I'm sure," Jocie said. "Do you think I should put him in the garage when we go to church tomorrow?"

"No. If he's going to be your dog, he'll stay."

"But what if he doesn't?"

"Then we'll find you another dog if you want one so bad."

"I don't want any dog now. I want Zebedee."

"Then maybe he'll stay. He's been sitting at the door waiting for you to get through with supper for about an hour now. Go on and take him for a walk or something." Her father gave her a little push. "You can wash the dishes later."

4

Jocie dumped the scraps out on the wide, flat rock that served as a bottom step off the back porch. Zeb ate them all, even the stinky cabbage, and then licked the rock until not even the smell of food could have remained.

Before supper, the dog had endured a dunking in the old washtub as if he knew there was a price to pay for the biscuits she'd given him. The soap and water had lightened the gray of his coat, but the dirty-looking spots hadn't disappeared even though she'd scrubbed until Zeb had yelped and poked her hand with his nose.

"Sorry, Zeb." Jocie had hugged the wet dog.

Now she ran her hand over the spots on his sides. Already, with just two feedings, his ribs were sinking back under his skin. "You know, those look a little like storm clouds. So you not only bark like thunder, you carry a storm along with you."

The dog sat up on his hind legs and put his front paws together. "No, no, Zeb. You're supposed to say grace before you eat, not after."

The dog dropped back down on all fours and grinned at her.

"I can't wait for Wes to see you. How about we go right now? Dad will be deep in the Scripture, and who knows when Aunt Love and Jezebel will come out of hiding."

Zeb cocked his head and stopped smiling.

"Oh, don't look so worried. We won't get into trouble. We'll be home before anybody even knows we're gone. But if it makes you feel better, I'll leave a note on the table. Nobody will see it, but I can still leave it there."

Jocie ran back inside, dropped the pan in the sink, scribbled out a note, and then went to get a piece of rope from the garage. When Zeb saw the rope, he scooted just out of her reach.

"But something might happen to you in town," she said.

The dog stared warily at her and moved back a few more steps.

"Okay, but you've got to promise not to get in trouble." Jocie stuck the rope in her pocket, and Zeb stood up on his hind legs and did a circle. Jocie laughed. "You must have escaped from the circus."

Normally she didn't pay the first bit of attention to cars when she was on her bike, but now she had Zeb. Dogs regularly got done in by cars. Her last dog had met that fate. Right in front of their house. She still sometimes cried when she thought about Stumpy even though he'd been gone for years. Now every time she heard a car coming, her heart jumped up in her throat, but Zeb seemed to be road smart and stayed out of the way when cars passed by.

The big old motorcycle was in its usual spot behind the news office. That meant Wes was home in his apartment upstairs. Her dad was always telling her Wes might be busy or something and she shouldn't just show up at his door, but Wes didn't have a phone. So how else could she find out if he was home except to knock on his door? And he always looked glad to see her.

Wes wasn't your average Hollyhiller, maybe because he hadn't been born there like most of the people in Hollyhill. He was what the locals called a "foreigner." She didn't know where he came from. Not really.

When she asked, he always trotted out this crazy tall tale about being from Jupiter. His story was that he fell out of a spaceship as it was passing over Hollyhill, of all the rotten luck. Every time he told the story, he picked a different place to want to be dropped—a spewed-out volcano in Hawaii, the middle of a kangaroo herd in the Australian outback, Disneyland in California. But no, he got Hollyhill in the middle of nowhere. Somebody forgot to turn on the magnetic seal, and when they went over an air bump, he fell against the door, and here he was. He was just hanging around till his fellow Jupiterians found the way back to pick him up.

"But what about the motorcycle?" Jocie sometimes asked when he told her his story, not because she believed him but because she liked hearing him embellish the tale. "Dad said you were riding it when you showed up at the paper that first morning looking for a job. Did you steal it from somebody?"

"Oh, no. We can't steal. Folks from Jupiter can't even lie. If we try it, purple spots pop out on our faces. But Jupiterians who cruise the galaxy are supplied with a few buttons in our pockets that we can push to help us out when things go bad. We don't have many. Usually just three—sort of like the wishes a genie might give you if you rubbed his lamp. Except with these buttons you can't pick what you wish. Jackson Jupiter—he's the one who runs the planet up there—he thinks he knows what you need better than you do, and he just sort of supplies. So I pushed a button, and violà, he put me in old blue jeans and a leather jacket and plopped me astride that old motorcycle. I haven't ever needed to punch the other two buttons."

"Why not?"

"Well, I liked the motorcycle, and I didn't want to take the chance that Mr. Jupiter might take it away if he sent me something new."

When Jocie was younger, she used to pester him to show her the magic buttons, but he had told her it was too dangerous to have them lying around where somebody might touch them by accident. Mr. Jupiter might turn him into a cow just for the fun of it, and then he wouldn't even be able to push the last button. Cows not only weren't that smart, they didn't have fingers.

When Jocie had laughed and said that could never happen, Wes had said, "What about that Bible guy Nebuchadnezzar? He was a king and then had to eat grass for a few years before the Lord decided he'd learned his lesson, took pity on him, and made him back into a king. But old Jackson Jupiter, he likes his jokes, and I might just end up eating grass from now on."

Wes could always make Jocie laugh even when he never cracked a smile. "That's not really in the Bible," Jocie had said. "You're making that up."

"Ask your daddy if you don't believe me. At any rate, those extra buttons are hid away good. So good I doubt if even I could find them."

She had asked her father, and he'd told her Nebuchadnezzar's story, had even preached on it a few weeks later, but the story had sounded different when her father told it. More biblical and full of lessons to be learned. When she'd told Wes that, he'd said, "I ain't never claimed to be a preacher. I just told the story the way I heard it."

"Who'd you hear it from up on Jupiter?"

"I didn't say I heard it up there. It was when I was on that flying saucer going over all the churches on Sunday mornings. Our supersensors would pick up the preaching, and that's where I learned most of my Bible. That and your daddy practicing his sermons while we're putting the paper to bed."

"Why don't you come to church with us and listen to him there?" Jocie found a way to ask Wes to come to church two or three times a month. Her daddy was always telling people they needed to be in church, and she worried about Wes not going ever. She'd asked him again just a few weeks ago as they worked in the pressroom cleaning the type.

He'd given her his usual excuse. "Now, what good Hollyhill

31

Baptist would want a Jupiterian plopping down on the pew beside him? I think they have a rule against aliens. Especially one with black fingers." Wes had held up his ink-stained hands.

"Aunt Love says anybody can come up with an excuse not to go to church when they want to. It's too hot. It's too cold. It's too windy. The pews are too hard. Whatever."

"Dirty fingernails ain't an excuse. They're a reason. I tell you what. If I wake up one Sunday morning and by some miracle the black is gone from under my fingernails, this old alien might just try the fit in a church pew." Wes had grinned and added, "If it's not too hot, that is."

"I don't think it matters if you have inky hands or not." Jocie had held up her own black-tinged hands.

"Is that a fact?" Wes had laughed at her. "You're probably right, but the truth is, I get enough religion listening to you and your daddy without having to involve too much soap and water."

"Me? I don't preach."

"No, I reckon not. But you do seem to be full up with questions now and again."

"Daddy says you have to ask stuff if you want to find out anything," Jocie had said. "And he says something the same about praying. He says the Bible tells us to ask and to keep asking, but sometimes it seems like the Lord would get tired of listening to the same thing every night and day. 'Thank you for my food.' 'Let the folks at the Mt. Pleasant Church plant something besides cabbage.' 'Keep me from sinning.' 'Help me do good in school.'"

"What about the sister prayer or the dog prayer? You still sending them up?"

Jocie had nodded. "But sometimes I don't think God is listening." Jocie had slapped her hand over her mouth, leaving a smudge of ink on her cheek. "I shouldn't have said that."

"You can't say anything to shock an old alien like me, kiddo, and fact is, I figure God has heard just about everything before now too. And who knows? Maybe you'll get an answer one of these days."

Jocie ran up the steps to the apartment with Zeb on her heels. She couldn't wait to see Wes's face when he saw how the Lord had answered her dog prayer. As she knocked on the door, she felt a flicker of guilt that this was the prayer God had answered instead of the sister prayer. But she'd asked for them both equally fervently. God had picked which one he wanted to answer first.

Wes opened the door. The smell of hamburger grease spilled out from behind him. "Well if it ain't Jocelyn come to see if I got any frenchy fried potatoes left over from my supper."

"Yum, and I bet Zebedee here would dance for a hamburger crumble." Jocie moved aside so Wes could see the dog. Zeb stared at Wes with wary eyes and then suddenly sat up on his back legs and let out a howl.

Wes peered out at the dog. "Holy moly, is that you, Harlan?"

5

Jocie's heart jumped up in her throat. "You know him?"

"I believe I do. The old home ship must have been coming back for me and hit another air bump, because this is a Jupiter dog if I've ever seen one."

Jocie was able to breath again. "You had dogs in your spaceship?"

"Oh, no. No dogs. The mission was much too dangerous for dogs, but I think this is Harlan."

"Harlan?"

"One of my fellow Jupiterians. He must have fallen out of the spaceship just like me and punched one of his buttons, and Mr. Jupiter decided he could best hide out as a dog." Wes stepped out onto the little porch at the top of the stairs. Wes was short, not much taller than Jocie, and bent in the shoulders from years of working on machinery in the pressroom. His thin gray hair was in its usual state of disarray, and he ran his hand through it as he gave the dog the once-over. "I have never felt so lucky in my life as I feel right this minute. Mr. Jupiter could have made me a dog instead of a beatnik on a motorcycle."

"You're crazy, Wes," Jocie said with a laugh. "This isn't Harlan. It's Zebedee."

"Harlan never much liked his name. He won't mind that you changed it. Zebedee, you say."

"You should hear him bark. Sounds like thunder. He took

on Jezebel the witch cat as soon as he came to the house, and he won."

"Beat up old Jezebel? It's a wonder your Aunt Love didn't shoot him."

"She's not happy, but when the Lord answers a prayer, you can't be chasing the answer off, now can you?"

"Your father's always saying the Lord works in mysterious ways." Wes pointed at the dog's back. "He hasn't been rolling in cow piles, now has he?"

"No, those spots are just him."

"Yep, Jupiterian dogs are all ugly as sin." Wes laughed. "Poor old Harlan. Well as I remember, he never even liked dogs."

"Did you?"

"Sure. I always thought the dogs on Jupiter were smarter than the people." Wes stood up and motioned them inside. "Come on in, and you can tell me all about him, since it looks like Harlan ain't talking."

"He hasn't yet." Jocie and Zeb followed Wes into the apartment. "Do dogs on Jupiter talk?"

"Not often. Maybe once or twice in a lifetime."

"What do they say?"

"It would surprise you. You'd think it would be something Jupiter shaking, but it's usually something as common as 'Where's the nearest tree?' or 'Pardon me, but I think you're standing on my tail.'" Wes grinned and touched Zeb's head. "Jupiterian dogs are always polite. Unlike Jupiterian people, who are notoriously rude, so I don't know what you'll get with Harlan-turned-Zebedee here."

"He hasn't bitten anyone. Just bonked old Jezebel." Jocie moved a stack of books off one of the chairs in the apartment and sat them on the floor.

Wes didn't waste any more time on housekeeping than he did on scrubbing the black out from under his fingernails. He said dust bunnies just ran behind curtains and under shelves till you put the broom away and then scooted right back out again, and he had better things to do than play hide-and-seek with dust bunnies. He, being from Jupiter and all, was way behind on his Earth reading. He read anything and everything from cowboy novels to biographies to science fiction. He said the science fiction writers got mostly everything about spaceships and outer space totally wrong, and someday he might write an Earth book to let the people down here in on some secrets about the universe.

Every once in a while when the books were on the verge of taking over all the space in the apartment, he'd cram them into boxes and carry them down to donate to the town library. Half the books in the Hollyhill Library had "Donated by Wesley Green" in the front of them.

Jocie didn't see any open books waiting for Wes, so she said, "Did we come at a bad time? Were you getting ready to go out?"

"Out? Where's there to go out to in Hollyhill?" Wes pulled a scrap of bread out of the trash can and rubbed it around the skillet still sitting on the hot plate that served as his stove. He offered it to Zeb, who politely took it between his teeth and then carefully held it in his mouth a moment before swallowing.

"I swear, for a second there I thought he was going to do like that cartoon dog that floats up in the air with his toes twirling after he has a doggy treat," Wes said.

"I think he hadn't found anything to eat for a while."

"Probably too slow to catch mice and too squeamish to eat possums squashed on the side of the road." Wes passed her a paper plate with some soggy french fries. Jocie covered the fries with a generous layer of salt and ate them with her fingers. She fed three of them to Zeb.

"Daddy says I shouldn't just pop in on you. He says you might have a date or something."

"A date with destiny? I already had that years ago."

"No, silly. With a girl."

"Your dad's the one who needs to be having a date with a girl. All my girls are up on Jupiter, but your dad could snap his fingers and have five running after him."

Jocie let Zeb lick the grease off her fingers. She used to wonder what it might be like having a mother in the house instead of just Aunt Love. Her friends' mothers were always making cookies or cleaning something or fussing about somebody making a mess. Jocie couldn't remember her own mother ever doing anything like that. She had tried once to remember her mother wearing an apron or telling her to pick up her toys, but if it had ever happened she couldn't recall it. What she could remember was her mother putting on makeup and getting dressed up. She could still call up the exotic smell of her mother's perfume and the cool touch of her mother's fingers when she'd dab a touch of it behind Jocie's ears if Jocie pestered her enough. She had always seemed to be going somewhere.

"I have a hard enough time getting along with Aunt Love," Jocie told Wes. "Now here you are pushing stepmothers at me."

"You've read too many fairy tales. A stepmother might be the very thing to keep you straight."

"Dad keeps me straight already." Jocie shifted in her chair. She liked Wes talking to her as if she was a grown-up most of the time, but sometimes he made her think about things she'd rather forget.

"Your father don't know where you are half the time. I'll bet he don't know where you are right now."

"I left him a note, but he won't read it. He's holed up in his room trying to come up with the sermon of the year."

"Oh yeah, the good people out there are voting tomorrow," Wes said. "But that's where a stepmother would come in handy. And I think we've got a candidate."

"A candidate? Who?" Jocie asked.

"That Leigh Jacobson who works down at the courthouse. Ain't you noticed how she keeps dropping by the paper to bring this or that notice for publication? I figure she's coming by to get a glimpse of a certain somebody."

"Maybe it's you she's stuck on."

"Well, I thought so too at first, but I asked her to take a spin on my bike, and she turned white as blank newsprint. But I've noticed she always gets a nice rosy hue when your daddy's around."

"Leigh Jacobson at the clerk's office?" Jocie made a face. "She's sort of fat, isn't she?"

"I heard her telling Zella that she's dieting. Already lost ten pounds. Besides, a woman with a little weight on her might be a good cook."

"I don't think we should pick out a girlfriend for Dad by how she can cook. He might have other ideas of what to look for."

"Cooking is a big plus." Wes waved his hand at his hot plate. "A man gets tired of beans and burgers after a while. And besides, Leigh's a nice girl. That's what your daddy needs. Somebody nice who can take care of him and make him happy."

"And keep me straight," Jocie said.

"Well, that might be too much to expect. Especially now that you got this Jupiterian dog. No telling the scrapes he'll get you into."

Jocie laughed. Then her smile disappeared as she said, "You were here before my mother left. Tell me about her."

Wes got up and took the skillet over to the sink. He ran some water in it and then let it set. Jocie waited. Wes always answered her sooner or later. Zebedee put his head down on top of her feet.

Wes got a soft drink out of his little refrigerator and popped off the top. He poured half of it into a glass and handed it to Jocie, then took a drink out of the bottle. He rubbed the palm of his hand over the top and sat back down in his easy chair next to the window. He stared out at the fading sunlight, and Jocie began to think she might have to leave for home before he answered her. Finally he said, "I didn't know her all that well. She hardly ever came to the office, and I didn't go to your house much then. If I wanted free food, I went to your Mama Mae's house. Now, she could cook."

"I loved her tomatoes and macaroni."

"Mmm, and those chocolate pies. She should have opened a restaurant and gotten rich. She had a gift."

"I don't remember my mother cooking, but surely she did. I mean, Daddy was preaching then too. People were bound to be giving him beans and stuff."

"If they did, your Mama Mae was probably the one who cooked it for you. Your mother, she wasn't Mrs. Sally Housewife, but she was a looker. Prettiest woman I ever saw, and I've seen my share, drifting around the country in a spaceship."

"Do I look like her?"

Wes gave her face a close look. "Can't say as I think you do."

"But I don't look like Daddy either."

"No," Wes said. "But sometimes it's good to just look like yourself."

"Tabitha looked like Mama, didn't she?"

"She did. Same coloring. Same eyes. She was at that twixt-and-tween age when I knew her, but she showed promise of being real pretty."

"Not something you'd say about me," Jocie said. Her face was too long, her eyes too big, her mouth too wide.

"That's true. Pretty don't suit you. It's too common. You're going to be a stunner—one of those girls who breaks all the boys' hearts."

"And that's going to happen any day now, I guess." Jocie grinned. "Why, next fall when school starts, I'll have to take Zeb with me to keep the boys away."

"I expect they'll make a special rule about guard dogs just for you, and old Harlan here will get to go to Earth school and store up all kinds of interesting information to take back to Jupiter. Maybe that's what Jackson Jupiter had in mind when he made him into a dog."

"You're crazy, Wes."

"I think the word is *Jupiterian*." He finished off the bottle of pop and blew into the top to make an odd tune.

"*I'll* be a Jupiterian before that ever happens. I'm not even sure I'd want it to happen." Jocie shuddered at the thought of any of the boys at school trying to kiss her. "You think there's something wrong with me feeling like that?"

"Naw. You'll change your mind in a few years."

"Tabitha had boyfriends before she left. One of them gave her a big red heart-shaped box of chocolates on Valentine's Day. The box is still in the closet at home."

"So?"

"Well, Dad says she was my age when they left, but when I think about her, it seems like she was older. I remember her looking grown-up, if you know what I mean. And me, I don't think I'm ever going to need a bra." Jocie's face went a little pink. "I guess I shouldn't talk about bras to you. Aunt Love would have a calf."

"She might, and truth is, I ain't no expert on the subject of female underwear, which is another argument for a stepmother."

"But Leigh Jacobson?" When Jocie thought about it, she had been running into the woman a lot lately. And she had been overly friendly, asking how Jocie was doing and asking after her father. Jocie was sort of used to that from church folks, who were always being nice to her to make points with the preacher. But Leigh Jacobson went to the First Baptist Church in town. Jocie's father never got invited to fill the pulpit there. "Daddy's not interested, is he?"

"Oh, you know your dad. He's either got his head up in the

clouds or down in the Scripture. Half the time he don't know what's going on."

"Was that why he didn't know my mother was going to leave him? He said he didn't know she was leaving till she was gone."

"Sometimes people don't want to know things. It was pretty plain that your mama wasn't happy in Hollyhill, had never been happy in Hollyhill."

"But Dad says she was born here."

"That don't mean she had to like it here."

"No, I guess not," Jocie said. "Dad says we can have a birthday party for Tabitha even if she isn't here. I'm going to make a chocolate cake, and we'll have ice cream. You want to come?"

"Free food. I'll be there. Are you sending out invites?"

"Maybe. I would send one to Tabitha for sure, but we don't have an address right now. Dad thinks they're still in California, but the last letter to Tabitha came back."

"California. Now there's a state."

"Have you been there?"

"Our spaceship landed there a few times. The people never notice you're Jupiterian there, because they're all crazier than your average run-of-the-mill outer-space guy. And from the stuff that's been coming along the news lines, it's crazier now than it was then, what with all this free love and peace stuff." Wes held up his hand with his fingers parted in a V.

"Peace is good."

"That's a fact, but oft as not hard to come by." Wes stared down at his empty pop bottle.

Jocie took a sip of her cola. She hated it when Wes got that sad look on his face. She wanted to get up and hug him or something, but when she'd asked her father about it once, he'd said everybody had their demons from the past to deal with and that Wes had his share and she should just wait out his sad times and not bother him about it.

After what seemed like a half hour but probably was only a couple of minutes, Jocie touched Zeb's head, and the dog raised up and put his nose on her knee. "Anyway, about the party—who knows? The Lord answered my dog prayer. Maybe he'll answer my sister prayer."

Wes looked up at Jocie. "Did you ever once imagine anything that looked like that dog there when you were sending up your dog prayers?"

"No, but I like him now that he's here."

"That's good. But what I'm trying to tell you is that if Tabitha were to suddenly appear out of the blue, she wouldn't be the sister you remember. A lot of years have passed since then."

"I know that. But it would still be good, wouldn't it? I mean, it would make Daddy happy and maybe scare off that Leigh Jacobson if Dad had two daughters."

"Double trouble for sure." Wes stood up and peered out the window. "Come on, kiddo. It's done got too dark for you to ride that old bike home. I'll give you a lift. You can come to work with your dad Monday and get your bike."

"What about Zeb?"

"He can ride too."

They sandwiched the dog between them, and he sat still as a stone when Wes revved up the motor and shook awake the sleepy streets of Hollyhill. Jocie loved the way her hair whipped back away from her face as they raced down the road with nothing but the wind and the roar of the motorcycle in her ears. Jocie waved at the people they passed. Some waved back. Others just frowned at this disturbance of the town's peace and quiet. Wes was always saying that if people didn't love her daddy so much, they would have run him out of town years ago.

Jocie could think of several Hollyhillers she'd rather run out of town. Mayor Palmor for one. He was always smiling, always shaking hands for votes, even if the election had just ended. Of course, he never paid much attention to Jocie, seeing as how she was too young to vote. Sometimes he didn't notice her at all. Jocie didn't care. That gave her the chance to do some eavesdropping, pick up all kinds of tidbits to pass on to her father. He hardly ever printed any of them. Said he couldn't publish stories on a hearsay basis. He needed stories with facts to back them up, not town gossips. Wes wasn't so worried about facts. He always laughed at the stories Jocie brought in and said maybe he'd add some of them to his Hollyhill Book of the Strange.

Maybe she could talk her father into starting a News of the Strange column. This, a dog riding a motorcycle, could be the lead story. Zebedee lifted his head and began barking at the trees rushing past them. His joyous barks would have hurt their ears if the motorcycle hadn't already been deafening them.

Jocie started laughing. She just had a feeling this was going to be her strangest and best summer ever.

6

David hadn't let himself think about being nervous. He had prayed and studied his Scripture. He knew the Bible story frontward and backward. He'd gotten up early to watch the sun come up as he tried to put himself in the crowd that trailed after Jesus hungrier for his words than for food that day so long ago. He had soaked his shoes in the early morning dew of the neighbor's cow pasture while his hunger pangs reminded him he hadn't had breakfast. He'd sat on a rock at the edge of the field and thought about sharing a little boy's lunch of two fish and five loaves with thousands of other hungry people and then seeing the baskets of leftovers after he was too full to eat more. He had his points all lined up in his head and listed one, two, three on the lined notepaper stuck in his Bible. And he'd been sure he was ready to deliver the best sermon of his life.

He wasn't a great preacher. He could take a person one-on-one through any story in the Bible and help them see the truths laid out there. He could pray with anyone who had a need and help them find comfort in the Lord. He could write a good sermon with all his points and life lessons drawn out clear and simple, but he struggled with his delivery.

He practiced in the woods. He practiced in front of a mirror. He practiced in his car driving to take this or that picture for the newspaper. He had even practiced that morning to Jocie's ugly stray dog, who had sat in front of him in the pasture and listened politely. But practice didn't always make perfect.

Here he was gripping the edges of the pulpit, looking out at pews loaded with Mt. Pleasant faithful while his much-practiced sermon gathered in a hard knot just below his heart. He wasn't sure he was going to be able to cough it up.

David amened Deacon Jackson's mumbled offertory prayer, and the congregation settled back into the pews, putting up their hymn books and digging in their pockets and purses for money to drop into the offering plates. David tried not to think about his sermon moments away and instead looked at the families. As usual, little Bobby Whitehead was giving his mother fits in the next to back row. She'd already tried Cheerios and a coloring book, but the Cheerios had rolled in four directions under the pews, and Bobby was chewing on the red crayon. She had the three-year-old's shoulder in a vise grip and was whispering intently in his ear. He was doing his best to wriggle free. She'd be lucky to hear a line of Scripture.

The McDermotts with their three children were on the fourth pew, smiling and ready to look favorably on whatever he said. Aunt Love, in her customary black hat and dress, sat in the pew in front of them, looking sternly expectant as always. Jocie was sitting alone in the second pew from the back even though three other girls near her age sat together about midway on the other side of the church. David wished she was sitting in the middle of the other girls, trying to keep from giggling as the offering plates were being passed.

But no, Jocie was a loner. Her best friend in the world was Wes, who was nearly five times her age. Of course, she had friends at school but none she invited home for the weekend. That's the kind of friend she needed. One she could hook pinkies and share secrets with. One she could be silly with. Wes said she needed a stepmother.

David tried not to think about that. Not with the sermon to deliver in a few minutes. But his eyes drifted to Leigh Jacobson, who had slipped in the back door during the opening hymn and settled in the back pew. She wasn't a member of Mt. Pleasant. She went to the First Baptist Church in town, but she'd said last week she might come listen to him preach sometime. He wished she'd picked some other morning. Any other morning.

It was beginning to look as if Wes was right about Leigh. Even Aunt Love had noticed, telling David that girl had her hat set for him, when they'd run into Leigh at the grocery store last week. David hadn't decided whether to be pleased or panicked.

Leigh was pleasant enough, but she didn't set his blood to boiling the way Adrienne had the first time he'd laid eyes on her at his father's funeral. Of course, his submarine had just come in for maintenance when he got word of his father's heart attack and was given leave to go home for the funeral. After months at the bottom of the sea, the sight of any female started the blood to pumping.

But it had been more than that. He'd seen Adrienne at the funeral home, and she'd invited him to her house the next day. He'd found her in the backyard in a red swimsuit working on her tan. She'd asked him if he believed in love at first sight, and when he'd said yes, she'd challenged him to marry her—not later after they got to know one another, but that very day.

He'd just seen his father's body lowered into the ground. His mother was grieving. His older brothers and sister and their families had come in from Ohio and Texas for the funeral. He hadn't seen them for over two years, had laid eyes on a couple of their grandchildren for the first time the day before. He and his brothers and sister had never been very close. They'd all been grown before he'd come along and surprised his parents when his mother was forty-three and his father fifty. Still, they were family, and he had obligations. Adrienne had smiled and said now or never. She hadn't even wanted him to call his mother, but he had done that at least. They had driven south across the state border, found a justice of the peace, and drove back the next day. His brothers and their families were gone. His sister, Esther, was still there, a frown fixed between her eyes every time she looked at David. The frown grew even deeper when she looked at Adrienne. But his mother had smiled and welcomed Adrienne into her house and heart when David had to catch the plane back to his submarine. David thought she was glad of an excuse not to go to Texas with Esther.

Of course, nobody had known then that Tabitha was already on the way. God's plan, his mother would write him later. He hadn't been so sure then, but that was before God had put his hand on his shoulder and called him to preach. That had come later in the bowels of the submarine with the ominous blips of the radar signaling death coming. Adrienne had never wanted him to preach, had refused to believe his call was real.

David watched the deacons coming back down the aisle to set the offering plates on the altar table. He spotted some fives and a ten sticking up through the ones. At least they'd have enough to pay him the full amount for today's sermon even if they didn't vote him in. That was good. His car needed tires. The last two Sundays he'd preached, they'd given him only half pay, since the church was having some financial problems. Aunt Love told him to preach on tithing, but he told her the Lord hadn't laid that message on his heart. Thank goodness. He doubted any preacher anywhere had ever been called to a church after preaching on tithing.

David spread his hands flat on the pages of his Bible and shut his eyes as if he could absorb the words and the message God wanted him to deliver. Jessica Sanderson hit the last notes of "What a Friend We Have in Jesus" and stood up to go back to her seat two rows back. The wives of the men who had taken up the collection were scooting over to make room for them in the pews, and that sudden expectant silence fell over the church, almost as if the people had sucked in their breath in unison and were afraid to breathe out again as they waited for God's message to come through him.

The silence stretched. David's throat tightened up, threatened to close off completely. He thought that was why preachers told jokes—to get past that first moment, but he was singularly untalented at telling funny stories. Of course, as long as he kept his eyes closed and his head bowed, the people would think he was praying instead of panicking.

And he was praying. Desperately. *Help me, Lord, to say something to help these people.* He paused and waited for some words to come. His mind was still blank. He could almost feel the Lord out there with the congregation, waiting. A few people began stirring in their seats as the wait stretched out too long. His prayer got more desperate. *Help me to say anything!*

There was a loud cough in the back of the church. He knew even before he looked up that it was Jocie. She was making her wide-mouth-and-eyes face, and he couldn't keep from smiling. The first line about a little boy with a lunch of five loaves and two fishes popped into his mind. He pushed it out of his mouth, and as always, the Lord took over and did the rest.

Jocie watched the people in front of her and tried to judge how her father was doing. Most of the people seemed to be listening, except a couple of toddlers who were banging their hands on the pew backs and making eyes at the people behind them. Her father wouldn't be worried about that. He liked babies in the church, even if they did draw attention away from the sermon sometimes. He was always saying that God could deliver a better sermon through the love of a baby than any he could ever think up.

The little boy and his lunch had been a good choice. Her father was telling the story so that all the church was trailing along with the little boy. Jocie wished Wes was there to hear her father, but as usual he hadn't shown up. Leigh Jacobson had. Wes must be right about her. Thank goodness she hadn't seen Jocie and scooted in beside her. Jocie would have rather sat by Aunt Love and let her pinch her arm if she noticed Jocie's eyes getting the least bit droopy.

She tried to keep her mind on Andrew bringing the boy and his lunch to Jesus, but Zeb pushed the Bible story right out of her head. She'd left him stretched out happily on the front porch, but what would happen when they were gone all day and into the night? He might drift off to another house in search of some leftover biscuits. But God wouldn't answer her dog prayer and then let the answer disappear after just one day. Zeb would be there.

She'd told her Sunday school class about the Lord answering her prayer and sending Zeb. She figured since the Lord had been good enough to answer her prayer, she ought to give him credit. A couple of boys had snickered, but Miss McMurtry had silenced them with a look as she'd said, "That's a wonderful story, Jocie, and a good lesson for us all. God wants us to pray about everything—the big and little things." And then she'd passed out some chewing gum before she told the Sunday school story about Jesus healing a blind man. The one where he made mud and smeared it on the man's eyes. It always seemed funny to think about Jesus spitting and making mud like any ordinary person instead of commanding down a splash of rainwater to make the mud.

Jocie scooted over a few inches until she could see the watch on Mr. Snyder's arm stretched out on the pew in front of her. Five minutes till twelve. She wondered if she should make the slit throat signal so her dad would know to stop. No matter how well you were preaching, the folks wanted to be home in time to take the roast out of the oven. She hoped there was a roast in Mrs. McDermott's oven and not just a kettle of cabbage on top of the stove. Maybe she could even beg a bone or two for Zeb. The McDermotts had dogs, but they probably got bones all the time.

Her father must have peeked at his watch, because he began winding up the points of the sermon and making his appeal for people to come down the aisle if they had any decisions to let the church in on. Jocie hoped a couple of people would join church to make a few extra points in her father's favor, but nobody walked the aisle, and they quit singing before they got to the last verse of the invitation hymn. Her father didn't allow much time for working up your nerve.

Still, everybody was smiling as they headed toward the door to shake her father's hand on the way out. Ronnie Martin, one of the boys who had laughed at her in Sunday school class, stopped at Jocie's pew. He was older than her, already in high school and always bragging about playing varsity football the next year.

He blocked her in the pew. "Aren't you a little old to be praying for puppy dogs?"

"What's it to you what I pray for?" Jocie glared at him. He was too big to shove out of her way. She might as well try to move a rock wall.

"You ought to be praying for boyfriends." He let his eyes drop down to her chest. "With your equipment it might take some heavy-duty praying."

Jocie's face got hot. She was already raising the hymnbook still in her hand to pop him upside the head when just in time she remembered the vote and Ronnie's deacon father. She took a deep breath and tried to think of one of Aunt Love's Bible verses to zap him with. She couldn't, so she made one up on the spot. "Foolish words spout out of a fool's mouth and propel him along the road to destruction. Proverbs something."

"You sound like a preacher's kid."

"I am a preacher's kid." Jocie stepped up on the pew. She wasn't going to let him block her in a minute longer.

"Yeah, but where's your mama, preacher's kid?"

As ladylike as possible, Jocie vaulted over the back of the pew. If Ronnie was right, she didn't have any "equipment" worth showing anyway. Her feet hit the floor hard enough to draw attention from the few people who hadn't made it out the door yet. She didn't dare look toward her father. Instead she glared at Ronnie and said, "Take a hike."

"Your little doggy can come with me."

Miss McMurtry was suddenly beside Jocie. "Is everything okay, dear?" She looked at Ronnie. "Are we having a misunderstanding?"

Jocie smiled her best smile. "Not at all, Miss McMurtry. Ronnie was just suggesting some new things I might pray for."

"Well, that was helpful of him, I'm sure." Miss McMurtry darted a sharp look his way. "Maybe we should have a little prayer right now, just the three of us."

"Yes, ma'am," Ronnie said.

Jocie didn't see any way to escape, so she bowed her head and let Miss McMurtry pretend to talk to God while she was really preaching at her and Ronnie about getting along and being brothers and sisters in Christ. At least her prayer was mercifully short. Ronnie must have felt the same way, because he was out the door the second Miss McMurtry whispered amen.

Miss McMurtry gave Jocie an extra pat on the shoulder and said, "He was probably just picking on you because he likes you."

"Oh boy. That makes me feel loads better," Jocie said before she thought. "Sorry, Miss McMurtry. It's just that I don't think Ronnie's my type. To tell the truth, I don't think I have a type right now."

Miss McMurtry laughed. "You're way too young to worry about it just yet, dear. The Lord will send the right type along when it's time."

"Good. I'll just trust him on that one."

Miss McMurtry put her arm around Jocie's waist and walked her toward where her father was waiting.

People were still gathered in clusters under the big oak tree out front. Jocie stayed by her father's side as they made the rounds one more time before joining Aunt Love, who was already in the car. She even managed to smile sweetly at Ronnie when they passed by the Martin family sharing fishing stories with the Sandersons.

After Sunday dinner, David and Mr. McDermott left to visit the sick. They figured to be gone all afternoon, since it had been a busy week at the Mt. Pleasant Church, with a gallbladder surgery, a sprained ankle, a broken arm (Herbert Haskins had been painting the eaves on his house when wasps dive-bombed him, and he'd taken the direct route to the ground), a new baby, a root canal, and a teenager threatening to run off to sing country music in Nashville.

When Jocie started helping clear away the dinner dishes, Mrs. McDermott shooed her out of the kitchen. "Go on outside with little Matt Jr. and Molly. It's too pretty a day for you to be stuck inside with us old ladies."

Jocie opened her mouth to inform Mrs. McDermott that she wasn't exactly a kid like Matt Jr. and Molly, but then she thought about sitting all afternoon hiding her yawns while Mrs. McDermott and Aunt Love talked about the best way to freeze green beans or how to keep the bugs off roses. She shut her mouth. The McDermott kids had to be more entertaining.

Before she went outside, she tiptoed down the hall to peek in at the baby, Murray, napping in his crib. Babies amazed her, and she stood there hoping Murray's eyes would pop open so she could offer to carry him outside for a while. She watched his little chest rise and fall at least ten times before giving up and heading for the door.

She found Matt Jr. and Molly watching wiggletails hatch out in the rain barrel. "They're baby mosquitoes, you know," Matt Jr. informed Jocie.

"Why don't you dump the water and kill them?" Jocie asked.

"Mom would shoot us. She likes having rainwater for her flowers. Besides, you'd never be able to kill all the wiggletails anyway," Matt Jr. said. "Hey, you want to go pet the horses out behind the barn?"

As Jocie sidestepped cow piles on the way to the barn, she told Matt Jr. and Molly how lucky they were to have so many animals around. Then she told them about Zeb, her one and only animal.

Matt Jr. made her tell the part about Zeb riding the motorcycle twice. He was a serious-looking kid with dark-rimmed glasses over sky-blue eyes. He'd changed out of his church clothes into blue jeans with a rip in the knee.

Molly had changed into a sundress with strawberries the same red as the ribbons on the ends of her braids, which bounced against her shoulders as she kept hold of Jocie's hand and tugged her along behind Matt Jr.

On the way to the barn, Molly tipped up rocks and dried hunks of cow manure so Matt Jr. could grab any worms under them before they sank back down into the ground. They were hoping to go fishing the next day. They let Jocie hold the coffee can half full of black dirt laced with fat, pink earthworms.

At the barn Matt Jr. stuck the can inside the milk room and found a piece of wood to lay on top of it. "You ever been fishing?" he asked Jocie.

"Once."

"Catch anything worth mentioning?"

"Nope. Just got eat up by mosquitoes." She'd gone with a family at the Sinai Church the summer before. They'd promised her it would be fun. Nobody had mentioned the mosquitoes and deer flies or having to squash stinky worms onto a hook. But as bad as worm juice had smelled, the unlucky fish that had taken the bait had smelled even worse. She'd had to take hold of the fish and work the hook out of its mouth. After catching two fingerlings that the others had told her to toss up on the bank to let die, she'd quit putting worms on her hook. The day hadn't been all that bad after that except for the mosquitoes and deer flies.

Out behind the barn, two old work horses raised their heads and plodded over to them when Matt Jr. climbed up on the fence and whistled through his teeth.

"We should have brought them some peppermint," Molly said.

"Peppermint? Peppermint candy?" Jocie asked.

"Yeah, they'll almost run if they think you've got candy. Almost. I doubt if anything could really make them run," Matt Jr. said. "But if you don't have candy, they'll eat grass out of your hand. I guess to them it's sort of like going to a restaurant. Having you pull the grass for them."

Jocie jerked up a handful of clover and let the biggest horse nibble it off her hand.

"Your fingers should be safe. He don't bite very often," Matt Jr. said.

"Oh, Matt," Molly said. "Ace and Annie have never bit anybody. But you do have to be careful not to let them step on you."

Jocie looked down at the horses' feet, which were as big around as Molly's waist. "Do you ride them?" she asked as she rubbed Ace's velvety nose.

"Yeah, but they won't do more than a plod," Matt Jr. said. "Daddy is going to get me a riding pony next year when I'm ten."

They gave the horses a last serving of grass and then went up to the hayloft to search for a new litter of kittens. The loft, half full of spring hay, smelled sweet and green. Dust and seeds floated in the air and caught in cobwebs that dripped down from the roof posts.

Jocie had to keep yanking loose hay straws out of the toes of her Sunday sandals, but the kittens were worth it. They found them in a small depression between a couple of bales of hay. Two were gray and white, one almost all white, and the other one black. The kittens were just beginning to open their eyes, and when Molly picked up the black kitten by the nape of his neck, they all set up a high-pitched mewing that brought the black-and-white mama cat running. She squeezed in between the bales of hay and wrapped her body around the kittens, who stopped mewing and started nursing.

"I bet she moves them again," Molly said as she carefully placed the black kitten back beside his mother. "She hates it when we find them."

"I just hope she doesn't lose them like she did the last bunch. Mama says Miss Kitty has some learning to do about being a good mother," Matt Jr. said.

"I thought all animal mothers were good mothers. You know, natural instinct and all that," Jocie said.

"Nah, that's not true," Matt Jr. said. "We have to bottle-feed a couple of lambs every year because the mama sheep decides the baby she just had isn't hers and kicks it away when it tries to suck. Of course, sheep are dumber than rocks."

The mama cat licked her babies in between glares over her shoulder at Jocie and the kids. Jocie said, "She looks like she's being a good mother now. She'd like us to disappear."

"Yeah, she does okay till they're big enough to follow her around. Then like as not, she'll lead them off and lose them in the woods."

"On purpose?" Jocie said.

Molly shrugged. "Mama says she probably doesn't aim to lose them, that maybe she hasn't figured out how to sneak off without them seeing her, and they just follow after her and get lost. Or then again, Mama says she could just get tired of being a mother."

"Does she? Your mother, I mean."

"No, of course not," Molly said. "People mothers don't get tired of their babies."

Jocie pushed aside the thought of her own mother. She hadn't been a baby when her mother had left. Far from it. She'd been five, the same age as Molly. One night she'd had a mother and a sister when she went to bed, and the next morning she hadn't.

Jocie wondered again for the thousandth time why her mother had taken Tabitha and not her. Of course, she wouldn't have gone. She would have grabbed hold of the porch posts and held on for dear life before she would have left her father and Hollyhill. Still, her mother could have said good-bye. But there had been no good-bye, no note from her mother to her or to her father, no anything.

Tabitha had left a note for her father. Jocie had seen it in one of her father's Bibles once. The paper was limp from being handled, and some of the folds were tearing in two. Tabitha had said she was leaving, that her mother wouldn't let her wake him up to say good-bye, and to make Jocie leave her stuff alone, because she'd be back someday. Except for her dolls. She'd said Jocie could have the dolls. But Jocie hadn't played with the dolls. Mama Mae had packed them away in boxes along with Tabitha's other stuff. It was all still there in the closet waiting for her.

Jocie was glad when Matt Jr. said he was thirsty, and they headed back to the house. She didn't really want to think about good mothers or bad mothers. Cats or otherwise.

Aunt Love nearly had a stroke when they came in, but Mrs. McDermott just laughed and made them go back out on the porch to brush off the hay seeds before pointing them to the bathroom to wash up.

"That girl," Jocie could hear Aunt Love saying. "Sometimes she acts more like ten than thirteen."

"Oh well," Mrs. McDermott said with another laugh. "Ten can

be more fun and lots easier on Brother David, I'd say. At thirteen, she could be starting to run after the boys instead of crawling around in a hayloft hunting kittens."

Jocie splashed cold water on her face to try to douse the red blooming on her cheeks. She hated getting embarrassed. Wes said people from Jupiter didn't turn red. Instead their ears tingled until they had to wiggle them to let the embarrassment out. Jocie opened her mouth wide and breathed out until the bathroom mirror in front of her was foggy and her cheeks were a nice normal pink instead of red. Who said you couldn't learn a few tricks from a Jupiterian?

8

That night after evening services, David stepped down from the pulpit and shook the hands of the people who stayed seated in the pews as he walked down the aisle toward the door. Most of them looked him in the eyes and smiled. Surely that was a sign the vote might go in his favor.

David wanted the position badly. While he'd filled a lot of pulpits when a pastor was sick or on vacation, no church had called him for any kind of permanent position since Adrienne had left.

He'd been the pastor at New Liberty over in the small community of Summersville when that had happened. It was an old church but with life. Around fifty faithful members had showed up every time the church doors opened, and he had been urging more back into the pews. The people had adopted Tabitha and Jocie into their hearts and had mostly overlooked Adrienne.

Adrienne had never taken to the idea of being a preacher's wife. "Why should I waste my every Sunday afternoon listening to some toothless old country woman telling me to plant peas in February and how to pick the worms off cabbages and that I should sew ruffles on my 'precious' little girls' dresses? I don't like peas. Cabbage with or without worms makes me puke. And I detest ruffles," Adrienne had told him on numerous occasions. She flat out refused to go to church more than once a month.

And while he always encouraged her to go, sometimes it was

worse when she did. David was afraid to let her out of earshot for fear of what she might say or do. If he asked her to be kind and careful about what she said, she'd say, "Thou shalt not lie."

He told her that didn't necessarily mean she had to run with arms flailing at the head deacon's wife to warn her that birds were circling her bouffant hairstyle for a prime nesting spot. Or tell the choir director that she could hear a better chorus around a pond. Adrienne would just laugh and say, "At least things were interesting for a few minutes."

She let him know every Sunday, every day really, that she hadn't married a preacher. She'd married a soldier who had freaked out in battle and insanely made promises to God for her that she couldn't keep. Being a good preacher's wife was as much a calling as being a preacher. Adrienne hadn't been called, and she didn't plan to pick up the phone if the Lord did dial her number.

"What is your calling?" he'd asked her once.

"Who says I have to have a calling?" she'd said with that smile that could make him forgive her almost anything. She'd lightly traced her fingers across the back of his neck. "At least from God."

A tingle tickled across his back and slammed him in the stomach even all these years later. She'd always known just what to do to get around his anger. At least until she was out of sight. Then the resentment would flood back, and he'd practice arguments in his head until they threatened to block out his sermons—Didn't he try to be a good father and husband? Didn't he work long hours to get her the things she wanted? Was it too much to ask her to support him in his calling by going to church on Sundays and being nice to the people there? He couldn't remember ever actually asking those questions, but he'd gotten an answer anyway. She'd left.

None of the churches they'd ever been part of had warmed to Adrienne. They had always hired David in spite of his wife, but once she was gone, she became an obstacle the churches could no longer overlook.

The deacons at New Liberty Church hadn't exactly fired him. They had just encouraged him to take some time off until he got his family situation under control. After all, a man who couldn't control his family certainly couldn't be expected to lead a church. So Paul had written to Timothy.

Now some of the people here at Mt. Pleasant seemed willing to look past his fractured marriage to give him a new chance. But would enough of them feel that way to vote him in as their interim pastor?

Aunt Love and Jocie followed him out. He shut the church door behind them and headed for the car. It felt strange to leave the church full of people, as if he was running scared.

In the car, Aunt Love sniffed loudly and said, "Did you ask for a unanimous vote? If so, we might as well tell this church good-bye for the last time right here and now."

"Ninety percent," David said as he started the engine.

Aunt Love dug into her pocketbook for a handkerchief. "You should have said eighty. It's only an interim position. They'll send you packing as soon as they get wind of a preacher they can call full-time."

"I don't expect it to last more than a few months, but however long, I didn't want there to be a lot of friction about me being here. I think I've got a chance at ninety. What do you think, Jocie?" He looked in the rearview mirror at Jocie in the backseat.

"If Mr. McDermott is counting the votes, you're a shoo-in."

"Matt likes us, but he wouldn't cheat on the count."

"Besides, you can rest assured Ogden Martin won't let him do the count alone," Aunt Love put in.

"Well, I daresay I don't have Brother Ogden's vote," David said. He hadn't figured out exactly what Ogden Martin held against him. He'd heard through the church grapevine that Ogden said there was no way a newspaperman could also be a preacher. David shook his head and went on, "But we'll just leave the vote up to God. That's whose hands I want it to be in anyway. 'A man's heart deviseth his way: but the LORD directeth his steps.'"

"Proverbs 16:9," Aunt Love said. She waited a minute and then said over her shoulder to Jocie, "Go ahead and look, child. I know you want to."

Jocie turned the whisper thin pages of her Bible in the last of the daylight. "Yep, right as usual."

"That's amazing, Aunt Love," David said. "I study and study, but I can't snatch Scripture references out of the air like that."

"I've got a few years on you, and I've always had a good mind for numbers. I don't know them all, by any means. Just the ones that are quoted most often."

"I know John 3:16 and Psalm 23. 'The LORD is my shepherd; I shall not want,'" Jocie volunteered from the backseat.

"And could know more if you spent any time with your Bible," Aunt Love said. "Even one verse a week gives a person a lot of heart Scripture after several years."

"I guess we could both try harder on that one, couldn't we, Jocie?"

"Yes sir," she said. "But you'll get the vote. You telling the story tonight about how God called you to preach should be good for a dozen votes." Jocie scooted up to lean on the back of the front seat beside David. "Did you really feel God's hand on your shoulder? I mean really feel it instead of just thinking you felt it." Jocie laid her hand on his shoulder. "Did it feel normal like this? Or did you know right away something spooky was happening?"

Jocie had always wanted to know more than he could explain about God calling him. He'd told it a thousand times to her and to others who had asked in the nearly twenty years since it had happened, but some things were beyond rational explanation. Still, it had been good to tell the story again tonight. He needed to keep reminding himself that he was doing what God had told him to do and not just drifting along under his own direction. David put his hand over Jocie's. "No, not like a normal hand, but not spooky either," he said.

"Then how did it feel?"

"It's hard to put into words." David pulled on the lights of the car and stared out at the shadows of the trees beside the road. Aunt Love was nodding off in the seat beside him, but he could feel Jocie's rapt attention waiting for him to try to explain the unexplainable.

He remembered trying to explain it to Adrienne. "Dear Adrienne, my darling," he'd written. "Last night my life, maybe I should say our lives, were changed forever. God laid his hand on me and told me to preach his Word."

All these years later, he could recall his exact words, probably because he had written and rewritten them so many times before stuffing the letter in an envelope and sliding it through the mail slot. Later he'd tried, without success, to get one of the guys in charge of bagging up the mail to fish out the letter and give it back to him. When that hadn't worked, he'd written another letter trying to explain and another until in the end Adrienne had received seven letters on the same day, since the mail was delayed going out when they were in a war zone.

It had been another lifetime, months, before he'd gotten an answer back from her. Mail call was infrequent on a submarine, and even if they had been on a regular mail line, Adrienne wasn't good at writing letters. She usually just scribbled a few lines to send along with his mother's letters, saying that she was sick of having a big belly and a backache and that it was too much for him to expect her to have this baby by herself and she needed him to come home right away. As for God calling him, she'd simply told him he must be half crazy and she hoped he got over it before he wrote again. And of course, she was right about the half crazy part.

Being in the submarine deep in the ocean had messed with his mind. No sunshine, no daylight, no grass, no trees. Only the dark. Even with the lights fully ablaze, he was always aware of the crushing blackness lurking a power failure or a depth charge away. He still had nightmares where he opened his eyes to total darkness.

"Just try," Jocie begged now.

"You've heard it a hundred times, Jocie. You just heard it again tonight."

"You didn't tell the church how it felt. You just told them it happened. You were in a submarine at the bottom of the ocean. The enemy ships were feeling through the waters to find you so they could blow you up. Your job was to tell where the enemy ships were so you could sneak up on them and blow them up first. It was war. Ships went down. Submarines took hits. People died." Jocie stopped and squeezed her father's shoulder. "I'm glad you didn't."

"Me too," David said. "I did tell it a little bit better than that tonight, didn't I?"

"Oh yeah. I'm doing a *Reader's Digest* version." She took a breath and went on. "You were more afraid of getting hit and not being able to get back to the top than of being blown up. One night when the sonar was going crazy, God showed up and let you know he was in control and that he had plans for you back in Hollyhill, so you weren't going to end up shark food."

Aunt Love roused up with a shudder. "Heavenly days, child. You shouldn't talk about your father being shark food."

"I shouldn't, should I? That was awful," Jocie said. "I'm sorry."

"That's okay," David said with a laugh. "I didn't end up shark food, and the image does give the story a certain dramatic flare. Maybe I'll throw that in the next time I tell the story."

"I think your usual version is quite dramatic enough without the mention of shark food," Aunt Love said.

"But you never say how you felt. Were you afraid?" Jocie asked.

"Of course I was afraid. Every day. But after a while it was like a bad toothache. You couldn't make it go away. You couldn't forget it. So you just blocked it back away from the front of your mind so you could keep breathing, keep cracking jokes, keep writing letters home, keep thinking it would be over."

"I don't mean the war. I mean were you afraid when God showed up?"

"If God or his angel showed up here in this car this very minute, would you be afraid?" David asked.

"We'd have to be unnatural human beings to not be afraid," Aunt Love said. "Just look in the Bible everywhere it says an angel showed up, and the first thing the angel always said was 'Be not afraid.'"

"That's right," David said. "So yes, I was afraid, but it was a different kind of fear. And you have to realize that at first I didn't know what was happening."

"What did happen first?" Jocie asked.

"I smelled locust blooms," David said.

"Locust blooms?" Jocie said.

"One of the sweetest scents on earth," Aunt Love said.

"Lilacs are better," Jocie said.

"Not to me," David said. "I used to be the first one to notice the locust trees blooming in the spring. Mama would always come right out on the porch to see if she could smell them too, but sometimes it would be a couple of days before she could. She used to say God must have gotten me mixed up with a dog when he gave out the noses."

"Everybody has a gift," Aunt Love said.

"A sensitive nose isn't always that great a gift. Plenty of smells are better unsmelt." David concentrated on the road for a moment. Funny how he could still call up the odor of those locust blooms.

Along with the metallic smells, the machine oil, and stale body odors that were the norm in the submarine.

"Are you saying God smells like locust blooms?" Jocie asked.

"No, no. I think he just used the locust blooms to get my attention. To tell you the truth, when I smelled the locust blooms, I thought I was going to die. That God had sent me this last blessing, like a gift from home before we got blown out of the water. It was certainly a possibility that night."

"And then his hand was on your shoulder. Was it hot? Or cold?" Jocie said.

"I wouldn't say hot, or cold either."

"It had to be something," Jocie said.

"True. Let's see, how can I describe it? Maybe like a towel you get off the line in the summertime that's warm from the heat of the sun. Comforting. Perfect. And while it wasn't heavy, it wasn't something you could shake off even if you wanted to."

That wasn't a particularly good description, but it seemed to satisfy Jocie.

"How did you know it was God's hand?"

"I really don't know. I don't think I did at first. I just knew I wasn't afraid of dying anymore, that I felt completely different than I had five minutes before."

"The peace that passeth understanding," Aunt Love put in.

"That must have been it," David agreed. He remembered thinking that if this was the way it felt to die, then it wasn't going to be so bad. He'd had regrets. Especially the baby on the way he'd never see. And then the peace had gone deeper into his soul and wiped away even the thought of regret.

The needle on the sonar screen had been going crazy. The submarine had been bouncing in the waters as the charges went off around them. The man next to him had been trembling as he tried to operate the controls to rotate the sonar, but David had been as calm as if he were drifting along in a rowboat baiting a hook to drop a line down into a sun-dappled stream.

And then a message had begun flashing on the screen in front of him. "YOU WILL PREACH MY WORD." All capitals. Dark green one flash. Red the next.

"I thought maybe I'd lost my mind," David told Jocie. "We weren't using that screen, didn't even have it turned on, and even if it had been operating, it showed echo signals, not words. But there they were. Red and green flashing words. I yelled at the officer in charge to come look. I don't know what I expected him to see."

"Flashing words, I suppose," Aunt Love said.

"But he didn't," Jocie said.

"Well, I've never been sure. Maybe he did see them and thought he was slipping over the edge. Or maybe he thought the message was for him. I always intended to catch him by himself and ask him straight out sometime, but I didn't." David could never decide whether he was afraid the chief officer did see the words or he didn't.

"But what happened?" Jocie asked.

"I came home and started working at the newspaper and preaching."

"No, I mean then. The officer came over, didn't act like he saw any flashing words anywhere, and then what?"

"The words disappeared. The locust bloom scent was gone. I could smell the guy next to me sweating again. My shoulder felt empty. Really empty. And the sonar showed an enemy ship practically right over top of us. The chief officer sounded the attack alarm, and we went into battle mode and sank the ship."

"But you weren't afraid anymore," Jocie said.

"Not of dying," David said. There had been new things to fear. Having hallucinations. Preaching. Telling Adrienne. And being a light in the crushing blackness that still surrounded them.

Knowing people were dying because radio waves had bounced off their ship and showed up on his sonar. It was war. War and death could not be separated.

He hadn't wanted to die. He hadn't wanted to be the reason others died. He hadn't wanted to preach. Not then. But God had said preach, so what else could he do?

ocie liked hearing the story of her father's calling. She knew her father was special, but the fact that God had singled him out just proved it that much more. Of course, her father said everybody was special in God's eyes, but everybody didn't have a story to tell like her father's.

She talked to God all the time. Mostly one-way stuff like the dog prayer and "Bless Daddy" and "Help me not drive Aunt Love completely batty since half batty is bad enough" and "Thank you for the mockingbird that sings and dances in the tree beside the house" and "Watch over Tabitha and my mother." Prayers like that were easy, but she never really expected to hear God talking back, saying do this or do that.

The idea that he might made her nervous. What if he told her to do something she didn't want to do? Like be a missionary in Africa, where she might have to eat fried ants or who knows what. She was happy with the way things were. Especially now that God had answered her dog prayer. But what if God expected some kind of payback for sending her Zeb?

Her father said that wasn't the way God worked, but fair seemed fair. God had given her Zeb. He might expect her to give him something back. Maybe not socking Ronnie Martin in the nose next Sunday if her father got voted in at Mt. Pleasant. Or actually learning her Sunday school memory verse before she got to Sunday school instead of just reading it over on the way to class and faking it. Or not complaining about Aunt Love burning the biscuits. Or even better, getting up early enough to be in the kitchen to rescue the biscuits before they burned.

If she promised to work at showing how thankful she was, surely God would let Zeb still be there on the porch. She offered up a silent prayer as they turned up the lane to their house. *Please, Lord, don't let Zeb go find another house.*

It was already dark, but the car lights would hit the porch as they pulled up. She'd be able to see if Zeb was there waiting for her. She scooted up on the edge of her seat again and peered through the windshield toward the house. There was a light on the front porch. Not the porch light. More like a flashlight with the batteries running down. Or a jar of lightning bugs. Or a candle flickering in the breeze.

"Look, Dad." She pointed past his head toward the porch. "What is that light?"

Aunt Love woke up with a little snort. "Light? What light?"

"It looks to be a candle," her father said.

"A candle? How odd." Aunt Love sat up straighter and peered out of the window.

"Somebody is on the porch," her father said.

"Who?" Jocie asked.

"I can't see who. It's too dark," her father said.

Jocie strained to see, but all she could make out was the shape of a person in the rocking chair on the porch. No shape of a dog was anywhere in sight. "I can't see Zeb. You don't think he's gone, do you?"

"Don't worry, Jocie. That dog knows a good thing when he's found it. He'll be here," her father said.

Jocie touched the sack beside her that held the bone she'd begged from Mrs. McDermott, and she suddenly had a terrible thought. "What if it's Zeb's owner come to claim him?"

"Nobody in their right mind would come hunting that dog,"

Aunt Love said shortly. "It's probably just Wes with something about the paper."

"I don't see his motorcycle. And Wes never walks anywhere," Jocie said.

"His motorcycle could have stripped a gear or whatever motorcycles do besides make an unholy racket," Aunt Love said.

"We don't have to do the five guesses game. We'll find out who it is as soon as we get there," her father said.

"But, Dad, somebody on our porch this time of night with no car anywhere around and with a candle lit? Don't you think that's weird? I mean, who sits on anybody's porch and brings a candle to light?"

"Somebody afraid of the dark who doesn't have a flashlight?" her father suggested.

"But it's too late to come visiting or anything normal," Jocie said.

"Unless they're bringing bad news," Aunt Love said. She too was leaning forward trying to get a better look at the mystery person on the porch.

"Hush, you two," her father said as he parked the car in front of the garage. "It's probably just somebody who knows I'm a preacher and needs to talk. Or somebody who's lost and needs a ride home."

"Carrying candles in their pocket?"

"People carry all kinds of things in their pockets. Or pocketbooks. Who knows? Aunt Love might be able to pull a candle out of her purse."

"No candles," Aunt Love said. "Matches, but no candles."

Paws hit against Jocie's door, and Zeb stuck his nose to her window. Jocie pushed open the door and let Zeb lick her face. For some reason her heart was banging around inside her. And it didn't have anything to do with the dog. It was whoever was on the porch. In spite of what her father said, it wasn't normal.

71

Something was up. The dog prayer had been answered. The father getting a call to a church prayer was being answered. Maybe God had just decided this was the week to answer all the Brooke family prayers.

People from California probably carried candles in their pockets. Jocie had seen pictures on TV of teenagers in wild clothes with candles everywhere. Hippies. Not something you'd find in Hollyhill. Here you might find birthday cake candles and candles for when a storm knocked the electricity out. Nothing anybody would carry in a pocket, but who knew what people in California carried around with them.

Jocie rubbed Zeb's head and gave him the bone. He plopped right down in the middle of the driveway to start chewing on it. Jocie trailed after her father and Aunt Love to the porch.

The person on the porch stood up, and the wicker chair rocked back and forth. The candle flame flickered and went out in the slight draft. The candle hadn't given off much light, but the night suddenly seemed intensely dark in spite of the bright glitter of millions of stars above their heads. The moon was in hiding. Somewhere far away an owl hooted, and chills shot up Jocie's back. She moved closer to her father and touched the back of his shirt. She held her breath and waited. It seemed as if the night was doing the same. She couldn't even hear Zeb chewing now.

Her father stopped at the bottom of the steps as if they were the visitors and the person on the porch the homebody. "Can we help you some way?" he asked.

The person on the porch stepped closer to the edge of the porch above them. The woman's voice was timid, almost afraid. "Hi, Daddy. I'm home."

Jocie's breath exploded out of her. "It *is* her. It's Tabitha!" she shouted. She pushed past her father and Aunt Love to run up the steps and grab her sister.

"You can't be Jocie," Tabitha said as she held Jocie out away from her. It was still too dark to see faces. "You're so tall."

Together they turned to look at their father, who was still standing in the same spot. Beside him, Aunt Love was clutching her chest and quoting Scripture. "O give thanks unto the LORD; for he is good: for his mercy endureth for ever."

"Say something, Daddy," they both said at practically the same instant. And then Tabitha went on, "You are glad to see me, aren't you, Daddy?"

David stared at the two girls, his two girls, looking down at him from the porch and felt as if someone had sucker punched him. One as familiar as his own hand, the other strange and un-known. He struggled for breath to answer Tabitha. How could it be possible that this tall, slim young woman peering through the dark at him could be Tabitha? He had carried the thirteen-year-old Tabitha in his heart all these years without letting her grow, as if he could stop time and not miss any of her life. Now here she was in front of him, years of her life totally lost to him, and he couldn't say a word.

"He can't talk. I've never seen Daddy not able to talk." Jocie tugged Tabitha down the porch steps toward David.

"Praise God," David finally said as he put his arms around Jocie and Tabitha and fought back the tears that threatened to render him speechless again. "I can't believe you're actually here. Welcome home, sweetheart." He gently touched his lips to her forehead.

Aunt Love was still quoting Scripture beside them, and Jocie's stray dog had deserted his bone to dance around them, his thun-derous barks at full volume.

Tabitha suddenly started laughing. "This is crazier than any-thing in California." She peered at Aunt Love and said, "Who are you?"

Aunt Love quit quoting Scripture and stepped up to Tabitha. "I'm your Aunt Love."

"Oh yeah. Mama Mae's sister. I remember Dad writing that you were living here now, but I forgot. Sorry," Tabitha said. "What is that you were saying? A hymn or something."

"No, dear. It was Scripture. Psalms mostly," Aunt Love said.

"Oh. Well, I haven't been to church much lately." Tabitha glanced at her father and then at the ground. "Well, any lately."

"Don't worry. Now that you're home, you'll get plenty of chances to make it up," Jocie said. "Every Sunday and then some."

"Let's go inside," David said. "I want to see how you've grown up." It was still too dark to see more than a shadow of her face, but in that shadow was Adrienne. "You are alone?"

Tabitha let David turn her toward the porch steps and the front door. "Sort of."

He heard echoes of the child's voice he remembered, but it was strange and new at the same time.

"Mother's not here?" Jocie's words sounded tight.

"Oh, no," Tabitha said. "DeeDee will never leave California. She belongs there. Says she should have been born there."

"But how did you get here?"

"On the bus. Man, it's a long ride from California."

"We don't have a bus stop in Hollyhill," David said.

"Tell me about it. I had to get off in Grundy and catch a ride with this truck driver," Tabitha said. "He was delivering potato chips to the restaurant where I was trying to call you from, and I guess he thought I looked lost or something, so he gave me a ride over here. Don't worry, Dad. He was nice. Said he had a granddaughter my age. I was beginning to think I was going to have to sleep in the park or something since I couldn't hang out in the bus station, seeing as how there wasn't one. The bus driver just fished my stuff out of the bottom of the bus and let me off at the corner by the courthouse and went on. I mean, that's what I asked him to do, but

I never expected the town to be so dead. Nobody anywhere. I was lucky to find a restaurant open so I could try to call you."

"You should have let me know you were coming, and I would have met you in Williamsburg, where there is a bus station." David didn't like to think about her alone, at the mercy of whoever came along.

"It was no big deal. I'd already spent a lot of hours hanging out in bus stations waiting to make the next connection. Another night somewhere wouldn't have been a problem. As long as somebody didn't want to share my bench and their life story. I've heard more life stories on the way cross country. Yawn city. You'd think that occasionally somebody would have something exciting happen to them, but no. Nothing but ruptured appendixes and long stories about their Einstein grandkids."

"I like hearing people's life stories," Jocie said as she went in the front door ahead of Tabitha and switched on the light.

"Well, I wish you'd been there to be my ears, little sister," Tabitha said as she shielded her eyes from the sudden burst of light. "Then I could've snoozed coast to heartland."

"You should have come on in and made yourself at home. The door wasn't locked," David said.

"Yeah, I know. I started to, but I got to thinking. What if you didn't live here anymore? I mean, it'd been a while since we got a letter and there wasn't a name on the mailbox and this dog was trying to bark us deaf and I didn't remember anything about a dog. I mean, I knew Stumpy got done in after I left. So I told Grandpop Jack I'd better wait on the porch. He would have waited around with me, but he had to get home and we decided that even if you had moved, nobody would get too excited about me staging a sit-in on their porch. He gave me a couple of bags of chips before he left. I finally got the dog to quit barking by pitching him some of the chips. Then I ate some. Too many, I guess, because I got sick and had to puke. I sure was glad to see your lights coming up the road."

The poor girl looked tired. Worse than tired, exhausted. She was too slim and too pale, with dark circles under her eyes. A painted rose adorned her upper left cheek. At least he hoped it was painted on. Her wrinkled, faded red top hung loosely over bright green pants. She had a red and green strip of material tied around her forehead like a farmer's sweatband. Her long hair, the same honey brown as Adrienne's, was caught at the nape of her neck in a plain rubber band.

Even mussed and in desperate need of a shower she looked so much like Adrienne the first time he'd seen her that David lost his breath again for a moment. She'd always been like Adrienne, from the six-month-old baby he'd first met when he got home from the war to the thirteen-year-old who had disappeared in the night with her mother.

But it was even more than the same color hair and the green eyes with thick dark lashes and the high cheekbones. Adrienne had always had secrets she'd never shared, and now Tabitha had that same shielded look to her eyes, as if there was more than she'd be willing to tell in spite of the way her words were streaming out practically tripping on one another.

She was looking around the living room. "I can't believe this. It's all exactly the same. The old piano in the corner with our school pictures on it and the books. Surely you've gotten some new books." She ran her hands over some of the bookends.

"Lots of new books," Jocie said. "And new pictures too. My school pictures."

"Well, sure, but it's still the same." Tabitha ran over to pick up an embroidered throw pillow off the couch. "Mama Mae made this. She let me pick out the colors of the threads and poke the needle through on some of the stitches." She hugged the pillow to her. A couple of tears slid out the corners of her eyes. "I keep thinking I'll see her too."

"She died a few years after you left," Jocie said, the only one of them besides Tabitha who seemed to be able to talk. "Daddy wrote and told you that."

"Yeah, I know. But I guess when you're not here, it's easier to keep somebody alive in your head. I just kept imagining everybody doing the same things. Mama Mae planting flowers. Daddy at the paper. You playing in the dirt. You were always playing in the dirt. It drove DeeDee crazy. She'd scream at you if you got close to her with your dirty hands."

"I don't play in the dirt now except when I have to help Aunt Love plant the garden."

"Well, of course not. You're all grown-up. What are you now? Eleven? Twelve?"

10

Aunt Love plopped her purse down on the table beside the stairs and said, "Thirteen. Your sister is thirteen. And you'd better sit down before you faint. I think there was some ham left over at breakfast. Maybe some applesauce. You need something besides potato chips to eat. And who in heaven's name is this DeeDee you keep talking about? Surely not your mother," Aunt Love said.

Tabitha looked at Aunt Love as if she'd shaken her out of a dream. "You're not the same. I don't remember you at all. Should I?"

Aunt Love stopped in front of her on the way to the kitchen. "I saw you a few times when you were a child. Nothing you'd have any reason to remember. I was never anybody's favorite aunt."

"Aunt Love. I knew a girl in California who wanted everybody to call her Love, but her name was actually Edith. Is that really your name—Love?"

"Lovella. I don't know where my mother came up with it. It's not a respectable Bible name like yours. Tabitha also called Dorcas." Aunt Love gently pushed Tabitha toward the couch. "Now sit. You've had a long trip, and you can't tell us everything tonight. You'll be staying awhile, I'm guessing."

"Awhile, and I am zonked. From my head bone to my big toe bones." Tabitha sank down on the couch and kicked off her sandals. The straps had made deep marks across the tops of her feet. She stretched her legs out in front of her and wiggled toes with bright

78

red toenails. She didn't bother trying to hide a yawn. "Does the rest of the house look the same too? I mean, is the same rose-covered bedspread on the bed? I used to think I could smell those roses when I lay on it."

"No, somebody gave us a log cabin patch quilt I use as a bedspread. I sleep there now," Jocie said. "But your stuff's still in the closet. The rose bedspread is probably in there somewhere too."

"What about your old bedroom?"

"Dad's now," Jocie said. "Aunt Love's in the bedroom down here."

"Oh, of course," Tabitha said, but she looked disappointed. "Not a problem. I'm used to sleeping on the couch. Most of our apartments only had one bedroom. That's all DeeDee could afford."

"There you go with the DeeDee again," Aunt Love said as she handed Tabitha a plate of ham and biscuits and applesauce. She sat a glass of lemonade on the glass-covered coffee table in front of the couch. "Is that some modern name for mothers in California?"

Tabitha laughed. "You're funny."

"A merry heart doeth good like a medicine," Aunt Love said.

"The Bible again, I presume," Tabitha said.

"You'll get used to it," Jocie said. "But do kids call their mothers DeeDee in California?"

"No, no. That doesn't have anything to do with California. That happened in Chicago right after we left. DeeDee told everybody we were sisters, so I couldn't very well keep calling her Mama. She threatened to send me back a hundred times before I got used to it, but I can't imagine calling DeeDee Mama now."

"I prayed she'd send you back. Every day. A dozen times a day," David said.

"Well, I guess your prayers finally got answered." Tabitha took a sip of lemonade and pinched a crumb off the biscuit as if testing the food to be sure it was safe.

"Mine too," Jocie said. "I've been saying the sister prayer for years. That and the dog prayer, and now I've got Zeb and you both in two days."

"The sister prayer?" Tabitha laughed again. "You guys are hilarious. DeeDee said I'd need to pack my sense of humor along with me if I was going to survive around here." She took another nibble of the biscuit and then sat the plate down on the coffee table. "I'm really not very hungry. Too many chips I guess, but the lemonade is delicious. Thank you, Aunt Love."

"She must have remembered to put sugar in it," Jocie muttered. David frowned at her, but she was saved by the phone ringing. "That'll be the church."

The phone rang again before David stood up to answer it. Maybe it would be better to just let it ring and wait until the next morning to find out the verdict. He didn't want anything ruining Tabitha's homecoming, but the rings kept on, demanding he answer it. As he moved slowly toward the phone on the little table by the door, he heard Jocie explaining to Tabitha about the church and the vote for him to be interim pastor.

"You mean Daddy's actually still preaching?" Tabitha said. "DeeDee didn't think he'd still be preaching, you know, because of the divorce and all. She said people in Hollyhill aren't very tolerant. Not like they are in California. Nobody cares how many times you've been married or even if you're married or not out there. Of course, I don't know about preachers. I'm not sure they even have preachers."

"Of course they have preachers in California," Aunt Love said shortly.

"You think so? I never met one if they do," Tabitha said. "And you'd think I would have. I mean, don't preachers go around advertising what they do? You know, saying things like 'Come to my church,' 'Believe in God or else,' 'Stop doing anything fun,' that sort of thing."

"My heavens, child. What a thing to say," Aunt Love said.

"Oh dear, I've shocked you," Tabitha said. "DeeDee said I'd have to be careful about that too. That my mouth would get me in trouble double-quick in Hollyhill."

David wanted to let the phone ring, turn around, and get Tabitha out of hot water, but if it was Matt McDermott, he'd think something was wrong if David didn't answer the phone and like as not would make the trip over here to be sure they hadn't had car trouble on the way home. Just today he'd told David that prayer was surely all that was keeping the wheels on David's car rolling. The old car had been making funny noises lately. Even Wes had been on him to get a new car, had told him he needed a dating car now that Leigh Jacobson was giving him the eye.

David pushed that thought away. He didn't have time to worry about new modes of transportation tonight. Or Leigh Jacobson. It was enough that Adrienne's memory had walked back into the house along with Tabitha, as sharp and piercing as the day she'd left. What he really needed was to go sit on the rock fence out back, look up at the stars until their sparkle calmed his soul, and let God help him make some sense of what was happening. But the phone kept ringing, surely on the twentieth ring by now. Tabitha was still talking. Aunt Love had started quoting Scripture. And he couldn't even whisper a prayer before he said, "Hello."

"Oh, good, you're there," Matt McDermott said. "I called earlier without an answer and was about to get afeared you were broke down somewhere."

David couldn't read anything in his voice. Matt was such a steady man that good and bad news would probably sound the same, something to be dealt with either way. "We were outside for a while." He thought about telling him Tabitha had come home, but that would mean too much explaining. Better to just find out the vote and get it over with.

"I guess the girl had to see to her dog. If I'd known she wanted a dog, I could have rounded one up for her. Somebody's always trying to get rid of pups."

"I think she's happy with the mutt that showed up here. But what about the vote? Am I preaching at Mt. Pleasant next Sunday?"

Matt hesitated before he said, "I'm thinking that might be up to you, Brother David."

"So I didn't get the vote." David tried to keep the disappointment out of his voice. How could he be disappointed about anything tonight with the daughter he had feared he might never see again sitting on the couch behind him?

"Well, you the same as did. It turned out eighty-eight point six percent, which is near the same as ninety, and would have been ninety if Stella Hoskins hadn't got the bug this afternoon. She's been telling everybody that you're God's answer to our prayers here at Mt. Pleasant. Somebody who'd know how to minister to the young and old alike. She called me a little bit ago and asked if she couldn't register her vote over the phone, but I figured it was too late for it to officially count, you know. Maybe if she'd called before church, but she said she was too busy losing her dinner to call then. Still, unofficially, I think you can be sure you got ninety percent."

"That's reaching a little," David said.

"Maybe, but it's a reach I hope—that ninety percent of the people at Mt. Pleasant hope—you'll make." Matt McDermott emphasized the ninety percent.

"Eighty-eight point six," David said.

It was suddenly quiet on the couch behind him. And then Jocie was at his elbow, whispering, "That rounds off to ninety."

He pointed her back to the couch. He couldn't decide now. But he wouldn't say no yet either. "I'll pray about it and let you know tomorrow," he told Matt.

"Well, I'd rather you just went ahead and said yes now, but a deacon can't argue with a preacher who wants to pray. Fact of the matter is, we shouldn't even have voted on this now. The pulpit committee could've just appointed you interim."

"I requested a vote."

"I know, and I understood where you were coming from on it. No need arguing that now." Matt let out a deep breath that whooshed over the phone lines. "So you pray about it, Brother David, and I'll be praying you decide to let the vote be near enough. It isn't but a baby step away. But if the good Lord leads you in another direction, you know I won't cancel my subscription to the *Hollyhill Banner* or anything. And you can still bring your girl out to go fishing in my pond whenever you want."

"That's good to hear," David said with a smile. "The *Banner* can't afford to lose any subscribers or me any fishing holes."

After a few more words, David hung up and turned back toward the couch. Jocie looked nearly ready to explode, but he shook his head at her. "God's the only one I'm talking to about it tonight. Pray tonight. Think tomorrow."

"Okay," Jocie said with a shrug. "It doesn't matter to me anyway. If you don't take it, I won't have to try to be nice to Ronnie Martin."

"Being nice to people you don't like is good for your Christian character," Aunt Love said. "But your father is right. We're all tired, and poor Tabitha is exhausted. We need to fix her a bed and let her rest."

Tabitha's eyes had drooped shut several times while David had been on the phone. "Sorry, crew. I don't mean to be a wet blanket, but I need some shut-eye," she said. "Get me a pillow and a blanket and I'll be set right here."

"Why don't you sleep in your old room?" Jocie said. "I can sleep out on the back porch. You know, I've been thinking about asking to sleep out there this summer anyway. It's cooler with the windows open."

"That's sweet of you, Jocie." David figured she planned on sneaking the dog in as soon as she heard the first snore, but he'd feign ignorance for now. Maybe the bath she'd given the mutt the day before had gotten rid of any fleas. And the fact was, David wasn't capable of one more decision on this night.

Jocie led Tabitha off to the bathroom and her bedroom. Aunt Love went off to the kitchen to rattle pans. David didn't know what she was doing. Sometimes he doubted if Aunt Love knew what she was doing. But if it helped her to rattle a pan, then he wasn't going to complain about a little noise.

David sat on the couch and let his household settle around him. He supposed he should pray, but his soul was too weary. He tried not to even think, but then Tabitha laughed upstairs in the bedroom and it was Adrienne's laugh. Adrienne laughing at him when he'd talked about having another baby when Tabitha was five. Adrienne saying she'd never go through what she went through with Tabitha again. Then two years later his elation to find out she was expecting followed by the rage when he caught her concocting some poisonous brew she hoped would make her miscarry.

There had been no laughter in the house for a long time after that. For months Adrienne had refused to come out of their bedroom or to let him in. He had slept on the back porch on the cot then and wondered at times if the stars he could see through the tall windows were all that kept him sane. He could have broken down the bedroom door, had considered it at least once every day during the last months before Jocie was born, but his mother, whom Adrienne allowed to carry meals to her, had said she was well physically and would surely regain some emotional stability once the baby came.

When the labor pains had started, she'd refused to go to the hospital. Dr. Markum had made a home delivery with David's mother's help. Two days later Adrienne had handed the screaming baby to him and said, "You wanted her. She's yours. Her name is Jocelyn. It's not in the Bible. I made sure before I picked it."

He'd agreed to the terms, all the terms—sleeping on the couch to better hear Jocie at night, not asking questions when Adrienne was late coming home from Grundy, living separate lives in the same house. A funny thing about hope. Even when there's not a spot of light in the east, you're still sure the sun will rise. And hope works like that for the sun, but other things aren't as sure as the sunrise.

He wondered now if somewhere inside him where he was afraid to look he'd held on to hope that someday not just Tabitha but Adrienne would return. In spite of the long-distance divorce when Adrienne had gotten to Las Vegas. In spite of the boyfriend. In spite of the fact that she'd left him long before she'd gotten in the car and driven away in the middle of the night.

Maybe Wes was right. It was time to move on. But Leigh Jacobson? She was so young. Her face as she'd watched him preach that morning came to mind. Eager. Smiling. Yet somehow anxious too, as though she was already worried about not saying the right thing when she shook his hand on the way out of the church.

He pushed her face away as Jocie came back carrying a pillow and sheets and a blanket for the cot on the porch.

"Are you sure you don't mind giving up your room?" he asked her.

"No, it'll be neat out there in the morning when the sun comes up."

"The stars aren't bad either," David said. "I used to sleep out there some years ago. Tabitha okay for the night?"

"Said she was still feeling a little woozy, but she was asleep before I got out of the room. It's great that she came home, isn't it, Daddy?"

"Yes, it is."

"And you almost got ninety percent. They do want you, and in another couple of weeks, you'll probably even get the Martin family to liking you."

"If you don't give Ronnie a black eye."

"I'll do something even sneakier. I'll be so nice to him he'll go crazy trying to figure out what I'm up to." Jocie grinned.

"Confuse the enemy."

"Exactly. Night, Daddy." Jocie kissed his cheek and looked around. "Aunt Love already turned in?"

"I think so. I don't hear any more pans rattling."

"Then maybe Jezebel isn't waiting on the other side of the kitchen door to attack. I forgot to warn Tabitha about the evil that lurks in the dark ready to pounce at unsuspecting toes."

"I'll shut the door to your bedroom when I go up."

"Good, but who knows? Jezzie hates me, but she may like Tabitha. We're nothing alike, are we?"

"She's been away from Hollyhill for a long time. But she seemed glad to be back."

"Yeah." Jocie hesitated a moment before she asked, "Do you wish Mother had come with her?"

"No," he said without thinking and surprised himself. When he stood up to go up to his bedroom, he felt lighter the way the biblical David must have felt when he took off King Saul's armor before going out to fight Goliath. Almost floating as he went out to meet the giant. But the shepherd David had seen the giant waiting for him and at least knew what he was up against. What giants were out there waiting for David Brooke?

Upstairs, David peeked in at Tabitha. Curled up in a ball with the sheet pulled up under her chin, she looked more like the Tabitha he remembered. Her honey brown hair fanned across the pillow. She'd left the headband on. His eyes touched on the rose on her cheek. A California girl in Hollyhill. That might be the first giant he had to face. He had a feeling he better add courage to his prayer list this night. And wisdom.

The door to the back porch barely squeaked when Jocie let the dog in. Nothing her father would hear upstairs with the fan running beside his bed. She told Zeb the rules—no barking or growling, no hiking his leg on the furniture, no chasing the evil cat. Zeb cocked his head to the left and intently watched her until she stopped talking. Then he settled on the rug beside the cot with a contented huff and closed his eyes. Jocie had a harder time settling down.

The long outside wall of the porch had four hinged windows that swung up and hooked to the ceiling to let in the cool night air along with the evening serenade. The tree frogs and katydids were going strong just outside. When an owl screeched over in Mr. Crutcher's woods, Jocie reached down to touch Zeb's head. The dog didn't move, not bothered at all by the night sounds or the novelty of being inside, or almost inside.

A whip-poor-will began his night chorus. The same notes over and over, "whip-poor-will," but there was something calming about the sound. Nothing unexpected. The bird never got bored with the song God had given him and switched it around to "poor-will-whip" or "whip-will-poor."

And her father was right about the stars. A couple of the windows were blocked by the maple outside, but the others were open to the sky with stars so thick it was as if God had spilled a whole package of them there and the angels had forgotten to pick them up and spread them around. How could she close her eyes on that and just go to sleep? It seemed disrespectful somehow.

Jocie started a thank-you prayer a dozen times, but her mind kept scooting away to other things. Tabitha sleeping in her bed. How to keep Zeb from barking if Jezebel made an unexpected appearance. The Mt. Pleasant vote. The kittens and the mother cat who might lead them off and lose them in the woods. Her own mother. DeeDee. Maybe she could write her a letter. She'd written her before and never gotten an answer, but maybe if she said "Dear DeeDee" instead of "Dear Mama."

Dear DeeDee, I hope you are doing okay. We're fine here and really glad to see Tabitha. Daddy was surprised. Why didn't you come back with her?

Jocie stopped and rubbed out that last question with a mental eraser. She couldn't ask that. After a few minutes she began to write the note in her mind again. *Do you look the same? I remember you were very pretty. I don't look the same. I'm thirteen. Do you think I should ask Dad if I can buy a bra? I'm skinny and don't much need one, but I can't start high school without bra straps. I got a dog. Well, actually, God sent me a dog. Dad says he's the ugliest dog he's ever seen, but I like him. Do you like dogs?*

I really don't know what you like. Sometimes I wonder if you were ever here. I mean, I know you were. I remember seeing you, but did you listen to the whip-poor-will at night and wish you could find his tree and see him singing? Did you ever peek in on me at night to see if I was sleeping? Did you ever kiss my bumped head to make the hurt go away? Did you teach me to say Mama? I can't remember any of that, and it seems like I should be able to remember something. I mean, I was five, almost six. Was I too young to be your sister and that's why you left me behind? I mean, that's okay. I don't think I could be a California girl. Wes says I could, that anybody can move anywhere and be okay after a while. I guess he should know. Being from Jupiter and all. But I like Hollyhill. The people are sometimes funny, but aren't people funny everywhere?

We'll take good care of Tabitha. Love, Jocie.

She went back and mentally crossed out the part about Wes and how she liked Hollyhill. Her mother would just laugh at that anyway. Of course, she probably wouldn't ever write any of it down to send. Not unless Tabitha said her mother wanted to get a letter from her. Maybe after Tabitha had a while to rest, Jocie would ask her about their mother. After all, shouldn't a person know something about her mother? Like her favorite color. And did she lick or bite ice cream cones? And did she still wear that icy pink lipstick and that tropical flower perfume? Did she ever talk about Hollyhill? Or Jocie?

Jocie swatted at a mosquito buzzing her ear, yanked the cover up over her head, and went to sleep.

The next morning Jocie was jerked awake by a mockingbird shouting out his songs. Normally she liked mockingbirds, but this one had not only variety but volume. She put her head under her pillow, but it was no use. Aunt Love started slamming skillets around in the kitchen, and Mr. Crutcher was hitting rocks as he bush-hogged his pasture just across the fence from them.

Beside her Zeb growled low in his throat. She'd forgotten about the dog. Jocie threw off the pillow, grabbed his muzzle, and whispered, "No barking." She slid off the cot, glanced over her shoulder toward the kitchen door, and then let Zeb out the back door. Just in time. Jezebel stuck her head around the corner of the kitchen door.

"Morning, Sugar," Jocie said sweetly. The white cat arched her back and took a swipe at the air before turning back to the kitchen.

Ten minutes later Jocie had washed her face, combed her hair, and sneaked into her room for some clean clothes. Tabitha didn't move so much as an eyelash while Jocie was getting her stuff, even when the dresser drawer groaned as she pulled it open. Tabitha was so still, in fact, that Jocie stared at her chest before she left the room to be sure she was breathing while crazy headlines ran through her head. "Sister Returns Home Only to Die in Her Sleep." "Chips from Unknown Truck Driver Poison Unsuspecting Girl." But Tabitha was breathing, her chest rising and falling quite naturally. Jocie whispered a thank-you prayer and pulled the door shut behind her.

She made it to the kitchen just in time to rescue the biscuits and turn the bacon. Breakfast was her favorite meal, since Aunt Love hadn't come up with any way to use up Mt. Pleasant's bountiful supply of cabbage for breakfast.

Aunt Love was nowhere to be seen. That was her problem lately. She'd start cooking and then go off to do something else and forget all about the food on the stove till the smoke reminded her. What Jocie couldn't understand was how come Aunt Love couldn't remember the beans she'd put on to cook ten minutes ago but could still come up with half the verses in the Bible. But her dad said that was the way it was with old people, and they'd just have to try to help Aunt Love with the things she kept forgetting.

It wasn't that Jocie didn't like Aunt Love. She was family. She had to like her, or maybe that was love her. Maybe it was the liking Aunt Love she had a choice on. Love thy neighbor could just as easily say love thy senile old aunt. It wasn't Aunt Love's fault that she wasn't like Mama Mae. Sisters, but not alike. Just like Jocie and Tabitha. Sisters, but nothing alike.

Jocie lifted the bacon strips out of the skillet and laid them out on a brown paper grocery bag to drain the grease. She was setting plates on the table when Aunt Love finally made her way back to the kitchen. If Jocie hadn't come to the rescue, the bacon grease would have surely been flaming to the ceiling by now. Maybe they should start eating cornflakes for breakfast. Her father had already asked Aunt Love not to cook at lunchtime if he or Jocie wasn't there. Some days he took the fuse for the stove out of the meter box.

"Rejoice! For this is the day the Lord hath made," Jocie said, beating Aunt Love to the punch with a little Scripture.

Aunt Love smiled. She wore her customary dark purple house-dress with a white apron tied over it. A few white cat hairs clung to the sleeves of the purple dress, but the cat was nowhere in sight. Aunt Love's iron gray hair was fastened tightly in a bun on the back of her head. Jocie had seen her cutting it one time. Aunt Love had washed her hair in the kitchen sink and combed it out down her back before gathering it all up in her hand to bring over her shoulder in a bunch. Then she'd unceremoniously snipped off a couple of inches. She'd said it didn't matter if the length was uneven. A hair shorter here or there wasn't going to make a penny's worth of difference all wound up in a bun.

"Did you ever cut your hair short?" Jocie had asked. Jocie's hair lapped her shoulders now, but she'd also had hair so short that she couldn't wear a barrette much less a ponytail holder.

"Once, but I didn't like it. So I let it grow back out," Aunt Love had said. "I've had it in a bun like this for some forty years, I'd say. Truth is, my head like as not would lop over on my chest if it wasn't anchored by that bun these days."

Jocie had been surprised by the attempt at humor from Aunt Love. Sometimes she almost seemed like a regular person, but it never lasted long.

But now Jocie was determined to make it last longer. She was determined to stay out of trouble with Aunt Love, to not let it bother her when Aunt Love found fault, as she surely would, with anything Jocie did. She was determined to listen to her advice and not do things opposite for spite.

Being nice to Aunt Love was an act of thanks to the Lord for answering her dog prayer and her sister prayer. She still didn't see why Tabitha had said the sister prayer was so hilarious. If she'd been praying the same thing for seven years, then she'd understand, but it didn't seem as if Tabitha had been praying any kind of prayer lately. Maybe Jocie could help her brush up her praying skills before somebody asked her to say grace or anything.

Now Aunt Love corrected Jocie's verse. "'This is the day which the LORD hath made; we will rejoice and be glad in it.' Psalm 118:24, but that's very good, Jocie."

"Thanks," Jocie said. "Do you want me to do the eggs for Dad? Where is he, anyway? He's usually up by now."

"He went out early to walk the fields and pray, I suppose," Aunt Love said.

"Oh, the vote. Do you think he'll take it?"

"He should, but I don't know what he'll do. Your father has to make up his own mind what's best," Aunt Love said. "With the help of the Lord, of course."

"Yeah," Jocie said.

Aunt Love took the basket of eggs from Jocie. "You did the bacon. I'll do the eggs." Then Aunt Love saw the pan of biscuits on top of the stove and remembered. "Oh dear, I did it again, didn't I? I say I'm not going to leave the kitchen after I put something on the stove, but then I end up back in the bedroom looking for something and lose my concentration."

"Don't worry about it, Aunt Love. Nothing burned." Jocie sat a jar of blackberry jam on the table beside the butter. "Tabitha's still dead to the world."

"I doubt she'll be up before noon, if then. The best thing for her is to sleep, get rested up. The next few weeks may be difficult for her."

"Why?" Jocie asked.

Aunt Love hesitated before she said, "Adjusting to being back here. Getting used to us."

"You mean laughing at us."

"I guess I did seem pretty odd to her. But then everybody thinks I'm pretty odd."

Jocie trotted out her new attitude. "No, Aunt Love. Maybe eccentric, but not odd."

"I think if you look those words up in the dictionary, you'll find they mean close to the same thing, Jocelyn," Aunt Love said, but she was smiling.

"Where's Jez—uh, Sugar?" Jocie asked to change the subject.

"Napping already. She was restless all night. Half had me worried, but I decided it was just a new person in the house."

Or dog, Jocie thought. "I'll go see if I can round Dad up for breakfast. Don't fix me an egg. I'll just eat biscuits and jam."

"You don't eat enough, child. You turn sideways, you'll disappear," Aunt Love muttered as Jocie went out the back door.

Zeb was waiting on the back step with a grin as if he hadn't seen her for a month instead of just being shoved out the door fifteen minutes ago. Jocie grinned back and let him lick her fingers. "Good dog."

Aunt Love came to the door. "Careful. He's smelling the bacon grease on your hand. Who knows with a stray like this? He might take a bite."

Jocie ignored Aunt Love and headed toward the rock fence at the end of the yard. She stepped into the coolness of the two old oaks that stood sentinel on either side of the gate that went into the apple orchard. The top hinge of the gate had been broken for years, and the iron gate stood open, its bottom iron pieces embedded in the grass and weeds. It didn't matter. They didn't have any cows or horses to keep out of the yard.

A few more rocks had bled down out of the wound in the fence. Jocie picked up one of the rocks and tried to place it back, but as soon as she turned it loose, it slid back to the ground. Her father said there was an art to placing the rocks so the fence would stand without mortar. He had tried to find someone to teach him, had even advertised in the *Banner*, but the fence had been built over a hundred years ago, and the men who knew the secret of placing the stones had all long since died out in Hollyhill.

Jocie usually found her father sitting on the flattest rock where the fence was spilling its guts as he contemplated the necessary arrangement to rebuild the fence. But today he wasn't there, so Jocie climbed through the gap in the fence to the orchard. The rocks still held the cool of the night.

The apple trees might not be as old as the rock fence, but they were gnarled and twisted by years of withstanding the weather. A couple had blown down, but enough of the roots still clung to the earth that the trees had leaves and sometimes apples. Jocie loved walking through the trees in the spring when the petals were floating in the breezes.

But the petals had fallen weeks ago, and small round apples dotted the limbs now, promising a bumper crop. One of those mixed blessings her dad sometimes talked about. It was good to pick up an apple to chomp whenever she walked this way, but Jocie dreaded the long hours peeling the apples for Aunt Love to can. Of course, stewed apples for supper beat stewed cabbage hands down.

She was about to give up and head back to the house, when she spotted her father at the far end of the orchard. He waved when he saw her.

She stopped and waited for him. He looked taller as he came through the trees with the sun at this back. He wasn't half bad looking for somebody his age. Not that he was all that old. She'd never really thought about what her dad might look like to other people, but Wes talking about stepmothers had sort of knocked her eyes open a bit. She could see why Leigh Jacobson might drive all the way out to Mt. Pleasant Church to listen to his sermon. Still, the idea sort of scared her. She and her dad had managed for a long time together.

Aunt Love hadn't changed that. They managed in spite of Aunt Love. She didn't know whether Tabitha would change that. But she was pretty sure Leigh Jacobson would change that if she became her stepmother. Still, she might know about bras. It didn't look like Tabitha would. She hadn't been wearing one.

12

David lengthened his stride when he spotted Jocie and the dog at the other end of the orchard. He hadn't intended to walk so long, but his prayer line to the Lord had been clogged with worries that had nothing to do with Mt. Pleasant Church. He'd hardly been able to think of anything but Tabitha. He hadn't slept well, and at the first gray light of dawn he'd gone to stand in Jocie's bedroom door to watch Tabitha sleep.

It seemed appropriate that the light was new. It was all going to be new, getting to know this daughter so long missing from his life and finding a way to help her. And she was going to need help. She hadn't ridden a bus all the way across the plains states because she was tired of California. Something was wrong.

But until she trusted him enough to tell him what it was, he'd have to be patient. Who knew what had happened to her over the years. Obviously there had been no thought of church. Of course, it wouldn't be all gone—the Bible teachings she had learned before she left. After all, she had been thirteen. Way past old enough to know right from wrong. And she had made a confession of faith when she was twelve, had been baptized, had joined New Liberty Church. Still was a member there, he supposed, unless the church had taken her off the roll. Not many churches did that anymore. No cleaning house just because a member no longer occupied a pew.

They would have to talk. He'd have to find out if the decision she'd made as a child meant anything to her now. He'd have to know if she loved the Lord. That was something he'd never had to wonder about for himself. He knew, had always known, the Lord was with him long before he felt his touch on his shoulder in the submarine. He hadn't always made the right decisions, but he'd never doubted the Lord was there rooting for him to choose the right path.

He wasn't sure he'd made the right decision this morning walking through Herman Crutcher's cow pasture. He'd prayed. He'd tried to put what he wanted aside. He'd listened and heard nothing but a baby calf bawling for his mother. But sometimes that was the way the Lord answered prayers. With no sure push one way or the other.

He could have asked for a sign. He could have prayed, "Lord, if you want me to keep preaching at Mt. Pleasant, let me hear a meadowlark call," but who was he to push the Lord for signs? And it didn't matter that three minutes after having the thought he had heard a meadowlark. He might have heard one earlier and that was what had given him the idea to begin with. He trusted the Lord to lead his thoughts, to lead him. Not just in what to do about the Mt. Pleasant vote, but in everything he did from what he published in the *Banner* to what he said to the people he talked to on the streets of Hollyhill. Wes told him that sometimes made him a sorry editor of a boring small-town paper not good for much more than lining dresser drawers.

At times David wished he could liven up the *Banner* a bit, but the facts were that Hollyhill was the town he had to write about and the folks in Hollyhill were upstanding, regular folks who didn't go around shooting one another. At least not very often. Thank God. The bank had never been robbed. As far as anybody knew, no city official had ever stuck city funds in his own pocket. The mayor might not be the sharpest pencil in the box, but the Hollyhill folks were comfortable with him and had elected him three terms running. The chief of police spent the better part of his day writing parking tickets.

There were scandals, of course. Junior Jackson's wife had just run off with the high school track coach three weeks ago. And there was Bennie Adams who'd been fired at the bank because he'd come to work drunk. Not to mention the Harrisons' divorce after little Stevie was born. Cutest baby in town, but gossip said the baby didn't look a thing like Seth Harrison for a reason. Several names of possible fathers had been bandied about, but David couldn't print that kind of news in the *Banner*. He'd been that kind of news when Adrienne left. Tabitha coming back might bring the story back to the gossip buzz line. If so, nobody would need to wait for the *Banner* to come out to get the scoop.

"Hi, Dad," Jocie said when he got close. "Breakfast's ready."

He was glad she didn't ask about his decision about the church. "And I'm ready for breakfast," he said with a glance at his watch. "I didn't mean to be out so long. Wes will wonder what's happened to us."

"Wes won't, but you'll hear it from Zella for being late. You'd think she was never late for anything."

"I doubt if she has been." David had inherited Zella Curtsinger from the last editor, who'd made him promise to keep her on. The *Banner* was all the family she had. Not that David would have fired her anyway. She knew where everything was. She sent out the bills on time, kept up with who paid and who didn't, made sure the paper sold enough ads to pay them to put it out. Without her, David would have sunk in red ink years ago.

"Of course, I left Aunt Love alone with the eggs," Jocie said. "We might not even have a kitchen to eat in by now. She needs to teach Jez—I mean Sugar—to yowl when something starts burning. I'll bet Zeb would do that."

"If he were allowed in the house." David looked straight at Jocie and almost smiled when she ducked her head. The child had never been good at hiding anything from him. Even as a four-year-old, if she jumped in a mud puddle with her Sunday shoes on, she'd run straight to show him. He knew every recess she'd lost for talking too much. She hadn't tried to hide the broken pieces or glue them back together when she'd broken Aunt Love's favorite candy dish. She'd faced right up to the music. The dog was no different.

"I know I didn't ask, but I let Zeb sleep beside my bed last night. You don't care, do you? I mean really care." She looked up. "He was good."

"If Sugar shows up on the porch in the middle of the night, we'll have World War III."

"Then he can keep coming in? I mean at night." Jocie's eyes were hopeful.

"If you can keep the peace. If war breaks out, it's outside. Sugar was here first."

"Deal," Jocie said. "But we shouldn't tell Aunt Love, should we? No need upsetting her for no reason, and I'll keep the porch clean."

"Agreed. Of course, I'm going to claim ignorance if war breaks out. You'll be on your own."

"Oh, Dad. You wouldn't do that. That would be lying."

"You call it what you want to. I'm calling it self-preservation." David laughed and put his arm around Jocie. "Preachers learn that early on. What you don't know you can't be blamed for."

⁂

Aunt Love hadn't forgotten the eggs. Breakfast looked good. David waited until after Aunt Love said grace to make his decision announcement. He buttered a biscuit half and said, "I've decided to accept the vote. We'll be at Mt. Pleasant Church for the summer at least."

"That's great, Dad. I can surely be nice to Ronnie Martin that long. With prayer and the Lord's help, of course," Jocie added as she broke up a piece of bacon to fit on her biscuit.

Aunt Love was briefer. "Good," she said.

David smiled. That's the way it was with decisions half the time. You wrestled with them. Let them keep you awake at night. Studied and pondered. Then the decision was made and life went on with barely a ripple in the surface of the day. "I'll call Matt McDermott when I get to the office."

"He'd be at the barn milking now anyway," Aunt Love said. "Do you want me to just let Tabitha sleep?"

"That might be best. She was worn out," David said.

"I can't wait to tell Wes. He'll never believe it. The dog prayer and now the sister prayer," Jocie said. "It's okay if I go to work with you, isn't it? I left my bike there the other night, and I promised to help Wes with those Bible school ads this morning. He has five to set up."

"Dorothy McDermott was talking about Mt. Pleasant's Bible school yesterday. I think they're expecting you to be there to lead the assemblies," Aunt Love said.

He'd have to figure out a way to handle the newspaper deadlines and drive to Mt. Pleasant Church every day. He didn't mind. It was a good problem to have again.

* * *

Zella looked up from her typewriter when they got to the *Banner* a little after nine. "Oh, you're here. I thought perhaps you'd taken the day off even though it wasn't written in on your calendar." She swiveled her chair around to face David and Jocie. With her index finger she pushed her green-rimmed glasses up on her nose and then lightly touched her dyed-black hair to make sure each round curl was still in place. David had never seen her with a hair ruffled even on the windiest days. Jocie said Zella's hair would break before it would blow out of place.

"Now, Zella, you know I wouldn't not let you know if I wasn't coming in. I'm sorry. I guess I should have called to let you know we were running late."

"Oh, that's okay. I'm sure you had more important things to worry about than whether the people at your workplace knew where you were. After all, it hardly matters if I have to tell the mayor you're not here and I have no idea whether you will be or not."

Jocie rolled her eyes at David. "Yikes, Zella. What did you eat for breakfast? Prunes?" Without waiting for an answer, Jocie opened the door to the pressroom. The sound of the machinery spilled out. She was yelling to Wes about Tabitha before the door closed.

"So the mayor called. Did he want anything special or just some free advertising for his next political campaign?"

"The election is not until next spring," Zella said.

"It's always election time with the mayor."

"True enough," Zella conceded. "But he says he wants to get with you about the community having a Fourth of July celebration. He says he thinks it's especially important this year after the tragic events of the fall, and I couldn't agree with him more. I still get tears in my eyes every time I think about little John-John saluting his father's coffin. Such a tragedy." She fished a tissue out of her skirt's waistband and dabbed her eyes. "What is the world coming to when they'll shoot down wonderful men like President Kennedy?"

"I don't know, Zella." He wished he was in the back with Wes and Jocie talking about Tabitha coming home. Not that he didn't agree with Zella about the tragedy of the Kennedy assassination. He did. But Zella wallowed in her grief, enjoying it as much as a pig loves mud.

"But as a preacher, what do you think, David? Do you think we're in the latter days with rumors of war and storms and up-heavals all around?"

"The Bible is pretty clear on that, Zella. It says no one can know, so I don't spend a lot of time trying to figure out God's plans."

"But they have those bombs that could wipe us out in a millisecond and those red phones and everything. It's scary when you think about it. I thought about having one of those bomb shelters built in my backyard, but I couldn't see tearing up my rose garden. My mother planted some of those rosebushes, you know. Besides, who wants to be all squirreled up under the ground while everything is dying above you? Better to go first and quick, I say." Zella bobbed her head up and down. Her curls didn't bounce out of place.

"You could be right," David agreed. "We just have to keep praying for peace."

"Well, of course, that goes without saying."

"Any other messages besides the mayor's?" David said as he edged past Zella's desk. Zella could talk nonstop for hours about the world going to the dogs, but she had no trouble jumping back to the business at hand.

"Just Harry Sanders. He called to say he had his paint on sale this week if you still needed some."

"Did you talk him into putting a sale ad in the paper?"

"Of course."

"You're worth your weight in gold," David said.

"A man doesn't advertise, he goes broke." Zella turned back to her typewriter to hide her pleased smile.

"And a paper that doesn't sell ads goes broke even faster." David was to the door to his small office. "Oh, by the way, I've got news. Good news."

Zella looked up at him again. "The church voted you in? Well, that's wonderful. Of course, they should have."

"That too," David said. "But more. Tabitha came home."

Zella frowned, at a loss, until it dawned on her what Tabitha he was talking about. Her eyes flew open wide. "Your Tabitha?"

"Yes, my Tabitha."

"Oh my heavens, David. That's fantastic news." Zella stood

up but didn't seem to know what to do next. "Is she okay? What about Adrienne? And my gracious, why didn't you tell me the minute you got here? This is so exciting."

"She's fine, Zella, and Adrienne's still in California."

"California suits her." Zella sat back down, her smile disappearing.

"How do you know? Have you ever been to California?"

"No, but Wesley has, and you see how he is." Zella rolled a fresh piece of paper into her typewriter. "You really shouldn't let him tell Jocelyn all those crazy stories about being from Jupiter. She half believes him."

"Oh, they're just having fun. Nothing to worry about."

"Wesley's something to worry about. Has he ever told you why he's hiding out here in Hollyhill? He has to be running from the law."

"I don't think he's hiding from the law," David said.

"He's hiding from something. But Tabitha." Zella gave him a hard look. "You surely didn't know she was coming and just keep it a secret from all of us."

"Nope, we came home from Mt. Pleasant Church last night, and there she was on the porch."

Zella's smile came back. "How amazing! How old is she now?"

"She'll be twenty next month."

"Twenty? It's been that long? That doesn't seem possible. Well, tell her to come in to see me. You know I taught her to type when she was just a little thing and showed her how to water my violets without getting water on the leaves. She used to sit out here with me and draw rainbows when she came to work with you. She was such a sweet little girl."

"Jocie could probably use some pointers about improving her typing."

Zella slid a look his way. "She'll be going to the high school in the fall. They have typing classes."

David gave it up and went on into his office to call the mayor. No, the mayor didn't have any concrete plans for the Fourth of July celebration. He was thinking some patriotic songs and maybe some preaching. Of course, they'd have to get the preacher at First Baptist for that. And the Christian Church preacher for the opening prayer. That wasn't exactly equal time, but there were more Baptists in Hollyhill than Christian Church members.

"What about the Methodists?" David asked.

"Oh, they can come too," the mayor said. "We don't discriminate on denominations. Do you think, if you put something in the paper, we can get some of the folks to donate a little cash for a few fireworks? I was over at Grundy last summer on the Fourth, and they had this American flag in fireworks. Made me want to salute or something."

"I'll write an editorial," David promised. "But we don't have much time. Not even a whole month. We should have started planning earlier."

"Well, I aimed to get started on it earlier, but you know how the time flies by. It feels like it ought to still be March instead of already June. Anyhow, we can't go back and do any of that different. And we don't have to have the fireworks. Just the singing and preaching and maybe the high school band out to play the national anthem. And Boy Scouts with flags. Girl Scouts too. Their cookie sale's over, isn't it? Maybe we could have a parade."

"Sounds good, Mayor. You checked with the council members to see what they think?"

"Who cares what they think," the mayor said shortly and then remembered who he was talking to. "Now, I don't want to see that in print next week, David, but you know how a couple of them are. If I said we should put a water fountain in the Sahara Desert, they'd say nobody was ever thirsty there and even if they were they could drink sand like their daddies before them and a water fountain would be a misuse of city funds. Now, you know that's true, David."

David laughed. "Well, maybe, but surely everybody will want to get on the patriotic bandwagon."

"They might climb aboard if they think they can push me off, but that's the kind of thing a public servant has to deal with every day. So you'll beat the drums a little to work up some interest? It'll have to be in this week or next week."

"Sure. Sounds like a great idea. Something to draw the community together."

"Great. I'll start passing the hat around the businesses on Main Street. If we get the parade idea going, that should mean some extra folks downtown shopping. A win-win situation for everybody."

"Are you sure it's not an election year?"

"If a man wants to stay mayor, every year's election year," Mayor Palmor said. "You just don't have to put ads in the local paper every year."

"You pay for them, we'll run them."

"Don't you worry. I'll be paying for plenty of ads next campaign, but right now you just make sure you remember who came up with the idea when you're writing that Fourth of July piece." The mayor laughed and hung up.

David dropped the receiver back on the phone and looked at the stacks of papers on his desk. All to-do piles instead of done piles. And he still had to call Matt McDermott. He pushed back from his desk and stood up. That could wait. It all could wait. He needed coffee and a good dose of banter from Wes. He'd get everything done. The Lord wouldn't throw opportunities his way and then not help him handle them.

13

Wes was always a step ahead of Jocie in any conversation and ready for the sneakiest curveball, but the news about Tabitha seemed to surprise him. "Tabitha home? All the way from California?" he said. "She come in on a spaceship like me?"

"Nope. A bus," Jocie said.

"All the way from California! Well, if that ain't something." Wes shook his head at the wonder of it. "Saturday the dog prayer. Sunday the sister prayer. You ain't been praying anything about me, have you?" Wes looked worried.

"Just the usual everyday stuff. 'God bless Wes and help him keep from mashing his fingers in the press, and don't let his space-ship come back for a few more years.' Nothing special."

Wes looked at his ink-stained fingers. "You know, I haven't got a single purple fingernail. I can't remember that ever happening since I went to work for your dad. The dog prayer. The sister prayer. The no mashed fingers prayer. What else you been praying about?"

Jocie shrugged. "I don't know. That Aunt Love doesn't burn the house down. Rain for the farmers. Lost people get saved. Sick people get well. I don't know. Daddy says half the time we don't expect an answer when we pray anyway. We just do these little prayer chants without thinking about what we're asking for."

"Did you expect to get an answer to the sister prayer?"

106

"Well, yeah, but maybe not so soon after the dog prayer. It's like God just looked down and said, 'Oh, there's Jocie. What is it she's been praying for? Oh yeah, dogs and sisters.' And wow, here they are."

"And what about Tabitha? How was she? She was just a little kid like you last time I saw her."

"I'm not a little kid. I'm thirteen."

"Okay, so you're almost grown and in another fifty years you'll be old like me. But tell me about Tabitha. Did she grow up as pretty as I thought she would?"

"She's pretty. Like I remember Mama. Of course, Tabitha didn't have on any makeup like Mama always wore. Not even lipstick. Nothing except this rose painted on her cheek. But she'd been on a bus for days before she hitched a ride out to our house with a potato chip truck driver. I thought Dad would go bananas over that, but he stayed pretty calm. Then she camped out on the porch till we got home."

"Why didn't she go on in the house?"

"Said she wasn't sure we still lived there. As if Dad would have moved without letting her know. Of course, he hadn't written her for a while, since we didn't have their latest address. Anyway, she'd had to rough it across country. Said she slept in the bus stations whenever she had a layover."

"She came all that way by herself?" Wes shook his head as if he couldn't believe it. "The Tabby I remember was a timid little thing, scared of her shadow. Bus stations have more than their share of shadows."

"I don't know, but she got here. I guess she might have looked a little nervous last night, but of course, everything was pretty crazy with Zeb barking and Aunt Love quoting Scripture and Dad just staring at her as if he couldn't believe his eyes and not saying anything."

"Your dad speechless? I should've been there to see that."

"Yeah, I know. Anyway, Tabitha doesn't look much like I remember. Her hair is long and straight, almost down to her waist. And she had on a funky loose top and bright green pants and sandals. And then that rose painted on her cheek. I think it's just painted on. I've never seen a girl with a real tattoo."

"I thought about getting a tattoo once," Wes said. "But I couldn't remember what the Jupiterian spaceship laws said about foreign ink coming back into the home planet zone. I didn't want to have to slice off a piece of my skin before I could go home."

"You're a nut," Jocie said with a grin and then looked over her shoulder as if she expected Zella or her father to be sneaking up on them. No one was in the pressroom but Wes and her, but still she kept her voice low as she asked Wes, "Do you think she's a hippie?"

"Could be. Coming from California and all. Why don't you ask her?"

"I might. Later, after she gets rested up. I might ask her lots of things," Jocie said, thinking about her mother again.

Nobody liked talking about her mother. Aunt Love said she had never said more than "How do you do?" to her a few times, and you didn't get to know much about a person that way. Wes said pretty much the same thing, that he didn't know enough about her to tell Jocie, and her father looked like she was poking him with needles every time she said anything about her mother. Most people in Hollyhill acted as if Jocie had never even had a mother. But Tabitha shouldn't mind talking about her. And she'd know things no one in Hollyhill could know.

The door opened, and her father came in the pressroom. "Any coffee left out here?" he asked.

"You bet, boss. Strong and so thick we can use it for ink if we run low," Wes said.

Jocie grabbed a cup off the shelf over the coffeepot and poured her dad a cup. She waved the coffee under her nose before she handed it to her father. "Whew. Maybe this was what Zella had for breakfast instead of prunes."

"Nah. This is too much coffee for a mere woman like Zella. It takes a man to swallow something this vile," Wes said as he finished off what was left in his cup and held it out to Jocie for more.

"It might be time to clean the pot," David said as he looked at the black liquid in his cup.

"I've heard that takes the taste away," Wes said.

"One could only hope." David took a swig and swallowed with a grimace. "But it does have a way of popping the eyes open."

"Wide open," Wes said. "Which is what a newspaperman wants. Jo was just telling me that Tabby showed up on your doorstep last night. She okay?"

"Tired. Half sick from the trip, but okay." David sipped the brew in his cup.

"She tell you why she's here?" Wes asked.

"Not yet," David said.

Jocie jumped in. "What do you mean why she's here? Maybe she just wanted to come. Maybe she wanted to see Dad."

"She say she's just visiting?" Wes asked.

"I think she's planning to stay awhile," David said.

"Hollyhill's going to be a change for her. Jo here says she looks like a real California girl."

"A flower child for sure," David said. "But still my daughter."

"A father should take care of his daughter." Wes stared down at his coffee.

"As best a father can. No father can keep every bad thing from happening," David said softly.

"Well, we ain't gonna get no paper out standing around yammering all day," Wes said. "Let's get started on those Bible school ads. Come one, come all. We'll teach you how to spell Jesus in macaroni on a plate."

"Oh, Wes," Jocie said. "Bible school is fun. You get to eat cookies till you're sick and sing and play tag. I never met a kid who didn't like Bible school."

"Homemade cookies?" Wes said.

"Sure. Sometimes even cupcakes."

"Am I too old to give it a try?" Wes asked, his smile back in place.

"I don't know. You'll have to ask the preacher," Jocie said.

Wes peered over at David. "Do we have one in the room? Am I looking at Mt. Pleasant's newest and finest? The Right Reverend Brooke?"

"Brother David will do," David said.

"So you got the vote," Wes said.

"Actually, one vote short of what I asked for, but one vote didn't seem to be enough reason to turn them down. It'll be just a few months till they find somebody full-time. Of course, I haven't talked to Matt McDermott yet this morning. He doesn't know Tabitha's home."

"What difference could that make? Give you sermon fodder. The prodigal daughter comes home." Wes put his hand on Jocie's shoulder. "And the faithful other daughter is as happy as you are. She's ready for the feast. You're going to invite me too, aren't you?"

Jocie giggled. She thought of Tabitha waking up in her room, maybe pulling the box of her old stuff out of the closet. Some of the stuff would make her laugh. Some would make her cry. And then she'd go downstairs, where Aunt Love would greet her with some Scripture. Maybe something like "Good sleep is a gift of God." Jocie wasn't sure that was in the Bible, but it might be. Maybe with somebody else in the house to pile Scripture on, Aunt Love would let up a little on her.

Jocie mashed her mouth together to keep from giggling again. Her father and Wes would think she'd been drinking giggle juice.

She thought of Zeb digging a hole in the dirt under the porch to stay cool till she got home. She thought of the stars through the window the night before. She remembered that "If you're happy and you know it" Bible school song. She wanted to clap her hands and stomp her feet and shout amen all at the same time.

"I'll plan the feast right after I figure out what we're going to run on the front page this week," her father was saying.

"You got the picture of the twin calves," Wes said. "And it's Bible school season in our little holy Hollyhill. You could let Jo here write up something about the wonders of Bible school. She seems to be a fan. We're sure to have some pictures of kids running wild around a churchyard in the files somewhere."

"You could write about Tabitha coming home," Jocie suggested.

"I don't think so," David said. "Tabitha might not like seeing her name in the paper the week she comes back. Of course, the mayor wants the town to start planning a big Fourth of July bash. I told him I'd do an editorial, but we might just spread it on the front. Make people notice."

"How about the new preacher at Mt. Pleasant? New preachers are always newsworthy," Wes said. "I could come out to the house and take a picture of you and Tabby and Jo and Love like you'd just moved in. Get the whole family. That way everybody would get a look at Tabby and wouldn't have to come up with excuses to drop by your house to see her with their own eyes."

"You may be on to something there," David said. "Folks are going to be curious for sure."

"Well, see. We've got the front page more than full already, and we've got Little League games and a bumper crop of wedding announcements," Wes said. "Who says exciting stuff doesn't happen in Hollyhill?"

"You, I think," Jocie said.

"None of that back talk." Wes gave her a little shove toward the composing table where the Bible school ads were waiting.

"You ain't got time. The presses have to start rolling tomorrow afternoon, and if I ain't missing my guess, you haven't got the first word of that Bible school piece written. Not to mention the ads set up."

"And maybe I could interview the mayor and some others about the Fourth," Jocie said. "We studied about it in school, but that was just history book stuff."

"Getting our town leaders to tell a kid what Independence Day means to them. That might work. And I could hunt up some kids to see what they think Independence Day is. Great idea, Jocie," her father said.

"I could start with you," Jocie said.

"I better save my thunder for my editorial. I have to fill up that page too."

"Well, then how about you, Wes? Just for practice. What's the Fourth mean to you?"

"Up on Jupiter, we don't have Independence Day, but . . ."

"Come on, Wes. You know I can't write about Jupiter for this," Jocie interrupted him. "It has to be all American pie. Stuff like that."

"Okay, no Jupiter history today. You might have liked the story, but oh well. If it's Earth stuff you want, it's Earth stuff you'll get." Wes looked at the press behind him as if words might be forming on the iron pieces. "Fireworks. Hot dogs. Ripe, juicy watermelons. Naps."

Jocie had grabbed a pencil to take notes. She looked up. "Naps?"

"Yeah, while the politicians tell you how great they are. You'll have to get toothpicks to prop open your eyes when you talk to the mayor," Wes said.

"I'll tell him he has to limit it to five things, no more than two words each."

"He couldn't even tell you his name without using more words than that," Wes said. He raised his voice a couple of octaves. "Mayor Raymond Palmor, that's me. But people just call me Buzz in the best little town in America. Because I made it that way. Single-handedly. Don't forget that when you vote next year. Keep the Buzz going in Hollyhill."

"Don't let him hear that one," David said as he turned to go back to his office. "He'd want us to change the name of the *Banner* to the *Buzz Banner*."

Jocie settled down to work on the ads, but while she was cutting and cropping and fitting in the words, she kept thinking about the other stories she was supposed to write. The Bible school piece would be easy. She had lots of experience with Bible school. The summer she was eight, the perfect Bible school age, she'd gone to ten different Bible schools. By the time summer was over, she could have taught the Bible lessons blindfolded, and she had a whole shelf full of egg carton caterpillars, pencil holders made from soup cans, macaroni-encrusted plates, and coasters with her picture stuck in the bottom.

Her Mama Mae had made a fuss over each of them as if they were works of art. When Mama Mae had died the following fall, Jocie had slipped one of the coasters into the coffin when nobody was looking. She could still remember how stiff and wrong her grandmother's arm had felt when she'd touched it. She'd had nightmares about it for months after that, but she'd never been sorry she'd put the coaster picture in the coffin. She didn't want her grandmother to forget what she looked like before she saw her again in heaven.

14

They ran the papers Tuesday afternoon. Even Zella got her hands black assembling the pages fresh off the press for distribution, but she was an old pro at it, folding papers long before David or Wes had even thought about working in a newspaper office. On Tuesdays she always wore a navy skirt and white button-up blouse that somehow stayed white. She never scratched her nose or rubbed her eyes until the last paper was folded, while the rest of them generally ended a folding session spotted like Dalmatian pups.

For David it was always the best moment of the work week when he took the first paper off the pile and sat down and unfolded it as if he were on his front porch settling in to catch up on the town's news. As he looked over this week's front page, he nodded his approval.

Jocie blew out a long breath and smiled. Her piece on Bible schools was on the bottom of the front page. The picture of the twin calves had made the top fold of the paper. Twin calves happened only once in a blue moon, and although everybody in the county had probably heard about the calves by now, David was banking on them wanting to see a picture for proof.

They hadn't been able to find a kids-in-the-churchyard picture, so Wes had designed a VBS logo that David figured some of the churches would cut out to use in their Sunday bulletins. Wes had worked in a Bible, a smiling kid's face, and a cross. David pulled the paper up for a closer look at the top of the S. "Wes, tell me I don't see snake eyes on that S."

"Snakes are biblical. One old serpent had a right important part at the beginning, I'm told," Wes said.

"Snake? Where's a snake?" Jocie said as she grabbed a paper off the pile.

Zella peered over Jocie's shoulder. "Wesley Green, if we have to run another front page, the cost is coming out of your pay," she said.

"We aren't doing a new run," David said. "The Lord mostly smudged it out for us, but Wes, there are some things you shouldn't play around with. If church people quit buying the *Banner*, we're sunk."

"Not to mention the danger of losing advertising dollars during Bible school and revival season," Zella put in.

Jocie clapped her hand over her mouth to hide her smile and smudged more black on her cheeks.

"It's not the least bit amusing, Jocelyn," Zella said.

Jocie couldn't help it. She laughed out loud. "Oh, come on, Zella. Nobody but us will know it's a snake, and if they do we'll give it a close-up look and admit that if you use your imagination that ink smudge the press made might look a little bit like snake eyes."

Zella gave Wes a withering look. "Wesley Green, someday you'll have to give an accounting of the ways you've led this child astray."

"Aw, Zell, it's just a couple of snake eyes. A body's got to have some fun," Wes said. "If you don't start practicing smiling every now and again, one of these days you're going to come across something so funny you won't be able to keep from smiling and then your face is liable to crack."

"Ha. Ha," Zella said without the trace of a smile before she stalked off to wash her hands.

David sighed. "Wes, you promised you'd lay off Zella for a while. I have to work out there beside her."

"Sorry, boss." Wes didn't look sorry as he began bundling the papers for delivery. Two thirds of the copies went to the post office for mail delivery. The other third went to grocery stores and the grill, any place that would put them out for sale. A few went into the stand out on the street in front of the office. For a quarter anybody could find out everything newsworthy that happened in Hollyhill the week before. Or not so newsworthy. If no news happened, they still had to fill the columns with words.

David scanned Jocie's Bible school article again. He could almost see freshly scrubbed kids marching into the churches, hear the pledges to the flags and Bible, and taste the orange drink and chocolate chip cookies. The girl was a natural with words, way better than him.

Of course, he'd never planned to be a newspaperman, had never given it the first thought. Had no real training for writing other than a lifetime of reading and practice writing up reports in the service. But a job had been open at the *Banner* when he'd come home after the war. Henry Lyster, the owner and editor then, had taken a liking to him and let him work crazy hours so he could attend seminary classes over in Louisville. David just had to make sure he was there when the presses were rolling and that he had his stories ready to run.

Henry had been putting out the Banner for over thirty years, and he liked to sum up his newspaper know-how by saying, "Prod the politicians every now and again and print the citizens' grandkids' pictures every chance you get."

After David had finished his seminary training, Henry had announced he was moving to Florida and selling the Banner to David. Every year since, David had sent him a percentage of the profits, which Henry put toward the purchase price. Henry had told him this year's payment would be the last if the *Banner* had a good year. That didn't exactly match David's records, but Henry said his records were the ones that mattered.

David opened up the paper, and the picture of the interim pastor of Mt. Pleasant Church and his family jumped out at him. Aunt Love hadn't wanted to be in the picture, had fussed with the combs in her hair and the white collar on her purple dress until Jocie had said, "Do not tarry, saith the Lord."

"Prove the Lord said that with chapter and verse reference," Aunt Love had retorted, but she'd finally let Wes take the picture. She wasn't smiling, but she looked regal and composed. No one could tell by just looking that her memory was leaking away from her.

Tabitha still looked pale, wan almost, but she had smiled. Her mother's smile. The one that meant I'm here, I'm doing what you want, but you might have to pay for it later. Thank goodness she had the cheek with the rose on it turned away from the camera. He hadn't gotten up the nerve to ask her if the rose was permanent or if there was a chance it might disappear by Sunday. He hadn't asked her anything. She hadn't told him anything. She just said she still wasn't feeling well. Aunt Love kept giving her looks and then looking at David as the lines deepened around her eyes.

Jocie was smiling like always. She'd wanted the dog to be in the picture but hadn't pouted when he'd said no. Tears sprang into his eyes as he looked at Jocie in the picture. It was funny how you could look at a person every day and not notice how she was changing until you saw it in a picture. She was losing the baby roundness to her face and was turning into a young woman. Such a gift God had given him when she was born.

"What you looking at, Dad?" Jocie said as she pushed up beside him to peek at the paper. "Uh-oh. Is the picture that bad?"

"Not bad at all. No shame to a few tears falling because I get to see my two daughters in the same picture."

"It would have looked even more American pie if you'd have let Zeb be in it," Jocie said.

"It might need more than a dog to qualify as the model family photo. Say, a wife?" David said.

Jocie grinned up at him. "I hear there are candidates actively campaigning for the position. I mean, it's a long drive out to Mt. Pleasant Church."

Wes picked up on what she said right away. "Leigh found her way out there, then. I heard Zell giving her directions." He raised his eyebrows. "Did she make any decisions?"

"Enough, you two." David looked back at the picture to hide the red crawling up his cheeks. "Leigh's a nice young woman. Emphasis on the young."

"Who's stuck on a certain preacher man we know," Wes said.

"She's way too young for me," David said, looking at his own picture. "When did I get so old?"

"It's a day-by-day kind of thing," Wes said. "But you've got a few days yet to go before you start grumbling about being old." Wes hoisted a couple of bundles of papers up into the cart they used to take them out to the car. "Wait till you get ancient like me. This job have any kind of retirement?"

"You can't retire, Wes," Jocie said. "We'd never get the paper out without you."

"She's right there." David looked at Wes to see if there was anything serious behind his talk. It had been ten years since Wes had driven his motorcycle up on the sidewalk in front of the newspaper offices to get a paper. The dispenser on the street had been empty, so he'd come banging through the front door, setting the bell above the door to jingling and sending Zella scurrying to the back room to get David. All he'd wanted was an odd job to buy more gas to go on down the road. He hadn't had a destination. He'd just been going.

The man, in his beat-up leather jacket, with a red bandanna

tied around his head, had looked used up and spent. David hadn't been looking for help, but he'd opened his mouth and offered him a job for as long as he wanted it, be that two weeks or a year. Zella had threatened to quit when she heard about it. Every morning for a year David had come to work expecting to find Wes gone, but every morning he'd been there waiting to do whatever needed doing to get the *Banner* out. And to play with Jocie, because even then Jocie had been David's shadow. She'd had to be. He couldn't leave her at home with Adrienne. He'd found that out the hard way when he'd come home one day to find Jocie toddling up the road in search of Daddy.

Adrienne had been on the porch, painting her toenails. "Oh, you found her," she'd said. "Tabitha was wondering where she got off to."

David had exploded. When Adrienne had just smiled at him and kept polishing her toenails, he'd snatched up the jar of nail polish and flung it against a tree out in the yard. Jocie had started screaming, and Tabitha had peered out the screen door with wide, round eyes.

Adrienne hadn't been bothered in the least. She'd picked up her purse and said, "Now I'll have to go to Grundy to get some more polish to finish my toenails. I don't know when I'll be home. It may take a while to find the same exact color."

He'd said he was sorry, but of course, she hadn't cared. She hadn't cared since before Jocie was born what he thought or said. They'd only pretended to be married, and she'd left most of the pretending up to him. Strange what love would make a man do. Or was it pride?

It was pride that had kept him from asking anybody to babysit Jocie, because if he did that he would have had to own up to how strange things were in his family. He was a preacher, for heaven's sake. He was supposed to be able to figure things like that out. Of course, his mother had known, even though no words about

Adrienne's indifference to Jocie had ever passed between them. And Wes had guessed and had become babysitter, best friend, and grandfather all wrapped up in one to Jocie.

Sometimes he'd wondered if maybe Zella was right, that maybe Wes wasn't the best influence with his Jupiter stories and his lack of religious observance. But there was never any doubt of his love for Jocie. If the ever-present sadness sometimes threatened to leak out of his eyes when Jocie was around, Wes would shake it off and tell her a Jupiter story or teach her a silly new tongue twister. "Lupiter from Jupiter jumped through a fiery hoopiter. Lupiter from Jupiter must be stupider than Jaturn from Saturn, who jumped over a lantern."

So David had stopped worrying about Wes going back on the road. Had never given it a moment's consideration till the Monday morning he'd shown up to find the note taped to the printing press. Even then he'd been unable to believe it. He'd run up the stairs to the apartment over the offices as if the letter he held in his hands didn't exist. The letter that said thanks for everything, but it was time to get back out on the road.

Jocie hadn't been with David, thank goodness. She'd started first grade the week before, and he'd dropped her off at school before he came to work. He'd watched her walk into the school building, her shoulders hunched up and her head pushed forward to be ready for whatever attack might come first. He'd wanted to run after her, to protect her from every hurt. But of course he couldn't.

Any more than he could have protected her from the pain of her mother and sister disappearing into the night two months before. At the time, Jocie had still run to the door with hope in her eyes every time she heard a car coming up their lane, and the night before he'd found her in Tabitha's room, standing stock-still in the middle of the floor as if she might be able to pull Tabitha out of the walls.

David had sunk down on the dusty brown couch in the middle of the apartment and wondered what he would tell Jocie. The note had said, "Tell Jocie I'll send her a message from Jupiter someday."

A message from Jupiter wasn't going to help. Nothing was going to help. His heart had broken just thinking about telling Jocie Wes was gone. Her mother and sister slipping away in the middle of the night had been bad, but this had been worse. Much worse. Adrienne had treated Jocie like a stray cat that had found its way to her porch. Any time the stray had gotten close to her, she'd kicked it away. But Wes had taken the stray cat to his heart, and the stray had curled up and found a favorite purring place there.

David had read the note again and then folded and refolded it while he'd prayed. His prayer had not had words, just desperation. He almost couldn't believe his ears when he'd heard the motorcycle. In fact, he'd stayed where he was on the couch, as if going to the window to look out might make the motorcycle sound disappear.

He'd left the door to the apartment open, and Wes had climbed halfway up the outside flight of stairs and called, "You up there, David?"

"I am."

"Jo at school?"

"Yes."

"Good."

Wes had finished climbing the stairs to the apartment, sat down on a box of books, and looked at his hands instead of at David. "I couldn't go. I got all the way to the Georgia state line and knew I couldn't go on. I've been riding all night."

"Are you okay?" David had asked.

"No."

"Do you want to talk about it?"

"No."

David had still been searching for what to say next when Wes went on. "Maybe. I don't know."

Again David had waited. The silence had stretched so long that David had wondered if he should just go on down to the newspaper office and let Wes have the time to himself. But just as he was about to get up and leave, Wes had started talking.

"I swore I'd never get attached to anybody again. Not really attached. Too much pain. I had the pain with Rosa and Lydia. Still have it. Bores down in my heart every day. I didn't want more of it. Didn't think I could bear more of it."

"Rosa and Lydia?" David had asked.

"My wife and daughter. Rosa liked to say we were the perfect family. A strong man, a beautiful woman, a good son, and a sweet daughter. We had twenty-three years. More than some folks, I guess."

"What happened?"

"Wesley Jr. got married. He was happy. After the wedding, me and Rosa and Lydia went to the beach for a week. We were happy. Me and Rosa talked about how everything was changing, with Wes Jr. married and Lydia going off to college in the fall. I didn't realize how much more things were going to change."

"What happened?" David had said.

"It ain't something I like to talk about. Fact is, I don't know what happened. I know we packed up and were headed home. I know I was driving. I know it was raining. The police said maybe a tire blew. I don't remember. I just know when I woke up in the ambulance the guy in there with me wouldn't look me in the eye when I asked him about Rosa and Lydia. I tried to kill him. I don't know why. It wasn't his fault. It was mine."

"I'm sorry." The words had been inadequate. "What about your son?"

"It was funny. We couldn't talk about it or anything else. The ghosts of Rosa and Lydia were always there between us. I figured if I didn't run, he'd have to, so I signed the house over to him and tried to lose myself out on the road. I don't know why I stopped running when I got here."

"You were tired."

"I was. That's a fact. And I liked the smell of ink."

"And then there was Jocie," David had said.

"Yeah, Jo. I should have left the first day I saw that little face looking up at me."

"Why didn't you?"

"I don't know. I aimed to, but I kept putting it off. You'd been nice to me and I didn't want to leave you in the lurch, I'd tell myself. Or I'd promised Jo another Jupiter story and a man should keep his promises. There was always a reason."

"Then why wasn't there a reason yesterday?"

"I don't know. When she was at the newspaper yesterday morning, she told me her dog got run over and she cried. I didn't have no way of making her smile. I just sat there and cried with her. Too much pain. I needed to get out on the road again."

"Then why are you here now?"

"Jo," Wes had said, and that had been enough explanation.

David had never told anybody else Wes's story. Not even Jocie. He figured that Wes might tell her himself someday but that if he wanted the people in Hollyhill to think he was from Jupiter, that was his right. He sometimes wondered about the son Wes had told him about, but he never asked.

Now Jocie waved her hand in front of David's face to bring him back to the present. "Hey, Dad, you in there?"

"He's probably thinking about a certain young somebody," Wes said. "He sure ain't thinking about helping us with these papers."

"I was thinking how lucky I am to have two such willing workers to pick up the slack while I'm daydreaming."

"I'll bet Leigh would help fold papers for you," Wes said. "Just for you. Especially if it was a private folding session."

"A date folding papers?" Jocie said. "She'd have to be crazy."

"If she's really stuck on this old man the way the two of you think she is, that's already established. She's definitely got a few screws missing." David turned away so they couldn't see him smile. This afternoon it didn't sound too bad having a woman ten plus years younger than him giving him the eye.

15

A week passed. And then another. Two issues of the *Banner* off the press. Two Sunday morning sermons. Two Sundays Jocie managed not to sock Ronnie Martin in the nose in Sunday school. Every time he said something stupid, she just smiled and told herself God loved everybody. If that didn't work, she imagined Zeb biting him.

Not that Zeb would bite anybody. Zeb was being a model dog, not digging up the first one of Aunt Love's flowers or chasing Jezebel. When Jezzie showed up on the back porch in the early morning hours, he just rumbled a warning growl that sent the cat scurrying back to Aunt Love's room.

Tabitha hadn't gone to church yet. She said she didn't feel up to it, and Aunt Love just looked at her and said okay instead of starting the great inquisition the way she did if Jocie ever said she was sick—"What hurts? How long has it hurt? How bad does it hurt? Are you throwing up? No? Then get ready for church." All Jocie could figure was they were hoping the rose on Tabitha's cheek would disappear before they had to introduce her to the Mt. Pleasant congregation.

It was strange how little Tabitha coming home had changed anything. Nobody made her do the first thing. She slept when she wanted to. If she didn't come to the table at supper time, Aunt Love just saved her a plate. Mostly she spent her days sitting on a blanket in the sun, plaiting her long hair, and painting her toenails different colors. Nobody seemed to mind that either. It was as if coming home from California gave her special freedom. Aunt Love didn't even bombard her with Bible verses. She saved all of those for Jocie.

A couple of times Jocie went out to sit on the grass beside Tabitha's blanket. She always intended to ask about her mother, but somehow the questions got stuck in her throat.

Jocie didn't usually have all that much problem asking questions. She interviewed practically the whole town for the Fourth of July article that was supposed to run in next week's *Banner* a week before the town's parade and celebration. She started with Mayor Palmor and got the expected responses. The flag, parades, civic pride, fireworks, patriotic speeches. Randy Simmons, the chief of police, said pretty much the same with an added pitch for celebrating in a responsible way. Judge Blakemore mentioned the military, since he had a son in Vietnam. Betty Moore, the city clerk, talked about family picnics.

Jocie even threw a few questions out at Leigh Jacobson, but they weren't the ones she really wanted to ask. Like why are you interested in my dad? And do you like dogs? And did you know that my dad thinks being a preacher's wife is a calling just like being a preacher? And by the way, have you been getting any calls? From God?

Instead she asked if Leigh liked the Fourth, and Leigh smiled at her and said, "Who wouldn't like the Fourth, with fireworks and a day off from work and watermelon and hot dogs?" She didn't say the first thing about the flag, and by the time Jocie asked all her Fourth of July questions, she was beginning to almost like Leigh a little. She even dared throw in one extra question—what was Leigh's favorite thing to cook for the Fourth?

When Leigh said chocolate cake with chocolate icing, it seemed like some kind of sign. Jocie needed a chocolate cake with chocolate icing for Tabitha's birthday on Saturday, and that wasn't something Leigh could have found out about unless maybe Wes had told her. It was almost enough to make Jocie ask Leigh where to shop for bras, but instead she asked her to help her bake the birthday cake. And of course, after she asked Leigh to help bake the cake, she couldn't very well not invite her over to help eat it.

Then she had to ask Zella because Leigh called up and blabbed to Zella all about the party Jocie was having for Tabitha. Zella came straight back to the pressroom to corner Jocie, and what could Jocie do but say, "Oh, Zella, didn't I tell you? It's just going to be cake and tea or lemonade. Nothing much."

"But I have been so anxious to see Tabitha," Zella said. "I keep expecting her to stop in when she comes to town."

"I don't think she's come to town since she's been home. She just wants to stay home and sit in the sun. Says tans are harder to get here than in California."

"The same sun shines here as out there," Zella asked.

"Well, yeah, I guess. But she says you tan better if there's an ocean around. Here she says you just sweat."

"Horses sweat, men perspire, and ladies glisten." Zella fished a pink tissue out from under the waistband of her rose-colored skirt and dabbed her glistening forehead. "Do you need me to bring anything Saturday? Perhaps some of those little pastel mints?"

"Sure, if you want to."

"Is Aunt Love helping you make the cake?" Zella raised her eyebrows.

Jocie could tell she was fishing, but sometimes the easiest way to get Zella out of the pressroom was to go ahead and play her games. "No. I figured you knew Leigh was going to help me with the cake."

"Oh, that's right. She did tell me that," Zella said as if she had just remembered. She looked particularly pleased with herself. "I've eaten her chocolate cake. It's delicious."

Wes waited until Zella went back out front to her desk before he said, "Next thing she'll want to be bridesmaid at the wedding."

"Wedding? Whoa, I just asked Leigh to help me bake a cake," Jocie said.

"A birthday cake today. A wedding cake tomorrow. Or whenever."

"I should've just bought a cake mix." Jocie sank down on the stool in front of the composing table.

"No, no. You've made two women very happy."

"Maybe I should warn Dad."

"Might be a good idea."

"And Tabitha. And Aunt Love."

"You haven't told your Aunt Love you're planning a party?"

"I wasn't planning a party. I was just planning for you to come over, and Aunt Love doesn't care if you see dust on the piano, but now we'll have to scrub down the walls and wash the woodwork. I won't get to do anything but clean till Saturday."

"Well, at least you'll have Tabitha to help you."

"Aunt Love doesn't make Tabitha do anything, not even set the table or peel potatoes. And if I say anything about it, Aunt Love just quotes me some Scripture that as far as I can tell has nothing at all to do with me or Tabitha, and then she tells me I shouldn't be worrying about what other people do, just what I do."

"Not bad advice," Wes said.

"Whose side are you on, anyway?" Jocie demanded.

"Hold on. I ain't got no sides in this battle. I'll just hang out on the sidelines and watch the fireworks from there."

"But it's not fair, Wes. I mean, I'm glad Tabitha's home and everything, but it's like she sent her body home but the rest of her stayed out in California." Jocie picked up a pen and began clicking the tip in and out as she talked.

Wes sat down on the stool next to her and picked up another

pen to click in rhythm with hers. "'Bout the only thing you can expect to be fair is the weather every so often."

"Or the face of a pretty girl or a passing grade or the county or state fairs. Why are they called fairs? Why not greats?" Jocie didn't wait for an answer. She just threw out the question she really wanted answered. "I mean, why did she come home if she didn't want to?"

"To answer somebody's prayers?"

Jocie dropped the pen on the desk. "She didn't know I was praying. She thought it was hilarious when I told her about the sister prayer."

"Well, then what is it your pop is always saying?—the Lord works in mysterious ways."

"Yeah, I guess."

"Well, just think about it. You're going to be baking a cake with Leigh Jacobson. Who'd have thought that would ever happen two weeks ago?"

It did seem weird biking to Leigh Jacobson's house on Friday afternoon. Jocie had hardly had a moment to do anything but scrub since she'd told Aunt Love about inviting Leigh and Zella to come for birthday cake Saturday afternoon. She'd had to wash every window in the house while Aunt Love was doing up the curtains. Then the floors had needed sweeping and mopping and shining, and the refrigerator had had to be defrosted and cleaned out. Thank goodness they only had three days to get ready or Aunt Love would have had them painting the house inside and out. As it was, her father had had to paint the porch floor.

Tabitha had watched them working, had even helped iron some of the curtains for Aunt Love when Aunt Love's face turned extra pink one hot afternoon. Nobody had told Tabitha why they were cleaning. She thought they were just having an attack of spring cleaning fever, even if it was the middle of the summer. Jocie had convinced her father it would be fun to surprise Tabitha, who hadn't mentioned her birthday coming up one time. Maybe she thought they'd forgotten when her birthday was. But that wasn't the real reason Jocie hadn't wanted to tell Tabitha about the birthday party. If nobody asked her, she couldn't say no.

Jocie kept telling herself that surely Tabitha would be happy to have a party. It was just Zella and Wes. They were practically family. And of course Leigh, who wanted to be family. This would be a good test to see if Jocie should campaign for or against that idea.

Jocie had shaken some quarters out of her piggy bank and gone to the Five and Dime store to buy Tabitha some nail polish and a brush and comb. She'd thought about buying her a new shirt or some shorts. As far as Jocie could tell, Tabitha only had two things she could wear besides her bathing suit, and they looked a little tight. Aunt Love's cooking wasn't great, but it must have been better than what Tabitha had been getting in California. But Jocie didn't have enough money for anything from the Fashion Shop, and besides, she had to save some in case she had to make an emergency bra run before school started.

She cringed at the idea of asking Mrs. Headley at the Fashion Shop to show her a bra. Mrs. Headley kept all the underwear in white boxes on shelves behind the counter and pulled them out one box at a time to lay the panties out on the counter. Mrs. Headley or Miss Paulie asked you for a size, but if you didn't know, they gave you the eye and matched you up with the right size. Jocie was afraid they might not have any sizes to match her top part in the underwear department. They'd probably just laugh her out of the shop.

But she didn't have to worry about that now. It was still weeks and weeks before school. Maybe Tabitha would wake up from her zombie state and offer to go to Grundy to help her school shop. Even if she didn't wear bras, she'd know about them. After all, she was going to be twenty on her birthday Saturday.

Leigh lived in an apartment in the upstairs of an old house on Water Street. When Jocie climbed the stairs, Leigh pulled open the door before Jocie could knock. Mrs. Simpson, the owner of the house, lived downstairs and complained about noises. Leigh practically tiptoed as she led the way back across the kitchen to the table, where a couple of iced soft drinks were still bubbling beside a plate of chocolate chip cookies.

Jocie's eyes slid around the kitchen taking in the light green tile counters, the yellow sink, and the white stove and refrigerator gleaming in the afternoon sunlight pouring through the window over the sink. No curtains hindered the light or the scant air drifting in the open window. A pink fringed violet bloomed on the window sill. A wooden cutting board with a large sunflower painted on it hung on the wall beside the stove. Fruit-shaped magnets were scattered across the top of the refrigerator door. Under the apple was the picture of Mt. Pleasant Church's new interim pastor and family.

Jocie didn't let her eyes linger on it but instead looked through the door into the living room, where she spotted a stereo. Just for something to say, she asked, "What happens when you want to dance?"

Leigh smiled. "I put on a waltz and dance sedately with my broom." Leigh's smile got wider. "Or I climb up on the couch and do the twist. So far I haven't fallen off and through the ceiling."

Jocie laughed.

"You think I'm kidding?" Leigh went into the living room, slipped a forty-five rpm record out of a wire holder and put it on. Chubby Checker's voice urging everybody to come on and do the twist came through the speakers. Leigh threw the cushions off the couch and demonstrated. Everything about her was bouncing and twisting as she let the music take her over. Jocie jumped on one of the couch cushions on the floor and joined in.

When the song ended, Leigh stepped off the couch and fanned

her face with her hand. "See, it's not too noisy that way. Of course, Mrs. Simpson still complains about the music, but there are some things you just have to do anyway." She turned on an oscillating fan and then stacked some more forty-fives on the turntable. "Elvis is the very best music for making chocolate cakes. They should put his picture on the cake mix instead of Betty Crocker's."

The strains of "Love Me Tender" followed them back to the kitchen, where Leigh gulped down her soft drink before she pulled an index card out of a recipe box and handed it to Jocie. "This is my mother's recipe. She's a great cook. One reason I'm too heavy. The other is that I like to cook too, and there's nobody but me to eat it, and it's a sin to be wasteful. Of course, it's a sin to be a glutton too."

"I'm sure you're not a glutton," Jocie said politely. She looked at the card. "I didn't bring any flour or stuff with me, but I could ride my bike over to the market on Model Street."

"No need for that," Leigh said as she took some butter out of the refrigerator. "I've got everything you'll need. Even birthday candles."

"Tabitha may think she's too old to blow out candles," Jocie said.

"Nobody ever gets too old for birthday wishes." Leigh held out the spoon. "You want to cream the butter?"

"If it won't mess up the cake if I do it wrong."

"You can't do it wrong. You just mash the heck out of it."

Jocie took the spoon and attacked the stick of butter Leigh had dropped in the mixing bowl on the counter. In the next room, a new record dropped down and Elvis was belting out "Hound Dog." Jocie kept mashing and thought about her father listening to Elvis. He liked Tennessee Ernie Ford. Singing hymns. Maybe her father was right. Maybe Leigh was too young for him.

Jocie peeked over at Leigh, who was standing beside her, watching her smash the butter. Jocie wondered just how old Leigh was. It was hard to tell. She looked way older than Tabitha and not nearly as old as Zella. She'd obviously been out of school awhile. She'd been working at the courthouse as long as Jocie could remember.

Of course, Jocie hadn't paid much attention to who worked where until a couple of years back. When she went to the courthouse with her father, she was more interested in the way her footsteps echoed in the hallway and how fast she could run up the winding staircase. She liked bouncing her voice off the marble walls and then slipping into the clerk's office to hide among the deed books when the sheriff's deputy came out into the hall to see who was disturbing the peace.

The first time she remembered seeing Leigh was when she was around ten and Leigh had given Jocie a nickel to put in the Lion's Club gumball dispenser. Jocie could always get free gum at the courthouse by standing by the gumball machine with sad eyes. The reason she remembered Leigh was that Leigh put in a nickel for herself as well and they'd both crossed their fingers and hoped for a blue gumball. Two blue gumballs had popped out of the machine. It was one of those times when Jocie felt as if she'd wasted a miracle, that she should have crossed her fingers and wished for something important like world peace or a letter from her mother instead of a blue gumball.

She said, "Do you remember the time we got the blue gumballs?"

"I do," Leigh said as she measured sugar and added it to the mashed butter in the bowl. "I don't think I've ever gotten another blue gumball out of that machine since then."

"Did you know who I was then?"

"Well, sure I did. You were the noisy brat Deputy Karsner kept threatening to put in jail if he ever collared you."

Jocie grinned. "Daddy used to threaten to turn me in."

"The sheriff talked about putting up a wanted poster," Leigh said.

"Surely I wasn't the only kid who liked to stomp my feet and make echoes in the courthouse hall."

"No indeed. Just the one who was there the most and whose daddy never told you to pipe down." Leigh broke a couple of eggs into a bowl and beat them for a few seconds before adding them to Jocie's mixing bowl. "It never bothered me. I still wear my clickiest shoes so I can break up the silence of the place. It's like a tomb in that hallway when nobody's around."

"Did you grow up here in Hollyhill? I mean, I guess you did. Everybody who works at the courthouse grew up here."

"Nope, not me." Leigh made a paste of cocoa and hot water to add to the cake mixture. "Now stir that in fast."

Jocie stirred fast. She licked a little of the chocolate paste off her finger and made a face. It was bitter.

"It does look as if it would taste good, doesn't it?" Leigh said as she handed Jocie her glass of soda. "You have to wait till the end to lick the bowl. There's no sugar in the cocoa paste."

"So how did you get a job in the courthouse if you're not a Hollyhill native? Zella says it can't be done."

"My mother was raised here, and my aunt works for the judge. Actually, the judge is my third or fourth cousin once removed or twice removed, whatever. I grew up in Grundy, but I always loved coming to Hollyhill to visit my grandmother. She died last year." Leigh looked teary.

"My grandmother died when I was nine."

"Yeah, I was lucky to have mine so long, but I still miss her," Leigh said as she sifted and measured the flour. She added the flour along with the milk. "Now we'll have to beat it three hundred strokes."

Jocie counted as she slapped the spoon through the batter and against the side of the bowl. By the time she got to sixty she was slowing down. Leigh took the bowl and spoon and beat the batter in a steady, easy rhythm as she counted under her breath.

"It looks easy when you do it," Jocie said.

"Lots of practice. Every time we have a church dinner, people go into fits if I don't bring my chocolate cake." She held the spoon up and let the batter drip off it back down into the bowl. "Here, you finish the last fifty while I grease and flour the pans."

The music had stopped in the living room, and Leigh went in to lift the pile of forty-fives up, flip them over, and start them playing again. She was singing along with Elvis when she came back to the kitchen and started greasing the pans.

"Dad says he's too old for you," Jocie said as she pushed through the last five beats.

16

Leigh's face turned bright pink.

Jocie looked up. "Uh-oh, I guess I shouldn't have said that."

"Well, probably not." Leigh fanned herself with the end of a dish towel spotted with sunflowers. "But I pink up easy as pie. One of the problems with having a fair complexion."

"Me too. Last time I flamed up, I opened my mouth and blew the heat out and off my face." Jocie opened her mouth wide and demonstrated. "It sort of helped."

Leigh stopped fanning and gave it a try. The pink on her cheeks faded. "I think it did help. Where'd you come up with that?"

"A slant on a Jupiterian idea."

"Oh, Wes. Zella's always fussing about him, but I think he's kind of fun." Leigh spooned the cake batter evenly into the two round pans and set them carefully in the oven. "Now we'll let them bake for about thirty minutes."

She closed the oven door, stood up, and looked straight at Jocie. "I guess we might as well talk about it now that you've brought it up. My mama always says there's no shame to getting embarrassed unless you tried to hide from what was embarrassing you. So you think I don't have a snowball's chance in you know where with your father."

Now Jocie's cheeks went hot. "I didn't exactly say that."

"Well, you can if that's what you think," Leigh said. "Come on. Let's go sit at the table while you tell me what you think. And just so you'll know, I'm the type of person who'd rather hear the truth straight out than to have somebody lie to me to keep from hurting my feelings."

Leigh pulled out a chair at the table for Jocie and then sat down across from her and waited.

"I wouldn't do that. I nearly always tell the truth," Jocie said as she sat down.

"Good, now we're getting somewhere." Leigh drummed her fingers on the table while staring at the wall over the top of Jocie's head before she said, "Surely your dad has had a girl-friend or two since your mother left. That's been forever ago, before I even came to Hollyhill."

"If he has, he never let me know about it."

"Really? No other woman has ever been after him?"

"Gee, I don't know." Jocie scooted the sunflower dish towel over in front of her and began tracing the petals with her finger. "I didn't know you were till Wes told me."

Leigh laughed. "I guess I've been too obvious, but I thought if I could get your dad to notice me, he might think going on a date was fun."

"I don't think Dad worries too much about having fun."

"You don't worry about having fun. You just have it."

"I guess," Jocie said.

Leigh broke off a piece of a chocolate chip cookie but didn't put it in her mouth. "Well, if he doesn't think about having fun, what does he do?"

"Work. Pray. Preach. Visit the sick."

"Surely he does something just for fun?" She picked a choco-late chip out of the cookie and put it in her mouth. "Read?"

"Mostly the Bible or other newspapers or magazines. For the *Banner* or for church."

"Does he like to take walks?"

"Yeah. Early in the morning when he's praying about something."

"Then he probably wouldn't want company. TV?"

"We have a TV, but it doesn't come in too good. Dad says we need a real antenna instead of just the rabbit ears on top of the set."

"Okay." Leigh studied the cookie and then picked out another chocolate chip. "Baseball?"

"He takes pictures of the kids playing Little League. That's sort of fun."

"I could watch little kids playing baseball," Leigh said. "But he'd be down on the field taking pictures, and I'd be on the sidelines looking like a mom who forgot to bring her kid. Not much of a date. Anything else he does for fun?"

Jocie thought about it. "He plays horseshoes with the men at church picnics, and they talk about going fishing."

"I'm horrible at horseshoes, and I hate fishing. Nasty, slimy fish." Leigh shuddered.

"Yeah, when I have to go, I just don't bait my hook."

"But that's the problem. I am trying to bait my hook and I can't think what bait might work. Music?"

"Not Elvis. We saw him once on Ed Sullivan, and Dad just thought he was funny. Of course, the screen was pretty snowy."

"At least he thought something was funny."

"Dad thinks lots of things are funny," Jocie said. "He'd probably think this was funny."

"This?"

"Us talking about him. He laughs a lot. He says God wants us to be happy."

"Is he happy?"

"I guess so. I don't know. He's got a lot on his mind right now with a new church and the paper and Tabitha coming home and Aunt Love going a little more bananas every day and trying to keep me out of trouble."

"Do you get into trouble often?" Leigh pulled the last chocolate chip out of the cookie and popped it into her mouth before she pushed the crumbs away from her.

"I try not to, but I have this bad habit of talking too much. I'm probably talking too much right now."

"I know I am. But your dad is just so nice, and he's not all that much older than me. I'm thirty-two and what's he? Forty?"

"Forty-four." Jocie bit off a piece of cookie. She hadn't tasted anything as yummy since the last dinner on the grounds at church. Maybe Wes was right and cooking was something important to consider in a stepmother.

"Well, that's still not so bad. I don't have to listen to Elvis." She pulled her shoulder-length hair back and twisted it into a bun on the back of her neck. "I could start wearing my hair like this and get some glasses. I may need some anyway. I have to squint my eyes to make out the small print."

Jocie laughed. "I don't think trying to look like Zella or Aunt Love will do the trick."

"Oh well." Leigh dropped her hair back onto her shoulders. The timer went off, and Leigh showed Jocie how to stick a toothpick down in the middle of the cake to see if it was done. When the toothpick came out clean, Leigh turned the cake layers out onto a cooling rack. "We'll give it a few minutes to cool and then make the icing."

"Can we go listen to some more records while we're waiting?" Jocie asked.

"Sure."

Jocie picked out some songs she'd never heard before and put them on the player. "I guess all songs are about somebody loving somebody or not. Even the church songs are about loving God or other people or God loving us."

"Love, it's what makes the world go round." Leigh sat on a cushion on the floor in front of the fan. "How about you? Have you ever had a boyfriend?"

Jocie made a face as she plopped down on the floor beside Leigh. She leaned back against the couch and said, "I don't like boys."

"I used to say that. All the way through high school I figured I was too fat for any of the boys to like me. Not that you'd ever have that problem. Being too fat, I mean. So I just said I didn't like them. The only date I had was with my cousin Kenny to the senior prom, and that was just because my mother nearly took to her bed when I said I wasn't going. She wanted to see me all decked out in a prom dress. She talked me into asking Kenny to go with me. He's a year older than me and didn't go to my high school, so I thought it might work. But you can't really date a cousin. It was awful."

"Why?"

"We just sat there drinking punch till we were about to float while all the couples were cuddling up on the dance floor. I was home by ten."

"You've surely had a boyfriend since then?"

"Nope. Half the kids in my class got married the summer we got out of school, and the rest of them went off somewhere looking for fresh faces. I thought about going off to college, but we didn't really have the money, and besides, I was chicken. So I got a job as a secretary in a transport business over in Grundy. Some of the truck drivers were nice, but every one was married. After a couple of years, I came here for a change of scenery, and it's just as bad here as it was back in Grundy. Maybe worse. All the good guys are married. Except, of course, for your dad. But him being single doesn't do me much good if he's not interested."

"Maybe he'll get interested. Wes says he should. That he needs to find somebody."

"Wes asked me to take a ride on his motorcycle. Maybe I should make eyes at him."

"He'd probably notice," Jocie said with a laugh. "And riding the motorcycle is fun."

"Really? I think I'd be scared silly."

"What do you do for fun?" Jocie asked. "Besides cook."

"Read. I've read nearly everything Wes has donated to the library. That man is in some strange book clubs. And I like to dance and listen to music."

"Some churches think dancing is sinful."

"How about your dad? Does he?"

"I've never heard him say so if he does."

"That's encouraging."

Jocie didn't think anything she'd said was encouraging for a romance between her father and Leigh, but she didn't say so. Instead she changed the subject. "Maybe we should make the frosting. I need to get home before dark."

The icing was easy, just a matter of mixing butter, powdered sugar, cocoa, and milk in the top of a double boiler and then using their beating muscles some more. Leigh put in extra cocoa, and when they smeared the icing on the cake, it hardened into a nice glistening dark-brown finish. Then Leigh made bright yellow icing and showed Jocie how to use her metal decorating tips to write "Happy birthday, Tabitha" and push out a ribbon of yellow around the edge of the layers.

"I hope it tastes as good as it looks," Jocie said as she licked yellow icing off her fingers.

"Hardly anything ever does. The cakes that usually taste the best are the ones that look the worst. I dropped a jam cake one time getting it out of the oven. I just scraped it up off the floor and put it on saucers and drizzled caramel over the top. Best cake I ever ate."

"You're funny, Leigh."

"Tell your dad that and that I'm way older than I look."

"But you're not."

"Oh shoot. And I thought I looked sixteen."

"You might to Dad."

"Then see, you wouldn't be lying."

The air was thickening into night as Jocie pedaled her bike through town. She thought about stopping at the *Banner* and getting Wes to take her home but decided if she pedaled fast she'd skid into her lane a few minutes before full darkness fell. It was a funny thing about night, she thought as she passed houses with lights shining out every window. Outside it was plenty light, but inside looking out it was dark already.

If her dad had noticed she wasn't home, he might be worried. But she'd told him where she was going. Maybe if he got worried enough, he'd call Leigh to see if she was still there. Leigh might like that, and Jocie owed her for all the help with the cake. Jocie stopped pedaling as fast.

Once she got out of town, she had the road to herself. She glided in and out of the deepening shadows of the trees. The hum of her tires on the blacktop blended with the crickets and katydids. Fingers of darkness crept up toward her from the sides of the road, and a shiver ran down her back. She began to pedal faster again.

When she was just a little girl, she'd cry out when she opened her eyes on a moonless or cloudy night and could see nothing but black. Her father would come out of the darkness to sit with her, but he never turned on a light. He'd said there had been times when he worried about the dark and that's when he reminded himself that God made the night as well as the day and that there was no dark so deep that Jocie couldn't still see God if she tried.

Jocie used to lie awake and stare up at the blackness after her father left to go back to his bed. The dark air would pull together and make circles in front of her eyes. She'd stare and stare trying to make the circles into a face, but she never could. Her father told her she didn't have to see a visible face, that God could be just a presence, just a feeling that everything was going to be all right.

And then Jocie would hear her father's step in the hallway or hear him snoring in his bedroom and she'd be asleep in a minute.

It was full dark when Jocie turned her bike into the lane that led up to the house. The porch light was on, so she had been missed. With a yelp of welcome, Zeb came running at the first crunch of her bicycle tires on the gravel lane. He ran alongside her bike to the garage where her father was leaning against the trunk of the car.

"I was just fixing to come hunt you," he said, but he didn't sound mad or anything.

"Sorry I'm late. It takes longer than I thought to make a birthday cake. You didn't say anything to Tabitha, did you?"

"No, she hasn't got a clue what's going on. I think she's forgotten it's her birthday tomorrow."

"It's okay that I asked Leigh and Zella, isn't it?" Jocie leaned her bike against the edge of the garage under the eave. The dew had already fallen, and the toes of her shoes were wet. "I mean, I couldn't very well ask Leigh to bring the cake and just deliver it after she helped me make it and everything without asking her to stay to eat a piece. And Zella sort of invited herself."

"I'm sure Tabitha will enjoy seeing Zella again and meeting Leigh." He was quiet for a minute before he said, "What'd you think about Leigh?"

143

Jocie tried to see her father's face, but the shadows were too deep. "She's a good cook," she said and then decided that wasn't fair to Leigh, who'd supplied everything she'd needed to make Tabitha a great cake. So she added, "Actually, she's funny." That was what Leigh had asked her to tell her father.

"Funny?"

"Yeah. And not all that young. She may have to get glasses soon." Jocie leaned over to rub Zeb's ears. The dog's teeth glistened in the moonlight as he grinned at her. "I'm so glad God sent me a dog."

"You're the one who's funny." Her father put his hand on her shoulder. "Come on. Let's go see if Aunt Love saved you any cabbage casserole."

Jocie held back a groan. "You know, Dad, I'm not very hungry. I must have eaten too much chocolate frosting."

"Well, there may be a baked potato left over too. That might go better with chocolate frosting."

Together they climbed up the porch steps. "I hope Tabitha still likes chocolate," Jocie said.

"She will," her father said, but he didn't sound all that sure. He'd said just last week that California changed people. California chocolate might taste different.

avid was up early the next morning. He had praying to do. Bible school was only a couple of weeks away at Mt. Pleasant, and they were still two or three helpers short, even after Ogden Martin's wife had finally agreed to teach.

The Martins were still hoping David would disappear. He hadn't gotten an inch closer to convincing Ogden Martin they could work together for the Lord. The man had sat like a stone through the deacons' meeting after church last Sunday and hadn't said so much as an amen during their season of prayer to close out the meeting.

Of course, the deacon had had a bad morning. A couple of renegade wasps had dive-bombed the poor man while he was taking up the offering. Ogden had swiped at the wasps with the offering plate, sending dollar bills and checks flying in the breeze coming in the open windows. Quarters, nickels, and pennies had hit the wooden floor and rolled for the corners. A couple of boys had given chase under the pews, and laughter had broken out all over the church until the only person not smiling was Ogden himself. Ogden's ears had gone pink as he replaced the felt lining in the bottom of the empty offering plate.

Then, with as much dignity as he could muster, Ogden had plucked a five-dollar bill out of old Mrs. Ramsey's hair and passed the plate around to those who'd snagged the other checks and bills. He'd had to wait for the two boys to crawl out from under the pews with the change before he could take the plate back up to the front. By the time he got back to his seat by his wife, the whole top of his bald head was pink.

All through the sermon, Ogden had glared at David as if he personally had sent the wasps to attack the man. After the deacons' meeting, David had caught up with Ogden before he got to his car, but Ogden wasn't about to forgive the wasps or David. He'd told David in no uncertain terms that there were some things that weren't a bit funny and as preacher it was David's duty to maintain a sense of decorum and reverence in the worship place. And by the way, what had he done about Sadie White?

"I'm not sure what you mean, Ogden. Sadie is looking forward to helping with the refreshments at Bible school. She told me last week she'd been doing that for over forty years and she'd never yet met a child she didn't like." David had kept his smile steady. Sometimes he wanted to just grab people by the shoulders and give them a good shake until they realized what was really important.

Ogden had frowned. "Who doesn't like kids? But the wife says Sadie's getting so senile that she can't remember half the time whether she put sugar in the drinks or not. Have you ever drank grape drink with no sugar, preacher? Lela says it'll make the mouth pucker."

"Well, tell Lela we'll try to work out something to stop the pucker mouth." That had made Ogden's frown deepen, so David had rushed on. "And tell her I really appreciate her volunteering to work with the juniors. That's a lively bunch to teach sometimes."

"Lela's always worked in Bible school, preacher. She's not doing it because you asked, but for the Lord."

"And the Lord will reward her," David had said. Even that had seemed to insult Ogden, who had hurried off to his car, where his wife and children waited.

David had been pastor at enough churches to know there were some people you couldn't please even if you did backflips. Maybe the problem was that David wasn't very good at backflips, and there was no way he was going to do any kind of flip about Miss Sadie. The fact was, it didn't seem like all that much of a problem to David. Just taste the drink and then dump in some sugar when Miss Sadie turned her back. If he had to do it himself, he would. For sure, he wasn't going to be the one to end a forty-plus-year run of loving kids.

David had never been good at replacing people in church jobs, or anywhere as far as that went. Look at Zella. And it would probably be easier to get her out from behind her desk than it would be to get Miss Sadie out from behind the church kitchen counter.

Look at Adrienne. She'd been gone for years, and he hadn't even thought about looking around for a replacement. At least not until Wes had started needling him about Leigh.

David climbed through the hole in the rock fence and walked through the apple trees. He picked up one of the June apples that were beginning to fall and rubbed it off on his shirt. It was still so tart it set his teeth on edge, but he kept eating around the bruises as he went through his prayer routine in the apple trees. As he passed each tree, he repeated one of the Beatitudes and prayed for someone on his prayer list.

"'Blessed are the poor in spirit: for theirs is the kingdom of heaven.' Dear God, please bless and protect Hazel Warren as she goes to the doctor this week. 'Blessed are they that mourn: for they shall be comforted.' Watch over James Perry as he continues to grieve the death of his wife."

And on he went past the trees and through his prayers. He didn't normally offer up his family prayers in the trees, but this morning when he got to the Beatitude about the pure in heart, he paused and prayed for Jocie's party.

"Lord, a birthday party may not seem all that important. But we need some help down here, and we're trusting you to know the sort of help we need."

He went through the rest of the trees before he let himself think about birthdays and birthday cake and who was bringing a cake today. He'd noticed Leigh this week. Really noticed her. He didn't know why he hadn't before. She seemed to be in his line of vision at least two or three times a day.

She was young but not all that young. She had an air about her as if she'd heard a funny story but she'd forgotten the ending and didn't know if she should laugh or not. He wanted to tell her to laugh, that no matter what the story was, it was better to laugh.

He'd heard her laughing with Zella a few days ago. He didn't know what they were talking about, had tried not to eavesdrop on their conversation, but Leigh's laugh had been so clear and honest that it had lifted his spirits and made him think about getting up to go see if he could find a way to get another laugh to bubble out into the office air. But while he was wavering on whether he should or shouldn't, the front door had opened and shut and Leigh was gone.

When he had stuck his head out of his office door, Zella had looked up and said, "Too late. The story of your life. Always a minute too late."

"I don't know what you're talking about," David had said.

"That's the truth if you ever spoke it." Zella had given a little snort as she turned back to her typewriter and began pounding it extra hard.

He'd retreated into his office knowing she was right. When Adrienne had left, he'd never thought about another woman. Adrienne was his wife. He'd made vows. For better or worse. Through sickness and health. Till death.

At first he'd thought Adrienne would come back. Weeks had passed and then months. And he'd known, but he'd put off thinking about it. Even when the divorce papers had come in the mail, even when he'd finally signed them, he'd still felt married, still felt as if he had to be faithful to those vows even though they were empty and meaningless now. Perhaps that was just because he was afraid of moving past those vows, afraid of starting over.

So now he looked straight into the eyes of that fear. The fear of being hurt again. The fear of not being worthy of a woman's love. The fear of failure. How could a young woman like Leigh think a man beginning to lose his hair like David was attractive? Maybe it was just an elaborate Jupiterian joke Wes had thought up, but no, Wes and Zella never worked together on anything. And even Jocie had been pushing Leigh at him last night. Of course, she'd also been humming "Hound Dog" all night. She'd said Leigh had all of Elvis Presley's records.

David didn't need another daughter. He didn't know what to do with the two he had. Especially one of the two. Tabitha had been a mystery ever since she'd shown up in the rocking chair on the front porch. That night she'd seemed happy enough to be home, but ever since then she'd acted half afraid to even look in his direction. He couldn't help wondering what Adrienne had told her during the years she'd been gone. And it wasn't just him. She would hardly talk to Jocie either. David just hoped she'd stay quiet and polite through the party today and not pitch an Adrienne birthday fit. Adrienne had hated having birthdays, had made you sorry if you mentioned the day. Surely Tabitha couldn't be worried about a birthday. Didn't kids want to turn twenty?

David forgot to pay attention to where he was walking and set his foot down in a squishy cow pile in the middle of Herman Crutcher's cow pasture. He scraped his shoe bottom and sides against a tall clump of grass. "Okay, Lord," he said. "You got my attention. I'll get back to praying and trust you to help me figure out all this other. I'm so confused I don't even know what I need to figure out first."

He was coming back through the apple trees when he spotted someone waiting for him at the gate. Not Jocie. Jocie would have been waiting at the hole in the rock fence, because she knew that's the way he went. He looked at Tabitha standing with her hand on the old unused gate, and a pain stabbed through him. She was a stranger. His daughter, but a stranger nonetheless.

abitha rubbed the rose on her cheek as she watched her father walking toward her through the apple trees. She remembered the apple trees being taller and not so gnarled.

That's the way everything had been since she'd come back. Of course, she remembered things. After all, she'd been thirteen when she'd left, but nothing was quite as big or bright or good as she remembered. She had treasured her thoughts of home until they had become a kind of fairy tale, a Hansel and Gretel gingerbread house without the witch.

But there wasn't any gingerbread. There was cabbage and burnt beans, and a weird aunt who wasn't so crazy that she didn't know why Tabitha kept flipping her breakfast, and a little sister who was nothing like the little kid she remembered, and a father who she didn't know anymore, who maybe she'd never known.

A thirteen-year-old can't know her father. She certainly hadn't known how much she had depended on him, how much she would miss him, until she went with DeeDee. A thousand times she'd wished she'd never awakened in the middle of that night and caught her mother packing.

DeeDee hadn't intended to take her, had told her to go back to bed and keep her mouth shut till morning. That's what she should have done, but instead she'd gone to her room, stuffed an armload of clothes into a duffel bag, scribbled a quick note to her dad, and gone to sit in the car till her mother came tiptoeing out of the house with her own bag. Tabitha's heart had pounded in her chest as the black night closed in on her. Off in the distance, a dog had started barking, and Stumpy had answered from behind the house. A train had passed through town a couple of miles away, and the sound of its whistle at the crossings had been like a signal to leave.

Her mother had ordered her out of the car, but Tabitha had grabbed hold of the steering wheel and threatened to scream if her mother tried to push her out. DeeDee had surprised her by laughing. "You're making a mistake, girlie. A big mistake."

"Then maybe we should both stay." Tabitha had turned loose of the steering wheel.

"It's not a mistake for me. The only mistake I made was not leaving about a hundred years ago." She'd started the engine and looked over at Tabitha. "Last chance for a normal life. I'm not leaving to find normal."

Tabitha had looked back at the house. No lights, everybody inside asleep. Not just asleep but practically petrified by their dullness. Nothing ever changed in Hollyhill, and Tabitha had been ready for things to change.

"Okay, girl. That's it. You can't start crying ten miles down the road and expect me to turn around. I'm driving out of here and never coming back. Ever."

Tabitha hadn't said anything, and her mother had slowly inched the car down the lane without the headlights on. In the years since, she'd often wondered what her life would have been like if she'd opened the door and gotten out. For sure she wouldn't be in the mess she was in now. She'd never have met Jerome in California.

She should have known better. DeeDee had told her over and over she should have known better, but Jerome had made her feel so special. It had been so long since she'd felt special. So loved. Of course, he hadn't loved her. Had split at the first hint of a problem. Left her to face the music alone. Her mother had asked her what else she expected from a musician, especially a drummer. Hadn't she been around enough of the sorry losers her mother had dragged in to know better?

Her father was close enough that she could see him smiling at her now, and she wanted to run back into the house and climb into the back of the closet and just stay there in the dark. She wouldn't think. She'd just breathe and count the spots that floated in the dark air. Her stomach rolled, and she started to stick her finger down her throat so she could go on and throw up and get it over with.

That's what Aunt Love kept telling her. That she needed to get it over with. She'd begged Aunt Love to tell her father for her, but Aunt Love said it was something she had to do herself. That hiding things didn't make them go away, especially not babies. That stomachs kept getting bigger and bigger and babies always came out eventually.

Sometimes Aunt Love didn't sound like an old spinster aunt. She sounded as if she really knew what she was talking about. Of course, she'd told her that the morning sickness should have ended a week or two ago, and Tabitha was still throwing up at least once every morning.

Tabitha swallowed down the nausea as best she could and pushed a smile across her face as her father got closer. "Hi, Daddy."

"Happy birthday, sweetheart. I'm so happy I can tell you that in person today."

"Birthday?" Tabitha hadn't looked at a calendar for weeks because she didn't want to think about the days passing, the baby growing inside her pushing out her belly. "Is it my birthday?"

"You didn't remember?"

"No. DeeDee never made much fuss over birthdays. I don't even know when hers is. She didn't want to have birthdays."

"But you always had fun celebrating birthdays when you were here."

"Things were different after we left. We had fun other ways."

"Did you have fun, Tabitha? I always hoped you did. You always

153

loved to laugh when you were a little girl. You used to laugh about the silliest things until you had to sit on the floor and hold your sides."

"I remember," Tabitha said. "I used to beg you to tickle me just so I'd have something to laugh about. I wish I could laugh like that now."

"Why can't you?" her father asked.

"Nothing's that funny anymore."

"I'm surprised to hear you say that. I'd have thought everything in Hollyhill might seem funny to you after California."

"I haven't been to Hollyhill. I've only been here with you and Jocie and Aunt Love."

"Well, there you go. That should be enough to keep you laughing for days, especially if you throw in Jocie's ugly mutt and Aunt Love's crazy cat."

Tabitha hadn't intended to cry. She hadn't cried when DeeDee had given her the money Jerome had left with DeeDee to get rid of the baby. She hadn't cried when DeeDee had told her she couldn't be a grandmother, that Eddie wouldn't be able to live with a grandmother.

Tabitha had understood. Always before it had been DeeDee who had gotten tired of the men she brought home and kicked them out, but ever since the first time DeeDee had heard Eddie singing with his band, she'd done whatever it took to keep Eddie happy. Even though he was years younger than her. Even though he drank too much. Even though he made no secret that he was just there till something better came along. But DeeDee wasn't willing to give up even a day with Eddie for Tabitha or her baby.

She didn't know what she'd expected from her mother. Not tears, but DeeDee had cried when she'd put her on the bus. Tabitha had been too surprised to cry then. She hadn't cried all the way across the country on those bouncy old buses. She'd just put her hands over her stomach and worried the baby might be jostled out. That had surprised her too—how much she wanted the baby to be okay when heaven only knew everything would be easier if the bumps had knocked her loose. She just knew the baby was a girl.

But now she cried. Great racking sobs that had to have been stored up inside her for weeks. Her father pulled her close and let her cry, still not knowing, still not guessing the trouble she'd brought him from California.

DeeDee had told her what to expect. Not from her father, but from the people in Hollyhill. Especially the church people. She said they'd whisper about her, point fingers of shame at her, shun her. And that it would just get worse after the baby came, especially if he took after Jerome.

But she'd said her father would help her. That he had an inner core of goodness that even DeeDee hadn't been able to dent, though she'd given it her best shot.

Of course, they hadn't thought about her father still preaching, much less having his own church. That's the reason Tabitha hadn't told him. She hadn't wanted to spoil things for him at Mt. Pleasant the way her mother had years ago at New Liberty.

Her father stroked her hair and spoke softly. "Let it all out, sweetheart. It's okay."

She yanked herself away from him. "No, it's not okay. It can't be okay."

He smiled and gathered her back into the circle of his arms. "If you'll let me help you, together we can handle whatever it is." He put his finger under her chin and tipped her face up until he was looking into her wet eyes. "I promise, and daddies don't make promises they can't keep."

"You used to tell me that when I was little."

"And did I ever make a promise to you that I didn't keep?"

"I don't remember."

"You would remember if I did. Now tell me what's wrong."

Tabitha looked at him, her tears suddenly drying up. A bead

of sweat rolled down her father's forehead and caught in his dark eyebrows. Jerome had sweated a lot. Sweat had soaked his shirt when he played the drums in Eddie's band. His sweat had dripped on her when they made love. When they made this baby. A baby he had wanted to kill but one she would face any shame, any pain, to have.

Tabitha put one hand on her stomach and the other hand on her father's arm as if somehow that would pass the love she felt for one to the other. "I'm going to have a baby." The words slipped out easy as pie, and most surprising of all, she wanted to smile when she said it.

19

David was surprised. He shouldn't have been. He'd known she was in trouble, and a girl in trouble at her age often meant a baby showing up before a husband.

That was his problem. Seeing her as a girl of her age. It wasn't reasonable or even sensible, but he'd kept her thirteen and, in his mind, too young, too innocent to be with a man, to have the results of that growing inside her. His grandbaby.

The wonder of it grabbed him. His eyes went to her swollen tummy, and he smiled. "I'm going to be a grandfather," he said almost to himself.

She nodded shyly as her lips trembled with an answering smile. "I know it's wrong, a sin even." Her smile faded away. "But please don't ask me to give her up. I can't. I love her already."

"Her?"

"The baby's a girl. I just know it is, but DeeDee said you might make me give her up for adoption. Send me to one of those homes, but I won't go. I'll run away first."

"I'm not going to send you anywhere, Tabitha." He reached out and folded her into his arms again. "You're my daughter. Your child is my grandchild. I wouldn't give that up for anything."

"Not even for God."

"God won't ask me to," David said. "God will want us to love this baby, to take care of her."

"I'm not married."

"I didn't think you were," David said. "Did you want to be? Did you love the father that much?"

"I thought I did. I thought he would marry me. DeeDee said I was stupid, and I guess she was right. Of course, she said he wasn't all bad since he did give me some money to 'fix' my problem before he split. DeeDee knew the name of a guy who did that kind of thing. Said she'd go with me and everything." Both her hands covered her belly now. "But I couldn't do that."

"Thank God."

"DeeDee wanted me to, said it would be the easiest way out of a hard spot. The best way. When I wouldn't listen to her, she blamed all that church you used to make me go to back here in Hollyhill for warping my good sense, but she didn't try to force me to do it. She just said I couldn't stick there, that she wasn't ready to be a grandmother or even a great-aunt. And that Eddie wouldn't be able to abide a baby in the house. He was pissed enough about Jerome splitting from the band. Said good drummers were hard to find. That I was old enough to know how to keep from getting knocked up. That DeeDee should have made sure I knew the facts of life."

David clenched his fists and breathed in and out slowly. The Bible verses about turning the other cheek came to him, but it was easier to turn your own cheek than to turn your child's. He gave up on counting to ten. "A nice guy, huh?"

"Oh, Eddie's okay," Tabitha said. "Anyway, I used the money Jerome gave DeeDee to buy a bus ticket here. I didn't know what else to do."

"You did the right thing." David put his arm around her and turned her toward the house. "Aunt Love knows?" It wasn't really a question.

"Since the first day. She may be sort of loopy about some things, but she knew that. She's been after me to tell you."

"She wasn't upset? She didn't quote Scripture to you or try to make you feel sorry?"

"Nope. She just said that people make mistakes, and once the mistake's been made you just have to move on and figure out what to do next while you try not to make a bigger mistake." Tabitha looked up at him. "She was never married, was she?"

"No. Why?"

"She seems to know a lot about what I'm supposed to be feeling with the baby and all."

"Really? Well, I guess she's seen a lot of expectant mothers over the years."

"Mother!" Tabitha said. "That's a scary word."

"It'll fit after a while. How about Jocie?"

"She's clueless. I doubt she even knows what makes babies." Tabitha gave him a sideways glance. "Maybe you should have a talk with her. She is starting high school next year."

"Did I ever have a talk with you?"

"No. But DeeDee did when we left. She wanted to make sure I didn't let any of the men she brought home mess with me. She said it was always better to know the facts straight out than to dress them up in pretty talk."

David went cold inside. "Did any of them bother you?"

Tabitha looked up at him. "No, don't look so worried. DeeDee always kicked them out pronto if they made a move on me. She couldn't stand any man who had eyes for anybody but her. At least until Eddie came along. I mean, he never much more than noticed I was alive, but girls are always hitting on him at the club, and sometimes he just doesn't come home for days at a time. DeeDee hates it, but she never throws his stuff out the door. She just pretends he was never gone when he comes back."

"What goes around comes around," David muttered.

"What?" Tabitha asked.

"Never mind," David said. What Adrienne had done years ago and he had endured meant nothing now. "It wasn't important."

"DeeDee did the best she could for me. She didn't say much

159

about waiting till I got married or anything, but nobody worried too much about rings on fingers where we were."

David bit his lip and kept silent.

"She did say I should be sure I was ready before I gave myself to anyone." Tabitha's face reddened a bit. "I did wait until Jerome. I thought he was the one."

"Some things can't be wished undone," David said.

Tabitha squared her jaw. "I don't want to wish it undone. If I did, I'd be wishing away my baby, and no matter what happens, I don't want to do that. Even if the people of Hollyhill make me wear a scarlet A."

"It probably won't come to that," David said with a little smile. "Oh, there'll be talk. There's always talk in a town like Hollyhill, but people will forget after a while and start talking about something else."

"But will the people at your church forget?"

"Some of them will. Some of them might not, but it doesn't matter. I'm just filling in till they find a regular pastor, so if they start searching harder, so be it." David kept smiling. No need to let Tabitha see his worry about losing the church. Besides, he believed most things happened for a reason. Could be he wasn't meant to be a preacher. Maybe God meant for him to serve in some other way. Through the printed word instead of the spoken word. Maybe he had misinterpreted God's message to him all those years ago in the submarine the way Adrienne had always said he had. Funny to think Adrienne might have been right about him not having a real calling after all. Maybe his real calling, a calling he'd almost missed at times, was to his family. To this unborn child his daughter was carrying.

As they came across the yard, Aunt Love peeked through the curtains on the window over the sink, then quickly stepped away from the window back into the shadows of the kitchen. For the first time since Tabitha had met him at the orchard gate, he thought about the time. It had to be past noon, just a couple of hours till Jocie's party. They could still call it off. It wasn't like they'd invited the whole town, but Jocie had worked so hard to do something for Tabitha. There had been no way they could have known today would be confession day. Tabitha hadn't even remembered it was her birthday.

"You do know we're having a party this afternoon," he said.

"A party?" She looked a little scared. "A church party?"

"No, silly. A birthday party."

Now she looked all the way scared. "Not for me?" It was more prayer than question.

He nodded, ignoring her panic. "I wasn't supposed to tell you. Jocie wanted it to be a surprise. Of course, we didn't think you'd totally forget your birthday." He put his arm around her.

"I can't face a bunch of people. Not yet. I haven't gotten my scarlet A sewed on my shirt."

"It's a small party. Just us and Wes and Zella and a woman named Leigh Jacobson who helped Jocie make the cake. Jocie started planning this party weeks ago before you even came home."

"How'd she know I was coming?"

"She didn't. It was just her way of keeping you part of our family." He tightened his arm on her shoulders. "You think you could put on a happy face for a couple of hours for Jocie? We've always made a big deal out of her birthday, and she wanted to do the same for you."

"I refuse to blow out candles."

"But that used to be your favorite part. You always wanted to make a dozen wishes."

"Yeah, I know." She smiled. "My first wish was always that I'd blow out all the candles so that the rest of my wishes could come true, but that was when I still thought wishes came true."

"All wishes don't come true, for sure. But some of them still do, and prayers are answered, and here you are, the answer to my wish and prayers, and Jocie's too. She's worked hard for this party because she thought it would make you happy."

"That's what all the window washing and floor scrubbing was about." Tabitha almost laughed. "No wonder she kept giving me mean looks while she was scrubbing."

"She hasn't figured out why Aunt Love is on her case all the time and never yours," David said. "She and Aunt Love rarely find a common ground spot."

"Maybe she needs to get pregnant."

"God forbid," David said.

"Sorry, Dad. It was a joke."

"Forgive me if I don't laugh," David said. "I can barely realize you're old enough to be a mother. I don't even want to imagine Jocie old enough."

"She's thirteen," Tabitha reminded him again.

"I know. The talk. I'll do it soon." He looked at her. "Then you will try to smile and look as if you're happy at the party?"

"I don't have to tell everybody today, do I?"

"You don't have to tell anybody any day. Let them figure it out on their own."

"And they might the way my tummy's poking out." Tabitha put her hand on her stomach again.

"How far along are you?"

"I went to a doctor in California. You know, just to be sure. I was about three months then. So I guess maybe five months now. Aunt Love says I'm going to start really 'blooming,' as she calls it, next month."

"We'll make you an appointment with an obstetrician in Grundy next week. You need vitamins and stuff."

"Okay." Tabitha tiptoed up and brushed his cheek with her lips. "Thanks, Daddy. And I'll try this afternoon. I'll even blow out candles if Jocie has candles. Maybe I'll wish something for her. She probably still believes in wishes. We used to play wishing games all the time when she was little."

"Wishing games? I don't remember that."

"It was our secret game. I watched her a lot." Tabitha hesitated before adding, "You know, because DeeDee didn't."

"I know."

"I was afraid something would happen to her, like she'd get lost or fall in a well." Tabitha shook her head. "We didn't even have a well, did we?"

"No, but we had a cistern. She could have fallen into that."

"Whatever. Anyway, every morning I'd say something like 'I wish you will stay in the yard and play today,' and she'd say she wished the moon would be purple just for one night, and I'd say, 'I wish your guardian angel would fly beside you,' and she'd say she wished guardian angels sparkled so she could see them and not run faster than they did. It was a silly game, but I thought it kept her safe."

"You were a good big sister. She missed you when you left."

"But she had Mama Mae to watch her then. I used to think about that after I left, about how Mama Mae would move in with you, and I used to wish I was here and not wherever we were. I never worried about Jocie. I figured you and Mama Mae and crazy old Wes surely would keep her safe and that I was the one needing all the guardian angels. I guess I must have finally outrun them."

"All things work for good to those who love the Lord."

"Yeah, Aunt Love keeps telling me the same thing, but sometimes she doesn't look as if she believes it."

"She does most of the time."

"Do you?" Tabitha asked with a kind of stillness in her eyes as if his answer was especially important.

He was careful to answer as honestly as possible. "I don't believe that all things that happen are good, but I do believe the Lord can make good come from even the worst things."

"Even DeeDee leaving? Even me having a baby with no father?"

"He has a grandfather and a heavenly father and a loving mother."

"She. It's going to be a girl."

"Okay, she. And it was bad when your mother left and took you, but God used that to make me stronger, pray more, and move closer to him even though I lost the church. And a new baby is always a blessing." He smiled. "God will want us to celebrate that."

"Thank you, Daddy, for not being ashamed of me."

"Ashamed? Never. I'm proud of you for having the courage to come home and let us help you." He hugged her again before they went on to the house.

20

*S*ince the heat had climbed into the living room with the morning sun and the fans were just stirring hot air, Jocie set up the card table and chairs in the front yard under the oak tree, where a little breeze was stirring. She brushed the dirt off some pretty rocks from Aunt Love's rock garden to hold the yellow tablecloth in place and tried not to think about all those hours scrubbing floors and walls inside that nobody was going to get a chance to look at now. Maybe she'd take Leigh on a tour of the house just so she could look out the sparkling windows.

Aunt Love said no housework was ever wasted, that it had to be done sooner or later anyway, but Jocie noticed the sooner you did it the sooner you had to do it again.

Her father had spilled the beans to Tabitha about the party. As if he was worried about Tabitha not being there or something. She hadn't gone anywhere since she'd come home. Still, her father said it was only fair to give Tabitha the chance to spruce up, since she was going to be seeing people she hadn't seen since she'd left with DeeDee.

Jocie grinned. It was funny how much easier it was to think about her mother as DeeDee. She wished Tabitha had written her about that years ago.

Zeb watched her getting everything ready as if hoping she was putting everything out for him. Every once in a while she wondered if Wes had been right about the dog being his Jupiterian buddy, Herman or Harlan or whatever. Zeb just seemed to know too much to be a regular dog. Dogs liked to jump in ponds and roll in cow manure and chew on bones. Zeb liked the bones, but he tiptoed around the shallowest puddles and didn't even sniff cow piles. And every time she went out the door, he was sitting there waiting for her with his silly dog grin and wagging tail. She'd stopped even worrying about him leaving.

The daisies she'd picked that morning in Mr. Crutcher's hay field looked perfect in the middle of the yellow table. The wind puffed a few of the green and yellow Happy Birthday napkins off the table. Jocie gathered them up and used the silver cake server Aunt Love had made her polish as a weight to hold them on the table. Two little silver serving dishes that had belonged to Aunt Love's mother waited for the mints Zella had promised to bring.

Jocie sat down in one of the chairs to wait, but the minutes dragged by as if it were Christmas Eve. She looked at her watch. Still almost an hour before time. Her father was closeted in his room working on tomorrow's sermon. Tabitha had taken up residence in the bathroom, and Aunt Love was in her rocker on the porch knitting something pink that Jocie fervently hoped wasn't for her. She hated pink.

Jocie got up and moved the silver dishes and counted the Happy Birthday plates. She wished Leigh would get there with the cake. It didn't look like a birthday till there was a cake. And presents. She'd forgotten the presents.

"Mercy sakes, child, what is it now?" Aunt Love said when Jocie ran up the porch steps. "If you keep fanning the door, you're going to let every fly in the country in."

"I forgot Tabitha's presents." Jocie stopped halfway through the door. "Can I bring out something to put them on? In case other people bring presents too."

"Bring out whatever you want. Just don't keep holding the door open."

"Oh, sorry."

"And don't slam the door."

Jocie tried to catch it, but it was too late. She yelled another sorry back at Aunt Love, who was muttering her tribulation worketh patience Scripture. Jocie heard that one a lot.

She cleared the pictures and the lamp off the oblong table in the living room. Then she fished Tabitha's present out from under the cot on the back porch. She'd forgotten to buy wrapping paper, so she'd colored daisies and rainbows and stars on white freezer paper to wrap it in. The brush and comb and fingernail polish didn't make a very big package, and it looked lonesome in the middle of the oblong table. Jocie moved her gift to the side to leave room for other presents. Wes would bring a book or something. And she could set the cake on that table if Leigh ever got there. Jocie looked at her watch. Still not time.

Aunt Love came down off the porch to pass judgment on Jocie's preparations. Jocie waited for her to say "Put the rocks back" or "Go find a cloth not so bright," but Aunt Love fooled her by smiling and saying, " 'He that loveth his brother abideth in the light.' First John 2:10. I'd think the good Lord meant that to go for sisters too." She held out a small, flat package wrapped in white tissue paper. "It's not much, but you can add it to your gift table."

"Gee, thanks, Aunt Love." Jocie was happier than if she'd been getting the present herself. "What is it?"

"A brooch. A lady's elongated face. I bought it years ago in a weak moment, but I never had the occasion to wear it. Perhaps Tabitha will like it."

"I'm sure she will. She likes weird stuff." Jocie put the present beside her own and then practically jumped up and down when she heard the motorcycle. "Listen, I hear Wes."

"Who couldn't? You'd think the sheriff would require him to get some kind of muffler for that thing."

Wes rode his motorcycle up into the yard. "Looks like I'm just in time for a party." He handed Jocie a book wrapped in an old newspaper. "Poetry. I figured a California flower child would have to like poetry."

"She's going to be so excited."

"Maybe half as excited as you," he said. "Good afternoon, Lovella. You haven't changed your mind about going for a spin on my hog, have you?"

Aunt Love actually smiled. Angels must have been sprinkling happy dust on them all. "Not yet, Wesley," she said. "But who knows? I might surprise you one of these days."

"I wouldn't be surprised. Only honored," Wes said. Zeb sniffed his boots. "Well, looks like old Harlan is still hanging around. I bet he never expected to be the answer to a dog prayer."

"He's not Harlan. He's Zebedee. And he likes it here. He wouldn't go back to Jupiter even if your old spaceship landed right in the front yard," Jocie said. "Oh, look, there's Leigh. I can't wait for you to see the cake."

"But does it bounce?" Wes asked. "That's the important question to ask about one of your cakes, Jo."

Jocie watched the 1959 Chevy crawl up the lane as if she could will it to go faster with her eyes. She couldn't wait to set the cake by the presents.

When Zella climbed out of the passenger's side of Leigh's car, Wes said, "Hey, Zell, why didn't you tell me you needed a ride?"

Zella didn't bother to answer as she handed Jocie the bag of pastel-colored mints and two more presents, these actually wrapped in birthday paper. Leigh was carrying the cake in an open box to keep the icing from getting mashed. Jocie gingerly lifted it out and placed it on the table beside the presents.

Leigh handed her a box of candles. "One per year? Or do you want to make the shape of 20? You said Tabitha was twenty, right?"

"One per year." Jocie stuck candles around the yellow roses. "The cake looks fantastic. Even better than yesterday."

"I added a little more decoration after you left. That's a lot of candles. I hope she's got lots of breath to blow with," Leigh said. "By the way, where is the birthday girl? And your father?" she added almost as an afterthought even as her face went pink.

"Dad's probably still working on his sermon. He forgets to look at the time when he's in the Scripture, and Tabitha is getting ready. Maybe I'd better go check," Jocie said. "You want to come in and look at the house?"

"Oh, I'll just visit with the folks out here. I wouldn't want to intrude."

Jocie didn't insist. Maybe they'd see how sparkling the windows were by looking at them from the outside.

Tabitha was blowing on her freshly painted fingernails as she sat cross-legged on the bed in a puddle of blue and purple silk skirt. The white shirt she'd tied loosely at the waist looked as if it could have been her father's. She hooked her still-damp hair back behind her ears and tried to smile when Jocie stuck her head in the door. "Am I keeping everybody waiting?"

"Everybody but Dad. I've got to get him next." Jocie stared at Tabitha. "You look very California. I mean, that's good. You're beautiful."

Tabitha glanced over at the mirror on the dresser and then away. "It was either this or my shorts and halter top, and I didn't want to shock Zella."

"Everything shocks Zella," Jocie said. "You'd think she never watched TV or read the news."

"Or maybe she likes to be shocked," their father said from the doorway. "But I don't think anybody is going to be shocked by you two unless it's by how lovely you both are."

"Tabitha maybe," Jocie said. "The only person who thinks I'm pretty is Wes, and that's just because he's from Jupiter and doesn't know any better."

"Jupiter?" Tabitha frowned.

Her father put his arm around Tabitha and said, "Don't ask."

"You don't remember that Wes is from Jupiter?" Jocie said.

"Jupiter, Indiana?"

Jocie laughed. "Is there a Jupiter, Indiana? Maybe that's where Wes has been talking about all these years." Jocie ran ahead of them to the stairs. "You two go on out. I've got to get the lemonade and tea out of the fridge. But don't look at the cake till I get out there."

"Are you sure it's not her birthday?" Tabitha said as Jocie ran down the stairs.

"It's more blessed to give than to receive," her father answered.

"And obviously more fun," Tabitha said. "Can't I pretend to be sick or something and let Jocie carry my cake in here to me?"

Her father laughed and tightened his arm around her shoulder as he guided her toward the stairs. "It won't be so bad. Just Zella—you remember Zella."

"Is she still as quirky as she used to be?"

"Quirkier. And Wes."

"I always thought he was from Mars."

"Close. And Leigh Jacobson, who I'm told helped bake you a cake."

"Who the heck is she? Am I supposed to know her?"

"No. She's a friend of Zella's."

Jocie came out of the kitchen carrying two pitchers. "But she wants to be Dad's friend. Real bad."

Tabitha looked back at the staircase with longing. "DeeDee was right about birthdays. This is getting too crazy."

21

Seeing the cake with candles made Tabitha feel like the kid who used to run out to the end of the lane to wait for Mama Mae to show up with her birthday cake and presents wrapped in white tissue paper. Mama Mae always made her a new dress and gave her a book or a puzzle and a bag of chocolate peanut clusters with cream in the middle. She wished her father had remembered about the peanut clusters, even if chocolate did set off the morning sickness.

But there weren't any peanut clusters. She got a brush and comb and bright red nail polish from Jocie; stationery decorated with violets from Zella, who kept sneaking peeks at the rose on Tabitha's cheek; a book of poems from Wes, who looked exactly the same; a card with a ten-dollar bill tucked inside from her father; and hair ribbons from Leigh, who'd either had too much sun that morning or had a permanent blush.

The biggest surprise had been Aunt Love's present, a wire pin twisted into the profile of a woman wearing a wide-brimmed hat. Tabitha could have worn it in California. If she'd thought about it, which she hadn't, she'd have expected Aunt Love to give her a Bible. Aunt Love had been reading the Bible to her. Some psalms. Some of the old Sunday school stories. None of the "thou shalt not" parts.

They'd made Tabitha sit in the middle of the rest of the chairs where she could be the main focus of everyone's eyes. Tabitha folded pleats in her skirt to keep her hands occupied and away from her tummy. She sipped the sugary lemonade and told herself over and over, *I won't get sick till everybody's gone. I won't get sick till everybody's gone.* Then just to get her mind off having to run behind the house to lose the chocolate cake she would have to eat if they ever got the candles lit, she let another silent thought run through her mind. *I won't laugh out loud till everybody's gone. I won't laugh out loud till everybody's gone.*

DeeDee would have laughed. Out loud whenever she wanted to. But she wasn't DeeDee. That's why she was here with her secret growing inside her. A secret she'd shared, or at least part of the secret. She'd been hoping, even praying at night before she went to sleep, that she might not have to tell the rest of the secret ever in Hollyhill. After all, the baby had just as much chance of looking like her as like Jerome.

Secrets. Everybody had secrets they never told. DeeDee said so. And to prove it she'd told some of them to Tabitha. Some Tabitha wished DeeDee had kept secret. Tabitha looked at Jocie. She was practically spinning she was having such fun.

Tabitha was still having a hard time connecting this Jocie to the little kid who had tagged after her with a book under her arm in case she might decide to read to her. Jocie had never cried even if she fell down and scraped her knees, and when she disappeared for any length of time, Tabitha usually could find her under the porch taking a nap with Stumpy. That was then. A little shadow of a girl with big eyes.

Now she was completely different. She still had the big eyes watching the world, but she was far from a shadow. She practically sparked with energy. She made Tabitha think of a girl she'd known in Chicago, or maybe it was in Kansas City. Tabitha couldn't keep the places straight, but it must have been Kansas City, because it had been summer and hot. Courtney had yanked her hair back out of her eyes into a ponytail with a plain rubber band. She'd carried a notebook and pencil with her everywhere and hadn't been a bit embarrassed when her tennis shoes had holes in the toes. One day she'd be cross-legged on the ground counting ants marching into an anthill and the next she'd be planting her rubber snake on the sidewalk to see how many people screamed. Tabitha had always been good for at least one shriek even though she knew the stupid thing was fake. Tabitha used to look Courtney up just to see what weird idea she would come up with next. The weirdest thing was that Courtney never knew she was weird.

Not that Jocie was weird exactly. But she did bounce from idea to idea like somebody riding one of those bumper cars at the fair. Had she bumped into any of the secrets? Tabitha probably would have never bumped into them if she'd stayed with her father in Hollyhill. Some things it was better not to bump into when you were a kid, or maybe ever. Tabitha's hands crept up to her midsection for a quick touch. She'd have secrets to keep from her baby for sure. No child ever needed to know her father wanted to scrape her out of existence before she had a chance to be born.

Tabitha's eyes went to her father, who had moved up behind the cake to make a windbreak to help the candles stay lit. The Leigh woman's face was flaming so red that she looked as if she could just lean over and light the whole mess of candles without a match. Tabitha couldn't remember the last time she'd blushed like that. Maybe before she left Hollyhill. Maybe never.

It was hard to keep secrets when your face gave you away like that. Her father wasn't blushing. He looked calm and in control. That's one of the things that had always driven DeeDee crazy—how he could stay so calm. She used to say he'd never come up out of his submarine after the war and still kept the tons of water between him and the world. Tabitha remembered their fights—DeeDee screaming or laughing according to the mood she was in and her father watching without the first clue of what to do to make DeeDee stop. He'd looked like a man who didn't know any secrets then, but now Tabitha wasn't so sure.

Maybe he knew the secrets but hid them deep inside so no one would ever guess he knew them. After all, he knew her secret, but there was no sign on his face that anything was any different today than it had been yesterday or the day before. And maybe he had secrets none of them knew anything about.

DeeDee had always said that no woman in her right mind could live with a man so deep down good that it took a war to make him mad. She hadn't had to worry about that after leaving Hollyhill. Some of the men she'd brought home had been nice enough. There was Bobby, who had taught Tabitha to play hearts and three kinds of solitaire, and Rick, who had helped her plant tulips in a window box. That was the year after she'd gotten the letter that Mama Mae had died, and Tabitha had cried every time a tulip bloomed until finally DeeDee had thrown the whole thing in the dumpster.

Tabitha had climbed into the dumpster after it, but all the tulip bulbs had been out of the dirt and the blooms had been broken. Rick had yelled at DeeDee when he found out about the tulips, and DeeDee had thrown his stuff out of the apartment. Tabitha missed Rick more than most of the men her mother brought home, but she was used to them coming and going. Eddie was the only one her mother let stay in spite of anything he did.

Finally the candles were mostly lit, and the whole bunch of them were yelling at her to make a wish. She felt twelve again, and it wasn't a bad feeling. Of course, she only had one wish, but she was almost afraid to wish it for fear she might jinx the wish if she left a candle burning.

The cake was blazing, and she took such a deep breath she felt dizzy. *Please let my baby look like me*, she whispered in her mind and blew, moving her head in a circle to get the most candles. Every candle went out, and everybody clapped, even Aunt Love, who surely believed wishing on candles was against Bible teaching. "Better prayers than wishes," she'd told Tabitha just last week. But a wish was sometimes like a prayer, and maybe there were birthday angels floating around the cake. Mama Mae used to talk about birthday angels. One of them could carry her wish up to heaven and turn it into a prayer.

22

The trouble with a weekly paper was that anything exciting seemed to always happen on the day the paper was printed, and then by the next week's issue, it was old news. So of course, the Fourth fell on Tuesday when they had to run the paper for distribution on Wednesday. Monday Jocie's father called them all together around Zella's desk to see if they could find a way to push back the deadline for printing. Wes said they could set up the inside pages and run them that day and leave the front and back pages for stories and pictures of the parade to run on Tuesday after the parade was over.

Zella looked up from filing her fingernails. "I'm not staying around here till midnight."

She and her over-forty Sunday school class had spent every night for two weeks stuffing red, white, and blue tissue paper into a flag-shaped chicken-wire frame Chester Hagan had built on his farm wagon. Zella said it even had a wind ripple in the middle, but chicken wire was murder on fingernails. She'd worn out two emery boards in a week.

"I might get a good shot of the First Baptist float," Jocie's father said.

Zella inspected her fingernails and didn't look at him. "Front page, top fold."

"Church kids riding on it?" Jocie's father asked.

"Ten last head count."

"Then agreed. Front page, top fold."

They left Zella to her nail filing and went back to the press-room to block out the inside pages and ads before Jocie's father left to interview Myron Haskins, a veteran of World War I who was always more than ready to share every detail of every battle and all the times between. Her father invited Jocie to ride along, but she'd heard Mr. Haskins talk before. On and on and on. She told her father she'd wait for the condensed version in the *Banner*.

Besides, she wanted to hear what Wes thought about the party. And about Tabitha. And about Leigh and her father. Her father had actually sat by Leigh and told her what he was preaching on the next day. Her father never told people what his sermon was going to be about. Said he was never sure the Lord might not change the subject at the last minute. Even more amazing, Leigh had almost stopped blushing while they talked about Peter step-ping out of the boat to walk on the water toward Jesus. Nobody had mentioned Elvis.

Jocie told Wes she tried to think about how the birthday cake had practically melted in her mouth and not worry about step-mothers who did the twist and knew every word of "Love Me Tender."

Wes laughed. "That ain't your worry, Jo. Your daddy is the one who'll have to worry about that one."

Wes and Jocie were just settling in to work when Zella came back to the pressroom waving a couple of letters.

Wes said, "We must have gotten a letter from the president to get Zella back here."

"I heard that," Zella said. "The fact is, I just came across a couple more letters in the mail that will go good this week."

"Happy letters?" Jocie asked.

"One is. From little Donnie Mason."

"He lives next door to you, doesn't he?" Jocie said.

"That doesn't mean he can't write a letter to the paper. He's made his list of the best things about the Fourth."

"Oh, cute," Jocie said.

"Don't be snitty." Zella pulled the letter up and started reading. "Red, white, and blue cupcakes. Fireworks. Loud booms. The flag. Cotton candy."

"Cotton candy? What does that have to do with the Fourth?" Jocie asked.

"I don't know. Something, I'm sure." Zella slapped the letter down on the desk and looked at the other one in her hand. "This one is from Betty Marshall complaining about the twin calf picture on the front page of the *Banner* a few weeks back. She says that just proves what a one-horse town we live in, or in this case a one-cow town."

"A cow with twins. That puts us up to a three-cow town at least." Wes took the letter from Zella and scanned it quickly. "Not bad. But she doesn't mention goats. I think Wilbur French has some new spotted goats out at his place. He wants to start making goat cheese to sell. New business venture. Cute goats. Sounds like a front page story to me."

Zella rolled her eyes. "Deliver us."

"Tell me where, and I'll do my best," Wes said.

Jocie twisted her mouth to keep from giggling. She expected Zella to storm back to her desk, but instead she said, "Ha. Ha. Very funny, I'm sure." Then she looked at Jocie. "Your party was very nice, Jocelyn. Thank you for inviting me. I'm sure Tabitha appreciated it even if it may have been a bit tame after what she was used to in California."

"Yeah, thanks for coming. And for bringing the mints," Jocie said.

"My pleasure." Zella took a couple of steps back toward the front office, then stopped. "Tabitha isn't the sweet little child who left here, is she? But I suppose that was to be expected. Heaven knows what the poor child has gone through with that mother of hers."

"She seems okay to me," Jocie said.

"Well, of course. I didn't mean to imply that she wasn't okay. She's just changed, you know," Zella said. "That rose. It is just painted on, isn't it? I mean, it surely isn't a tattoo."

"What's wrong with tattoos?" Wes said. "I almost got one once."

"Well, we expect that kind of thing from you, Wesley," Zella said. "But certainly not from a young girl like Tabitha. What do the people at Mt. Pleasant think?"

"I don't know," Jocie said. "She hasn't gone to church with us yet."

"She hasn't gone to church?" Zella looked ready to faint.

"Not yet. The trip home wore her out, and Dad's giving her time to rest up."

"Time for the tattoo to disappear, more likely," Zella said.

"Tattoos don't disappear, do they?" Jocie asked Wes.

"Nope, not even on Jupiter," Wes agreed.

"You two. I don't know why I even bother trying to talk to you."

"Because you like us so much?" Wes said.

"Hmph." Zella headed toward the door but then stopped again. "Leigh called a bit ago. Said David had called her to thank her for helping you with the cake, Jocelyn. That's surely a good sign, don't you think?"

"I hope it's a sign that she might make us another cake," Jocie said. "We ate the last of it last night after we got home from church. Even Aunt Love said it was the best chocolate cake she'd ever eaten."

"You should try to get your Aunt Love to invite Leigh for supper sometime."

"I thought it was Dad you wanted to invite Leigh somewhere."

"Well, we can't depend on David. Leave it up to him and he'd

179

never get past go with any girl," Zella said. "And this may be his only opportunity to get a really nice girl."

"Who can cook," Wes chimed in.

"And do the twist," Jocie said. "And sing along with Elvis."

"There's nothing wrong with being young," Zella said.

"That's not what you usually tell me," Jocie said.

"Young and nice is different than young and smart-alecky, Jocelyn Brooke," Zella said as she went back out into the front office. The pressroom door slammed shut behind her.

"Uh-oh. Now she'll tell Dad, and I'll have to listen to the 'be respectful to my elders' lecture," Jocie said. "And I've been trying really hard to stay out of trouble."

"Nah, Zell won't be telling on you this week. She wants you to help her with her matchmaking plans with Leigh."

"I liked Leigh. She talked to me like you do, not like I'm some stupid kid who doesn't know straight up about anything. But I just can't imagine Daddy listening to Elvis or doing the twist."

"Folks will surprise you sometimes. Even daddies." Wes put his hand on Jocie's shoulder. "But we've done our part. We brought it to your father's attention that Leigh is female and has recognized that he is male. Now we have to let him do his part, whether it's listening to Elvis or just ignoring the whole thing and letting Leigh move on to some other feller."

"Leigh says there aren't any other single men in Hollyhill besides you, and she's too afraid of your motorcycle to make eyes at you."

"Plus, I could be her father. Maybe her grandfather."

"You're not that old. Of course, it could be she just doesn't want to intrude on Zella's territory."

Wes laughed. "That's a good one. I'd have more chance with your Aunt Love than old Zell out there. She has a positive aversion to anything Jupiterian."

The next day dawned clear and hot. By the time the parade started forming in the high school parking lot at noon, heat was rising off the sidewalks and people were crowding in under the scarce midday shade of storefront awnings. They tried to wave back the heat with the "Service with Dignity" Hazelton Funeral Home fans Junior and Rita Hazelton were passing out for their father. Hazelton's was the only funeral home in Hollyhill, but Gordon Hazelton didn't want folks to think he took their dying and coming to him for their funerals for granted.

Nobody could remember Hollyhill ever having a Fourth of July parade before, and plenty of folks had come out to see what there was to see. The stores along Main Street all had "Sale" signs in the windows to entice people inside. Fans swished around the hot air in the older stores, while the newer ones cranked up their air conditioners to fight against the swinging doors as customers streamed in and out more in search of cool air than bargains.

The *Banner* offices didn't have air-conditioning, but fans were roaring. Aunt Love and Tabitha had come to watch the parade from the big front window. Zella was out at the high school, ready with extra tissue paper if a hole was spotted in the First Baptist float. Jocie loaded her camera, stuck an extra roll of film in her pocket, and went out hunting some paper-selling shots. Her father told her to zero in on kids watching the parade or kids on the floats. He would take pictures of the floats and the politicians.

Wes went up the street to get Aunt Love and Tabitha some lemonade from the Girl Scouts' stand by the post office. The high school pep club and the Hollyhill Church of God had bake sales going in front of the banks. The icing on the cupcakes was melting in the heat, but nobody seemed to care as they licked their fingers and listened for the high school band to get the parade started.

Jocie snapped a couple of shots of kids sitting on the edge of the sidewalk peering down toward the high school. Then she took a picture of little Jamie Ray Jones up on his daddy's shoulders. She felt lucky when she caught sight of Myron Haskins sitting on the bench in front of the courthouse, both hands resting on his cane propped out in front of him like a podium. She took three pictures from different angles and even took the chance of asking Mr. Haskins what he thought about the parade. The band was still just tooting and drumming haphazardly, which surely meant the parade hadn't formed ranks.

He frowned at her. "It's a fine thing if it'll get you young folks to see that freedom's worth fighting for, to know that it has been fought for, that men died so we can march down this street."

"Yes, sir," Jocie said and began edging away.

"A man should be proud to serve his country, not try to get out of being drafted the way boys do nowadays." He reached out and thumped Jocie on the arm. "We ran to the enlistment office in my day."

"Yes, sir," Jocie repeated. "I'm sure the mayor will be recognizing your service when he gives his speech later." Jocie glanced over at the empty wagon set up across from the courthouse where the dignitaries would gather after they rode in the parade. "And everybody in Hollyhill knows what you did for your country."

Mr. Haskins raised his cane and stabbed it toward her. Jocie backed out of range. "Nobody can know what we did except the ones who were there. War isn't something you can know about unless you're a soldier."

"Yes, sir," Jocie said one last time and slipped out of sight behind the Civil War monument beside Mr. Haskins. She crossed the street and headed back toward the high school to see if the parade had started. The crowd was growing, and a couple of kids from school yelled at her to take their pictures. She pretended to push the shutter while they struck a pose. She didn't like posed pictures. She liked catching people unaware. Like Jimmy Sanders sitting cross-legged on top of the metal awning in front of his father's hardware store. He must have climbed out the upstairs window and slid into position.

The even rat-a-tat of drums signaled that the parade had at long last left the high school and was headed downtown. The people edged away from the shade of the buildings, closer to the street, pushing their kids in front of them. Jocie eased through the crowd to take up position in front of the concrete trash can by the Five and Dime store.

A couple of Eagle Scouts carried the American and Kentucky flags in front of the mayor in the first car. He'd appointed himself grand marshal of the parade, since the whole thing had been his idea and nobody had come up with anybody famous. They'd thought about asking Stu Williams, who had been a starter on the University of Kentucky basketball team twenty years ago, but he'd moved to South Carolina some years back and hadn't been back to Hollyhill more than twice since he'd got out of college. As Jocie watched the mayor ride by, she thought they should have asked old Mr. Haskins.

The next few cars carried the city council members and the county judge. Jocie didn't bother even to practice focus. She wasn't going to waste her film on yawner pictures. The band marched into view, and Jocie caught a shot of William Pickens twirling his drumsticks and Judy Lester carrying her trumpet. Judy, a junior next year, rode Jocie's bus and had promised to show her the ropes when she went to high school next fall.

The mayor's granddaughter and Hollyhill High prom queen, Judith Palmor, smiled and waved from her perch on the top of the backseat of a red and white Corvette convertible. She wore a blue sundress and held a small American flag. Every few feet she threw some peppermint candy out on the street where kids pounced on it. Jocie snapped a picture of Judith waving, then grabbed a piece of peppermint to see if the mayor's name was on the candy wrapper, but it was just plain cellophane.

Zella's float was first. The tissue paper flag wasn't half bad. At least you could tell it was supposed to be a flag. The kids on the float stood with their hands over their hearts repeating the pledge over and over. Next, 4-H Club members dressed in green and white held up paper four-leaf clovers with white H's. Jocie ran alongside the float to get a shot of Heather Byrd's border collie sitting at attention on the front of the wagon. Jocie wished her father would let Zeb come to work with them. Boys in the Future Farmers of America Club dangled their feet off the edge of their wagon and waved as they passed. They hadn't bothered decorating the wagon, but they were wearing their blue FFA jackets in spite of the heat. Scout troops and Little League baseball teams decked out in their uniforms walked behind the floats. Jocie took pictures as fast as she could focus and wind.

Five or six kids followed on bikes decorated with red crepe paper, flags, and signs. Bennie Drury spotted Jocie with her camera and popped a wheelie right in front of her, but she shrugged and pretended she'd used up her film. She didn't want Bennie to get the idea she liked him or something.

Ponies and horses with tiny American flags stuck in their bridles and saddle horns spread out across the street after the bikes. Jocie spotted five-year-old Marvin Sims in an oversized cowboy hat sitting on top of a big Appaloosa. Jocie crouched down low to focus in so the horse would look even bigger and Marvin even littler.

Bringing up the rear of the parade was the town's new fire truck. Fire chief Baxter Hill hit the siren every few minutes and kept his lights flashing. A couple of volunteer firemen hung on to the back and pitched out more candy. Jocie used up the rest of her film on kids scrambling for the candy. She could hear the band playing "The Star Spangled Banner" down in front of the courthouse, but she headed for the news office to turn in her film to Wes instead of going down the street. Her dad had said he'd cover the politicians.

She'd forgotten about Aunt Love and Tabitha watching the parade from the office until she pushed through the door and set the bell on top to jangling. "Where's the fire?" Tabitha asked.

"No fire. Just the paper to run." Jocie paused in her headlong rush back to the pressroom to look at Tabitha, who was sitting alone in a line of three chairs pulled up to the window. "Where's Aunt Love?"

"She and that Leigh woman went down the street to hear the speeches. I told them I'd rather stay here and nap."

"Leigh was here?"

"Yep. Dad saw her on the street and told her to come up and watch from here."

"Oh," Jocie said.

"Yeah," Tabitha said. "I think Dad might finally be over DeeDee."

"Well, Leigh's nice."

"Nice." Tabitha made a face. "That's the worst thing you can say about anybody. Better to be pretty. Or fun. Best of all, sexy. That's what makes men notice."

"I think Dad might rather have nice."

"No, all guys like sexy. Even old guys in the Bible. Remember King David and Bathsheba? That's a pretty hot story."

"I thought you'd forgotten everything you knew about the Bible," Jocie said.

"Aunt Love's been reading some Bible stories to me to refresh my memory."

"Well, if it's true that all guys want sexy, then I guess we won't have to worry about Leigh being our stepmother."

Tabitha smiled. "I don't know about that. Just because we don't think Leigh's sexy doesn't mean Dad might not. Besides, it might be good if he was married." Tabitha's smile disappeared. "It might be good if I was married."

"You probably could be if you wanted to be. You're pretty, and you look sexy."

"Oh yeah. No doubt. That's my problem. I'm too sexy for my own good." Tabitha looked straight at Jocie. "Guess now's as good a time to tell you as any, since you're way too innocent to ever notice on your own. I'm going to have a baby."

23

Y ou're going to have a baby?" Jocie echoed. "So that explains it."

"Explains what?" Tabitha asked.

"How you're getting fat eating Aunt Love's cooking."

Tabitha put her hands on her stomach and burst out laughing. Jocie looked at her as if she were crazy. "It wasn't that funny."

Finally Tabitha wiped her eyes and said, "You guys are a hoot. Here I worry overtime about how everybody is going to be ashamed of me, and Daddy just says wow, he's going to be a grandfather and you just look relieved you weren't wrong about Aunt Love's cooking. Maybe I won't have to wear a scarlet A after all."

"Well, I guess it would be better if you were married, wouldn't it?"

"Oh yeah. Even DeeDee would agree to that one. At least I think she would."

"And Aunt Love." Jocie's eyes got big. "Does she know?"

"Since day one. Figured it out the first time I upchucked my toast."

"And she didn't flip out and start quoting Bible verses about thou shalt not or something?"

"No, I don't get why you complain about Aunt Love. She's been nothing but sweet to me."

"And I guess Jezebel—I mean Sugar—purrs when you rub her too."

"Well, yeah, but what's that got to do with anything?"

"Nothing. Just curious."

Tabitha stood up and came over to Jocie. "Maybe you're just too full of energy for Aunt Love. She doesn't know what to do with you. Me, I'm older and sort of mellowed out right now, and I think she's actually excited about me having a baby. Like it could be the grandchild she never had. She must have been lonely a lot. She told me her fiancé got killed in France in the First World War. Said she didn't want to marry after that. Besides, she had to take care of her father."

"I thought it was her brother who died in the war."

"The brother got sick and died on a ship on the way overseas."

"Oh. How come she's telling you all this stuff and she's never told me the first thing about it?"

"You've probably never sat still long enough for her to tell you anything."

"She finds plenty of time to quote me Scripture," Jocie said.

"That's different. She's just trying to help you with those."

"She beats me over the head with those." Jocie pulled up her camera. "We've got a while before the baby comes, right? I mean, I've got to get this film to Wes so we can run the paper."

"A few months," Tabitha said with another smile. "Lots of *Banner* issues before then. And time to talk."

Jocie headed for the pressroom, then turned around. "Is it a secret? I mean, you don't want me to tell anybody?"

"It's okay if you let it slip to Wes, if that's what you mean. He probably already knows anyway. Doesn't much get past him. You weren't doing a baby prayer, were you?"

"Nope. Just a sister prayer, but I guess I'd better start with a baby prayer now. What do you want me to pray?"

Tabitha put her hands on her belly. "That she'll be healthy and happy and look like me."

"Why? Was her father ugly or something?"

"No, he looked fine, but he didn't want her. And I do, so it only seems fair that she look like me, don't you think?"

"I guess so. I'm glad you want your baby, Tabitha."

"Why?"

"Because all babies should be wanted by their mothers."

"You're thinking about DeeDee, aren't you?"

"Maybe." Jocie shrugged. "It just seems funny that she'd take you and not even say good-bye to me."

"DeeDee's not much on good-byes. And she wasn't planning to take me. I just woke up and caught her packing. She told me to go back to bed, but I went out and got in the car."

"But she let you go. She would have pushed me out of the car."

"You wouldn't have gotten in the car to begin with, Jocie. You wouldn't have left Dad." Tabitha reached out and hugged Jocie. "Besides, you were the lucky one."

"I know." Jocie pulled away from Tabitha and said, "I really have to get this film started developing or we'll never get the paper going."

"Sure, go ahead. I'll just sit here and watch to see if Dad and that Leigh woman come back holding hands."

"They were that friendly?"

Tabitha grinned. "Not then, but maybe by now."

Jocie stopped at the pressroom door. "You know, you could have just told us you were married. That your husband died in some kind of freak accident or something. We'd have never known the difference."

"That's what DeeDee told me to do. Said to think up some kind of story on the way across the country. She'd have done it in a minute. Said sometimes lies saved everybody a lot of trouble. But I guess I have too much of Dad in me. I mean, I haven't been to church since I left here, but that's one of the big things, isn't it? Don't lie."

"Thou shalt not bear false witness." Jocie made a face. "Oh no, I'm sounding like Aunt Love."

"So anyway, while I don't know exactly why the Lord should pay any attention to anything I want, I do want him to bless my baby, and how could I ask that if I was lying to everybody? Am I making any sense?"

"God will pay attention, Tabitha. Get Aunt Love to quote you her verses about praying. She's got some good ones. 'Ask and it shall be given you' and things like that. I've been paying more attention since Zeb and you showed up."

Tabitha laughed again. "I don't know whether I should be mad or glad about being paired with a dog."

"A dog from Jupiter."

Tabitha rolled her eyes. "And I thought it was crazy in California with everybody saying love conquers all."

"God's love does. Just ask Dad."

"You keep giving me things to ask, I'm going to have to take notes."

Jocie disappeared through the door into the pressroom, and Tabitha settled back into the chair by the window. She stared out at the street. The traffic was still blocked off Main, and the sound of the speeches echoed up from in front of the courthouse. She listened but couldn't make out the first word. She could have walked down there, but then people would be looking at her as if she had two heads and telling her how great it was that she was home while they wondered why she was. Nobody came back to Hollyhill from California.

She'd already been the focus of a lot of stares in through the window, and two girls who said they'd gone to school with her had come in to say hello. That was about all they knew to say, and after an awkward exchange of "It's great to have you back" and "It's great to be back," they were glad to get back to the parade.

Tabitha hadn't known them. Even after they'd told her their names, nothing but a foggy almost-memory came to mind. She'd been gone too long, gone to too many different schools with too many different kids. But they had expected her to know them as if she had been frozen in time the way Hollyhill had.

She'd ridden across the country through a time tunnel and had ended up in Hollyhill not more than a week or two after she left. The storefronts still needed paint. The same cracks she'd jumped over to keep from breaking her mother's back as a kid still ran across the sidewalks. Even some of the people seemed frozen in time. Zella with her tight, windproof curls and Wes with black ink still imbedded under his fingernails. Mayor Palmor with a few more pounds around his middle but with the same running-for-office handshake.

Of course, she wasn't the same. Or Jocie. She could hear Jocie and Wes back in the pressroom, and she thought about going back to see them, but that rank ink odor might be bad for her baby. Tabitha wrapped her hands around her belly and rocked back and forth. She would be a good mother, a loving mother, a mother who wanted to be a mother. A mother who kept secrets that didn't need to be told. She wouldn't be anything like DeeDee.

Somebody tapped on the window, and Tabitha almost fell out of her chair. A man had his nose pressed against the glass peering in. When Tabitha jumped, he opened his mouth to show no teeth and laughed without making any sound. Lines traced ridges on the weathered skin of his face through the stubble of gray whiskers, but his brown eyes were surprisingly bright. His green shirt flopped loosely around his shoulders. He stepped back from the window and brought the guitar on his back around to strum the strings a couple of times. Then he pointed at the door, almost as if he were a kid asking her to come out to play.

He was older and grayer, but just like everything else about Hollyhill, the same. A name floated up out of her memory. Sallie.

When she was a little girl, she'd been afraid of him and curious at the same time. She'd edged up close to her father's leg whenever he stopped to listen to Sallie playing his guitar on the street. When they went on up the street, she'd ask her father questions. "Where's his teeth, Daddy? Why are there quarters in his hat? Is his name really Sallie? Isn't that a funny name for a man? What is that stinky smell?"

When she got older, she always crossed to the other side of the street when she spotted Sallie playing his guitar with his hat beside him for donations. He always sang louder when he saw her, and any quarters she had in her pocket got heavier. But she never crossed the street to drop any money into his hat.

She felt in her pocket now, but she hadn't brought any money. Not even a quarter. But he was still grinning at her and pointing at the door, so she got up and opened it. He didn't wait for her to come outside. He came inside and without the first hello or how are you went right to singing. "Tabitha Jane, Tabitha same. Tabitha Lee, Tabitha free. Tabitha Rose, Tabitha nose." And then he reached toward her nose with a pinch. She moved her head back quickly. He just laughed again and started in on "The Yellow Rose of Texas," one of his favorites from years before. His voice wavered a bit, but it just made the ballad sound truer.

"I don't have any money, Sallie," she said when he paused between verses. It only seemed fair to warn him that he was singing for nothing.

He just grinned bigger and kept singing. Jocie came out of the pressroom to save her. "I thought I heard old Sallie out here. Are you singing for your paper?" She handed him one of last week's *Banner*s. "We haven't got the new one out yet. We're late because of the parade. Come back in the morning, and we'll have this week's issue ready."

Sallie took the old paper. "Old news is still good news," he sang.

Jocie looked over at Tabitha. "Sallie wants to be in the know when he's singing out the news on the streets of Hollyhill." Jocie looked back at the old man. "Sallie knows everybody's secrets, don't you, Sallie?"

The old man strummed his guitar and hummed a couple of minutes before singing, "Sallie knows, but Sallie don't tell. Not in Hollyhill."

"Oh, the songs Sallie could sing if Sallie did," Jocie sang.

Tabitha kept smiling, but she wished she was on the other side of the street. The old man was staring at her, still grinning that stupid toothless grin, but it was as if he were pulling things out of her mind without her permission. And the smell was getting stronger. Just like she remembered. She put her hand over her nose.

He laughed again as he tucked the paper up under his arm, slung his guitar around behind him, and went out the door singing, "Rock-a-bye, baby."

Her baby did a flip inside her, and Tabitha felt faint. "How did he know that?"

"He probably just saw a baby down the street and had the song in his head. You never know what old Sallie will sing next. But it was kind of weird, wasn't it? Me talking about him knowing secrets and then him singing that."

"Does he really know secrets? I remember him, but I don't remember him telling fortunes or anything."

"He doesn't. I just tease him about knowing secrets because he stands out there on the street watching people and eavesdropping when he gets a chance and then sometimes makes up songs about what he hears."

"Is he going to make up a song about me?" Tabitha turned even paler under her tan.

"Not one anybody could put a face to. He'll probably just sing the Yellow Rose of Texas is having a baby, or maybe just sing

Rock-a-Bye, Baby, California T." Jocie frowned at Tabitha. "You look funny. Maybe you'd better sit down."

"I'm fine," Tabitha said, but she let Jocie guide her to the chair. "Aunt Love says expecting will make you feel light-headed sometimes."

Jocie frowned again. "How would she know?"

"I don't know. Maybe she read a book about it or something."

"I guess. But anyway, you don't have to worry about Sallie. He's harmless. Really. He wouldn't hurt a flea. I followed him around and wrote a story about him last year. Dad wouldn't print it, said it might upset some of his subscribers putting Sallie on the front page. But he did put his picture in the middle along with the lyrics of one of his songs I wrote down. It was good."

"What was it about?"

"I don't remember. Something about the rain washing all his blues away or Hollyhill away or something away. It's probably still around here if you wanted to dig through the back issues to find it."

"I'm not that interested."

"Don't they have characters like Sallie out in California?"

"Sure, worse than him, but you don't know them out there. You just walk past them like they're nothing more than another trash can."

"That sounds kind of mean. I thought you said everybody was all into love out there."

"Some of the people I hung out with talked a lot about it, but it's easy to say love. It's harder to do love."

"Oh, it's not all that hard to love Sallie the way the Bible says we're supposed to love one another. Now, giving him a hug—that would be harder. Lots harder." Jocie picked up another paper and waved it through the air toward the screen door. "When Zella's here, she has her air freshener out and ready before poor old Sallie can get through the door."

After Jocie disappeared back into the pressroom, Tabitha scooted her chair back away from the window. She didn't want anybody else peeking in at her. She wanted to hide out in the shadows as long as possible.

24

After the parade Leigh offered to drive Aunt Love and Tabitha home so David could get started on the headline piece with quotes from the speeches and an overview of the day. Zella went home to eat supper and feed her cat but promised to be back in time to help fold after the run. Wes and Jocie worked without talking to get the stories and pictures laid out and ready. Wes rushed the film through the developer, and they picked three photos for the front page and four more for the back. Of course, the First Baptist float had to be on the top of page one. David had promised.

Jocie argued for Heather Byrd's border collie, but it was pushed off till another issue. Marvin Sims on his Appaloosa made the bottom of the front page. David told her he might enter that one in the annual newspaper awards competition come September. By the time they quit picking, about a third of the families in Hollyhill were represented in one picture or another, which couldn't hurt circulation.

They were just beginning the run of the front page when there was a timid knock on the pressroom door and Leigh came in with a tray of chicken salad sandwiches on wheat, a bag of potato chips, and a plate of brownies. "Thought maybe you would be hungry," she said as she looked around for an empty spot to set the tray.

"Food is always welcome," Wes said as he pushed some stacks

out of the way and cleared a corner on one of the tables. "Right, boss?"

"Always," David said with a smile directly at Leigh. Pink touched her cheeks, but they didn't flame. In fact, David felt heat in his own cheeks when she met his glance with a shy smile. But maybe that was just from being out in the sun all afternoon listening to the mayor and the judge making speeches. Still, he was glad to see Leigh there, glad to feel the way she seemed to belong, glad to hear Jocie laughing with her, surprised to feel that tingle inside his belly that had nothing at all to do with hunger. He rubbed his sweaty palms off on his pants before he reached for one of the sandwiches.

"You going to say grace, Daddy, or can we just dig in?" Jocie asked.

"We'll say grace. It's been a good day. We should thank the Lord for it and for this food." David raised his eyes toward the ceiling. "We do thank you, Lord, for the blessings of the day, for the parade and the safety of all those in it. Thank you for our freedom and for the men and women who fought in wars to keep that freedom. Be with our local officials as they lead our town. And thank you for this food and for the one who prepared it. Amen."

"And thank you that I didn't have to listen to the speeches. Amen," Jocie said before she stuck some potato chips inside her sandwich. "Um, yum. Aunt Love doesn't believe in wasting money on potato chips, but there's nothing like a sandwich with a little crunch."

"Any kind of sandwich sounds good to me," Wes said. "Thank you, Miss Leigh. The boss here never thinks about food, so we'd have been out of luck with growling stomachs without you showing up."

"Don't call me Miss, Wes. You make me sound like an old Sunday school teacher or something."

"I'd miss my guess if you aren't a Sunday school teacher," Wes said between bites.

"Well, actually, I am, but not your Sunday school teacher."

"If you took brownies like this to Sunday school, I might give it a try," Wes said. "Try one, boss. It'll make your ears flap."

Leigh laughed, and it just felt natural to laugh along with her as he reached for one of the brownies. Jocie shot David a grin, but she kept chewing and didn't say anything.

David asked Leigh, "You want to stick around and watch us run the papers?"

Her eyes lit up. "That sounds like fun. Maybe I could even help a little if somebody would show me what to do."

She had pretty eyes. Light blue and clear like a summer sky with the sunshine exploding right through them. Funny, he'd never really noticed that before. He reminded himself of how young she was and realized he didn't know how young that was. He could ask Zella, but age was a touchy subject with Zella. Besides, even if he didn't know her age, it was obvious she was too young for him. He could just imagine the talk around town if he asked her out. And how in the heck would he go about asking her out? He was way too old to start in with sweaty palms and awkward invitations. So what if he had to wipe his palms off on his pants again. It was hot in the pressroom. It was always hot in the pressroom in July.

What did people do on a date anymore? He hadn't been on a date since he'd enlisted in the navy. The girls he'd met in this or that port before he'd married hardly counted as dates. Not the kind where you called up days in advance and took flowers or candy. He'd never even had a date with Adrienne. They'd met one day, run off to get married the next. Not the best way to pick a wife, but he'd been the one picked, not the one picking. Adrienne had thought he was her ticket out of Hollyhill, but he'd had to report back to the submarine and leave her in Hollyhill with Tabitha on the way. Still, she might have gotten him to leave Hollyhill after the war ended if he hadn't felt God's hand on his shoulder. That's when everything changed. Everything but Adrienne.

So really he'd never had a wife—a helpmate, a partner. He thought of Harry and Floradell Sanders, who worked together every day at their hardware store across the street, or Matt and Dorothy McDermott at Mt. Pleasant Church. Two become one. He'd said it dozens of time in marriage ceremonies. He and Adrienne had promised it, but it had never happened.

Since Adrienne had left, he'd gone it alone rather than risk failure again. One time was bad enough, but a lot of couples had been stampeded into marriage by the war. Letting it happen a second time would show a serious lack of judgment. And that's what asking Leigh for a date would be. A serious lack of judgment. A middle-aged man having delusions that he had anything to offer a young woman like Leigh. She needed someone who would give her babies, not grandbabies. Maybe he should tell her that. He knew about counseling people. He was a pastor, after all.

He'd tell her that he was divorced with two daughters and an aged aunt he was responsible for. Of course, she already knew that. He could tell her that a preacher was pulled in twenty directions at once and often had little energy to spare on his own family. Of course, he might not have a church much longer. He could tell her he was about to be a grandfather. That should give her pause. It gave him pause even while his soul was glad.

But maybe the best thing for him to do was nothing. Without encouragement, her infatuation with the idea of dating him would surely fade and she'd soon cast her net out for a better fish. He was suddenly hoping her net would be full of big holes.

She must have been reading his thoughts, because she brought over the plate with one last brownie on it to him. "If you don't eat it, I'll have to, and then there will go my diet," she said with a smile. He took the brownie, and her face glowed a little pinker. "Oh, and by the way, just in case Jocie didn't tell you and you were wondering, I'm thirty-two. Ages older than Tabitha, if that matters to you. It doesn't to me."

She hesitated a moment. He thought he should say something, but he wasn't sure what. Something like "You're older than you look" or "That's still years younger than me" or "You're scaring the heck out of me." His palms were sweaty again, and now sweat was running down his ribs inside his shirt. Finally he said, "I'm forty-four, almost forty-five." He felt like a preteen comparing ages. Thank goodness Wes was running the papers and he and Jocie couldn't hear anything but the press.

"Yeah, I know. Look, if you'd rather I just disappeared, say so. But I'm not asking for a proposal or anything. Oh gosh, I shouldn't have said that." Leigh's face got redder, but she didn't drop the tray and run for the door. "I just thought it might be fun to get together sometime. We don't have to do anything major. It was fun this afternoon, and when listening to the mayor can be fun, it has to be something besides the speeches." She blew air out of her mouth, and the red on her cheeks faded. "Anyway, I take a walk every morning in the park before I go to work. Maybe sometime you'd like to come down and give me moral support, although heaven knows you don't need to lose any weight."

"But I do go walking a lot in the mornings. That's when I pray."

"We can pray together." Leigh ducked her eyes at her boldness. "I mean, that is if you want to. I guess you might want to keep your prayers just between you and God."

He took pity on her in her embarrassment and his own. He rubbed his hands off on his printing apron and smiled. "Two prayers are surely better than one. I'd like to come walk with you some morning."

"Really? You're not just saying that because I put you on the spot?"

"Really. How about tomorrow?" He couldn't believe he'd actually set a date, but he was glad he had. Her face lit up like a flower opening to the sun. Her eyes were really extraordinary. She'd probably been told a thousand times how pretty she'd be if only she'd lose weight. Actually, the extra pounds didn't take a thing away from how pretty she was. David wanted to tell her that, but he'd already said too much. Way too much. He felt as if he'd stepped into a rain-swollen river and lost his footing and was being swept downstream with no way to stop himself. He should grab for a limb of sanity, but he kept letting the water carry him away. The really scary part was that he was beginning to enjoy the ride.

David had to wipe his hands off on his pants again as he picked up the papers off the press and carried them to the big flat table to put the sheets together in the proper order. Leigh watched him a minute and then joined in pulling the papers together. Zella came in a few minutes later and was so excited to see Leigh there shoulder to shoulder with David that she got two black smudges on her nose right away. Jocie laughed so hard she had to sit down for a while, and Wes just kept grinning at David as he pulled the papers off the press.

25

The next morning her father had already left for the paper before Jocie got up. He'd told Aunt Love he was going to get breakfast at the Grill and catch up on what was going on in town.

"I'll bet he's meeting Leigh for breakfast," Jocie said as she tried to stir the lumps out of her oatmeal. Oatmeal for breakfast was almost as bad as cabbage, but at least oatmeal meant she got to have toast, and Miss Pansy at church had given them a couple of jars of strawberry preserves Sunday. That made up for two or three heads of cabbage and a bucket of zucchini.

Aunt Love looked thoughtful. "He did seem a bit undone this morning. I thought he was worried about Tabitha."

"You mean because she's having a baby?"

"So she told you. Good."

Jocie spread some more strawberry preserves on her toast and studied Aunt Love, who was stirring her oatmeal as if she didn't like it any better than Jocie. Tabitha hadn't gotten up yet. "You think people will talk?"

"Of course people will talk. People always talk. Especially about preachers and their families. As if they weren't human like everybody else."

"I thought you might be upset. I mean, you're supposed to get married and then have babies, right?"

"That's the best way." Aunt Love put down her spoon and stared

202

at her oatmeal as if she'd lost her appetite. "But things don't always happen in the best way, and once some things have happened, we can't go back and change them to the best way." She looked up at Jocie. "But it's my belief that every child the Lord sends is a gift, and even when things aren't as they should be, God can make a way out of no way."

"Is that in the Bible?"

"Many times in many stories. Remember how the angel Gabriel told Mary, 'With God nothing shall be impossible'?"

"Yeah, and what was that Dad preached about one time where Jesus said a camel could go through the needle's eye?" Jocie frowned. "I just can't imagine that no matter how I try to put my mind around it. I can barely get a piece of thread through a needle's eye."

"'With God all things are possible.' Matthew 19:26. But that's the key, child. Only with God. Only with God. We have to put our trust in him."

"Do you think the Mt. Pleasant folks will kick Dad out when they find out?'

"Who can say." Aunt Love got up and scraped her oats into Jezebel's bowl. Jocie wondered if she could get away with giving hers to Zeb. Probably not after the four spoonfuls of sugar Aunt Love had watched her stir in. "But if they do, it will be their loss." Aunt Love straightened up and looked out the window. Suddenly she smiled. "So the girl got him to notice her. What did you say her name was again?"

"Leigh. Leigh Jacobson."

"I can't remember any Jacobsons."

"She's from Grundy, but she's the judge's niece or cousin or something." Jocie shoveled in a few bites of oats just to get it over with.

"Oh, I'll bet she's Polly Wilson's granddaughter. I used to go to church with Polly. A fine woman. She died a year or so back. Cancer, as I recall. Everybody dies from cancer."

Jocie choked down another bite of oatmeal and wondered if Aunt Love would notice if she added more sugar. It could be Aunt Love had already forgotten the first four spoonfuls, but you never knew with Aunt Love. Some things she forgot right off and others she remembered. Like what Leigh's grandmother died from. Old people were always trying to figure out what people died from or how many sisters and brothers they had and what they died from. That made up half the conversations Jocie had to sit through on Sunday afternoons while her father was out visiting.

"So this girl—what did you say her name was again?"

"Leigh. Leigh Jacobson. You want me to write it down for you?"

"That might help. I used to not have a bit of trouble remembering names. I clerked at Masterson's Market for years and could call everybody who came in by name, but lately I just can't seem to get hold of names. I don't know what's the matter with me. I forget everything."

"You remembered going to church with Polly Wilson," Jocie said as she took her bowl to the sink and quickly dumped the rest of her oats into Zeb's pan before she found some paper to write down Leigh's name.

"Oh yes, I can recall things that happened years ago. It's what happened last week that wanders away from me. I can't even remember what your father preached on last Sunday morning."

Jocie paused in her writing to think. "Me either."

"You probably weren't paying proper attention."

"I listened. I always listen to Dad preach. Seems like it was from Corinthians, or maybe that was the week before. This week was something about freedom. You know, because of the Fourth. You can ask Dad. He'll remember." Jocie finished printing out Leigh's name and handed it to Aunt Love before she picked up Zeb's food.

"Leigh Jacobson." Aunt Love stared at the paper. "This could be an answer to prayer."

"What?" Jocie stopped on the way out to feed Zeb and looked back at Aunt Love. "Have you been doing a girlfriend prayer for Dad?"

Aunt Love actually smiled. "I pray for your father every day. I pray the Lord will bless and guide him. If the Lord has decided to bless him with a good woman, then who am I to second-guess the Lord? Besides, your father has been alone too long."

"He's not alone. He's got us."

"But he needs a companion, a helpmate. All men do."

"What about women? I know lots of women who aren't married. Zella. You. Didn't you ever pray for a husband for yourself?" Too late Jocie remembered Tabitha telling her about Aunt Love's fiancé getting killed in the war, but there was no way to take back the words.

Aunt Love sat down at the table again and wrapped both her hands around her teacup. She didn't take a drink. She just stared down the reddish-brown liquid. "I did, and the Lord answered my prayer. But the Lord giveth and the Lord taketh away."

"I'm sorry. Tabitha told me the man you were going to marry got killed in the First World War."

"He did, but I didn't know that for years. I just knew he never came back for me."

"How did you find out?"

"When my father passed on, I found a letter in his Bible from one of Gil's army friends. They had made a pact to write to the other's sweetheart if anything happened to either of them in the war. His name was Albert Wiseman. He was from Missouri. He said Gil was killed in the Meuse-Argonne battle. I didn't even know where that was, but I went to the library and found out it was in France."

"Why didn't your father give you the letter when it came?"

"He didn't let me read any of Gil's letters. I found one in the mail one time that I suppose he'd overlooked, and he yanked it away from me and threw it in the stove. I tried to snatch it out, but the flames got it first." Aunt Love rubbed a scar on her arm. "Father didn't approve of Gilbert."

"That was an awful thing to do."

"Yes." Aunt Love took a sip of her tea. "Yes, it was."

Jocie wasn't sure what to do. She couldn't hug Aunt Love. She never hugged Aunt Love. It might give her a real heart attack if she did. So she just put her hand on her shoulder and said, "I'm sorry."

Aunt Love covered Jocie's hand with her own. Her skin felt dry and scratchy like oak leaves in the fall. "You should give thanks every day for the blessing of a kind and good father. You and Tabitha both."

"I do," Jocie said.

Aunt Love pushed Jocie's hand away and picked up her teacup. "Now get on with your chores."

As Jocie went out the door, she looked back at Aunt Love. Imagining her young and in love was almost as impossible as imagining that camel through the eye of a needle. But just because Jocie couldn't imagine it didn't mean it wasn't true. Or that the memory of it didn't still make Aunt Love sad. Jocie wanted to say something to make her feel better, but she didn't know what. She couldn't very well say maybe Aunt Love would forget about it the way she forgot other things and then she wouldn't have to be sad. She hadn't forgotten it in fifty years. That memory was probably stuck in there with the Bible verses. A Bible verse might help, but all Jocie could think of was one of the Beatitudes. She decided to try it. "Blessed are they that mourn: for they shall be comforted."

Aunt Love looked around at her. "'To every thing there is a season. A time to mourn, and a time to dance.' It's your time to dance, Jocelyn."

"I can't dance," Jocie said.

"You dance every day to the tune of life."

Zeb, impatient for his food, jumped up on the screen door, and Jocie hurried on out the door before he pushed the screen loose from the frame. She didn't know what Aunt Love was trying to tell her anyway with that Bible verse. She'd always figured Aunt Love was one of those people who didn't exactly approve of dancing.

Zeb gulped down the food, licking up every bit of the oats with relish. As usual, when he was sure every speck was gone, he sat up and put his paws together as if saying doggy grace. Jocie had quit trying to get him to do it differently. She figured that where he'd come from he'd had to eat first and thank the Lord second to be sure nothing grabbed his food.

Jocie stuck her head back through the screen door. Aunt Love was still holding her teacup at the table. "I'm going for a walk. I'll wash the dishes and sweep the floors when I get back, okay?"

"All right, but don't forget we have to hull those lima beans that Janie Brown gave your father."

Jocie groaned. "Why are all vegetables green?"

"Beets and carrots aren't green."

Jocie got her bike out. She'd told Aunt Love she was going on a walk, but Aunt Love wouldn't remember what she'd said ten minutes from now anyway, so it wouldn't matter. She hoped Aunt Love would forget to save the lima beans and have them already in the pan cooking by the time Jocie got home. Jocie didn't mind hulling peas. Pea hulls popped right open and the fat peas shelled out easy as pie, but a person could make airplane glue out of whatever was on the inside of some lima bean hulls.

She hadn't been to her grandfather's old woods since the day she'd found Zeb. But today the sun was shining and the wind was blowing in her face. A perfect day to go exploring. Zeb was her dog now. He wouldn't disappear on her. Not even if the Jupiter spaceship did come back for him.

She stashed her bike behind some bushes and followed Zeb into the shade of the trees. The air was immediately cooler, and the noise of cars passing on the road faded away. Shadows blended together, and she imagined animal eyes watching her and Zeb as they followed a faint path. Zeb scooted back and forth in front of her sniffing rocks and tree trunks. A few times he stopped, stared intently into the shadows, and barked his thunder barks.

"We won't see so much as a squirrel with you making all that racket," Jocie told him, but she didn't mind. It was good having company in the woods. She found a blackberry bush and shared a few ripe berries with Zeb. A rabbit must have peeked out of the brush and made a face at Zeb, because the dog suddenly took off through the woods. Jocie yelled at him to come back, but he didn't even slow down.

She pushed through the bushes trying to keep Zeb in sight, but he outran her in minutes. She paused to catch her breath and look for a path, but there was nothing but more bushes and trees. Worse, she couldn't hear Zeb now. She whistled and called, "Zeb, here boy." Above her a crow complained as if she'd interrupted his morning nap. The bird flapped off through the trees when Jocie whistled again.

Then it was quiet. Spooky quiet. Nothing looked familiar. "Don't be stupid," she told herself. "All trees look sort of alike." She looked for moss, which they said grew on the north side of trees, but the problem was she didn't know whether she needed to go north or south or east or west to get back to her bike. She never paid any attention to directions. Well, she knew you went north to Grundy and south to West Liberty, but that didn't do her much good out here in the woods. Besides, she couldn't go home without Zeb.

So she wasn't lost. Zeb was the one who was lost. She began walking south, if the moss on the trees was right. She just kept pushing under tree limbs and circling briar thickets. Every few steps she whistled till her lips were dry. At last she heard barks in the distance, and she plunged through the trees toward the sound.

She stumbled out on an old tractor road. She'd never found it before, and she wondered if she was even still on her grandfather's old farm. She started following the old road, but Zeb barked again off to the left. She ducked under some cedar trees and followed the sound. The cedars were thick, and Jocie had to practically crawl through them. Under her feet, the ground was cushy with fallen cedar needles, so she made hardly any noise as she hurried toward Zeb. The dog's barks were getting louder. He must have treed something. Jocie hoped for a cat or maybe a possum, nothing too big.

The cedars began to thin out a little, and she could stand up and weave her way through them. She came out into a small clearing. Zeb's barks were louder than ever, but she still couldn't spot him. At the edge of the clearing, the log part of an old barn still stood with bent pieces of rusted tin roofing and weathered planks scattered around it. Past the barn, purple phlox was blooming around what was left of a rock chimney. A good-sized maple grew up in the middle of where a house must have once stood, and poison ivy vines climbed on the chimney rocks. A rusted old bucket with no bottom lay on its side in the grass near an old cistern.

Jocie peered down through the rusting top of the cistern held down by a huge rock and saw the glint of water. Beyond the cistern, the spiky stems of a yucca plant stuck up out of a circle of rocks. More rocks, mostly geodes, were scattered willy-nilly through the grass. It looked like Aunt Love's rock garden gone wild. Jocie picked up a sparkling splinter of a geode and put it in her pocket to take to Aunt Love for her rock garden.

Jocie moved on down an incline toward a creek. Zeb was still barking, but he was nowhere in sight. She whistled again, and Zeb poked his head out from behind some rocks down by the creek.

Jocie picked up another couple of rocks just in case Zeb had treed something wild and vicious.

A small cave was tucked up behind some large rocks, and whatever Zeb had treed there must have long since found another way out, because when Jocie peeked inside she couldn't see the first glint of animal eyes or anything else. Even Zeb, now that she was there, lost interest and stopped barking.

"No spaceships, eh?" Jocie sat down on the biggest rock and gazed back toward where the house had once sat in the clearing. "Wonder if whoever lived here ever went in this cave."

Zeb seemed to take that as permission and scooted inside. Jocie got down on all fours and crawled part of the way through the entrance after him. Light sifted in around her and through a chink in the top of the rocks. The cave was bigger than Jocie had expected. Plenty of room for snakes and spiders. It didn't matter that Zeb was nosing around in every corner. The snakes might be on the rocks above her head. Cold chills tiptoed across the back of her neck.

She jerked her head out of the hole, but then curiosity got the better of her. She gingerly stuck her head back in the hole and waited till her eyes adjusted to the dim light. Zeb looked around at her before he went back to digging around a small mound of rocks at the back of the cave. He pulled out something and carried it toward Jocie. Jocie pulled her head out of the cave opening to let Zeb carry it out into the sunlight.

When Zeb dropped it at her feet, Jocie shrieked. It was a skull. Jocie put her hand over her mouth and leaned over for a closer look. A very small human skull.

26

ocie jumped back. She wanted to run up the bank and through the woods to the road where her bike was hidden. But she stood stock-still, closed her eyes, and whispered a prayer. "Help me, Lord. I don't know what I should do." She kept her eyes closed an extra minute in case the Lord wanted to plant an answer in her head, but nothing happened. She still didn't know what to do.

Of course, she did know some things. She knew she shouldn't let Zeb have the skull, and really, he didn't appear to want it now that he had presented it to her. He was sitting back, his head cocked to the side, waiting for her to do something. A chill tickled her spine as she imagined a baby's tiny ghost beside Zeb also watching and waiting.

She couldn't just leave the skull there on the ground, and she didn't think she should carry it home with her. She looked over at Zeb. "I don't guess you'd like to put this back where you found it." Zeb just kept panting.

"That's what I thought. Then I guess I'll have to do it, snakes or no snakes." Jocie picked up the skull. It was so small it fit in her palm. "Poor little baby. Wonder what happened to you. Why are you buried down here all alone in this cave? At least, I guess you're alone." Suddenly more ghosts popped up around her.

Jocie carried the skull very carefully toward the hole into the cave. She placed it inside the cave as far as she could reach and then crawled in after it. Zeb sniffed her feet as she pulled them into the cave and would have followed her in, but she made him stay out. He'd done more than enough digging for one day.

Something rustled in the cave behind her. Jocie froze on all fours, imagining snakes slithering toward her. She slowly turned her head and studied every inch of ground around her, but nothing was there. At least nothing she could see. She picked up the tiny skull and got a whole new crop of shivers up and down her spine as she crept toward the mound of rocks at the back of the cave.

"I'm sorry Zeb dug up your grave." Jocie's voice echoed in the cave. "He's just a dog, or at least I think he is. Anyway, we didn't mean any harm." Jocie laid the skull down and began gingerly replacing the rocks Zeb had disturbed as she recited the Lord's Prayer. She talked fast, but she didn't skip any words before she said amen and scrambled back out of the cave.

Zeb licked her face when she stuck it out into the sunshine. She pulled herself out of the cave and gave Zeb a hug. "Now what do we do?" she asked the dog as he licked her face again. "Tell somebody, I guess. You wouldn't happen to know the way home, would you?"

Zeb barked, made a circle around her, then stopped and waited. "I take it that means you're as lost as I am. You could at least look worried." Jocie looked up at the sun. It had to be noon already. She licked her lips and looked longingly at the creek, but her father said drinking out of a creek could give you the pukes. She remembered the glint of water in the old cistern, but snakes came to mind again. Zeb waded into the creek and lay down in the water while he lapped up a drink.

"Guess there's no need in both of us being thirsty," Jocie said. "Or are you trying to tell me we should follow the creek? Up or down creek?"

Zeb climbed out of the creek and shook, showering Jocie, before he trotted off downstream.

"As good a direction as any." Jocie followed him. They'd hardly gone fifteen steps before the trees swallowed them up again as they left the clearing behind. It was easy walking on the flat rocks in the shallow creek. Zeb jumped out of the creek to chase a grasshopper but came back when Jocie whistled.

When the creek ran under an old wire fence, Jocie deserted the creek to follow the fence line. The trees began to thin out, and they came out in a pasture full of cows who stopped eating long enough to give them the eye. Jocie climbed the fence and headed across the field. Nobody could be lost in a pasture field. They topped a rise on the other side of the cows and saw the road. A half hour later she was back where she'd left her bike. She looked back at the woods and wondered if she could find the cave again.

The midday sun was hot, and Jocie's sweat burned the scratches she'd gotten chasing after Zeb as she pedaled toward home. She thought about just going straight to the newspaper office to tell her father about the skull, but she was too thirsty. And Aunt Love might have remembered that she should have been home hours ago.

Aunt Love looked up from the pan of lima beans in her lap when Jocie burst through the kitchen door. "For mercy's sake, child, you look like you've been crawling through a briar patch."

Jocie wiped the sweat off her face with her shirt tail and went straight for the water pitcher in the refrigerator. She gulped down a glassful before she said, "I have to call Dad at the paper."

"He's not there," Aunt Love said. "He's taken Tabitha to Grundy. No telling when they'll be back."

"Grundy?" Jocie sank down in one of the kitchen chairs. Jezebel sniffed Jocie's feet and hissed.

"He got her in to see a doctor over there." Aunt Love split

open one of the lima bean hulls with a paring knife and pushed the beans out into the pan. "What's so important anyway? Have you hurt yourself somehow?" Aunt Love looked half worried, half irritated. "For heaven's sake, you need to learn to be careful. Your arm's bleeding."

"I'm not hurt, Aunt Love." Jocie rubbed at the dried blood on her arm. "But I found something."

"Ticks and chiggers, from the looks of you." Aunt Love picked up another lima bean and slit the hull. "You need to check through your head for the ticks. Better to find them before they dig in."

Jocie ran her fingers through her hair absentmindedly. She wasn't worried about ticks. She poured herself another glass of water. She couldn't wait till her father got back from Grundy. She had to tell somebody. Aunt Love might know what she should do.

"I was over in Grandfather's woods where I walk sometimes, and Zeb took off. I got worried he'd get lost or something."

"He'd have found his way home before supper time."

"Well, yeah, maybe, but that's where I found him, or he found me. Anyway, I didn't want to lose him, you know, so I went after him."

"You can hull while you talk." Aunt Love pushed a handful of lima beans toward Jocie on the table. "So your mongrel took off and you followed him. Then you got lost, I suppose."

"I don't know that I was actually lost lost, but I didn't know exactly where I was." Jocie broke open a lima bean hull. "Anyway, I came across this clearing with an old log barn and a stone chimney where a house used to be." Jocie pulled the rock out of her pocket and laid it on the table by Aunt Love. "There was even a rock garden like yours."

Aunt Love rested her hands in the pan of shelled lima beans in her lap and looked at the rock. "So you found a rock garden.

Were there rosebushes? There used to be rosebushes. Red and pink and yellow and white."

"You know the place?"

"I do."

"Then maybe you can tell me about the baby."

"Baby?" Aunt Love's voice sounded funny. "You found a baby?"

"Sort of. Zeb did. A baby's grave."

Aunt Love's face went white, and she grabbed her chest. Jezebel yowled and jumped up on Aunt Love's lap. The lima bean pan crashed to the floor, and beans bounced all over the kitchen.

"Look upon mine affliction and my pain; and forgive all my sins," Aunt Love whispered.

27

Aunt Love was always clutching her chest and quoting Scripture, but Jocie had never seen her turn so white. Jocie grabbed the wet dishrag out of the sink and dabbed Aunt Love's forehead with it. "Are you okay, Aunt Love?" Jezebel snarled and took a swipe at Jocie's arm, but Jocie ignored the cat. "Should I call the ambulance?"

"No. No ambulance." Aunt Love took hold of Jocie's wrist with more strength than Jocie thought possible. "Take me there."

"Where? To the hospital? But Dad has the car."

"No." Aunt Love's hand tightened on Jocie's wrist. "To the place where you found the ba—where your dog found the grave."

Jocie stared at Aunt Love. "It's way off in the woods, Aunt Love. You could never walk that far even if I could find it again, which I'm not sure I could."

"I can find it. Come on." Aunt Love pushed Jocie's hand aside and stood up, dumping Jezebel on the floor with the lima beans. Aunt Love went straight toward the door, not even noticing the beans she was smashing underfoot.

Jocie scooted along beside her. "It's miles, Aunt Love. You'd never make it."

Aunt Love stared out the back door as if trying to see across the distance to the place Jocie had told her about. Finally she leaned her forehead against the doorjamb. "You're right. It is too far."

Jocie breathed a sigh of relief. She watched Aunt Love warily, but color was back in her face and she didn't seem about to faint or anything. After a moment Jocie fished the bean pan out from under the table and began picking up the lima beans. Jezebel peeked out at Aunt Love from under a chair with wide, round eyes.

Aunt Love turned from the door and said, "Forget about those beans and go call Wesley."

Jocie stood up. "What do you want me to tell him? To bring Dr. Markum out?"

"I'm not in need of a doctor, child. Just do as I say and call Wesley at the paper. Tell him to come straightaway on that machine of his."

By the time Wes roared up to the house a half hour later, Jocie had finished picking up the lima beans, Jezebel was sulking under Aunt Love's bed, and Aunt Love had changed into her gardening shoes and was waiting in the rocking chair on the front porch. Before Wes got there, Jocie had ventured a couple of questions, but Aunt Love had shook her head. "Later, child. I can't talk right now."

So they had waited in silence. And Jocie had wished Aunt Love would quote Bible verses at her or something. Anything would have been better than the silence that was louder than the birds singing or the sound of Mr. Crutcher baling hay two fields over.

Wes drove the motorcycle right up to the porch. Aunt Love was down the steps before he stopped. "What's going on, girls?" he asked, balancing the bike with one foot on the ground.

Aunt Love didn't give Jocie time to say anything. "Can you get down a tractor road in the field on that contraption?"

Wes frowned a little. "I expect so, if it's not too rough. Why?"

"Then I'm taking you up on that offer of a ride. Help me climb on and let's go. The child can follow on her bicycle." Aunt Love lifted her skirts and eyed the motorcycle.

Wes looked too surprised to speak, so Jocie said, "Aunt Love, you can't ride on a motorcycle."

"I can and I will. Now are the two of you going to help me or do I have to climb on the thing by myself?"

Wes kicked down the motorcycle's stand, got off, and took Aunt Love's arm. "Is somebody going to tell me where we're going?"

"Jocelyn found a baby's grave. I want to go there." Aunt Love stared straight at Wes. "There's more to the story, but that's for later. Are you going to help me on this monster or not?"

Wes stared back at Aunt Love. "I've never seen you like this, Lovella."

"No, you haven't. But I'm in need of your help, Wesley. It's a long walk, and I think Jocelyn is right that I might not make it, but if you refuse to help me, I will walk."

Wes looked at Jocie, who shrugged and threw her hands up. "Don't ask me. I told her I found the grave. She went bonkers and here we are."

Wes eyed Aunt Love's dress. "You'll have to bundle up your skirt."

Aunt Love hiked her skirt up higher. Wes steadied the motorcycle, and Aunt Love used Jocie's shoulder for balance while she eased her leg over the passenger's seat. She tucked her skirt under her thighs and didn't seem a bit concerned about her white knees shining in the sun.

"You'll have to hang on to my waist," Wes said as he got on in front of her. Aunt Love grabbed hold of him as if it were the most natural thing in the world. She said, "I'll poke you when it's time to turn."

Jocie pedaled hard to keep up, but they kept disappearing around curves. Zeb stayed in front of her too, running ahead of her bike as if to keep them in sight and then running back to make sure Jocie was still following. They waited for her at the turnoff into the field. The sagging wooden gate had a couple of broken planks and clung to the post by the top hinge. Jocie pushed the gate open just enough for Wes to get through and then let the gate fall back against the post. The tractor ruts were so rough that she ditched her bike and walked. Ahead of her Wes carefully nosed out the smoothest path, but it was still bumpy. Aunt Love's dark purple skirt jerked loose from under her leg and snagged on a branch.

Love sneaked a hand loose from Wesley's waist and stuffed her skirt back under her. She didn't care about the torn material or her knees shining in the wind or the bumps jostling her insides loose. She hadn't been down this road since she'd moved to town after her father had finally passed on, but the bone-rattling bumps were familiar. Her father had never done anything to smooth the road, just drove their old car around the rocks where he could. Her father had never worried about smoothing out anything for anybody.

Love turned her mind away from her father. She didn't let herself think about him, hadn't for years, even before he died. She'd taken care of him. She'd cooked his meals, fed him with a spoon, and kept him clean in his later years, but she hadn't thought about him. He'd been a task, his care a chore that had to be done. Everyone thought she was a devoted daughter. They didn't know about the can of rat poison in the top of the cabinet over the stove or the times she'd actually held the open can in her hand while she scrambled her father's eggs in the morning. She'd never shaken the first drop out of the can, but she'd wanted to. And that was a sin. The Lord had said as much in the Sermon on the Mount. If the desire was in the heart, the sin was already committed.

She'd asked the Lord for forgiveness, but the Bible also said the Lord would forgive if you forgave, and she couldn't forgive her father. After her mother died, she should have left. Should have laced up her shoes and walked away with the clothes on her back. But she'd thought Gil might still come back. She'd known in her heart he wasn't coming when the first long year after the war had passed with no word, but she couldn't desert her hope that he might. She hadn't seen the letter that said he was dead. If she had, perhaps her life would have been different. But she'd stayed there and waited for what would, what could, never happen.

Gil had been her father's hired hand. He'd hired him on after her younger brother, Homer, joined the army. Poor Homer had died on the ship to France before he heard the first shot. Some kind of sickness. He'd been buried at sea. They had read the letter and known it was true, but at the same time, without the proof of a body to mourn, it was like the words weren't talking about Homer. Not their Homer. They had half expected to see him coming up the road carrying his pack for months after they got the news. A person shouldn't just disappear.

That's the way she'd felt about Gil. One day he was there, catching her away from the house and begging her to run away with him. And she had. Her mistake was coming back. It hadn't seemed such a mistake at first. Just a bit of a wait till the war was over.

The road got some smoother as they came out into the clearing and saw what was left of the barn up ahead. It looked funny with no house behind the barn, but Mae's husband hadn't wanted to sell the farm or rent the house. So he'd let Junior Perkins salvage what he could out of it. Junior had used some of the lumber to build a garage out behind his house. The rest he'd sold. A piece here. A piece there. The living room mantle was in a house over in Grundy, and the doors were in Davis Norville's house on Bush Avenue uptown. Wilbur Smith had used the tin off the roof to build a chicken house. They'd come in the store and told her where each piece went while she poked the keys on the cash register to total up their groceries. They had thought she would care.

The chimney looked lonely sticking up from where the house had been. Nobody had wanted to haul out the rocks. Rocks weren't that scarce in Holly County. Wesley stopped the motorcycle next to the forsaken steps and held it steady while Jocelyn helped her climb off. The child kept sneaking looks at her as if expecting to see the top of her head flipped off and her brains scattered on the wind. Love patted Jocelyn's cheek after she climbed off the monster machine. Her whole backside felt numb, but the thing had gotten them there.

"Where is it?" Love asked.

"Down by the creek. There's a cave down there," Jocelyn said.

Wesley took her arm. "So this is the home place. I guess as how it's sad seeing it gone and not like you remember."

"Not a bit sad. I tried to burn the thing down when I left, but Mae's John happened by before the fire got going and put it out. Scorched the living room wall, they told me. Said they figured I'd spilled a coal out of the fire onto some papers, and I said that's how it might have happened. It wasn't how it happened, but it might have been. I should've dropped that coal on the papers closer to the drapes."

Jocelyn's eyes got big. "Why ever would you want to burn down your own house, Aunt Love?"

"I guess I shouldn't have told you about that, but I never felt the least bit guilty about it. I was ready to put an end to this part of my life, child, and it just seemed burning was a good way to put a seal on it."

"I can relate to that," Wesley said. "I've done some bridge burning in my day as well."

Love looked at Wesley and nodded. She'd always known he was running away from something. That's why he came up with those crazy stories about Jupiter. So he'd never have to tell the truth. Just the way she'd never told the truth after she'd run away from this place. She hadn't exactly lied or made up stories, but she'd never told the truth. Never. Maybe because she'd never known the whole truth. Not till now.

She leaned on Wesley as they moved down past her rock garden toward the creek. Sometimes she thought that rock garden was all that had kept her sane before her father died. There, still standing in the middle of the garden, was the birdbath she'd fashioned out of pebbles and shards of geodes and an old sack of mixing cement she'd come across in the barn after her father could no longer get out of the house, but her mother's rosebushes were gone. She remembered the times she'd stood in the garden and tried to think of nothing but the sweet scent of those roses. If she shut her eyes, she could still almost smell them. Almost.

This was where she had always imagined the grave to be. She'd always hoped there was a grave, but she'd never been able to find it. She'd never once thought of the cave, although Homer used to hide in it when he was a boy and wanted to get out of his chores. He was the baby, and oft as not she'd do his chores for him along with her own to keep him out of trouble with their father. He'd been the only person in the world outside of Gil and her mother who she'd ever felt loved her. Homer had a way of smiling that could bring sunshine through the dingiest window into the soul. It had been too hard to think of both Homer and Gil dying in the war. That's why she had stayed and waited so long for Gil to come back for her. She couldn't believe God would take both of them so close together. But of course, God never promised that troubles wouldn't come. That had taken her some years to understand and even more years to accept.

But the cave made sense. She should have thought of it. It had been January. The coldest on record until about ten years back. Some days the thermometer on the back porch had never made it past zero. Her father couldn't have dug a hole in the frozen ground.

The baby would have been forty-six last January. Love always remembered his birthday. It seemed funny to think about him older than David. She'd known the baby was a boy. Her mother had seen that much before her father had taken him away.

28

Wesley crawled through the hole Jocelyn pointed out. The dog tried to follow him, but the child grabbed him around the neck and pulled him back away from the opening into the cave.

After Wesley's feet disappeared into the darkness of the cave, Love thought she should pray or at least whisper some Bible verses, but nothing came to mind. Instead, echoing across the years was the cry of a newborn. She wanted to put her hands over her ears, but of course that wouldn't stop it. It never had.

"Are you okay, Aunt Love?" Jocelyn asked. "Maybe you should find someplace to sit down."

She did feel a bit faint as her heart pounded inside her chest, so she sank down on a boulder. The warmth of the rock surprised her. She'd barely noticed the bright sunshine. She'd been standing too deep in the shadows of the past.

She tried to hear Wesley moving inside the cave, but all she could hear was the dog panting beside her and a crow cawing in some trees out behind the barn. The child was still staring at her as if she expected her to keel over any second. That was one of the problems with getting old. Folks kept expecting you to die right in front of their eyes. There had been times when she'd wished it was that easy, that she could just close her eyes down here and open them up in heaven, but a person couldn't pick her time. "To every thing there is a season, and a time to every purpose under the heaven. A time to be born, and a time to die."

She didn't realize she'd spoken the Bible verse aloud until the child said, "That's in Ecclesiastes, isn't it? Where it starts out 'Vanity of vanities. All is vanity.' What does that mean, Aunt Love?"

It wasn't a time for a Bible lesson. Too much of her mind and heart was inside that hole of a cave with Wesley. But the child kept looking at her expecting an answer, so she said, "That our lives don't matter all that much in the whole of time. We're born. We die."

"But what about all the years in between?"

"That's when it's time to sow and reap, to weep and laugh, to dance, to mourn. 'But if a man live many years, and rejoice in them all; yet let him remember the days of darkness; for they shall be many.' Ecclesiastes 11:8." Love had committed most of Ecclesiastes to memory years ago.

"Why not remember the days of joy and try to forget the darkness ones?" Jocelyn asked.

"I don't know, child. Maybe because it's the dark days that bring us closer to the Lord." Love stared at the cave and wished she'd just told the child to ask her father. David could have explained it to her without losing the joy.

"Is that why you're so close to the Lord, Aunt Love? Because you've had a lot of dark days?" Jocelyn asked softly.

"Knowing the Scriptures and knowing the Lord aren't the same thing," Love said. "I know the Scriptures because I searched for answers there."

"About God?"

Love looked down. It still surprised her sometimes to see her mother's hands lying in her lap. Slimmer but still liver spotted just the way she remembered her mother's hands. Her mother's hands knitting a tiny pastel yellow sweater. "God and other things," she said after a moment.

"Did you find the answers you wanted?"

"Sometimes there are no answers."

The child frowned. "But Dad says you can always find the answer in the Bible."

Love herself had once wanted the answers to be clear and simple, had thought she just wasn't searching hard enough, praying fervently enough. "Sometimes the answer is that there is no answer." Love looked up from her hands toward the hole Wesley had slid through what seemed like hours ago. "Do you think he's gotten stuck in there?"

"It's bigger than you think it would be inside. It opens up where you can almost stand up. Didn't you ever go inside it when you were a kid?"

Love almost smiled at the sight of Jocelyn struggling to think of her as a child. "No. I never cared for caves. Homer—that was my brother—he liked to go crawling about under the ground, but I prefer to see my spiders and snakes before they fall on my neck."

The girl's eyes widened a bit. "I felt the same way when I crawled in there. Spiders are creepy." She shivered, and the dog licked her face.

"Yet spiders are surely one of God's most amazing creations." She couldn't believe she was talking about spiders. Shouldn't she be screaming? Or crying? At the very least praying? But what was there to pray for now?

At last Wesley stuck his head out of the cave and crawled back out. She didn't know why her heart started beating faster. She knew what was in the cave. The child had already told her. Still, it seemed to need confirmation.

Wesley was somber. She appreciated that. He laid his hand on her shoulder and looked her in the eye. "It's like Jo said. There's a grave in there. A baby's skeleton under a pile of rocks. That big flood last spring must have shifted some of the stones, and that's how come the dog found it."

"I see." Love looked away from Wes toward the sky. It was blue, very blue with no clouds. The kind of blue that as a child made her think that God was in his heavens and all was right with the world. But now there should have been clouds. Love could feel the child's eyes on her, but for once she was quiet. Not a common thing for Jocelyn.

After a while, Wesley asked, "What do we do now, Lovella?"

"I don't know," Love said.

"Do you want to tell us about it?"

"I don't know if I can. It's something that's never been told." Love looked at Wesley. "I wasn't married, you see."

Wesley wiped the sweat off his forehead with a rumpled bandanna before he sat down beside Jocelyn and leaned back against a rock as if he had all day to hear whatever she had to say. But what could she tell? Especially with the child there staring at her as though she'd suddenly grown two heads. And maybe she had. Maybe it was the second head that started talking about something she never thought she would.

"We aimed to be married," she said softly. "We ran away that weekend for the sole purpose of marrying before Gil went overseas to fight in the war. That was the First World War. But when we got to Louisville that day, it was late and the courthouse was closed, and we didn't know where to find a judge or a preacher. So we had our wedding night early."

Even now, all these years later, the pure pleasure of lying beside Gil, knowing he loved her, knowing she was going to be his wife, still caused her to feel warm in places her father would have told her it was sinful to even acknowledge were there. "Our plan was to get up early the next morning and find a preacher before Gil had to catch his train."

"What happened?" Jocelyn asked.

"We didn't wake up in time." Love's heart had clunked in her chest when she'd opened her eyes to the sunlight pushing through the dingy window in the hotel where they'd spent the night. She had stared at Gil's watch for a good two minutes before she could believe the hands. After she'd shaken him awake, they'd had no time for anything but a mad rush through the streets to get Gil to his unit. The train was leaving. Gil had to get on it. There was a war on, and if he hadn't gotten on the train, he'd have been a deserter. Funny how a few hours of sleep could so change a whole life.

"He promised he'd come back. And I thought he would. I wasn't a child. I was into my twenties, but I didn't know about war. And the boys were all so sure they'd go over there and take care of business and come home."

"I remember," Wesley said. "There were signs about enlisting everywhere. I lied about my age and tried to sign up, but I was a little squirt and didn't even look thirteen. They laughed at me and sent me home."

"That was lucky for you," Love said. She'd watched the tracks long after the train had disappeared. Finally somebody had asked if she'd needed help, and of course, she had. But she'd said no and walked back to the hotel. She'd worried about paying the hotel bill. She'd worried about what she'd tell her father when she went home. She'd worried about how she'd stand it till the war was over. But she'd never once worried about Gil not coming home. "I thought Gil would be lucky too. He was so strong. He could do anything and nothing scared him. Not even my father."

She'd used the money Gil had given her to pay the hotel bill, then walked to her aunt's house, her father's widowed sister. She'd said she was going to Aunt Betty's in the letter she'd left on the kitchen table back at the house. She hadn't cared whether her father believed it or not. Not when she left. But once Gil was gone, her courage had collapsed. Aunt Betty had let her stay one night, but she couldn't stand up to Love's father any more than Love could.

Besides, there had been Love's mother to consider. She wasn't well. Hadn't been well since Homer was born. Love suspected she didn't want to be well, but that didn't change the fact that she was no longer capable of taking care of herself, much less the house. She was a fleshy woman, and there were nights she didn't bother to heave herself out of her favorite chair to go to bed but just slept where she was. Love often got up in the night and spread a blanket over her.

Her mother hadn't been in good health, but she hadn't been idle. Her hands were always busy, quilting, braiding rugs, or tatting the intricate lace Love sold to the neighbors. But Love had been taking care of the house since she was twelve. She hadn't minded the work. They'd all had to work to scrape a living out of their rocky old farm. Her father had set the example. He'd rarely sat for more than long enough to eat his meals, and then he'd attacked the food on his plate with the same single-minded purpose he'd used when plowing and planting.

Love's mother had disgusted him. And that's why Love had to go home. She shouldn't have. Mae could have seen to their mother, could have made sure she had food and clean clothes. But Mae couldn't have stayed to be a buffer for their father's anger. She had a family of her own. Three boys and a girl already. David still hadn't been born. He'd been a late-life blessing. And what a blessing, though at the time Love could barely force herself to look at him or any other baby.

So, wrong as it turned out to be, she'd gone home. Her father had backhanded her across the face and knocked her down. After that he'd acted as if she didn't exist except as the means of getting a myriad of chores done. Of course, then he hadn't known about the baby. She hadn't either.

Love looked at Wesley and the child. Wesley had his eyes half closed, giving her time to think. The child was trying to be as patient, but she was fidgeting. The child never sat still very long.

It wasn't in her nature. Love had once been that way, as if by her pure busyness she could make sure she wouldn't end up sapped of energy like her mother. Love hadn't understood then the many things that could rob a body's life energy.

Love stared at the opening into the cave for a long moment. The truth was almost half a century old. She wasn't sure it should be told. She wasn't sure she even knew the truth. At last she took a deep breath and began talking. "My father was strong in the church. If the preacher wasn't able to come, the people looked to my father to lead the services. He had a deep voice and a knowledge of the Scripture and assurance in what he said. When he prayed it was easy to imagine God's head bent over to listen.

"I was the next to youngest child. Homer was two years my junior. Mother's health was bad from the time I can remember. I took over the house and vegetable garden completely after Mae married when I was twelve. I didn't mind the work. We all worked. Even Mother as much as she was able, peeling and such and with her needlework. Father said idle hands were an invitation for the devil to get you into trouble.

"Father never thought about a war taking Homer or me marrying. He planned to keep us two youngest children home to help him keep the place going. I was a homely child and backward socially besides, so he wasn't worried about any suitors showing up on our doorstep. And he knew how Homer loved the farm. It was always a great sadness to me that Homer wasn't buried on the land. He wasn't a thing like Father. Everything fascinated him. A rock shining in the sun. A pretty leaf. He made a pet out of a groundhog once. And Father let him keep it for a spell. I never could understand that. Father wouldn't let us keep more than three or four barn cats. If too many kittens showed up, he just swung them by the tail up against a tree trunk. It was one of my chores to carry off the carcasses. One time he caught me crying over a dead kitten, and told me there wasn't enough milk for the cats and us too. When I told him they could have my share of the milk, he just boxed my jaws for being mouthy."

Love looked up at the sky again. Still blue. Still no clouds. Wesley's eyes were kind and sympathetic, but the child looked half peaked. She shouldn't have told about the kittens. She wished she could forget about the cat brains on the tree trunks herself. But after the baby had come, the kittens had been all she could think about for a long time.

"I guess you're wondering what too many kittens has to do with a baby's grave."

"You tell the story however you want to tell it, Lovella. The shade's about made it over to us, and we ain't in a bit of hurry," Wesley said.

29

ove wanted to reach out and touch him. To thank him for his kindness. Once when her father was on his deathbed, she had tried to recall a kindness he'd done for her. Just one single kind thing. She had thought about it through those long days while her father clung to life one raspy breath at a time. She'd made her mind travel back over the years, searching in every least important memory, and was not able to remember even one kind moment. Not even when her mother died, but that had been only a few months after the baby.

She'd wanted to be wrong. She'd wanted to stumble across a forgotten memory when he had taught her to put a worm on a hook or had smiled or tousled her hair when she was a small child. And perhaps he had. Perhaps it had just been blocked out by the misery of the years in between.

He'd been kind to Mae's children. In his later years he'd sat on the porch swatting flies in the summertime and watching for one of the grandchildren to come by. He'd given them peppermint sticks and told Love to make sugar cookies. And she'd seen the ghost of her own child in the shadow of Mae's children.

She started talking again, the words struggling up to the surface of her mind like the thick popping bubbles of apple butter cooking. She had never been able to stir apple butter without having burns to show for it. "I wore loose dresses and never complained about being ill, so no one knew I was in the family way. Not even

Mae. No one except Mother. Mother sometimes pretended not to notice things just so she wouldn't have to be bothered, but her eyes were sharp, and she started knitting the baby a sweater when I was seven months along. We didn't talk about it, but she let me lay my head in her lap and stroked my hair on the days I felt the worst. I don't know what we thought was going to happen. Maybe that the war would be over and Gil would get home before the baby came and make an honest woman of me. I don't think we were thinking. We were just letting it happen because we didn't know what else to do."

She'd loved the baby from the first moment she'd known he was growing inside her. She'd written Gil and told him, but she never knew if he got the news. Her father wouldn't let her have Gil's letters. He'd burned them unopened in the cookstove. Even now she could see the letters of her name on the envelopes turning black in the fire. She'd always wondered why he hadn't burned the one she'd found in his Bible after he died that told of Gil's death in the war. Perhaps that was the one kindness he'd done her, not burning the letter so that she could know Gil hadn't just broken his promise and not come back for her even if she found the letter years too late for it to make a difference in her life.

"The baby was strong and healthy. He kicked and boxed inside me until sometimes I thought he was going to break right out of me. I'd helped Mae and others in the neighborhood during their confinements, so I knew what to expect. Or at least I thought I did." Could any woman ever know what it was like for a baby to fight his way to freedom until she'd experienced it?

"I had a bad confinement. We still hadn't told my father what was wrong with me. Mother just told him it was female problems, which was certainly no lie. Before my pains got too bad, we came up with a plan of sorts. Mother would help me deliver the child. We'd hide him out like Moses in the Bible until I got my strength back, and then I'd go to my mother's sister who lived in another state. Mother had some money put back from selling the lace she made. We'd say my husband had gone to war. It was close to the truth. I even planned to take Gil's name. Gil would have wanted me to. When I worried how Gil would find me, Mother said she'd tell him where I was."

It had been such a good plan. Love had felt hope for the first time in weeks. She could feel the ground under her feet walking away from the farm, and for a while the pain hadn't been so hard to bear. But the hours had dragged on. The pains had strengthened. The baby hadn't come. She looked down at her hands again and wondered if she would have the courage to tell the rest of the story. Maybe she should just leave it there and say no more. She used to wish she could think to that spot and not remember the rest. But of course, she couldn't.

After a few minutes, Jocelyn reached over and touched Love's hand in her lap. "What happened, Aunt Love? What went wrong?"

She looked up at the child and tried to keep her face expressionless. "I screamed. Heaven knows I tried not to. When my pains started, my father was out sawing wood. It was dreadfully cold, but Father never surrendered to the elements. But he came to the house at dark after seeing to the animals. I'd labored all day with no progress. The pains banged against me, tore through every inch of my body, attacked me like a wild animal. Mother rolled up a piece of cloth for me to bite, but there comes a level of pain where there is no control. I screamed. We had barred the door with a chair, but it wasn't enough to keep my father out." Her father had slung the chair across the room, yanked the covers back, and cursed her. "I thought he was going to kill me, and I didn't even care. I just wanted to be free of the pain. Mother grabbed his arms and begged him to go for the doctor or at least Mae, but he refused. He would not allow me to shame him in the neighborhood."

Love took a breath and looked back at the sky. Still blue but somehow different, as though the blue was fading into evening. "The pain devoured me. I drifted in and out of consciousness. I don't know how long it was before the poor little thing finally made it out. From somewhere far away I heard Mother say it was a boy, but my father took him away from my mother. He wouldn't let me see the baby. He said the baby was dead."

She had screamed again and tried to get up to follow her father when he went toward the door holding the child. Her mother had wrapped the baby in a towel while she was cutting the cord, and all Love had been able see was the towel in her father's hands. She hadn't been able to get out of the bed. Her legs and arms wouldn't move. It had been as if the air was mashing her against the bed. She'd gotten her head up. Her mother's hands and dress had been covered with blood, and tears had been streaming down her cheeks as she'd gently held down Love's shoulders. She'd tried to fight her, but the bed had begun spinning. She'd begun falling down a deep hole. And that's when she'd heard the baby cry. She'd tried to climb back out of the hole, but the sides had been shiny with blood and she'd kept slipping deeper down into it.

She tried to turn her mind away from the echo of the baby's cry. It had all been so long ago. She looked at Wesley and Jocelyn. Tears were sliding unnoticed down the child's cheeks. Love shouldn't have told so much, but it was too late to take back her words. Now she was anxious to finish the telling of it. "Mother thought I was going to die. I don't know why I didn't. I wanted to. Mother and Mae nursed me. I don't know whether Mother told her about the baby or not. I don't think she did or surely Mae would have said something. Father told everyone I had rheumatic fever. Every church in the county prayed for me. I drifted in and out of consciousness. I had visions of the war. I dreamed about Gil. The baby haunted me. And I couldn't die. I decided it was part of my punishment to have to live. I had sinned, and sin brings its own punishment. In the spring I finally got out of bed and went back out into the sunshine. But I didn't feel its warmth for a long time."

She had been little more than a ghost searching for some sight of the ghost of her baby. She'd begged her father to tell her what he'd done with the baby, but he'd forbidden her ever to mention it again. So she had searched every inch of the farm for some sign of a grave. "That was when I started my rock garden. It was something to keep me sane until Gil came for me. I still thought he'd come. The war was ending, and the soldier boys were coming home. But he didn't come. And my mother died in June. I came in from hunting rocks for my garden and found her dead in her chair. And still I couldn't leave. Not only might Gil come for me, but the baby was there on the farm." She looked over at Wesley. "You do see that I had to stay."

Wesley nodded. "Life can sure serve us up a pot of misery sometimes."

Love saw the pain in Wesley's eyes. "I shouldn't have burdened you with my story when you have troubling memories of your own."

"Sometimes there's healing in the telling," Wesley said.

"Some things never heal. I think you know that." Love looked from Wesley to the child and reached out to touch the tears on her cheek. "Everybody has troubles, child, and secrets that might be best untold. But shared sorrows get lighter. Thank you for your tears."

"I'm sorry, Aunt Love, for every time I've ever been mean to you," the child said.

Love managed a smile. "There have been times when you have surely tried my patience, Jocelyn, but never a day when I didn't thank the Lord for the kindness of your father and for him allowing me to be part of your family."

"Does he know about the baby?" Jocelyn asked.

"No. It didn't seem to be something I should burden a young preacher with. Especially one who had enough burdens already of his own."

"You mean my mother leaving him?" Jocelyn said.

"She was a burden before she left."

"I don't remember much about her," Jocelyn said.

"Just as well." Love fished a handkerchief out of a pocket and handed it to the child. "I'd have been better off if I'd been half the country away from my father. Perhaps I could have stopped hating him then, but no, my hate was like a poison that soured everything around me."

"How did you get over it?" the child asked.

"Some griefs are too deep to ever get over, but once I knew I wasn't going to be able to just sit down and die, I had to find a way to keep living." Love looked back to where the house had once sat. "There were my rocks. And there was the Bible. Psalms like 'Give thy strength unto thy servant.' The Lord picked me up and carried me through the blackest days. And the sun keeps rising. Apple trees keep blooming. Bean seeds keep sprouting. And rocks keep rising to the top of the ground after spring rains."

"And you kept cooking and cleaning for your father?" Wesley asked.

"I did. I didn't seem to see much other choice till he died. Then, as I said, I tried to burn the house down and start over. I guess it was just as well Little John came by and put the fire out. Nothing else I'd ever done had gone right. Why should that?" Love pushed down on the rock and stood up. Her joints set up a painful complaint, and she wondered how she'd ever ride Wesley's monster machine back to the house. Another time it might be easier just to sit down and die. If the Lord would only allow it. She looked back at the cave.

Wes and the child stood up too. They were waiting for her to make the first step back toward home, but she couldn't. "I always

237

wanted him to have a proper funeral and burial. Do you think we could do that for him?"

"I don't see why not if we can find a shovel," Wesley said.

"And David to say the words over his grave. He should be home by now. Jocelyn can go fetch him while we get the grave ready. There used to be some shovels in the barn." She looked at the sky again. "We still have a few hours before dark."

"What should I tell Dad, Aunt Love?" the child asked, a frown between her eyes.

"That you and your dog found the remains of a baby who needs a proper burial," Love said.

"But he might think we need to call the sheriff."

"I thought once of calling the sheriff, but I couldn't think what good it would do. I had no proof of wrongdoing. I didn't even know where the baby's body lay. It was a hard birth. The poor child might very well have been dead as my father said."

"You think your father . . ." The child couldn't finish the thought as her eyes got wide.

"I think my father could have done what I feared." Love thought she should say no more, but she seemed unable to stop talking. "But whatever happened, my father is long past any earthly punishment, and I can't see how telling the tale can do anyone any good now. But if, after you tell your father what I've told you, he decides the sheriff should be told, then so be it. I'm past caring what people think of me."

"Your dad will know the right thing to do, Jo," Wes said. "You go on and fetch him while Lovella and I hunt a shovel."

"We'll bring one in case you can't find one."

"Yes," Love said, "and bring the wooden box under my bed. I had Mae's husband make it for me years ago. He never knew what I wanted it for, but all these years it's been waiting."

30

It was after sundown when they gathered around the hole her father had helped Wes finish digging when they got back to the farm. They'd talked about waiting till the next day, but Aunt Love hadn't wanted to. She'd said they could pull the car up and shine the lights on the grave site if it got too dark. But it was still light enough to see in spite of the heavy feel to the air as night crept up on them.

Jocie's father stood at the top of the small grave with his Bible open in his hands while the wooden box waited beside the small heap of dirt. Wes had crawled back inside the cave with a flashlight to place the baby's bones on a blanket in the box. Her father had thought to bring the flashlight and the blanket left over from Jocie's baby days.

He had known what to do just the way Wes had said he would. While he'd found the box and got his Bible, he'd sent Tabitha and Jocie out to cut every rose in bloom to take with them. He hadn't said a thing about the sheriff. At the turnoff he'd pushed the gate open wide enough to drive the car through. He'd straddled the ruts and driven back through the field, slowing to a creep when the bottom of the car scraped against a rock but not stopping. Tabitha had kept her hands on her belly as though she had to steady her baby through the jostles.

When Wes had handed Aunt Love the box with the baby's bones in it, she'd cradled it in her lap while tears slid down her cheeks. As she'd whispered the words of the Twenty-third Psalm, the world around them had held its breath. No bird had sung. No dog had barked in the distance. No airplane had passed overhead. Even the breeze had lain still in the branches and the creek had been whisper quiet as it rolled over the rocks downstream. Jocie wouldn't have been a bit surprised to have heard an angel choir break out into "The Sweet Bye and Bye" or "In the Garden" after that, but instead the silence had followed them up from the creek to Aunt Love's rock garden where the tiny grave awaited.

Into the silence her father read some Scriptures before he led them in prayer. Aunt Love had stopped crying, and after they put the box down into the grave, she dropped in the first handful of dirt. When she stepped back from the grave, Tabitha put her arm around her waist, and Jocie took Aunt Love's hand. She thought maybe she should hug Aunt Love, but she wasn't the sort of person who invited hugs. Even holding her hand seemed strange. Necessary, but strange.

When the dirt was all pushed back into the hole and Wes had gently tamped it down, Tabitha and Jocie laid the roses on top of the grave. Aunt Love pointed out a rock chiseled square on the corners. When Jocie's father and Wes lifted it up, Aunt Love took the hem of her skirt and rubbed the dirt off it until the name Stephen appeared.

Wes propped the stone up at the end of the tiny grave, and they bent their heads again as David offered one final prayer. "We thank thee, O Lord, for giving us the opportunity to lay this tiny baby's remains to rest. We know that these many years this child has been in heaven with you, and we praise thee and thank thee for this truth. And now we ask for comfort for this mother's heart. Honor her grief and grant her peace. Amen."

As her father gently turned Aunt Love away from the grave, he promised, "I'll come back and set the stone properly."

Night fell before they reached the car, as if the dark, which had been holding off until they had finished, couldn't delay another second. Slowly the noises of the night came back. Frogs and whip-poor-wills and katydids. Wes started up his motorcycle, and the noise of his motor seemed wrong, blasphemous almost. At the same time, Jocie wished she could ride with him through the velvety darkness instead of in the car. Still, she didn't dare ask, but climbed into the backseat beside Tabitha, who had her hands firmly clasped over her rounded tummy even before the car started moving down the rutted road.

None of them said anything as her father slowly guided the car back toward the road. It was harder picking the best path in the dark, and they all held their breath each time the bottom of the car scraped against a rock. Jocie thought about praying for the oil pan or the muffler, but she didn't know if she should. Then when they made it out to the paved road, she wanted to ask her father if he'd been praying. But the silence in the car made the words stick in her throat.

They were almost back to their house before Tabitha broke the silence. "I've always liked the name Stephanie. Stephanie Grace. That's what I'll name my little girl when she's born."

Aunt Love didn't say anything, but after a moment she pulled the edge of her collar up to dab at her eyes.

⸙

Back at the house, Aunt Love washed her hands in the kitchen sink, thanked the family formally as if they'd just come back from a funeral home, picked up Jezebel, and went to her room. Jocie stared at the closed door of Aunt Love's bedroom for a moment and then looked at her father.

"Don't you think you should go talk to her? Pray with her or something?" she asked.

"I think she wants to be alone," her father said.

"But I didn't tell you the whole story," Jocie said.

"She'll tell me if she wants to," her father said.

"But it was worse than what I had time to tell you earlier."

Her father put his arms around Jocie. "Then maybe telling you and Wes will give her the peace she needs."

"I don't think I can sleep," Jocie said.

Tabitha came over, took one of Jocie's hands, and put it on her stomach. "Do you feel her moving?"

Jocie couldn't feel a thing. "Maybe," she said, because she could tell Tabitha wanted her to feel something.

"She gets bigger, you'll feel it for certain. The doctor says she's supposed to be born somewhere around the first of October. He says I'll start getting big, really big, in a month."

"People will know you're expecting then," Jocie said.

"Does that bother you?" Tabitha asked.

"No, does it you?"

Tabitha smiled. "Not at all. I thought it might, but now I just want her here safe where I can hold her and watch her grow. I don't even care anymore who she looks like."

"You keep saying she. How do you know the baby's going to be a girl?" Jocie asked.

"I just know." Tabitha grinned at Jocie. "The same way I knew you were going to be a girl before you were born."

Their father frowned. "You remember when Jocie was born?"

"Well, yeah, Dad, of course. I was almost seven. I sort of felt bad being so excited with DeeDee being so mad about it all. You remember, don't you, Dad? She didn't come out of her bedroom for weeks. Months maybe." Tabitha looked at Jocie. "It didn't have anything to do with you, Jocie. She hated being pregnant when I came along too. She wouldn't let anybody see her but Mama Mae for months before either of us were born. DeeDee can't stand not being skinny. She told me I'd hate it too, but so far it hasn't bothered me except for needing some bigger clothes."

"Mrs. McDermott out at church might have some maternity clothes. Her baby's not very old. Of course, she's not very skinny, but I'll bet she knows somebody your size you could borrow some from," Jocie said.

"At church? I don't know what she'd think." A worried frown scooted across Tabitha's face.

"She's way too nice to say anything mean, isn't she, Daddy? I've never heard her fuss about anything."

"She's a good woman," their father agreed.

"I guess I could go to church this week," Tabitha said. "Aunt Love's been after me to go, and maybe if I went it would make her feel better. Think it would mess things up too much for you, Daddy?"

"Nothing that the Lord can't take care of, sweetie," her father said.

Tabitha laughed. "We know how to keep him busy around here, don't we?"

"Maybe we should ask Leigh to come along too so the folks out there won't know what to talk about first." Jocie looked up at her father's face. "I could call her and ask her for you if you want me too."

"That won't be necessary," her father said without really meeting Jocie's eyes.

Jocie grinned. "You've already asked her. Gee whiz, things are getting too crazy around here. You should have seen Aunt Love getting on Wes's motorcycle. I wish I'd had a camera."

"People can surprise us," her father said.

Jocie's grin disappeared. "I didn't mean to make fun."

"I know," her father said. He put one hand on Tabitha's shoulder and the other on Jocie's and drew them in a circle. "Come on. Let's pray for Aunt Love and for ourselves.

"Dear Lord, forgive us our sins this day and help us to be full of forgiveness toward others. Especially send down your loving-kindness on Aunt Love this night and help her to make peace with her past. Give Tabitha courage and strength and love. Bless Jocie and help her to know to do what's right. Use me, Lord, in your service and help me know how to help others in their spiritual journeys. Thank thee for the blessings of the day and for the trials that move us closer to the center of thy will. Amen."

***

Once Jocie lay down on the cot out on the porch, her bones ached. She was that tired, but still she couldn't go to sleep. Too many thoughts were zapping around in her head. She dangled her hand over the edge of the cot to touch Zeb's head and stared out the windows at the stars. Suddenly one of the stars fell in a flash of light. Seeing a shooting star always made her feel honored, as if God had staged a show just for her. "O the mighty works of thy heavens," she whispered. Aunt Love said something like that whenever they were outside at night. Psalm something.

Would Aunt Love get up in the morning and burn the biscuits and quote Scripture to Jocie the same as every other morning? And what would Jocie say if she did? Or if she didn't. She thought about getting up and going to ask her father, but he was going to be different too. Asking Leigh to church. Maybe to get married next. Then Tabitha going to church—tummy poking out and painted rose and all. Sunday was sure to be interesting.

Of course, if the Mt. Pleasant folk voted them out, they wouldn't have to deal with the sacks of cabbage and zucchini anymore, although Jocie was beginning to like zucchini bread.

And she could stop worrying about being nice to Ronnie Martin. She'd been struggling with that a little more each week anyway.

Paulette Riley had told her last week she should just go ahead and punch Ronnie in the nose and get it over with. She and Paulette had both helped with the babies during Bible school, and Jocie had found out Paulette was just as worried about starting high school as she was.

Of course, with everything else that had happened, starting

high school wasn't all that big a problem. Thousands of people started high school every year. And as Paulette liked to say, it was rarely ever fatal. Of course, Paulette had a mother who had already noticed her need for the proper undergarments.

Jocie pushed that worry out of her head. She still had over a month before school started, and bras just didn't seem that important tonight. Not when Aunt Love's words kept echoing in her head. About her father and the baby. And trying to burn down the house. Jocie wouldn't be making any more jokes about the house burning down because Aunt Love forgot the bacon.

Jocie shifted on the cot to try to get more comfortable. She shut her eyes on the stars and tried to think of nothing, but crazy thoughts kept shooting through her mind. Her mother had hated being in the family way. But why had her father frowned when Tabitha talked about it? Maybe if she asked, Tabitha would tell her more. Maybe she could go ask her right now. Shake her awake and say, "Tell me about when I was born. Did it make everybody happy?" Everybody always seemed to be happy when a new baby was born in the church. Had her father laughed?

And who picked her name—Jocelyn Ruth? Jocelyn wasn't in the Bible. It sounded like a Bible name, but a Sunday school teacher had checked for her years ago in this big book where every word in the Bible was written down. She'd shown Jocie how it went right from Jobab to Job's to Jochebed.

Jocie had felt lucky at the time that she hadn't been named Jochebed. But at the same time she figured her daddy would have picked a Bible name, so her mother must have named her. For some reason, she'd been afraid to ask her father. Just like she had always been afraid to ask him much about her mother. He always looked so sad whenever her mother was mentioned. Not just for himself, but for her too. But now if he was going to start noticing Leigh, things would be different.

Things would be different all right. But different good or different bad? In the house she heard the clock strike twelve. Tomorrow already. Maybe if she said a prayer, the Lord would settle her thoughts down and she could go to sleep.

Dear Lord, I'm not praying a stepmother prayer. I'm going to leave that up to Daddy. But I do thank you that Daddy is my father. Help me be the kind of daughter he can be proud of. Bless Aunt Love and forgive me for the times I've been mean to her. And thank you for letting me see the shooting star. Now help me to quit thinking so much so I can go to sleep. Amen.

She opened her eyes and looked at the stars again. She started counting in the top left corner of the window frame. She was asleep before she got to fifty. She dreamed about babies.

ocie didn't know who was the most nervous Sunday morning—Tabitha or Leigh. Or maybe Jocie herself, since she was nervous for both of them. Even her father seemed half undone when they got to Mt. Pleasant and saw Leigh's car parked across the way. He jerked the car to a stop a cat's whisker away from the concrete retaining wall at the edge of the parking area and muttered something about the brakes needing work. He ran his hand through his hair and straightened his tie before he climbed out of the car.

Leigh was still sitting in her car in the parking area across the road as if she hadn't worked up the courage to climb out and join the folk chatting in the churchyard. A few of them were shooting curious glances toward her car, but they were politely waiting for Leigh to get out before descending on her to welcome her to Mt. Pleasant.

Jocie's father helped Aunt Love out of the car and gave Tabitha's shoulder a little squeeze. Then he smoothed down his tie one more time, tucked his Bible under his arm, and marched straight across to Leigh's car. When she saw him coming, Leigh climbed out of the car and started toward him, but her full yellow skirt had caught in the car door and she almost fell. David reached out a hand to steady her. For a moment Leigh looked mortified, but then she laughed. Jocie's father laughed too as he opened the car door to free her skirt.

Jocie still wasn't so sure about this stepmother idea, but from the look on her father's face, he was getting surer by the minute. Jocie looked around for Paulette's car but didn't see it. She would pick this Sunday to miss.

Silence fell over the churchyard as the folks still outside the church shifted their eyes between the preacher and his family. Tabitha moved closer to Aunt Love and whispered, "Can I just stay out here in the car? They look like they're going to eat me alive."

"It will be all right. I'll be right beside you, and your father won't be far away." Aunt Love took hold of Tabitha's arm and moved her gently toward the steps.

"I haven't been to church since I was Jocie's age. Not even at Easter. I won't know what to do."

"Church hasn't changed that much," Aunt Love assured her.

"Yeah, it's easy," Jocie said. "Just smile and nod when people talk to you, bow your head when somebody's praying, don't talk when the Sunday school teacher's reading the lesson, and sing when everybody else sings."

"Sing?" Tabitha croaked. "I can't sing."

"Nobody else here can either. Wait till you hear. So it'll be okay," Jocie said, then added with a grin as Leigh and her father walked up, "Except Leigh. She can sing. Maybe you can get her to do a special, Dad."

Leigh grabbed her neck as panic flashed through her eyes, but then she laughed again. "Are you trying to make trouble, Jocie? Tell you what, we'll make it a duet. The two of us. I'll let you pick the song."

"How about 'Hound Dog'?" Jocie suggested.

Leigh twisted her mouth to keep from smiling as Jocie's father gave Jocie his stern church look. "No 'Hound Dog,' even in the churchyard."

"It might make them quit staring at Tabitha and Leigh and start staring at me. I'm used to it, so it wouldn't bother me. But if you don't want me to sing, I could do cartwheels or something."

"Just behave, okay?" her father said.

Jocie sighed as they climbed the concrete steps. "Just trying to help."

"If you want to help, go be nice to somebody," her father suggested. "Say, Ronnie Martin."

Leigh grabbed Jocie's arm before she got too far away and whispered to her, "You can be nice to me. If I get much more nervous, I may be the one doing cartwheels."

Mrs. McDermott came toward them carrying little Murray, who was reaching toward Jocie. "Here, Jocie. He's crying for you already."

Jocie took the baby and swung him in a little circle while her father said, "Good morning, Dorothy. I'm sure you know my friend Leigh." When Mrs. McDermott smiled and nodded, he went on. "I guess Leigh knows everybody, working at the courthouse the way she does. And this is my daughter Tabitha."

"It's so good to have you here with us this morning. Both of you." Mrs. McDermott said. She gave Leigh a knowing look and then settled her eyes on Tabitha. "My heavenly days, dear. You look just like your mother did when she was about your age. I used to ride the school bus with your mother. She was already in high school when I started school, but I remember how pretty she was. And you're every bit as pretty."

"Thank you," Tabitha murmured.

"I suppose you're finding things a lot different here than in California," Mrs. McDermott said. "But I'm sure you'll enjoy hearing your father preach. We just love Brother David here at Mt. Pleasant and, of course, all his family."

She paused for Tabitha to say something, but Tabitha just kept smiling while at the same time looking as if she might have to throw up any second. She moved a step closer to Aunt Love.

Mrs. McDermott took pity on her and turned to Aunt Love. "And how are you this morning, Miss Love?"

Aunt Love looked the same as on any other of a hundred Sundays. Her navy dress was neatly pressed, with a few white cat hairs clinging to it here and there. Her gray hair was coiled tightly in the bun at the back of her head as always. It was as if the day when they'd buried the baby's bones had never happened. Nothing had changed. Except for the red hat perched on her head. Jocie didn't even know Aunt Love owned a red hat. Maybe she had forgotten which colors were which. Or maybe she was turning somersaults in her own way.

Aunt Love smiled at Mrs. McDermott and said, "I'm well, Dorothy. And how are you?"

"Fine. Except I'm sick to death of green beans. I've been picking and canning all week. I'll bring you some to take home this evening."

"That would be kind of you," Aunt Love said as Jocie held back a groan. At least it wasn't cabbage.

Mrs. McDermott looked at Aunt Love's hat. "Is that a new hat, Miss Love? I don't think I've ever seen you wear it before."

"I've been saving it for a special occasion," Aunt Love said.

"And what occasion is this? It's not your birthday. That's in December, isn't it?" Mrs. McDermott said.

"Some special days don't have titles," Aunt Love said. "The Lord just tells you to rejoice and why not with a red hat if you've a mind to."

Jocie looked over Murray's head at Aunt Love. Maybe she had been too quick to decide Aunt Love was the same as any other Sunday. Mrs. McDermott kept smiling as she said, "Well, it's a lovely red hat."

Several other women drifted over to their group to welcome Tabitha and Leigh. Tabitha kept her smile going, but she looked nervous. Jocie asked her if she wanted to hold Murray, but that seemed to scare her even more. The sound of Jessica Sanderson playing a hymn drifted out the open front door.

"Sounds like it's time for Sunday school assembly," Mrs. Mc-Dermott said as she reached for Murray.

Jocie gave him up reluctantly. She'd just as soon stay outside with the baby instead of having to go try to be nice to Ronnie Martin. Some things were just too hard to do week after week.

She gave her father a sympathetic look as Ogden Martin way-laid him before they got to the door. "Brother David, I want to talk to you."

"Of course, Ogden. But Sunday school is about to start now."

"We can miss a bit of Sunday school. This won't take but a minute." Ogden didn't even seem to notice Tabitha or Leigh as he pulled David aside.

Jocie hung back to listen just enough to be sure it didn't have anything to do with her. The man was upset about something that had gone awry for Mrs. Martin during Bible school. Jocie caught up with Leigh as she went in the front door with Tabitha and Aunt Love.

"Do you think this can count as a date?" Leigh whispered as they went in the church.

"I don't know. It might have to be night church," Jocie said.

"I could come back tonight, and we could practice on that duet. Maybe make it a trio with your Dad."

"If so, we'll have to change songs. No 'Hound Dog' for sure."

"It didn't sound as if it was one of your father's favorites, but Elvis isn't the only guy out there making records. I've been think-ing about getting Tennessee Ernie Ford's 'Sixteen Tons.' That surely means we're making progress, don't you think?"

"He knows you're a girl now," Jocie said.

Leigh blushed. "Now if I can just get him to think of me as a woman."

Tabitha came back to get Leigh. "Aunt Love says I can't go in her Sunday school class. That I have to go to the young women's class. Will you stay with me? These people are scaring me to death."

"They do sort of look as if they don't know which one of us to go after first," Leigh said.

"Well, at least you're not expecting."

"Expecting? No way. It'd have to be another virgin birth." Leigh's eyes widened. "But you?"

"No virgin birth," Tabitha said.

"Oh." Pink flooded Leigh's cheeks. "I'm sorry. I mean, I'm not sorry about you expecting. That's wonderful, I suppose, isn't it? I'm just . . . I just don't know what to say." Leigh fanned herself with her hand.

"Oh, jeez, don't faint on me. I shouldn't have spilled the beans to you right here in the middle of church. No telling how many people were eavesdropping, but I figured you'd already noticed the way my stomach's sticking out." Tabitha looked around. Most of the other people had already headed off to their Sunday school classes.

Leigh took a peek at Tabitha's midsection. "I hadn't looked, I guess. How far along?"

"Due the first of October."

"You're not very big for that."

"Been throwing up nonstop for months," Tabitha said.

"I'd probably want to eat nonstop and get big as a cow," Leigh said.

"I feel like a cow already," Tabitha said.

The women in the senior adult women's class that met in the choir area at the front of the sanctuary were gazing curiously back at Jocie, Tabitha, and Leigh. The only one not paying the least bit of attention to them was Aunt Love, who normally wouldn't have let Jocie miss one second of Sunday school. Through the door, Jocie could see Ogden Martin still bending her father's ear.

Her father didn't look happy. If their discussion broke up and he came in and caught them dillydallying in the vestibule, he might be even more upset. And he'd probably blame Jocie, because he couldn't very well get upset with Tabitha on her first day at church or Leigh the first time he'd invited her to come.

"Look, guys, we'd better go to Sunday school before Miss Mc-Murtry sends a search party after me. Besides, we don't want to upset Dad. He might forget his sermon, and everything's crazy enough already without that happening." Jocie felt strange being the responsible one. "Come on, I'll show you to your Sunday school room."

❦

Outside, David was trying hard to hold on to his temper as he listened to Ogden Martin's complaints. The man had no intention of ever being happy. Something would always be wrong. David wondered if he'd always been this way or if it was just because he was so unhappy with David as pastor. David started to interrupt Ogden's litany of the problems with Bible school and just ask the man straight out what his problem with him was, but he didn't really want to spend rest of the Sunday school hour listening.

Instead he wanted to be inside to help Tabitha and Leigh, especially Tabitha, not feel so on display. Leigh might color up, but she'd just laugh about it. That was one of the things he was beginning to like the most about Leigh—how she could find a reason to laugh. She'd said it was because everybody expected plump people to be jolly, but David knew plenty of people who were plump and sour. Besides, she wasn't all that plump. Not Miss America shapely like Adrienne had been, but it was the shape of the heart inside that was the most important.

Of course, she was still so young. Half the people in the church would be counting up the years between them while he preached today. He probably shouldn't have invited her, but he'd had no way of knowing this would be the Sunday Tabitha would decide to make her first appearance at church. Or that they'd discover a baby in Aunt Love's past and she'd discover a red hat in her closet. He hoped that was a sign that she was surrendering some of the sadness of her past.

He'd asked her if she wanted to talk to him about it, but she'd said she'd already talked about it to Wes and Jocie, and now that she'd let the story out, she needed time to get some things straight in her head before she talked about it again. Then she'd said, "Let the child tell you about it. Some of the things I told her might have better gone unspoken, but I've always been too honest. I suppose that's a strange thing to say, what with nobody knowing about my baby and all, but I never lied about it. I just didn't tell it. Still, Jocelyn is so young. I shouldn't have burdened her with my misery."

"Bad things happen, Aunt Love. She knows that. Has known it since she was a little kid and Adrienne left."

"I know, David, but you're strong and good. I told her about another kind of father. Just let her talk to you so my misery won't dim her joy in life."

"I thought you wanted her to be a bit less joyful on occasion."

"Less boisterous perhaps. More respectful at times. But never less joyful. In fact, I'm going to start praying for joy in my own heart. And I'd covet your prayers for the same."

Maybe more joy was what he needed to pray for Ogden Martin, or more patience for himself.

"Are you even listening to me, Preacher?" Ogden said.

"Of course I'm listening, Brother Ogden, and I'm sorry if you're not happy with the way Bible school went. Still, it seemed to me the children enjoyed themselves and learned some good things, many of them from Mrs. Martin. She did a great job teaching the juniors the Bible books. Of course, there were a few problems, but then aren't there always a few problems?"

David tried to look as if he cared about the problems Ogden

had been talking about. Miss Sadie had forgotten the sugar again, one of the classes had spent more money than the others on craft supplies, and somebody had threatened to ship the youngest Martin, Paul, into outer space if he didn't behave. His father claimed the boy was almost afraid to get out of the car at church anymore.

David had cringed until after Ogden placed the blame on one of the younger Sunday school teachers. At least it hadn't been Jocie. He was sort of ashamed of himself for thinking it might have been her. Jocie had been a model Bible school worker, helping out with the little ones in the nursery. She had even managed to continue being nice to Ronnie Martin even though he went out of his way to pick on her.

David supposed he could have complained about that to Ogden, but David had bigger problems to worry about than a couple of kids working out a way to get along for a few hours every week in church. Such as whether he'd be back at square one trying to get a church, any church, to let him preach once he told the Mt. Pleasant deacons about Tabitha. He figured he might as well get it over with. Half the women would notice her condition this morning anyway.

When he told Ogden he wanted to have a special deacons' meeting that night after services, the man smiled for the first time all morning. David didn't know if it was because Ogden thought he was taking his complaints that seriously or if the deacon was hoping David had called the meeting to resign.

As he followed the other man into the church, David glanced at his watch. Still a half hour before worship service. He had time to find a quiet place to look over his Scripture and pray and prepare himself to deliver God's message to the people at Mt. Pleasant. His people. At least for one more Sunday.

The Lord had led him to the passage about forgiveness in the Sermon on the Mount. Now he wondered if he should search for a new Scripture. Ogden Martin would be sure to think he was directing his words at him. But then everybody needed forgiveness. "Forgive us our debts as we forgive our debtors." He hadn't planned to use that line out of the Lord's Prayer, but now it seemed right. Perhaps he'd have the church stand and repeat the prayer together. Before that, David himself needed to pray for forgiveness for his impatience with Ogden.

32

David looked down at his people from the pulpit. The pews were fuller than the first Sunday he'd preached at Mt. Pleasant. That could just be because it was summer and the early hay had been cut and the crops had been laid by. Or it could be the work he'd been doing in the church field. Most of the faces looking toward him as he again thanked the Bible school workers and made the announcements were smiling.

Of course, Ogden Martin wasn't smiling as he sat in the second pew on the left with three other deacons waiting to take up the offering after the song service. Even the offerings had been better the last few weeks. They'd taken care of the Bible school expenses, with some money left over to bank for a rainy day. Matt McDermott and Jim Sanderson, sitting with Ogden, looked a little worried when David announced the special deacons' meeting. David was glad they weren't going to Matt McDermott's house for Sunday dinner. He'd be too tempted to ask his advice before the meeting.

David's eyes drifted back to his women sitting a couple of rows behind the deacons. His women. Was he ready to include Leigh in his women? The thought didn't make sweat pop out on his forehead anymore. Just when he'd about decided he had a gift for being single the way Paul said in the Bible, the Lord had shoved Leigh into his path. The fact was, he liked her, had even spent some minutes wondering if he'd forgotten how to kiss a woman.

He felt as awkward as a sixteen-year-old thinking about it. And now wasn't the best time to think about it, with the offering hymn winding down through the last verse. The deacons were moving up to the front to pick up the offering plates, and he was thinking about kissing a woman twelve years younger than he was. Still, she wasn't young enough to be his daughter. Quite.

After Ogden Martin spoke the offertory prayer, David sat down in the chair on the podium behind the pulpit to wait while the men passed the plates and Jessica played "I Come to the Garden Alone." At least no wasps were flying around the sanctuary to distract attention from the message. Of course, it wasn't the people who were distracted this morning; it was the preacher.

And maybe his family. Tabitha still looked scared as she sat close to Aunt Love. She'd left the hymnbook open on her lap as if trying to cover up the evidence. He'd thought she was going to crawl under the pew and hide when he'd introduced her from the pulpit at the beginning of the service, but he had to do it. The people expected it. Adrienne used to ask him if he had to do everything the people expected. She said it was the unexpected that jolted people awake. She was good at the unexpected. Even better at the unacceptable. Thank heavens that although Tabitha looked like Adrienne she wasn't like her. The way she loved her unborn baby proved that well enough.

Aunt Love reached over and patted Tabitha's arm. No wonder Aunt Love had been so kind to Tabitha. She'd gone through some of the same thing. Talk about the unexpected. He had never heard the first hint of that story in his family. Surely his mother hadn't known. But then perhaps she had just kept the secret. There were other secrets kept in the family almost as well. Secrets so secret that sometimes David wondered if they were true or if Adrienne had just whispered them into his mind as some kind of cruel joke.

David's eyes went to Jocie, who was doing sentinel duty at the end of the pew next to the aisle. Nobody would get past her to harm the others. Two of the deacons were coming back down the aisle with the plates of money. He should close his eyes and pray over his sermon, but instead he kept his eyes on Jocie and thanked the Lord for giving her to him.

She noticed him looking at her and made a silly face. He grinned back at her and felt a surge of love. He wished that somehow he could shield her from the hurts of the world. They'd talked about Aunt Love the morning before out on the rock fence in the back. Tears had streamed down Jocie's face as she'd said, "But how could her father have done that to her?"

"I don't know," David had answered as honestly as he could. "It must have been a bad time for all of them."

"He would have been my great-grandfather. I didn't know him, did I?"

"No, he died many years before you were born."

"Do you remember him? Was he mean to you?"

"He was already well on in years and not in good health by the time I can remember, but my sister and brothers remembered him fondly. Said he told them stories about the farm and when he was growing up."

"I'll bet he didn't tell them stories about Aunt Love."

"No, I suppose not," David had said. "But nobody is all good or all bad. Just remember that."

"But do you think he killed the baby?"

Jocie had needed him to say no, that nobody could be that cruel, but David had never lied to her. He could only say the truth. "I don't know. You said even Aunt Love didn't know that." He'd pulled Jocie close and kissed the top of her head. "Whatever happened, it was all a long time ago, before even I was born. No amount of worrying is going to change any of it now."

"I know, Daddy, but I just can't keep from crying when I think about it."

"It is sad, and I know Aunt Love appreciates the way you care."

Jocie had pushed her hands across her cheeks to wipe away her tears. "Can I go with you when you fix the stone on the baby's grave? Maybe I could hold it up for you or something."

"Sure. We'll do it one day next week after we get the paper out."

She had ducked her head and directed her next words at the ground. "You know, I was never very happy about Aunt Love moving in with us after Mama Mae died. I used to wish she'd get tired of us and move out. That wasn't very nice of me."

He'd tipped up her face until she was looking into his eyes. "But she didn't move out, and now you realize she needs us."

"She told me that she prays for you every day and that I should be thankful to have such a good father," Jocie had said. "And I am."

The deacons had placed the offering plates back on the table in the front and made their way back to their families. Jessica finished up the song and went back to her seat. David gathered his thoughts and pushed them aside so that the Scripture could come to the forefront. Forgiveness. Perhaps it was time he forgave Adrienne. For everything. Perhaps that was why the Lord had laid this Scripture on his heart. Not for the Mt. Pleasant congregation. Not for Aunt Love. Not for Ogden Martin. But for him.

They went to the Sandersons for dinner. Jessica Sanderson always cooked twice as much as she needed whenever she had the preacher, or maybe every Sunday for all David knew. She had several grown children, and she never knew when they'd decide to show up for Sunday dinner. So she'd insisted Leigh join them. Two more than she was expecting was no problem at all.

Leigh's cheeks stayed rosy all through dinner, but she had no problem being the perfect guest. By the time Jessica brought out her fresh-baked apple pie, she was sending meaningful glances between David and Leigh.

After Leigh helped with the dishes, she thanked Jessica profusely for the delicious dinner and said she'd best go home. David took pity on Tabitha and let her ride home with Leigh. It might be better if she wasn't at church after the deacons' meeting that night.

That night after the evening services, David and the deacons went back into the men's Sunday school room. He waited till the five deacons present settled into the metal folding chairs. Ogden Martin, Matt McDermott, Jim Sanderson, Harvey McMurtry, and Joe Bottoms. Two weren't there. Whit Jackson was visiting his new grandbaby in Tennessee, and Dale Whitehead had called to say one of his cows was having trouble calving and he'd had to call the vet.

If there was going to be any dividing into sides, it would be Ogden and Joe on one side and Jim and Matt on the other with Harvey somewhere in the middle. That's the way it usually went, although David thought Joe had voted for him to be interim pastor. That's what he needed to remember now, that the Mt. Pleasant position was just an interim position anyway. If the deacons voted to boot him out, then the Lord would lead him to a new way to serve.

He hadn't planned to beat around the bush—just get the news told and leave, but Matt, who was chairman of the deacons, told David he had something to say first. Beside Matt, Ogden shifted in his chair and looked about as happy as a man who was watching it rain on ten acres of alfalfa he'd just cut.

Matt ignored him and started talking. "You've been here now for about six weeks, I think, Brother David, and folks have responded well to your sermons and leadership. You've been faithful to visit the sick and anyone who has a special need, and we appreciate that in a preacher. You know we usually have a seminary student down from Louisville, and there ain't no way those boys can be around to see to anybody during the week. Members here have to plan the day they die so they can have their funeral on a weekend. I mean, we know the boys have to go to class and then it's a long drive and gas prices are steep, but it would be good for a change to have a man who lives in our area as pastor."

"I always figured it was part of our church's mission giving those boys experience," Ogden said.

Matt hardly missed a beat. "And so it has been. But there's some of us who feel the Lord wants our church to go in a new direction, and we feel you're the man to lead us in that direction, Brother David. We're asking you to consider taking the church on a full-time basis."

Jim spoke up. "Well, full-time for us. We don't expect you to quit putting out the *Banner*, Brother David. Fact is, we feel that's a plus for our church. You being so well known in the community and all."

David held up his hand to stop them. Sometimes the Lord had a funny sense of humor. Here David was getting offered what he'd been wanting for years, a church full of good people to serve, and he had to present them with a dilemma instead of the simple yes he wanted to give them. At least he didn't have to tell them that his grandfather might have been a murderer. "There's nothing I'd like better, men, but first we need to talk about the reason I called this meeting."

Matt didn't let him finish. "We're prepared to raise the salary to sixty a week."

"Give me a chance to talk, Matt. I do appreciate everything you've said, but what I have to say is more of a personal nature." He looked at the men one at a time. Ogden wouldn't meet his eyes, stared out the window instead. It was getting dark. David thought of all the families out in the churchyard waiting on their husbands and fathers and getting impatient. "You met my daughter Tabitha today. Most of you, if not all of you, know that she's been with her mother since she was thirteen. There have been times over the last seven years when I thought I might never see her again. But the Lord answered my prayers and brought her back to me."

"Praise the Lord," Jim said.

"Yes," David said. "As you know, she came home the Sunday you voted me in as interim pastor here. So I had plenty of reasons to rejoice that night. Still, I knew something had brought her home all the way from California. It turns out she came home because she's expecting a baby and she didn't have anywhere else to turn."

All the men looked surprised except Matt. Dorothy must have noticed Tabitha's condition that morning.

Ogden was smiling a bit again. "I take it that this is without the benefit of matrimony."

"That's right. She wanted to get married. The father of the baby did not," David said.

"Do you know who the father is?" Ogden asked, looking happier by the moment.

"I know his name, if that's what you mean. But that hardly matters now. He's out of the picture," David said.

"Is she giving the baby up for adoption?" Joe asked. "I know a couple who has been on the adoption waiting list for over a year."

"She's keeping the baby," David said.

"But it would be better for the baby if he had a mother and a father," Joe said.

"He'll have me as a grandfather," David said. "And no doubt in time, Tabitha will find the right man to marry and that man will be the child's father."

"It seems you're always having some kind of family problems, aren't you, Reverend?" Ogden said.

263

"I don't look upon this baby as a problem, only a blessing, Brother Ogden." David stared straight at the man for a moment before looking at Matt. "However, I realize that everyone might not have the same feeling about this."

"Are you handing in your resignation?" Ogden asked.

"No, I'm not. If you want it, you'll have to ask for it." David stood up. "Now, I'm sure you'd feel freer discussing this without me here, so I'm going home. I'll see you men Wednesday night for prayer meeting."

Harvey McMurtry pushed himself up out of his chair before David got to the door. "Pastor, don't you think we should pray together before you leave?" Harvey was in his late seventies and had been coming to Mt. Pleasant since he was three weeks old.

"Of course, Harvey." David came back and knelt down in the middle of the men. "Dear Lord, we praise thee for this day of worship that we have had. And we thank thee for every man here and the family of God they serve so ably. Help us to always seek thy will, O Lord, and to allow thee to guide and direct our lives in service to thee. Forgive us our shortcomings, and thank thee for the many blessings thou dost shower down on us each and every day. Comfort those in our church family who are grieving, heal those who are sick, and convict those who are lost. In thy precious and holy name we pray. Amen."

When he went outside, Aunt Love had already gone to the car. Jocie gave the McDermott baby a hug and handed him back to his mother when she saw David come out of the church. As he headed for the car, he promised the families chatting in the yard that the other men would be out soon.

Jocie waited till they climbed inside before she said, "You told them about Tabitha?"

"I did."

"Good," Aunt Love said.

"Did they fire you?" Jocie asked.

"Not yet."

"Are they going to fire you?" Jocie asked.

"That remains to be seen, but whatever happens, the Lord will take care of us. And Tabitha." He backed the car out onto the road and turned it toward home.

"Dorothy McDermott brought us two bushels of beans and a bucket of tomatoes," Aunt Love said. "You'll have to remember to thank her, David."

"I will on Wednesday night. They're good people."

Aunt Love smiled. "She didn't know what to think of my red hat."

"I guess you surprised us all with that," David said.

They drove a little way in silence before Aunt Love said, "That girl, I can't ever remember her name, but the one that's stuck on you. She seems nice."

"Leigh," David said. "Yes, she does."

"Maybe she'll make us another chocolate cake," Jocie said from the backseat. "Paulette told me last week that her mother always says the way to a man's heart is through his stomach. Maybe I should tell Leigh that. Or even better, maybe we can invite her over to help string beans."

David glanced in the rearview mirror at Jocie. "Maybe it would be better if you leave the inviting up to me."

Jocie grinned. "Oh dear. I think my daddy has fell in love."

"Well, maybe not yet, but I'm not saying it couldn't happen. It's been a pretty wild summer so far. Who knows what might happen next?"

"Something good, I hope," Jocie said.

" 'Truth shall spring out of the earth; and righteousness shall look down from heaven. Yea, the LORD shall give that which is good.' Psalm 85, I think," Aunt Love said. "I'm thankful the truth did spring out of the earth this week, and I'm thankful for my family."

"And we're thankful for you," David said.

Again there was a moment of silence as they drove along before Jocie said, "I like your red hat, Aunt Love."

"That's sweet of you, child. I'm thinking about putting a flower on the one I wear next week, or maybe a feather."

David smiled out at the road and silently thanked the Lord for the blessings of the week. Even for the ones that hadn't especially felt like blessings at the time. He even planned on working on forgiving Adrienne during his prayer times next week. After all, hadn't he profited from some of the wrongs she'd done against him? He glanced up in the rearview mirror again. Jocie was dozing off. Again he felt that terrible need to protect her, even to make sure whatever she was dreaming was good and happy.

But then he remembered the way the tears had flowed down her cheeks when she'd talked about Aunt Love and her baby. There would be other times when life would knock her off her feet. He couldn't keep that from happening. Not every time. He could only try to be there to help her up and make her smile again.

33

onday morning, Jocie had to help Aunt Love with the green beans. She would have rather been helping Wes set up the paper, but her father said they couldn't very well leave Aunt Love alone with two bushels of beans and a pressure canner. Just last summer old Mrs. Cranfield out on Benson Creek had put a canner full of beans on the stove and gone out on the porch to check her flowers. She hadn't thought about the canner again till its top blew off and jars of beans went everywhere. Her grandson had even found a jar on a rafter in the attic. David had gone out and taken a picture of the unbroken jar of beans for the *Banner*.

So there was no way they could trust Aunt Love's memory when it came to pressure canners. When Jocie pointed out that Tabitha wasn't having memory lapses yet, her father said Tabitha probably didn't have the least idea how to can beans.

So Jocie sighed and accepted her fate. At least she didn't have to grate head after head of cabbage to salt down in crocks until it rotted into sauerkraut. She still hadn't figured out how people ate that stuff.

Actually, stringing beans wasn't so bad except for it taking forever. They sat on the front porch surrounded by the buckets of beans. Even Tabitha helped. She said it brought back memories of helping Mama Mae years ago. Zeb lay by Jocie's chair, ready to pounce when she dropped a bean.

"I don't think I ever saw a dog eat a green bean," Aunt Love said.

"Wes would say it's because he's a Jupiterian dog." Jocie dropped another bean on purpose.

"Wes isn't from Jupiter," Tabitha said. "He's from Illinois."

"How do you know that?" Jocie asked.

"DeeDee told me. She said Wes was the original beatnik and that when he first came to Hollyhill, she tried to get him to tell her stories about some of the places he'd been."

"And he told her?" Jocie carefully pulled the strings off the long green bean in her hand. For some reason, it bothered her that Wes might have told her mother things he had never told her.

"Not a lot. Said he wouldn't talk about his past at all. She said there were times when she wondered if Zella was right and the man was running from the law."

"He hasn't done much running for the last ten years or so," Aunt Love said.

"I didn't say I thought that," Tabitha said. "Anyway, DeeDee said about all she ever got out of him was that he used to live in Illinois. At least, I think she said Illinois. Maybe it was Ohio. Somewhere up north. I can't remember for sure."

Jocie broke up her handful of beans and threw them into the big kettle sitting in the middle of their chairs. She practiced what she was going to ask a couple of times in her head before she said it out loud. "Did you talk a lot about things here in Hollyhill?"

"Some. DeeDee said she didn't plan on ever thinking about Hollyhill again after she left, but then she decided some of the stories were just too good not to tell."

Again Jocie practiced, but her voice still sounded a little tight when she asked, "Did she ever talk about me?"

Tabitha picked a bean up off the pile on the newspaper in her lap and studied it as if it was the first green bean she'd ever seen before she answered, "I talked about you. I missed you, Jocie."

"But what about Moth—DeeDee?"

Tabitha dropped the bean back down on the pile in her lap and looked up at Jocie. "Do you want the truth?"

Jocie didn't hesitate. "Of course."

"Well, okay. DeeDee didn't talk about you. I would try sometimes to get her to write after we got a letter from you, but she always either acted like she didn't hear me or told me to write myself if I wanted to. She said she didn't have any claim on you, that she gave you to Daddy when you were born. She said Daddy wanted you, so Daddy could have you." Tabitha's eyes were moist with tears. "I'm sorry, Jocie. I know that sounds awful, but the truth was, DeeDee was never a mother to you even before we left. Surely you remember that."

"What do you mean?" Jocie asked. "She was my mother, wasn't she?"

"She gave birth to you, if that's what you mean, but I never saw her holding you or feeding you or changing you. Daddy did all that. If Mama Mae couldn't watch you, Daddy took you to the paper with him or to church, visiting, wherever he went."

Aunt Love was the only one still breaking beans. "That's true," she said. "I remember everybody in town talking about what a good father he was. And he was. Nobody talked about your mother. At least, not about her being a good mother."

"But how could she do that?" Jocie asked. Zeb stood up and put his nose on her knee.

"I don't know." Tabitha laid her hand on her stomach. "I can't understand it. I already know I'd do anything to keep from hurting little Stephanie Grace."

Aunt Love dumped her bean tips and ends into one of the empty buckets. "That's the way the good Lord intended a mother to feel. It's built into us to love and protect our babies, but obviously Adrienne was not a natural mother." Aunt Love reached across the space between their chairs, laid her hand on Jocie's, and waited until Jocie looked up at her. "But the Lord blessed you with a father who was willing to also be your mother. And he's been a good one. For that you can be thankful."

"I know," Jocie said. "Dad's the greatest."

"Gracious is the Lord." Aunt Love sat back and filled her lap with more beans.

Jocie concentrated on pulling the ends off a few beans. She didn't want to appear ungrateful for a good father. She really did thank the Lord for her father every day. Well, every time she prayed, which was nearly every day. Still, that didn't keep her from being curious about the woman who had given birth to her. After a moment, she said, "But even if I wouldn't change anything, I'm still curious about DeeDee. I don't remember much about her other than what her perfume smelled like." Jocie looked at Tabitha. "I mean, someday your baby might want to know more about his father. What he looked like or what he did."

Tabitha tightened her mouth before she said, "Or why he didn't stick around? I don't know what I'll say. There won't be much I can tell. His name is Jerome. He played drums with DeeDee's boyfriend's band. I fell in love with him the first time I saw him. I thought he loved me too, but if he did, he didn't love me enough. He didn't want to be a father."

"Do you still love him?" Jocie asked.

"No. I think the last little trace of love that hung on after he split on me drained out somewhere in Arkansas. I wouldn't have yelled a warning at him if he'd been standing in the middle of the road and hadn't seen the bus coming. I thought we'd never get through Arkansas. Twisty little roads up and down hills. I wanted to throw up every five minutes, but bus drivers don't stop for that. And the restrooms on those buses. They'd gag a maggot."

"As long as you didn't push him out in the road in front of the bus," Aunt Love said.

"I wouldn't have done that. At least, I don't think I would have. But I'll be just as happy if I never see him again."

"But isn't there something good about him you can tell the baby when she gets older?" Jocie asked.

"I'm sure there is." Tabitha broke up a handful of beans while she thought. "He was a good drummer. Really good. He could keep the beat going on any song. He had deep brown eyes. He laughed at stupid jokes. It was a good laugh, made other people smile just hearing it. Is that the kind of thing you're talking about?"

"I guess. It just seems like your mother or father should be a real person to you. And you'd think DeeDee would be real to me. She was here till I was five, but I can't remember much about her. If it wasn't for the picture in the living room, I probably wouldn't even be able to remember how she looked."

"She still looks sort of like that. Older, and she put some blond highlights in her hair to hide the gray, but that's about all. But ask me whatever you want. If I know the answer, I'll tell you."

Again Jocie concentrated on the beans in her lap. Strange how she couldn't think of a thing to ask. Now that she knew her mother had deserted her from day one instead of when she was five, she didn't seem to care whether she liked red or blue the best or what her favorite flower was. Jocie shoved her mother back into a closet in her mind as if she were an old game Jocie didn't care about playing anymore. "Thanks, Tabitha. If I think of anything, I'll ask."

For a while the only sounds between them were the snap of the beans and the creak of Aunt Love's rocker. Then Zeb jumped off the porch to chase a squirrel, and the mockingbird lit on the electric pole out beside the house and began running through his repertoire. Aunt Love asked Jocie if she remembered what David had preached on the day before and whether they'd washed the quart jars for the beans yet.

They didn't take the last canner full of beans off the stove until almost six. A whole day given over to beans. Twenty-one quarts of beans lined up on the counter to cool before she had to carry them to the cellar for storing till winter. Jocie hated going down

271

in the cold, dank cellar. There were no lights down there, and if the flashlight needed batteries, the way it usually did, she had to carry a candle that flickered and tried to go out every time she took a step while it cast spooky shadows on the walls.

Her father told her it built character to do things she didn't want to do, but she wasn't looking forward to five or six trips of character building to get all these jars to the cellar the next day. Maybe she could talk Tabitha into holding the candle or entice Zeb to go in the cellar with her to scare away any spiders hiding in and around the jars of pickles and apples left over from last year.

The next morning Aunt Love said she couldn't make biscuits till the jars of beans were out of the way. Jocie suggested toast, but Aunt Love just quoted some Bible verse about not putting off till tomorrow what needed to be done today. At least it sounded like a Bible verse. The flashlight was dim when Jocie switched it on as she went down the stone steps with her first load, but it was still better than a candle.

She didn't have anybody to help her. Not even Zeb, who was off hunting in Mr. Crutcher's hay field. Tabitha was still asleep, and Jocie couldn't ask Aunt Love, because she might fall down the steps and break a hip or something. Old ladies were always breaking hips. And her father was off praying somewhere.

He'd gotten another call from Matt McDermott about the church. They didn't want to fire him. They still wanted to hire him, except of course for Ogden Martin, who had never wanted to hire him in the first place. Jocie half hoped her father wouldn't decide the Lord was calling him to stay at Mt. Pleasant. She'd miss seeing Paulette, but she was sick of being nice to Ronnie Martin.

The temperature dropped a few degrees every step down into the cellar. Jocie started saying, "Yea, though I walk through the valley of the shadow of death." Then she thought of Aunt Love saying that as she held the bones of her long-dead baby and felt as if going into the cellar wasn't worthy of the same Scripture, so she started singing, "Yes, Jesus loves me." She changed the words a little. "He won't let the spiders get on my head. Yes, Jesus loves me."

Jocie kicked the wooden cellar door open as far as she could to let in a little extra light as she set the jars down in the space they always saved for the green beans. Tomatoes and apples on the left, pears and sauerkraut and pickles on the right, and green beans in the middle. She didn't bother counting how many jars were left from last year before she ran out of the dark cellar. Jezebel was peering down at her from the wall beside the steps. The cat waved her tail back and forth. "Jump on me now, cat, and I'll lock you in the cellar all day."

The cat meowed as if she knew Jocie was bluffing.

The flashlight went out on her last trip. The spiders over the door waiting to drop on her head got bigger. Snakes peered out from behind every jar. The shadows deepened and pointed fingers at her. But she was already in the cellar. She couldn't just drop the jars and run. She had to go through the dank air of the cellar and set the jars down one by one on the rock floor. She switched songs and started singing, "Do Lord, oh do Lord, oh do remember me."

She was out of the cellar in two seconds flat after the bottom of the last jar touched the floor. She ran over top of Jezebel, who had been lying in wait for her on the top step, and barreled into her father.

"Whoa," he said as he caught hold of her shoulders. "Where's the fire?"

"No fire." Jocie looked over her shoulder at the steps down to the cellar. "Just spiders and snakes and heaven only knows what else." Jocie ran her hands through her hair to shake out any stray spiders that might have a hitched a ride up the stairs.

Her father laughed. "There's absolutely nothing in that cellar that will hurt you."

273

"That's what you say."

"Have I ever lied to you?"

"But you don't know the things I can imagine," Jocie said, her heart slowing to a normal beat again. "And Jezebel was on the steps. She can hurt me."

Her father hugged her. "If I could protect you from all the Jezebels of the world, I would, but—"

"Yeah, I know. I have to develop character, and nobody can develop character if they have smooth sailing all the time. But if I could do the choosing, I'd rather develop character in the daylight and not in creepy old cellars."

"Tell you what. Next time we have stuff to carry down to the cellar, you can leave it till I can help you. We'll do the multiplication table while we carry the jars down. You won't have time to imagine anything bad."

"Ugh. Math. Spiders and snakes might be better."

"You'll get to take algebra next year. I can't believe my baby girl will be a freshman in high school."

It seemed the perfect opening. "Yeah, Dad. I need to get some clothes before school starts. Do you think Tabitha would go shopping with me next time you go to Grundy? Just for a few things. You know, some of the basics I can't get at the Fashion Shop uptown."

"That's a great idea. Leigh might even like to go along. She's from over in Grundy, you know, so she'd know which stores were best."

"Yeah, that would be great." Jocie really didn't care who went along as long as she didn't have to ask the prune-faced ladies at the Fashion Shop to show her the boxes of bras. Still, she couldn't keep from asking, "Is she going to be like one of the family now?"

"Let's just say a friend of the family right now," her father said. "You do like her okay, don't you?"

"She makes great brownies."

"She does. And she's nice in other ways too. She handled things at church pretty good Sunday."

"What things?"

"Oh, people staring at her, adding two and two and coming up with five. That sort of thing." Her father took off his wet shoes and set them by the door into the kitchen. "Did you get that story about the 4-H Club summer projects finished for the paper today?"

"Don't I always beat my deadlines?"

"You do. Always. I don't know what I'd do without you."

Jocie hugged him. "Thank you for wanting me, Daddy."

"What brought that on?" her father asked.

"Tabitha told me that my mother—that DeeDee—didn't want me. That she gave me to you and never did anything for me."

"She shouldn't have told you that."

"I asked her to tell me the truth. It was the truth, wasn't it?"

"Well, yes. Your mother wasn't happy when she found out you were on the way. I wanted more children, but she didn't. Still, there are some things better not told."

"But isn't it better to know the truth? I mean, my mother didn't want me. Plain and simple."

"Nothing is ever that simple." Her father frowned and asked, "What else did Tabitha tell you?"

"Nothing." Jocie studied her father's face. "Is there more that I should know?" Her father turned away from her and picked up his town shoes. "I'm sure there are lots of things neither of us know about your mother. Things better left unknown. Now, I think I smell something burning. We'd better go rescue breakfast."

34

They had the paper ready to run by noon. Nothing very newsworthy had happened in Hollyhill since the last issue. Then, as Wes was fond of pointing out, nothing very newsworthy had happened in Hollyhill since he'd been there except the tornado that blew through town in '59.

This week the weather had been calm, so about the most exciting thing in the *Banner* was old Mr. Petrey running up on the curb in front of Haskell's Drugs. Nobody had been hurt, but the parking meter had been bent over double. When Jocie's father had run up the street to take a picture, Mr. Petrey had been bent over trying to put his nickel in the meter before going in to pick up his medicine. Wes had said they ought to run that picture, but Zella had reminded them that Mr. Petrey had ten kids and twenty-nine grandkids and who knew how many great-grandkids, and most of them were *Banner* subscribers. So they'd just run the picture of the sheriff and Mr. Petrey looking over the damage.

Jocie had finally gotten to use her parade picture of Heather Boyd's collie with her 4-H story. The mayor and the city council had argued over Christmas decorations for the street. Mayor Palmor had accused the council members of not having any town spirit because they refused to vote for new lights, and the council members had accused the mayor of being reckless with the taxpayers' money. The Downtown Merchants' Association was advertising "Sidewalk Days." Her father had taken a whole roll of film of kids playing softball at the community park. They had wedding announcements, just-born baby pictures, summer revival ads. Regular, routine stuff.

"This sucker will put the press to sleep it's so dull," Wes said as he got the first page ready to run. They hadn't run more than ten copies when Wes stopped the press. "I hear something that ain't right, and it ain't snoring."

"I didn't hear anything," Jocie said.

"That's because you don't have Jupiterian ears," Wes said.

"Neither do you. Tabitha says you're from Illinois or Ohio."

"People just listen to half the story and think they've got the truth. Fact is, Illinois and Ohio are outer regions on the westernmost part of Jupiter's frontier. I guess being raised out there on the edge is what made me sign up for space travel. Then I get down here and you Earth people have copied half our names. Course, who knows? Could be some of my folks got stranded down here and started up settlements."

Jocie laughed. "You're never going to tell me the truth, are you?"

"I always tell you the truth, and the truth right now is that if we don't oil down this old boy, something might break big time and the folks would have to do without all the news that is the news in Hollyhill." Wes picked up his oil can. "Uh-uh. Not near enough. You'd better go up the street and get some more at the hardware store. No telling when your dad will come back in from the courthouse now that he's found out a certain somebody down there will laugh at his jokes."

"Yeah, it's getting serious."

"Dang right, it's serious. I don't get this press moving soon, we'll be here all night, and I'm right in the middle of the latest Rex Stout mystery and I ain't figured out who done it yet."

"I didn't mean the press. I meant Leigh and Dad. He invited her to church Sunday morning."

"You don't say. You think he was trying to scare her off?" Wes said.

"Nobody stared too much. They were all staring at Tabitha."

"She went too, huh?"

"I think because of Aunt Love. To make her feel better, you know. She thought Aunt Love would be sad, because of us finding the baby and everything."

"And she's not?" Wes squirted some oil on one of the gears.

"She wore a red hat to church Sunday."

Wes looked around. "A red hat? Your Aunt Love?"

"She's different. I mean, she still can't remember to take the biscuits out of the oven, but it's like she's remembered something more important."

"What's that?"

"I don't know. Maybe that the Bible says there's a time to laugh as well as a time to cry."

"Your Aunt Love quote that one to you?"

"She has before. It's in Ecclesiastes. Aunt Love practically knows that book by heart. But you know, now that I think about it, she hasn't been bashing me over the head with Scripture all that much this week. All she wants to talk about is Tabitha's baby coming. She's not worried a whit about what the church people or anybody else in Hollyhill might think. It's like she forgot who she used to be."

"Then again, Jo, maybe you never really knew who she used to be." Wes looked over his shoulder at her again. "She lived a lot of her life before you even discovered America. There's a lot you can never know about her."

"Or about you," Jocie said.

"Now, we ain't talking about me. We're talking about your Aunt Love."

"But you lived a lot of your life before you came to Hollyhill."

"Mostly just cruising around in spaceships. Don't much happen in spaceships. It's like when you're on vacation and you're looking out at the scenery and saying, 'Wow, look at that,' but you don't really do anything. You just look. Until, of course, you fall out."

"But you had your years on Jupiter."

"Not a bit interesting to Earth people. Sort of like this news here." Wes waved at the paper they had ready to run. "Only a Hollyhiller would ever think about reading more than two lines of this snooze news. I ain't even sure why they would, but they do expect to get something in their mailboxes on Wednesdays. So we mustn't disappoint them. Now run on up the street and get me some more oil and maybe a grease gun while you're at it. Nero Wolfe is waiting."

Once he had the oil, Wes worked his usual magic and had the press purring as it spit out the pages of the *Banner*. Jocie didn't think a thing about it when Leigh dropped by after work to help finish up folding the papers. It was as if she was part of the crew now. And maybe part of the family. Her dad said they'd all be going to Grundy the next day after lunch. Tabitha had to do some blood tests at the doctor's office, and Leigh was more than willing to help Jocie shop for school. And then they might just all go out to eat. Aunt Love was even thinking about going.

Zella overheard the plans and said, "Well, my word, David, why don't you ask me and Wesley along too?"

"Well, I would, Zella, but I don't think we have any more room in the car," he said. "I'll tell you what. You could ride over with Wes on his motorcycle."

Zella rolled her eyes. "I don't know what Leigh sees in you."

"Me either," he agreed.

"It's okay, Zella," Leigh said. "I love to go shopping."

"I think you might as well leave David at home," Zella said.

"Oh, no. He's paying for dinner," Leigh said.

Later Leigh caught Jocie alone as they bundled up the papers. "Do you think going to Grundy tomorrow can count as a date?"

"Closer than Sunday morning church," Jocie said. "But maybe not quite there yet. But then again, I'm no expert. Maybe you'd better ask Zella. She seems to know the rules. You think she used to have a boyfriend?"

"Who knows? After the last couple of weeks, I'm ready to believe anything is possible," Leigh said.

"Maybe you picked the wrong guy to make eyes at. The Lord seems to have overloaded Dad with family blessings."

"I don't think anybody can ever have an overload of blessings. I just want your father to start counting me in those blessings." She looked over to where David was helping Wes load the papers on the cart. He must have felt her eyes on him, because he looked around and smiled. Leigh's face lit up as if she'd just opened a gift she'd been wanting for months.

Jocie didn't know whether she was trying to encourage or discourage Leigh when she said, "Don't you have to have a goodnight kiss for it to be a real date?"

Leigh's cheeks turned red. "I haven't kissed a boy since I was in eighth grade and we played spin the bottle at one of the kids' houses. I won't know how."

Jocie took pity on her. "Dad won't be in practice either. You'll be in the same boat."

Leigh laughed. "The same boat sounds nice."

"Even with all the rest of us in there too?"

"Especially with all the rest of you in there too," Leigh said. "Instant family. I'm an only child, and I've always wanted more family."

The next day Jocie made a list of things she'd need for school. New shoes, socks, skirts and blouses, bras. Maybe she'd just hand the list to Leigh so she wouldn't have to ask out loud. Still, she'd already talked to Leigh about her and her dad kissing. Talking about bras should be a piece of cake after that.

She had her list finished and rewritten twice by nine o'clock. She couldn't just sit around watching Aunt Love knit and Tabitha nap till her father showed up after lunch, so she rode her bike into town to help Wes clean the press or something.

But Wes wasn't there. He had taken a piece off the press to the welding shop for repairs. Her father was gone too, out to Hungry Run Road to take pictures of Harvey Smith's tobacco field that had been hit by a hailstorm the night before. That just left Zella, who put Jocie to work stuffing envelopes with subscription renewal notices so she could pump her about how the stepmother quest was going.

"So I hear your father invited Leigh to church last Sunday," Zella said as she handed Jocie a pile of renewal notices.

"Dad invites lots of people to church every week. That's part of his job."

"Every Christian's job, in fact," Zella agreed. "But he doesn't invite Leigh to his church every Sunday. How did it go?"

"You mean church? Fine, I guess," Jocie said before licking an envelope and sealing it. "I don't know. Like church always goes, I suppose."

"But at least your father asked her. That's a huge step forward for him. Of course, it would be better if he invited her on a picnic. Just the two of them with a wicker basket full of food, some lemonade, and a blanket to sit on." Zella got a dreamy look on her face and sighed. "Now that would be romantic."

"Did you ever go on a picnic like that?" Jocie asked.

Zella's eyes narrowed. "I could have if I'd wanted to. I never wanted to."

"Maybe Dad doesn't want to either." Jocie folded another renewal notice. "And even if he did, knowing his luck, something would go wrong. There'd be ants, or he'd forget the glasses for the lemonade, or there would be a bull who didn't want to share his pasture."

"Or you'd decide to go along so you could mess things up," Zella said.

"What makes you think I'd want to mess things up? I like Leigh. She's going to teach me to dance."

"Dance? If she teaches anybody to dance, it should be your father."

"I don't think preachers do much dancing," Jocie said.

"Then neither should preachers' daughters."

"Of course, Dad might not be a preacher much longer. He's trying to decide whether to stay on at Mt. Pleasant. Some of them still want him to stay, and some of them don't since they found out about Tabitha having a baby."

"Tabitha has a baby?" Zella's voice sounded stretched and thin.

"Well, not yet, but she's going to. In a few months. I'm sorry. I figured somebody had told you. Like, maybe Leigh." Jocie peeked at Zella over the top of the envelope she was licking. She should have let her father tell her, but it was sort of fun causing Zella to go into shock mode. "She knows. But just since Sunday. It was a surprise to her too."

"My word! She's just like Adrienne."

Jocie was suddenly more interested. "What do you mean, like my mother? She didn't have a baby before she was married."

The top of Zella's cheeks turned pink. She snatched a tissue out of the box on her desk and dabbed her nose. "Well, no, I didn't say that she did." Zella crumpled the tissue and tossed it toward the trash can. She didn't seem to notice that she missed. "But she didn't exactly show much respect for the institution of matrimony."

"You mean because she ran off and left Dad?" Jocie had never seen Zella so rattled. She'd actually touched her hair and knocked a curl out of place.

"These are questions you should ask your father."

"But you knew her, didn't you? I mean, she grew up here in Hollyhill, didn't she?"

"Oh, I knew her all right." Zella got a mirror out of her desk drawer and carefully smoothed down her hair. "Everybody in Hollyhill knew Adrienne, but she didn't have much time for the likes of me." Zella looked over the mirror at Jocie. "I mean, if it hadn't been for me, your father would have gone broke that first year after he took over the *Banner*. Just ask him. He'll tell you it's so, but did she have any appreciation for what I did? Oh no. She never even bothered getting my name straight. Always called me Stella."

"You didn't like her?"

"Well, no, if you must know, I didn't. Not that she cared one bit if I did. Or if any other woman liked her. Now, if I'd have worn pants, that might have been different."

"Are you saying she liked men better than women?"

Zella peered into the mirror another minute before carefully placing it back into the drawer and pushing the drawer closed. "I told you these are things you should ask your father, although heaven knows he'd never say anything bad about anybody, not even Adrienne after all she did to him."

"What did she do to him? I mean, besides leaving."

"Leaving was the nicest thing she ever did to him," Zella said. "Now, I'm not answering one more question about your mother. We didn't get along. She wasn't good to your father, or to you for that matter, but my mother taught me that if I couldn't say something good about somebody to not say anything at all, so that's what I'm going to do. Not say anything at all."

"You can say whatever you want," Jocie said. "It won't bother me. Tabitha has already told me that my mother didn't want me. What could be worse than that? I'm just curious about her. Wouldn't you be curious about your mother if you didn't already know her?"

"Some things are better not known."

"Like what?" Jocie asked.

"Like lots of things."

"Dad always says it's better to know the truth."

"Then he can tell it to you."

"What do you mean?"

"I mean you ask too many questions. The very idea of trying to get me to tell you things a child of your age shouldn't even be thinking about." Zella picked up one of the renewal notices and began fanning herself with it. "And telling me Tabitha is having a baby without the least bit of embarrassment."

"I'm not embarrassed about it. I think it'll be fun to have a baby around."

"Well, at least nobody can blame your father for not raising her right since she's been gone these many years. Seven or eight, isn't it?"

"Seven. I guess he won't have that excuse with me."

"Heaven knows what he'll have to live down with you," Zella said. "You act like a heathen half the time as it is."

"I go to church two or three times a week."

"Going to church isn't always the answer. Your mother went to church."

"She doesn't now. Tabitha said she hadn't been to church since she left Hollyhill. I can't imagine."

"Well, I should say not. Nor should you imagine such a thing. Not if you want to be a good Christian girl."

"A week off every now and again wouldn't be so bad," Jocie said, mostly just to aggravate Zella.

"Dear Lord, deliver me." Zella rolled her eyes.

"I'm sorry, Zella. I know I'm being a pest. I'll get lost if you want me to."

"That would be an answer to prayer, but you aren't leaving until you finish those envelopes. Then when you're done with that, you can run up and get some coffee at the store. If I'm going to have to put up with you, you might as well be useful. Besides, now that you've told me about Tabitha, you'll have to tell me how she's doing and when the baby's due and if she's picked out a name, and what about the father?"

"She's fine. October. Stephanie Grace. And you'll have to ask Tabitha about the father. All I know is he had nice eyes."

"How in the world do you know that? About his eyes." Zella frowned at her. "He is in California, isn't he?"

"I don't know where he is. I don't think Tabitha does either, but the only good thing she could think of to tell me was that he had nice eyes. And that he was a good drummer. But she's going to be here this afternoon. You can get her to tell you anything else you want to know."

"Oh, that's right. The family expedition to Grundy. Lord help him, maybe David will remember how to treat a woman before Leigh gets fed up."

"She said she likes having instant family."

"There's family, and then there's family." Zella reached into a side drawer and pulled out a couple of dollar bills. "Here, never mind those envelopes. Go on and get the coffee before you have to go to Grundy. Who knows what Wesley might do if he doesn't have his coffee. You know he's bound to be running from the law somewhere."

"So you think he might kill somebody if the coffee runs out?"

"I'm not saying he would. I'm just saying it isn't a chance I want to take."

35

Jocie had the coffee and was on the way back to the *Banner* when she spotted old Sallie in a rickety folding chair out in front of the Grill strumming his guitar. His hat was upside down in front of his feet in case anybody was feeling generous. She hadn't seen him for a few days, so she crossed over to see if he was okay.

"Hey, Sallie. How's things going? You haven't been sick, have you?" She stayed back several steps. It wasn't good to get too close to Sallie.

"Not sick, just old." Sallie strummed his guitar a couple of times before he started singing. "I like pie. I like cake, but I ain't got no dough. No dough, no dough, dough, dough."

"Okay, I get the message. If I'm going to listen, I have to come up with the dough." Jocie dropped the change she had from the coffee into his hat. Zella would yell, but her dad wouldn't care.

"Dough, dough, dough. Do, re, me. Me, me, me." Sallie grinned at her as he tuned up his voice. "I was born in Hollyhill where folks know my name. I was born in Hollyhill where nobody cares. I was born in Hollyhill where we're all the same. I was born in Hollyhill where nobody cares."

Ronnie Martin and Jesse Smith came out of the Grill in time to hear old Sallie's song. "You've got that right, old man," Ronnie said. "Nobody cares. Everybody wishes you'd just go on and die. The sooner the better."

Sallie kept grinning and strumming, but he hooked his foot out and pulled his hat under his chair. Without missing a beat, he changed songs. "Nobody knows the trouble I've seen. Nobody knows but Jesus."

"And he's going to see you have some more," Ronnie said as he grabbed Sallie's chair and shook it. Jesse tried to snatch the old man's hat out from under the chair, but Sallie grabbed it up, bent the straw hat double, and stuffed it under his thigh.

Jocie grabbed Ronnie's arm. "Leave him alone," she said.

Sallie was still singing. "I see trouble. Trouble coming. Trouble coming down the road."

Ronnie looked at Jocie as if he hadn't even noticed she was there until she'd grabbed him. He changed targets. "Well, well, if it isn't Miss I Love Doggies preacher's kid. Course, your daddy isn't going to be preacher much longer."

Jocie counted to ten. She wasn't worried about being nice to Ronnie. She was just trying to keep from swinging the coffee can at his head. "Nothing you or your father can do or say will keep my father from being a preacher."

"Maybe he needs to do less preaching at church and more preaching at home," Ronnie said with a sneer. "I hear your sister has a bun in the oven. A little bastard bun."

Behind him, Jesse giggled and Sallie changed songs to "Rock-a-Bye, Baby." Jocie stopped counting and began rumpling the top of the sack that held the coffee can to get a better hold before she took a swipe at Ronnie's head. "I think you'd better quit talking about my sister."

"Oh yeah, what are you going to do about it?" Ronnie laughed and looked over at Jesse. "I'll bet she doesn't even know what *bastard* means, even if she's nothing but a bastard herself."

Sallie stopped singing. Jesse stopped giggling and said, "Come on, Ronnie. We'd better go."

Ronnie laughed. "What's the matter, Jesse? You ain't feeling sorry for her, are you? But then maybe we should feel sorry for her, seeing as how she don't have the first idea who her real father is. That's what a bastard is. Somebody who doesn't have a father."

A terrible stillness came over Jocie. Everything seemed to freeze in place and be surrounded by bold lines as if they had stepped into a scene in a comic book. Sallie was holding his guitar up over his heart as if to protect himself and staring at her with big round eyes. Jesse was up on his toes as if he wanted to run. Ronnie was smiling at her, an awful smile full of teeth. A blood red pimple was popping out on his chin. She wanted to smash him in the face with the coffee can, but she couldn't lift her arms. The air around her was pressing against her, making it hard to breath.

She heard Jesse's words as if they came through a tunnel. "What are you talking about, Ronnie? She ain't no bastard. She's your preacher's kid."

Sallie started singing again. No words, just a mournful moaning sound. Jocie hardly noticed.

"That ain't what my father says. He says her mama broke up my aunt's marriage nine months before this poor excuse for a girl was born. My aunt kicked her husband's sorry butt out, but not the preacher man. He pretended like nothing whatever had happened. He even pretended the bastard baby was his own." Ronnie's eyes bored into Jocie. "My daddy says some folks can carry turning the other cheek too far."

Old Sallie started singing "Amazing Grace" as loud as he could. Jocie gripped the top of the grocery sack so hard it tore. "You're lying," she said.

"You think so? Why don't you ask your pretend-like daddy? He wouldn't lie, now would he? Being a preacher and all." Ronnie grinned at her. "Or ask old Sallie here. I'll bet he knows. Old Sallie knows lots of things about people in Hollyhill that they'd just as soon nobody ever knew, don't you, Sallie? I dare you. Ask him."

Old Sallie wouldn't meet Jocie's eyes. He just started in on a new verse of "Amazing Grace," singing louder than ever and banging his hand against his guitar to keep time.

She didn't ask him anything. It would have been a betrayal of her father. She looked back at Ronnie. "You don't know anything. My father has never lied to me."

"Maybe not. But then again, maybe he's just never told you the truth, the whole truth, nothing but the truth, so help him God."

"You wouldn't know the truth if it hit you in the face," Jocie said. "And I hope it does. I hope it knocks you down and stomps on you."

"Looks to me like you're the one getting stomped on," Ronnie said.

Jocie whirled away from him to stalk away. There wasn't any more to say. He was lying. Plain and simple. He was just making up stories about her because his family hadn't been able to chase her father away from Mt. Pleasant. So what if everybody in Hollyhill acted as if she'd asked them to grab hold of a hot poker every time she mentioned her mother. That didn't mean anything. There was no doubt who her mother was whether she'd wanted Jocie or not.

There was no doubt who her father was either. None whatsoever. She didn't have the first doubt about that. *But you don't look like your father or your mother*, a little voice whispered in a back corner of her mind. And Zella had acted strange that morning talking about her mother. But Zella had been born strange, and lots of kids didn't look that much like their parents. Who was Ronnie Martin's aunt anyway? Maybe more important—who was her husband?

Jocie shook her head. This was stupid. Ronnie Martin could say whatever he wanted. She knew who her father was. There was no need for her heart to start beating funny inside her. No need at all. Nothing he'd said had been true. Nothing.

She could ask Wes. She could ask Wes anything. He'd tell her she was being stupid, but at least he'd tell her. His words would push Ronnie Martin's words right out of her ears, and then everything would be okay. She'd tell Wes what Ronnie had said, and Wes would say Ronnie should be sent to Neptune, and they'd laugh and figure out how to get him there.

But when she got back to the *Banner* offices, Wes was still gone. Tabitha and Aunt Love were in the chairs in front of Zella's desk waiting for her father to get back from picking Leigh up at the courthouse so they could leave for Grundy. Zella was smiling too big and sneaking peeks at Tabitha's waistline.

Jocie set the sack with the coffee in it down on Zella's desk.

"Where's the change?" Zella asked.

"I gave it to old Sallie. He was hungry."

"Hungry, my foot. He probably has hundreds of dollars stuffed in his mattress at the county poorhouse," Zella said.

"He didn't say anything about me, did he?" Tabitha asked a bit uneasily.

"Nope. He just sang. Ronnie Martin wasn't as nice. He called me a bastard," Jocie said.

Zella sucked in her breath at the word, and Aunt Love frowned as she said, "Put off the filthy communication out of your mouth."

"I didn't say it. He did." Once Jocie started talking she didn't seem to be able to stop. "He said my mother broke up his aunt's marriage."

Zella looked down at her desk, and Aunt Love seemed to be thumbing through her mind to come up with another Bible verse. Only Tabitha looked her straight in the eye. "She probably did, Jocie. DeeDee never worried much about who was married to who."

Jocie didn't want to keep looking at Tabitha. She didn't want to keep talking to her. She wanted Wes to be there. She wanted to talk to Wes about sending Ronnie Martin to Neptune. Jocie swallowed and licked her lips. Finally she said, "But it isn't true what he said."

"He shouldn't have called you a bastard," Tabitha said.

"But it isn't true what he said," Jocie said again.

Tabitha didn't say anything. She just looked at Jocie. She had tears in her eyes.

"Tell me it isn't true what he said," Jocie said again.

"Do you want the truth?" Tabitha asked softly.

"No!" Jocie screamed.

36

She didn't know how she got out of the building and on her bike. She spotted her father coming up the street with Leigh and spun her bike around the other direction. He yelled at her, but she just pedaled harder. She couldn't see him now. She couldn't hear him telling her the truth. She couldn't hear the truth. How could that be the truth?

She pedaled faster. Once out of town, she swerved across the road. Two cars honked at her and the third almost hit her, but she made it onto the side street. She didn't even know what street she'd turned on. She just wanted to get away from the cars, away from Hollyhill, away from her father.

He was her father. He had to be her father. But then why was she running away? Why hadn't she stopped and asked him? Why was she afraid of the truth?

What seemed like hours later, she had no idea where she was as she rode along a narrow, winding strip of blacktop between grass and weeds as high as the fence tops on the side of the road. No cars had passed her for a good while, and she hadn't even seen a house for what must have been a couple of miles. She did pass a field where a farmer was mowing hay, but he was watching his mower and didn't notice her. She didn't recognize him.

She was glad it was hot. Glad she was thirsty. Glad the muscles in her legs were burning. That gave her something to think about. She felt a little dizzy, but she kept pedaling. Her shadow was behind her. That must mean she was going west now, but who knew what direction she'd started out. North out of Hollyhill, she supposed, since she'd turned off North Main, but she had no idea how many times she'd turned since then. It didn't matter. She didn't want to go back. Not yet, anyway. Maybe never.

So she just kept riding, coasting down a steep road carved into the side of a rocky, tree-covered slope. There was no sign of people. She stopped at the bottom of the hill and heard water running in a creek not far from the road. Birds were singing their summer songs. A bee buzzed by her ear. She didn't hear the faintest sound of traffic or the faraway whistle of a train or even the drone of an airplane overhead. She was totally alone. Lost and alone. And very thirsty.

She pushed her bike off the road in behind a thick growth of stinkweed, careful not to touch the weeds. She pulled her shirt up over her nose and held her breath to block out the sickening odor of the white blooms and hurried along a faint path that led through the bushes to the creek. There were probably snakes, but she didn't care. She didn't even care if the water made her puke. She cupped her hand under a rivulet flowing over some limestone rocks and took a drink. Then she sat down in the middle of the creek and watched the water run over her tennis shoes. She wished Zeb was with her. Then maybe she wouldn't feel so alone.

The limestone rock was flat and smooth under her bottom. The water swirling gently past her was clear and cool. Tree limbs hung down over the creek, but here and there the sun pushed through to spark off the water. Up ahead of her the creek curved to the right, which would take it closer to the road. She wondered if this was the creek where they'd washed the car a few summers ago. A gravel road had passed right through the water. Her father had turned off the road and stopped the car in the middle of the creek. They'd scooped water up in buckets to throw over the car. Her father had slipped on the mossy rocks and fallen in. Then since he'd fallen down, she had too, on purpose. Their laughter echoed in her head until she wanted to put her hands over her ears, but that wouldn't stop what was inside her head. No more than she could block out the awful things Ronnie Martin had said or the shine of tears in Tabitha's eyes when she couldn't say it wasn't true.

But how could it be true? How could her father not be her father?

She ran her fingers through the water. Maybe she ought to pray, but what good would it do? Whatever the truth was, she couldn't change it. She supposed God could, because nothing was impossible with God. A camel could go through the eye of a needle. A virgin could have a baby. Lazarus could come out of the grave. But she'd never heard of God changing who anybody's father was. She splashed some water on her face and let it drip off.

Maybe it wasn't true. People liked to start stories in Hollyhill. Her father had always said she shouldn't listen to gossip. And now she had and here she was in the middle of a creek, her shorts soaking wet, with not the first idea of where she was. Or who she was.

She looked down at the water. A crawdad poked his head out from under a rock. Jocie sat very still as the crawdad came toward her with his claws raised. She wasn't sure if he thought she was just a big rock or supper. She stuck her finger slowly down in the water in front of him. He stopped and then hightailed it back under his rock. She picked the rock up, and he disappeared under another rock. She started to follow him, to keep picking up his hiding places and make him keep running, but then she put the first rock back in the same place.

The sunlight faded. Jocie thought it was just getting late until thunder sounded in the distance and black clouds rolled in above the treetops. She remembered another story when a flash flood had ripped down the very same creek where they'd washed their car and taken out trees and barns along the creek. They'd put pictures in the *Banner*. Wes had said it was almost as newsy as the '59 tornado. It was hard to believe that such a gentle creek could turn into something that could uproot trees.

She stayed in the middle of the creek. The clouds overhead were getting blacker by the second. The thunder boomed louder. She imagined a wall of water coming around the curve in the creek toward her, washing away her hiding place.

And her with it. She imagined herself bouncing in the flood water, being thrown against rocks and trees. The storm swept closer. Lightning lit up the sky. She counted one one thousand, two one thousand, three one thousand, four one thousand. The thunder sounded. The tree limbs began dipping down into the water and then up toward the sky as if they could shake free of the wind ripping through them.

Jocie stood up. Water dripped out of her shorts. She might want to keep hiding, but she didn't want to just sit there and wash away downstream.

"Good-bye, little crawdad," she said before sloshing out of the creek and back out to where her bike was hidden.

She pushed her bike up the hill. The whole sky was black now with a layer of gray clouds racing around under the heavy storm clouds as if trying to find a place to jump in and join the game. A streak of lightning popped down toward the ground in front of her.

If Jocie had been home, she'd have been out on the porch, watching the lightning and counting the seconds till the thunder sounded. She liked the way the wind threw raindrops under the porch roof into her face. She liked how the rain pounding down on the tin roof of their house shut out every other noise. If Aunt Love came to the door to yell at her to get in the house, she'd go inside and pretend to go up to her room before she sneaked back out the side door under the eave. But she'd never been totally out in the open in the middle of a storm. And wasn't there something about metal drawing lightning? She started to ditch her bicycle, but she was almost to the top of the hill. She'd make better time to shelter on her bike. There was nothing but trees here.

She couldn't take shelter under a tree. Just last summer the *Banner* had run a picture of Mr. Anderson's cows after lightning had struck the tree they were under. Five big black-and-white cows in a circle around the tree. Five big dead cows.

All at once rain came down in a sheet. She wished a car would come by. Somebody who would give her a ride somewhere. But no car appeared out of the rain, so she kept pushing her bike on up the road against the wind. The lightning flashed so close she saw spots. She didn't have time for even one one thousand before the thunder crashed. Surely there was a barn around here where she could wait out the storm.

That was something she could pray for. A barn. *Dear Lord, you know everything. You know I'm not usually afraid of storms, but this one's different. I mean, I know I ran from the truth, but it just doesn't seem right that lightning might strike me without me finding out. Anyway, I'm not asking for much. Just any kind of old barn, and I'll try not to complain if it has snakes.*

She stood still a moment and waited for the Lord to answer some way she could see, like a fork of lightning pointing to the left or right, but nothing happened except more thunder and lightning and the rain pounding down harder. She was at the top of the hill now, and the road leveled out. So she got on her bike. She was riding straight into the rain and could hardly see five feet in front of her. She tried not to think of anything except pushing the pedals on her bike. There had to be a house or a barn somewhere.

She was about ready to just plop down in the ditch beside the road when a flash of light lit up a building up ahead. Not a barn. A church. The sign out front said Clay's Creek Baptist Church.

Wasn't her father always saying that the Lord sometimes answered your prayers better than you expected?

The front door was locked. Jocie was pushing on the side door when lightning flashed so close she could smell it. She screamed, but the sound was lost in the boom that shook the ground. With her eyes shut against the blinding light, she shoved hard against the door. It popped open. She slammed it shut behind her. The wind pushing against the building sounded even louder than it had while she was outside in the middle of it.

It was dark inside the church. Jocie flipped one of the switches in the narrow hallway, but nothing happened. The storm must have knocked out the electricity. Slowly her eyes adjusted to the dim light between lightning flashes.

She'd been in a lot of churches but never all by herself. Her father had always been there with her. In spite of the storm still raging outside, it felt almost too quiet inside. Ghosts were watching her.

Church ghosts, she told herself firmly. They couldn't be too mean. Just curious, maybe. Church people were always curious. Especially about the preacher's family. How old are you? What's your name? Are you your daddy's little helper? Do you like Sunday school? Can you sing "Jesus Loves Me"? Where's your mother? Do you make good grades in school? What do you want to be when you grow up? A preacher's wife?

Right now she just wanted to be the preacher's daughter.

37

"Dear Lord, help me know which way she went," David prayed as he drove. He knew she'd gone north out of town. Jeffrey Wilkerson had waved him down on Court Street to tell him he'd almost hit Jocie when she'd swerved right out in front of him onto Bale Street. Jeffrey had been red in the face, and his hands had been shaking. "You need to tell your girl to pay attention when she's on that bike. I could have killed her," he'd said.

David hadn't had time to appease him. He'd just hoped Jocie's guardian angels were still keeping up with her as he headed toward Bale. A dozen other streets turned off it and wound around every direction, so he'd had no idea which way to go from there. The others were out searching too. Wes on his motorcycle. Leigh with Tabitha riding shotgun. Even Zella was helping. She'd taken Aunt Love home in case Jocie showed up there or called, and then she'd gone back to the office to call everybody she could think of to see if anybody else had spotted Jocie on her bike so they could narrow down the search area.

He hadn't called the sheriff. He thought he'd find her and talk to her and everything would be okay. At least as okay as it could be after what the Martin boy had told her. Why had she believed it? Why hadn't she asked him what the truth was?

She was his daughter. Had always been his daughter from the first day he knew she was growing in Adrienne's womb. It didn't matter what Adrienne said. What she'd obviously told Tabitha. Jocie was his daughter.

He'd known about the man in Grundy, but he'd never known his name. Hadn't wanted to know his name. What good would it have done? He didn't plan to ever confront the man, accuse him of destroying his marriage. It wouldn't have been true anyway. His marriage had gone belly-up long before that. There were times when he doubted if he and Adrienne had ever had a marriage, just the illusion of one that he'd held in his mind through the end of the war before he came home and they tried to live together.

So he'd known but he hadn't known. He'd thought it was better that way. He'd never wanted the other man to have a face in case someday the man was in a church where he was preaching. He'd never given the first thought to the other man's family. The pain and betrayal they might have felt. He supposed now, when he thought about it, that he assumed the other man's family wouldn't know. Of course, he should have known better. Adrienne had probably found a way to tell the man's wife herself just as she had told David the day he'd caught her concocting the poison she hoped would end the pregnancy. "What do you care?" she'd screamed at him after he'd knocked the stuff out of her hand. "It's not even yours."

She'd told him again the day she'd handed the baby to him to raise. "Now we'll see if you can live what you preach. You wanted her, so you can have her. But she's not yours. Some other seed made her."

But Adrienne was wrong. Jocie was his in every way that mattered. Even if she wasn't the seed of his loins, she was the seed of his heart. He'd never thought once that she was not his. Never once. Maybe he should have. Maybe if he had, he would have been able to prepare her. He should have known that nothing stayed secret in Hollyhill forever. Not if more than one person knew about it.

He was driving aimlessly, turning down one road and then another with not the least idea of whether he was going in the right direction or in circles. Of course, Jocie could be going in circles too. He knew her mind must be.

Why hadn't it been Wes or him she'd seen first? Why did it have to be Tabitha?

Tabitha had been crying when he'd gone in the *Banner* offices to see why Jocie had taken off on her bike like a swarm of bees was after her. Aunt Love had been patting Tabitha's hand murmuring something that could have been Bible verses. He wasn't sure. Zella had practically attacked him as soon as he'd come through the door.

"You should have already told the poor child. You had to know she'd find out sooner or later," she'd said.

"Told who what?" David had asked.

"That you aren't really her father," Zella had said.

"Not really whose father?"

"Honestly, David, sometimes you keep your head too far up in the clouds."

"I don't know what you're talking about." He really hadn't.

Zella had rolled her eyes and sighed heavily. "I really believe you don't. Jocelyn! I'm talking about Jocelyn."

"What about Jocie? What's wrong with her? She took off on her bike like she'd heard the school was on fire or something."

"She saw that horrid Martin boy up in town, and he called her a bastard. Told her you weren't her father. I wouldn't have even thought she knew what that meant, but she reads everything she can get her hands on. No telling where . . ."

Zella had kept talking, but David had stopped listening. He'd gone cold all over. "Jocie is my daughter," he'd said quietly.

Zella had looked at him. "Well, I know she is in every way that really counts. She couldn't have a better father, but everybody knows that Adrienne was messing around with Ogden Martin's sister's husband over in Grundy before she was born. And Adrienne told me herself there was a good reason Jocelyn didn't look like you. I remember the very day. Jocelyn was asleep in the playpen beside your desk, but you had gone up the street to the fiscal court meeting. I don't know where Tabitha was. Anyway, Adrienne had come in to get some money. That's the only reason she ever came in—to see if I had any money in the petty cash drawer. I always gave it to her to get rid of her. I figured I could buy a can of coffee out of my own pocket easier than I could put up with her."

"I don't care about coffee," David had said.

Zella had mashed her lips together for a second before she nodded and said, "I suppose not. Anyway, Adrienne wanted me to know you'd been cuckolded. Said I could put it in the paper if I wanted to. Of course, I didn't want to. I was glad when she left Hollyhill."

"Jocie is my daughter," David had repeated. "Adrienne may have never been my wife, but Tabitha and Jocie are my daughters."

Tabitha had looked up. "I'm sorry, Dad. I should have lied, but she asked me, and I only knew what DeeDee told me."

"Why would she tell you such a thing?" David had asked.

"I don't know. We'd get a letter from you asking us to come home, and she'd go berserk. She'd tear it up into little pieces and throw the pieces up in the air like confetti and do her freedom dance. She'd say that she didn't even want to think about Hollyhill or you ever again." Tabitha had peeked up at him as though worried that her words would upset him.

He hadn't been upset. Just impatient. She needed him to listen to her, but he needed to find Jocie, to put his words into her ears over top of the Martin boy's words. "Go on."

"She said nobody could live with a man who didn't even care who fathered his children. The first time she said that, I thought maybe she was talking about me, and I started crying. That made her even madder, but I couldn't quit crying. I wanted you to be my daddy. Even if I had left with her. I wanted to know you were here in Hollyhill waiting to be my daddy if I ever found my way home."

David had felt divided. He needed to be out looking for Jocie, but this child needed him too. He knelt down and put his arms around her. "I always wanted to come after you, but I didn't think you would come home with me."

"And I probably wouldn't have." Tabitha had wiped her eyes. "But anyway, it drove DeeDee crazy for me to cry, so after she smacked me and I still wouldn't stop, she told me I didn't have to worry. That she might have rushed you into marrying her thinking she could ride your soldier back out of Hollyhill when you went back to the war but that I was yours without the first doubt. An accident, but yours. That she'd been too stupid to know how to keep it from happening then. She said Jocie was an accident too. Something hadn't worked the way it was supposed to. So she decided to use Jocie to get back at you for all those years you'd trapped her in Hollyhill. That it served you right having to raise some other man's child for not letting her free."

"But did you ever think she might be lying?" David had said. "She lied about everything else. Why not that?"

Tabitha had looked at him. "I never knew her to lie to me. Not even when I wished she would."

Maybe that had always been his problem, David thought as he turned down yet another road, that he'd always thought Adrienne was lying when she never had. He'd been the one who had pretended they had a marriage, who had pretended she could be a preacher's wife, who had pretended that things would get better. He thought of Leigh's face as he'd left the *Banner* to search for Jocie. The caring concern there, the truth of her feelings for him. Not the brutal truth Adrienne had always pushed at him, but a kind truth, a loving truth. He had stopped on the way out the door and let her hug him. It had surprised both of them, but it had felt right.

It had never felt right with Adrienne. Heady, exciting, intoxicating, head spinning, and in the later years desperate, but never that comfortable right he'd just felt with Leigh. Maybe she wasn't too young. Maybe the Lord's hand was in this. He didn't know where she was searching with Tabitha. He hadn't crossed paths with her car. He and Wes had met at a crossroads earlier and had split the area.

"She can't have gone far," Wes had said. "She's a sensible girl, David. She'll get her mind around this and come back to talk to you. Course, maybe not before this weather hits. They're calling for bad storms. High winds. Hail. Lightning. The whole bit. I heard it on the radio over at the welding shop." Wes had looked up at the clouds rolling in from the west.

Until then David hadn't even noticed that the sun had gone into hiding. He'd frowned up at the clouds and said, "Maybe you'd better park your motorcycle and ride with me, Wes."

"Nah, we can cover more ground separate. Besides, the storm's a while away yet, and who knows? It might even blow over. Those weather guys miss more'n they hit. If it gets bad, I'll take shelter in a barn or on somebody's front porch."

"Not many houses out this way," David had said. "We're on Bohon Road, aren't we?"

"Beats the heck out of me. I'm from Jupiter, remember. You're the one who grew up around here." Wes had pointed down the road. "What's that road that turns down there?"

"That's Whitson Road."

"I think I've been on that one. When I first came around here, I used to ride around just for the heck of it. There's some kind of creek down in there, isn't there?"

"You go far enough and turn at the right place, you can get to Clay's Creek," David had said. "We should have brought maps and marked off the roads. But why would she be way out here anyway? Maybe she's at home already."

"Could be. Why don't you go find a house and call Zell or Lovella and see? Could be they're hunting us now."

"You don't believe that." David had stated it as fact.

"Nope."

"What do you think, Wes?"

"I think she took off like a bat out of . . . well, you know where, and then when she went a ways she looked around and didn't have the first idea how to get back to town. I think she's lost with no idea how to get home."

"Maybe I should call the sheriff."

"Might not be a bad idea. He could recruit us some help."

The thunder that had been rumbling in the distance had sounded louder. "I hope she doesn't get caught out in this on that bike."

"She's no dummy, David. She knows about lightning storms."

"But she's not afraid of them. Aunt Love's always fussing about her going out on the porch when it's lightning. She might think she can just stand out in it and let it pass. We've got to find her, Wes."

"We will." Wes had started to kick his motorcycle back in gear, then put his foot back on the ground for a minute. "What do you want me to tell her if I find her first?"

"The truth."

"Do I know the truth?" Wes had asked.

"I'm her father."

"I ain't never doubted that. Not for a minute." Wes had revved his motor and swerved away from David's car and made the turn onto Whitson Road toward Clay's Creek.

Now David prayed aloud as he drove the other direction. "Dear Lord, you gave me Jocie. Watch over her now in this storm, both the wind and lightning storm and the storm in her head. Help her to have faith in me as her father as you help me to lean on my faith in you."

The Lord would watch over her, David told himself, as lightning streaked down out of the sky to pop somewhere not that far away. Unbidden, the memory of little Carolyn Winthrop lying in her casket popped into his mind. A beautiful child with long curly brown hair and bright eyes. She'd been playing on an iced-over pond last winter. The ice had broken. They hadn't been able to get her out in time. She'd been ten. He'd preached the funeral. Josephine and Harold Winthrop were fine Christian people. The Lord hadn't reached down and pulled their little Carolyn off the ice. At the funeral David had told the tearful family that bad things just happened, and they did. But that was small comfort when the bad things happened to your child.

Lightning popped in front of him again, and he prayed harder.

ocie moved along the narrow hallway past the Sunday school rooms, where coloring books and crayons lay scattered on child-size tables. She could smell paste. At the end of the hall a door opened into the small sanctuary, where two rows of eight pews lined the middle aisle. She didn't need lights here. Outside, lightning was popping like zillion-watt flashbulbs, making the reds and golds in the stained-glass windows flicker as if on fire.

Thunder shook the building. The wind whistled down the chimney on the side of the church and rattled the windows. Rain banged against the glass. Jocie was grateful for the church walls around her. Even with the ghosts in the pews staring at her.

Actually, it was easier thinking about the storm and the ghosts than about anything else. Still, she had to think about it. And about what she was going to do once the storm moved on. But then the wind pushed harder against the little church until Jocie worried the church wouldn't be strong enough to stand against the storm. Maybe she should pray for the church. Not for herself so much as for the people who expected to come back there on Sunday and find a building to have church in.

She slid through one of the pews to the center aisle and went down to the pulpit. She never knew why people were so timid about walking the aisle. It was just a stretch of floor between pews. Of course, her father had been the preacher waiting when she'd walked down the aisle.

She imagined her father there now in front of the pulpit with his hands outstretched, welcoming her, telling her she belonged when maybe she never had. She couldn't hold on to the picture of her father in her head. He faded back in with all the other ghosts. She sank down on her knees in front of the offering table. She'd never been on her knees in church before. She knelt by her bed at home to pray, but never in church. They always just bowed their heads. Sometimes her father got down on his knees beside the front pew to pray a special prayer with someone. She wished he was there to say a special prayer with her. She never doubted the Lord was listening when her father prayed.

She looked down at the floor while she thought about what to pray. A puddle was forming around her as the water dripped from her drenched clothes. The deacons would be up on the roof looking for leaks next week. Maybe she should leave them a note. But she couldn't worry about that right now. She cleared her throat and started praying. "Dear Lord, I don't know whether you can hear me over the storm, but if you can, thank you for helping me find this church so I could get out of the rain, and forgive me for dripping all over everything."

"Of course he can hear you, child," Aunt Love's voice echoed in her head. *"Nothing can separate you from God. 'Neither death, nor life, nor angels, nor principalities, nor powers, nor things present, nor things to come, nor height, nor depth, nor any other creature, shall be able to separate us from the love of God.'"*

Was a storm a creature? And what was a principality? She'd always aimed to ask her father that and had never remembered to. Jocie put her mind back to her prayer. "Anyway, God, I don't know what to pray except maybe to keep me safe till the storm's over and then for you to show me the way home. Not home to heaven. At least, not just yet. I mean to my house. Maybe you could send Zeb out to find me. I mean, I'm not telling you how to do it. I'm willing to take whatever help you send me." Jocie was quiet as the storm kept going outside and inside her heart too. After a moment, she started talking out loud again but more softly, so she barely heard the words herself over the wind and rain. "And you know what else I want to know, but I'm afraid to pray about that, because you can't lie and maybe I want to be lied to."

Had her father lied to her?

She didn't say amen. She wanted to keep the line open. She smelled something different when she stood up. A flowery scent. But the flowers on the offering table were plastic. She touched them to be sure. No smell there. Her heart crashed inside her as loud as the rain against the windows. Lilacs. Not locust blooms, but lilacs. The sweetest smell on earth. She looked up toward the ceiling as if she expected to see an angel there or flashing words or something. Nothing. Not even the peace that passeth understanding her father and Aunt Love had talked about.

Definitely not that as a baseball-size hailstone crashed through a window in the back of the church and then the one closest to her. Glass shattered all over the floor. Wind roared into the church like a live thing. Jocie started to dive under one of the pews, but something propelled her down the aisle toward the front door. No hand on her shoulder. No nudge in the back, but still she couldn't stop and cower under one of the pews the way she wanted. The hail was attacking the church with fists of ice, and more windows shattered. The noise was fearsome.

She couldn't go outside into that. But the lilac scent enveloped her, and she reached up to turn the dead-bolt lock. Once the lock sprung open, Jocie hesitated before she pulled open the door. "Are you sure about this, Lord?"

"*Trust and obey, for there's no other way.*" The hymn popped into her head, but she wasn't sure who she was obeying. Maybe it was the devil pushing her out the door into the storm. Why would the Lord want her to go out there? But she had prayed, and her father was always preaching about how when you prayed you shouldn't second-guess the Lord's answer.

She pulled open the door, and the hail stopped as if someone had turned off a switch in the sky. Baseball-size chunks of ice littered the front walkway amid leaves and broken branches from the big oak tree beside the walk. Jocie tried to remember exactly what she'd prayed. To be safe. To be home.

She stepped out on the square concrete stoop. The scent of lilacs came at her from every direction as if it had been raining lilac blooms. The downpour changed to a gentle spray of water, and the lightning and thunder was moving away. But it was too still, and the clouds had a funny green tinge that bled out into the air. Suddenly the wind hissed like a huge snake in the sky and began swirling madly overhead.

The lilac scent faded. "Wait, Lord," Jocie said. "I'm scared. Show me what to do next."

She could hardly believe her ears when she heard the motorcycle. It had to be Wes. She ran toward the road waving her arms. The hiss of the wind turned into a roar. She looked up. The clouds had swirled into a funnel. It lifted two trees out of the ground like somebody plucking weeds. Wes tackled her and knocked her to the ground. He shielded her body with his as he yelled into her ear. "Hold on to the dirt for all you're worth, Jo."

She tried to answer him, but it was like four freight trains at once passing over them. The wind was sucking the very breath out of her and lifting Wes away from her. Things popped and cracked as debris pelted them. A churchyard might be as good a place as you could find to pass over to the other side, but she dug her fingers into the ground to stay earthbound and clenched her eyes shut. Her father was there in her mind, praying and singing and preaching and pecking on his old typewriter and laughing. *Oh, please, Lord.* She wanted to laugh with him at least one more time.

"Daddy," she screamed, but who knew if any sound made it out into the bedlam of the wind.

David didn't like the looks of the sky. It had steadily grown more ominous ever since he and Wes had talked. Gertrude Wilson had just told him the radio was putting out storm warnings for the whole county. David had gone up to her house to call Aunt Love and Zella, but her phone was out. She said she lost service nearly every time it thundered.

"You'd best stay here, Brother David, till the storm passes on," Gertrude told him.

Gertrude was in her seventies, widowed these many years, but her daughter couldn't talk her into moving to town. Miss Gertrude said if she had to live in one of those little shoe-box houses where you could practically reach out the window and hold your neighbor's hand, she would just die on the spot. Here she had everything she needed. A cow for milk. A few hens for eggs. A good garden spot. Trees all over with wood enough to keep her warm in the winter. She said now that they'd come out with those fancy chain saws, it wasn't even much of a chore getting in the wood. Not like it had been when she and Wallace had first married.

And she knew the weather from years of watching it. "We're in for a humdinger, or I miss my guess. I was out a while ago to check on my old setting hen, and even that old rooster of mine who's dumber than a bag of rocks was in the henhouse hiding out under the nests. Look around and see for yourself. You won't see the first bird."

She'd walked out on the porch to talk to him. "I haven't been paying much attention to the birds," David said.

"I reckon not with your little girl lost out there somewhere, but it won't do her a bit a good if you get blowed away in a storm. And birds always know."

"I'll be in the car."

"I seen the wind pick up a tractor once and flip it end over end. That storm gets close, you get out of that car and find you a ditch."

"We don't have tornadoes in July," David said.

She gave him a look up through her gray eyebrows. "You're a preacher man, Brother David. Surely you know the Lord can send us whatever kind of weather he wants to whenever he wants to. Take it from me. Them clouds is promising us a twister a-coming."

David couldn't say she was wrong. There was an odd cast to the sky. "You could be right, Miss Gertrude. And I'll keep an eye out if the wind gets worse. Maybe you ought to go to the cellar."

"I will if it turns my way, but if it just passes by, I'll be wanting to see it. It ain't too often you get to see tractors flipping and trees yanked straight up out of the ground."

David could almost see her with a glass of lemonade and a bowl of popcorn in her rocker on the porch waiting for the show to begin. "I'm hoping you're wrong."

"I could be, but them birds hardly ever are." Miss Gertrude patted his arm. "But even if the twister does hit, it might not hit wherever your little girl is. I'll say a prayer for her that the Lord will keep her safe. And you too."

"I appreciate that," David said as he went down the porch steps. By the time he got to the end of Miss Gertrude's driveway, the rain was peppering down. He'd planned to turn left and go on up to Liberty Road, but at the end of the driveway he turned right and went back the way he'd come.

He'd already covered this ground, and Wes had taken the roads off it, but it was as if he could almost see Jocie standing just out of sight motioning him to come that way. Or maybe it was an angel. He quit thinking about where he was driving and just drove. Each turn he made took him closer to the storm.

His wipers slashed back and forth, but they were little use against the buckets of rain hitting his windshield. He slowed the car to a creep. He was going uphill now, but he had no idea where he was. He was lost in a sea of rain and lightning. Was this how the disciples had felt when the storm had overtaken them on the Sea of Galilee? And Jesus had slept through it. He knew the Father was in control. That's what David needed to remember now. That the Lord was in control. David needed to give it over to him, to stop thinking he himself could do a better job of handling things than the Lord.

Still, he didn't stop. He kept pressing on the gas, kept creeping up the road. Hail the size of walnuts peppered the car. David hoped Wes had found shelter. And Jocie. Of course, Jocie. He couldn't bear to think about her out in this alone. He could almost feel the Lord's disapproving look, so he whispered, "Not alone, Lord. Never alone, Lord. Watch over her. Protect her."

39

Suddenly the roar swept past and was gone. Jocie warily opened one eye and saw grass. Still green. Still rooted to the ground. She opened the other eye and looked for Wes. He wasn't on top of her anymore. She felt light. Too light.

She rolled over and sat up. The world was no longer the same. She closed her eyes and slowly opened them again, but nothing was changed. Rather, everything was changed. The church was gone. Nothing was left but an open floor with the pulpit and one of the pews. Another pew sat in the middle of the churchyard. Everything else that had made up the church was gone. Doors, walls, windows, roof gone. Simply gone. Swept away. Except the big oak that lay twisted and torn asunder in the yard.

"Wes," she whispered as if she were afraid to yell for fear the wind would hear her and come back to get what it had forgotten. She stood up. The rain was gentle now, like tears falling out of the sky. "Wes!" She said it louder this time, but there was still no answer.

She tried to pray, but somehow the wind had sucked all the prayers out of her already. Maybe she hadn't made it through the storm. Maybe she was on the other side and that's why everything looked so weird. "Don't be stupid," she told herself. "Churches wouldn't get blown away in heaven."

She still didn't see Wes, but his motorcycle sat on its handlebars across the road against the fence. On the other side of the fence the trees were still tall and straight, untouched by the storm. But where was Wes?

Panic ballooned up inside her, and her heart began pounding. He couldn't have been carried away with the church building. The rain mixed with the tears on her face as she screamed, "Wes!"

She heard a groan, and her heart stopped pounding quite so hard. She scrambled over the fallen tree branches until she saw a boot among the leaves. For a moment she was almost afraid to look, but then there was another groan. Wes had to be alive to groan.

She picked her way through the branches that covered him until she could see his face streaked with bright red blood from a gash on his head. He looked way too still, way too white. She tore a piece off her shirt to press against the wound on his head. "Don't you dare die," she told him. "You can go back to Jupiter, but you can't die."

His eyes flickered open. He tried to smile. "I think I missed my ride to Jupiter."

Jocie put her head down on his chest, hugged him as best she could with the tree limbs in the way, and sobbed.

"Stop all that caterwauling, Jo, and get this here tree off me. What in the world happened, anyhow?"

Jocie sat up and wiped the tears off her cheeks. "It must have been a tornado. The church building is gone. Just gone."

Wes turned his head and tried to see. "I can't see diddly squat for this tree in my face, but I reckon as how that proves what I've been telling you all these years. That if I ever did show up at a church, it would just fall down from the shock."

"This one didn't fall down. I'd say it fell up."

Wes grimaced. "Up first, but no doubt down somewhere."

Jocie looked around. "Nowhere I can see. Maybe on Jupiter."

"I guess that could be. Old Mr. Jupiter might have decided he could use a church building up there." Wes tried to lift his head again, but the tree branches were in the way. "If he was the one doing it, I wish he hadn't dropped this tree on me. You think you can get me out of here?"

Jocie pulled some of the branches back from his arms and chest. She had him pretty much in the clear except for the part of the tree that had trapped his right leg, but that limb was nearly as big around as she was. She couldn't budge it.

"Maybe you could wedge another branch under it and use that to lift it enough that I could wiggle free," Wes said.

Jocie found a strong-looking branch, jammed the end under the limb, and leaned her weight on it. Nothing happened. "I don't think I can move it," she said.

"It might have given a little. Hold it there while I try to move my leg." Wes mashed his lips together and tried to pull his leg free. His face went ghost white as fresh, red blood soaked his jeans.

"Stop, Wes!" Jocie screamed. "You're making it bleed." She let go of the branch and knelt down beside him. She didn't know what to do. She'd never seen so much blood.

Wes pushed up on his elbows a few inches to look. "Does appear to be bleeding some. Funny it ain't hurting all that much." He dropped back to the ground. Jocie thought he'd passed out, but after a moment he said, "Well, I guess old Zell will be surprised. She always figured I'd get banged up on my bike, but who'd have thunk a tree would do me in instead."

"Don't talk like that, Wes. We'll get you out."

He looked straight at her. "And then what? It's a long way to a doctor's office. Heck, it's a long way to a house if any houses are left standing around here. And for sure I ain't walking nowhere anytime soon."

"I can go get help."

"That you can, Jo. Might be a good idea, in fact." Wes shut his eyes. "You just go on down the road and find somebody. I'll lay right here and wait on you."

She didn't like the way he'd agreed with her so easily without arguing the best way to do it or anything. She banged him on the chest. "I'm not letting you just shut your eyes and give up. You have to fight."

He opened one eye and peeked up at her. "Fight what? I think I'm already down for the count."

"Nobody's counting." Jocie was crying again. "You can't die. Not now. It would be all my fault, and I couldn't stand it."

"The tornado wasn't your fault, Jo."

"Maybe not, but you wouldn't have even been out here if you hadn't been looking for me. I shouldn't have run away."

He opened the other eye. "Why did you run away? It ain't like you not to talk to somebody."

"I did talk to somebody. Tabitha. She knew. And Zella knew. Did you know too?"

"Know what?"

"You know what," Jocie said. "That Daddy isn't my father."

"I ain't never known that." Wes lifted a hand up to touch Jocie's face. "Your daddy has always been your daddy."

"But is he my *father*? I mean like in the Bible. Adam begat Seth, and Seth begat Enos. You know what I mean."

"I ain't never exactly lied to you, Jo. Told you some interesting stories but never exactly lied. At least about anything important. So I can't say for sure about the begatting. But wouldn't you rather have a daddy than just be begatted?"

Jocie almost smiled. "I don't think that's a word."

"We ain't setting a story in type here. Anyway, your daddy's out looking for you. He loves you maybe even more than I do, though I don't know how he could. And there's no way I can claim any kind of kin to you. We're not even from the same planet." Wes smiled at her. "But no matter how much I love you, I'm gonna have to take a little rest. I'm seeing Jupiter circles."

"What are Jupiter circles?"

"I ain't sure, but I'm seeing them." Wes shut his eyes.

Jocie looked at his chest again. It was still rising and falling. She leaned down close to his ear. "I take it back. You can't go back to Jupiter either. The Lord's going to help us." Jocie looked up at the sky that was clearing out and showing blue again. "You are, aren't you, Lord? Please."

She'd barely gotten the words out when she heard a car coming up the road.

40

David drove through the storm. The trees lining the road-side were bending and shaking, warring with the wind. He thought about stopping, but his foot kept pressing the gas. Besides, if he stopped, it might be under the very tree that lost the battle with the wind. Of course, he could get out of the car and burrow into the ditch beside the road the way Miss Gertrude had advised. It would probably be the sensible thing to do, what with the funny greenish cast to the air and the menacing black clouds he could see through the frantically dancing treetops. But tornadoes came in the spring, not midsummer. He kept telling himself that. At least the hail had stopped and the rain was letting up.

He was almost to the top of the hill when he came around a curve into the storm's battlefield. The wind had definitely won. Trees lay like matchsticks tossed out for a game of pick up sticks, but the roadway was amazingly clear except for a church pew right in the middle of it. David blinked to be sure he wasn't seeing things. But the wooden bench was there. Where in the world had it come from?

The pew screeched on the blacktop as David scooted it out of the way. He had it off the road before he thought he should have taken a picture of it for the *Banner*. That was the kind of picture that moved papers. Not that he was worried about moving papers right now. He had to find Jocie.

He was almost back to the car when he spotted the wheel. It was crumpled and bent with spokes shooting out in every direction, but there was no doubt it was a bicycle wheel. David picked it up. He wanted it to be old and rusty, but the chrome was shiny and speckled with bright blue paint. The same bright blue Jocie had used to spruce up her bike in the spring.

He didn't let himself think. He just looked toward the sky and said, "Dear God." He stayed still a moment waiting for some kind of sign. A finger pointing the way or a cry for help perhaps. He would have been thankful for just a feeling that he should go this direction or that to look for Jocie. But rain kept hitting his face, and all he saw was a spot of blue pushing back the gray clouds up over his head.

He didn't see any other pieces of her bike. She wouldn't have been on the bike. She would have found shelter. He just needed to find that shelter. He gently lay the mangled bike wheel in the backseat and drove on up the road. Whatever shelter she had found would be along the road. She wouldn't have tried to go across the fields on her bike. And Wes had gone this way. She could be with him. David's heart suddenly felt lighter. He pictured her on the back of Wes's motorcycle way ahead of the storm, perhaps back to town by now. "Let it be so, Lord," he whispered as he nosed his car around the branches in the road.

Another curve and he was at the top of the hill where Clay's Creek Baptist Church had stood for nearly a century, but it was there no longer. The church building was gone. Wiped clean off its foundation. All that the wind had left behind was the pulpit and a couple more pews, one sitting amid the broken branches of what was left of the massive oak tree that had surely been there when the church was built.

David's heart sank. Wes hadn't found her in time to escape the storm. His motorcycle was standing on its handlebars against the fence across from what was left of the church. There was no sign of Wes. Or Jocie. God help them if they'd taken shelter inside the church.

He was getting out of his car when a head popped up out of the oak leaves.

"Daddy!"

He could hardly believe his eyes as Jocie climbed out of the branches and ran toward him. He grabbed and held her so tightly that he knew she couldn't breathe, but she didn't seem to mind as she held on to him just as tightly. He loosened his hold just a little, and she started talking.

"Daddy, I can't believe it's you. Everything's so crazy. I was in the church and I smelled lilacs." She peeked up at him. "Just like your locust blooms. I couldn't believe it, but then the Lord pushed me right out of the church into the middle of the storm and I didn't know whether he was helping me or letting me know it was my time. Then Wes came out of nowhere, sort of like you did just now, and knocked me down to the ground, and then everything blew away. I mean really away and I thought I might blow away too, but then I didn't. But Wes was gone and I couldn't find him. And then I did, but he's hurt and I didn't know what to do. So I asked the Lord for help. And here you are."

"Are you okay, Jocie?" He let go of her enough to look at her face. Blood was smeared across her cheek. "You're bleeding."

She swiped at her cheek and looked at her hand. "Not me, or at least I don't think so. It's Wes. The tree fell on him, and I can't get him out." She pulled away from David and tugged on his hand. "He's hurt bad." She stopped and looked back at him. "You won't let him die, will you, Daddy?"

"Not if I can help it, Jocie." He was already praying nonstop as he climbed across the branches, following Jocie. He prayed harder when he saw Wes. The man had a nasty gash on his head, and his eyes were closed. He was so white that David was afraid it might already be too late for prayers for him this side of eternity.

Jocie scrambled down beside Wes. "Daddy's here, Wes. You're going to be all right. The Lord sent us help just the way I told you he would."

David pushed through the branches till he was crouched on the other side of Wes. "Can you hear me, Wes?"

Wes opened one of his eyes and peered at David. "Of course I can hear you. A tree fell on me. I didn't go deaf."

"How bad is it?" David asked. "Can you feel your toes?"

"If I still have toes, I don't know it," Wes said. "But that might be good. I might not be wanting to feel my toes right now. Don't hurt much at all, to be truthful. My head smarts a mite but not my leg. Course, if you move that tree, I expect it will. And could sprout some real bleeders too."

"Well, we can't leave you under there," David said before he sent Jocie to the car for some of the string they used to tie up the bundles of papers. "I'll put a tourniquet on it till we see what's going to happen. You were right out in the middle of this one, weren't you? Get any pictures?"

"Sorry, boss. There wasn't time. I came up the hill just as them clouds started twisting together and came right at us. And there was Jo right out in the middle of the churchyard just staring at the funnel. We didn't have time to get inside, which is just as well, I guess. Jo says it took that old church here clean away."

"Not much left," David said.

"You could get some pictures now. It'd be a doggone shame not to take some for the paper. It ain't every day that you're Johnny on the Spot for a tornado. First real news in Holly County for years."

"We're not worrying about pictures for the paper." David broke a stick off one of the branches beside his head.

"Might sell enough extra papers to buy me some crutches and fix my motorcycle. And I ain't budging till you do it."

"You can't budge anyway," David said.

Wes grabbed hold of David's arm. "Let Jo take the pictures while you get me out of here. I don't want the girl to see it."

"She'll have to see it. She'll have to help me get you to the car."

"Let her take the pictures first. Give her something to think about instead of me yelling."

Jocie was back with the string. David wound it together before he worked it under Wes's leg. He glanced up at Jocie. "Go take some pictures. My camera's on the front seat. Finish off the whole roll, but do it quick. We need to move."

"I don't want to take pictures now," Jocie said.

"But you have to, Jo," Wes said. "Me and you lived to tell the story, but ain't nobody gonna believe we were all here and nobody took a picture. They'll think we're making it up for certain. So go on and snap a few, and don't pay me no mind if I let out a few Jupiter whoops back here."

"Take the pictures, Jocie." David looked Jocie in the eye. "Wes wants you to. But first clear out the backseat of the car and bring me a bunch of those old papers in the trunk. I'll have to try to fashion some kind of splint out of them. Oh, and move the car up as close as you can." When she just looked at him, David gave her shoulder a little nudge. "Go on. Do it. I'll yell if I need more help."

Jocie had been driving the car up and down their driveway since she was ten, so she didn't have any problem pulling up into the churchyard once she'd cleared out a path through the branches and pushed the church pew out of the way. She took her father the papers and more string and then grabbed the camera. It had a fresh roll of film.

The sun had come out, and the sky was mostly blue. Somehow that made the devastation look that much worse. She took a couple of shots of Wes stuck under the tree, several different angles of what was left of the church, a picture of the pew in the churchyard, a close-up of a hymnbook amid the rubble open to "When the Roll Is Called Up Yonder." She started to flip the pages to find "Amazing Grace," since she didn't want to think about the roll being called up there right now, but then she left it the way it was. Maybe the Lord had made the wind open it to that page for a reason.

Behind her, Wes let out a yell. Jocie cringed, but she kept shooting and winding. The sooner she got through, the sooner she could go help. And Wes was right. They had to take pictures. She finished up the film with a shot of her father working on Wes, who looked totally lost in one of those Jupiterian circles he'd talked about. His eyes were shut, and he was breathing hard.

When her father looked up at her, sweat was dripping off his nose. "That's enough pictures. Come hold these papers while I tie them in place." He glanced out toward the road. "You'd think somebody would have come out to see what the storm did by now. I'm going to need help getting Wes to the car."

"I'll help," Jocie said.

Wes passed out when her father picked him up to lift him out of the tree branches. Jocie held his mangled leg as straight as she could as they stepped over the limbs toward the car. *Please, Lord, don't let me hurt him,* she prayed every step.

Her father laid Wes gently in the backseat, and Jocie crawled in the other door to hold his head and steady him on the seat. He was still unconscious. "Will he be okay, Dad?"

Her father met her eyes. "I don't know, Jocie. I want him to be, but I don't know. His leg's bad."

Jocie looked down at Wes. "I'm sorry I ran away."

"You should have come to me," her father said. "But we can't talk about this now. We need to get Wes to the hospital."

Jocie looked up again. "But you will tell me the truth?"

"I've always told you the truth, Jocie." He laid his hand on her cheek. "I am your father. I've always been your father, and I will always be your father. You couldn't change that even if you wanted to."

She didn't want to change it. But she still had questions even though she knew she couldn't ask them now. Not with Wes pale and bleeding as she held his head in her lap. Some of them maybe she'd never be able to ask. She looked back at what was left of Clay's Creek Baptist Church as her father headed the car down the road. And she remembered the scent of lilacs.

41

Hollyhill didn't have a hospital. Dr. Markum had been trying for the last few years to get the town behind the idea
of building one, but most of the local folks balked at the
idea of extra taxes. The ones who hadn't had heart attacks and
had to actually make the trip with death knocking on the door
said it wasn't all that far to the emergency room over in Grundy,
where they could patch you up or ship you on to one of the big
hospitals in Lexington.

Dr. Markum took one look at Wes and said Lexington was
where he had to go if he was going to have any hope of ever walking again. Jocie's father had driven straight to the doctor's house,
since it was past regular office hours. Dr. Markum had carried his
doctor's bag out to the car while his wife called Gordon Hazelton,
who had an old hearse the town used for an ambulance.

"No need moving him twice. We'll just leave him where he is
till Gordon gets here," Dr. Markum said as he filled a hypodermic
needle. "This might ease the pain a little."

Jocie held Wes tighter as the doctor shoved in the needle. Wes
never opened his eyes. He hadn't opened his eyes all the way
through the country to the doctor's house. But he'd kept breathing
and didn't seem totally unconscious, just in one of his Jupiterian
circles, floating along in another dimension.

The doctor looked at his watch when Gordon Hazelton came
speeding up the street and said he'd made it in six and a half

minutes. "Fastest time ever," he said, but it had seemed like an hour to Jocie.

The three men lifted Wes as gently as possible out of the car and laid him on the stretcher. Jocie scrambled out of the car. "I'm going with him," Jocie said as they lifted the stretcher into the back of the hearse.

"No, no, child." Dr. Markum caught hold of her shoulder before she could climb in after Wes. "You go on inside and let Mrs. Markum check you out."

"I don't need checking out. I'm going with Wes." Jocie looked at her father. Not for permission, but for confirmation.

Dr. Markum looked over the top of her head at her father. "That wouldn't be wise, David. Who knows what might happen on the way to the hospital? The child would be in the way."

Jocie didn't wait for her father to answer. "I won't get in the way. Wes needs me."

"Dr. Markum will take care of Wes, Jocie," her father said. "We'll follow in the car."

"You can follow in the car. I'm riding with Wes." Jocie lifted her chin and stared not at her father but at the doctor.

Dr. Markum leaned down and lowered his voice almost to a whisper. "Jocie, Wes is gravely injured. There's a chance he might not survive the trip to Lexington."

Jocie didn't waver. "Even more reason I have to go. I'm his family."

Dr. Markum pressed his lips together and stood up.

"Let her go, doctor," her father said. "She's right. Wes would want her with him."

"It's against my better judgment, David."

Jocie didn't wait to hear any more. She climbed up into the hearse beside Wes. "I'm right here, Wes. They're going to take you to Lexington, where they'll fix you up good as new. Well, maybe not that good, but good enough to crank out a few more banner issues of the *Banner*."

Wes's eyelids twitched as if he were trying to open his eyes but didn't quite have the strength. He lifted his hand a few inches, and Jocie grabbed it and held on. He mumbled something, but even though Jocie leaned down close to listen, she couldn't make out exactly what he was saying. Something about hearses and motorcycles and spaceships.

Gordon Hazelton put the flashing light out on the roof of the hearse and fired up the sirens he'd installed for his ambulance runs. Jocie tried to keep her balance beside the stretcher as the hearse barreled around curves and between cars. Dr. Markum waited till they were on a straight stretch of road before he checked Wes again.

"You're doing good, Wes. Just keep hanging in there," the doctor said. Before he sat back down on the bench against the wall, he told Jocie. "Since you're here, it might help if you talk to him."

"You think he can hear me?"

"I'd be surprised if he couldn't. He's got a pretty good grip on your hand."

So Jocie started talking. Not about anything much. Just about riding in a hearse and what a story that was going to make for the *Banner*. She told him he'd have to help her write the story about the tornado and how she was afraid her hands had been shaking when she'd taken the pictures so none of them would turn out. And how she wondered what had happened to her bicycle but that she guessed she shouldn't be worried about that with how the Clay's Creek people lost their whole church except for the pulpit and a pew here and there. They didn't even have a shade tree to stand under and talk anymore.

She rattled on and on about anything and everything while under her words she kept a prayer going in her head. *Please, Lord, let Wes be okay.* She didn't let herself think about why he'd been in the path of the storm. She didn't let herself think about what Ronnie Martin had said. There would be time enough for that after Wes stopped bleeding and had his leg in a cast.

Jocie slid her eyes down to the bottom of the stretcher. His leg was covered up, but that didn't keep the memory of what it had looked like out of her mind. She started talking a little faster about the latest confrontation between Zeb and Jezzie. And all the way to the hospital, she wished she had never crossed the street to listen to old Sallie sing. She wished she had never seen Ronnie Martin. She wished Tabitha hadn't been at the newspaper office. She wished Tabitha had never asked her if she wanted the truth.

She'd always wanted to know the truth, or thought she had. She could accept the truth that her mother had deserted her with never a look back. She could accept the truth that she might never lay eyes on her mother again. But she couldn't accept that her very name might be a lie. She couldn't accept that Wes might die and that if he did, it would be because she had tried to run away from the truth.

She wanted to pray about it. Something more than just *Let Wes live*. She wanted to go back in time and make the wind turn a different way. Maybe go back even farther in time and make her mother never meet up with Ronnie Martin's aunt's husband.

Almost as if Wes knew what she was thinking behind her words, his fingers tightened around her hand as though afraid she might wish her very existence away.

A church song popped into her head. "Just As I Am." She had to have sung that song a million times. That's the song the church had been singing at Fern Creek when she'd walked down the aisle to join church and say she believed in Jesus. She had been seven years old. She'd wanted to go forward the summer before when she was six, but her father had said she needed to wait till she was older so that she'd know she was responding to the Spirit and not just to him.

She hadn't waited for her father's permission when she was seven. She'd just shot down the aisle at the first notes of the song, "Just as I am, without one plea." Her father had shaken his head at her, but she hadn't paid any attention. She hadn't been able to pay any attention with the way the Lord was pushing her. Sort of like he'd pushed her out the door before the tornado carried the church building away.

They had to peel Wes's fingers off Jocie's hand when they got to the hospital. Men in white came running out of the emergency room door to whisk Wes out of the hearse and inside. Dr. Markum's wife had called ahead, and they had an operating room ready. Jocie tried to keep up with the stretcher, but they pushed her aside when they reached two large metal swinging doors. "Sorry, kid. You can't go in here," one of the men said. "Don't worry. We'll take good care of your granddaddy."

The doors closed behind them, and the hospital swallowed Wes and the men pushing his stretcher.

She was still staring at the cold iron-gray doors when her father found her a few moments later. "Come on, Jocie." He put his arm around her shoulders, but he didn't try to make her turn away from the doors. "We can't wait here."

Jocie kept her eyes on the doors. "Tell me he'll tell me another Jupiter story."

"We'll pray that the Lord will let that happen," her father said.

"I have been praying, but how do I know God's listening?" Jocie said.

"God's always listening, and he answers. You shouldn't have any doubts about that after this summer with your dog showing up and Tabitha coming home."

"The sister prayer and the dog prayer." Jocie let her father turn her away from the swinging doors toward the waiting area. "But maybe I've had my quota of answered prayers already this summer."

"I don't think God works on the quota system," her father said with a smile.

"But he doesn't always answer the way we want either," Jocie said.

"That's true enough, but we've done all we can. Now we just have to leave it in the doctors' hands and trust in the Lord and wait."

The people in the waiting room looked up when they came in, then looked back down at their magazines or went back to their conversations. One large family had taken over the back side of the waiting room. Across from them, a man was scooted down in his chair, his head back, sleeping. Jocie and her father sat down beside a boy who had an ice bag on his arm. Next to him, his mother kept stroking his hair as she started telling Jocie's dad all about how the boy had fallen out of his top bunk. Jocie didn't listen. She couldn't think about anything but Wes.

Dr. Markum and Gordon Hazelton came in the waiting room, and it was odd seeing familiar faces in this strange place. Jocie's father stood up to talk to them.

Dr. Markum said, "I told them you'd check Wes in at the office, that you were the nearest thing to family he had as far as I knew. They asked about hospital or accident insurance."

"I don't know whether he has any or not," her father said. "I haven't given the first thought to money."

"Well, don't worry about it now," Gordon Hazelton said. "We'll have a benefit for him if we have to. Hollyhill folks take care of their own."

After Dr. Markum and Gordon Hazelton left and her father filled out all the forms to officially admit Wes to the hospital, a nurse directed them to the surgical waiting room, a smaller group of chairs at the end of a long hallway on the third floor of the hospital. No one else was there.

"It's late. They probably only do emergency surgeries this time of the day," her father said.

"Will Aunt Love and Tabitha be worried about us?" Jocie asked.

"Mrs. Markum was going to call and tell them about Wes and where we were."

"Oh." The couch let out a groaning sigh as she sat down and pushed the air out of the vinyl-covered cushions. "I hate noisy seats."

Her father sat down beside her, and the seat groaned again. "And we thought rickety wooden pews were bad."

Jocie couldn't remember ever being uncomfortable with her father. Even when she'd done something she shouldn't have and knew he was going to fuss at her, she had never tried to hide from him. She'd trusted his love to be there for her no matter what she did. He was her father.

But now Ronnie Martin and Tabitha and Zella said he wasn't, and she didn't know what to say or do. She stared down at her dirty, blood-smeared hands. Her jeans were torn and streaked with blood stains as well. Who knew what her face looked like. No wonder everybody kept looking at her as if she'd gotten lost on the way to the emergency room.

"Maybe I should go wash up a little before the nurses start spraying me with something antiseptic," Jocie said.

"There's a restroom about halfway down the hall," her father said. "Or maybe we should get a nurse to check you out."

"No, no. I just need to wash up." Jocie stood up quickly and took off down the hall.

The restroom was barely large enough for the commode and a sink. When she turned sideways to shut the door, she was staring straight into the small mirror on the wall. The face that looked back at her was scary. She quit looking at her eyes and ran her fingers through her hair. A couple of twigs were imbedded in the tangles. She didn't have a comb, so she just picked out the twigs and hooked her hair behind her ears to get it out of her face.

She let the water run over her hands until most of the dirt and blood went down the drain, but not all the blood had been from Wes. She'd banged up her knuckles trying to get the tree limbs off him. And there was a nasty scratch on her face from who knew when. Maybe she needed that antiseptic spray after all.

When she was finished, most of the blood and dirt was gone, but her eyes in the mirror still looked as scary. She stood there a long time, letting the water run over her hands and down the drain while she stared at her face in the mirror. She didn't want to go back out to the couch in the waiting room. She no longer wanted to know the truth. And that scared her most of all.

42

David had to make himself stay where he was instead of running after Jocie as she walked up the hallway to the restroom. She wasn't a baby, but he wanted to hold her hand. No, more than that. He wanted to pick her up and cradle her to him. He wanted to scare away the boogeymen and smooth the bumps out of her path.

He'd not done very well at that over the years. He'd tried, but the heartaches seemed to make a point of seeking her out. And now this.

Would she ever forgive him for not planting the seed in her mother's body that had caused her to be born? He couldn't say would she ever forgive him for not being her father. He was her father. The very thought that anybody would say he wasn't made him want to hit something. Or somebody. But how could he make her believe that? How could he get her to trust him again?

And what if Wes died? That didn't even bear thinking about.

He knew about death. He was a preacher, after all, and part of a preacher's job was shepherding his people through hard times, like seeing a loved one pass over to the other side. It was a pastor's job to comfort, to reassure, to help families accept the truth of death as part of life.

Some deaths were joyous, a time of celebration when the person had lived to a fine age and left a family confident in knowing their loved one was heaven bound. Comforting words came easily then. Still, the family wasn't always able to accept them right away. He himself had warred against the truth of his mother's death for months when he should have been celebrating her life and her move to heaven. Jocie would be even less ready to give up Wes. *Lord, I need a miracle. Again*, he prayed silently as Jocie disappeared into the restroom.

People didn't pray for miracles much anymore. Not really. They might speak prayers asking for healing, but most of them didn't believe it would happen. Not to them or anyone they knew. They could believe it had happened in Bible times, especially when Jesus and the disciples walked on the earth. David had preached once on how people had been healed just by being touched by Peter's shadow in the early days of the church, and the congregation had shaken David's hand on the way out and said it was a good sermon. None of them had told him it was too hard to believe. They believed what the Bible said, but it was quite another thing to believe that their mother, father, sister, brother, or they themselves were going to be miraculously healed of their cancers, crippled limbs, or heart problems.

Had the Bible-times families who had laid their ailing loved ones along the way Peter walked to the temple believed, or had it been a matter of thinking they had nothing to lose by trying? Was faith that the miracle would happen necessary? And if so, how much faith?

In the Bible, Jesus said that with faith the size of a mustard seed a person could tell a mountain to get up and move to another spot and it would. A mustard seed was so small David could hold dozens, even hundreds, of them in his hand. Yet he could not summon up even a fraction of that much faith in his heart that he could move a mountain from here to there.

David wanted to have that kind of faith for Wes, but he didn't really believe Wes's leg would miraculously knit back together while the doctors were getting ready to insert screws and rods to hold the pieces of bone together while it healed. He believed it was possible. He believed God could make the bone whole again. He truly believed anything was possible with God. Yet he didn't believe it would actually happen this hour to this man—that the doctors were even now turning back to the operating table and blinking their eyes in disbelief as Wes flexed his leg and tried to get off the table. He thought about the doctors looking at the X-rays and wondering what could have happened—how the bone in this man's leg could be miraculously whole again. And then David felt foolish even imagining such a thing happening. The best he could honestly pray was that the doctors would be skilled and that Wes would survive the surgery. He had the faith to pray that.

And that Jocie would listen to and believe him. She'd listened to his words in the churchyard, but she'd kept her eyes away from him. She'd been afraid to believe him. And now she was afraid to sit with him, afraid of being alone with him, afraid of what truth he might tell her.

She'd been in the restroom for a long time. Too long. He waited another minute, trying to pray as he watched the second hand on his watch creep around in a circle. The restroom door didn't open. He could feel the space between them growing wider as every second ticked past. He had to jump across the space before it got to be such a chasm that he would have no chance of landing on the other side.

He prayed for the right words to say as he walked down the hall to the restroom and knocked softly on the door. "Jocie, are you okay?" he asked.

It was a few seconds before she answered, "Yes."

"Come on out and we'll talk."

"I'm not sure I want to right now."

"If you don't come out, I'll come in," he told her.

"You can't. One of us would have to stand on the john."

"Then I'll stand on the john," he said as he turned the door handle.

The door bumped into Jocie as her father started to push it open. She almost giggled as she stuck her head out the half-open door. "Dad! It's a girls' room."

"And I want to talk to the girl who's in it." He kept pushing on the door.

"Okay, okay," she said as she stepped back out into the hall. She concentrated on keeping her feet within the square tiles as she walked back toward the waiting area. She should have known she couldn't hide from her father any more than she had been able to run away earlier. And why was she afraid of the truth? He'd already assured her he was her father. Why couldn't she just grab on to that and let the rest of it be swept out of her mind the way the wind had swept away the church building?

The nurse spoke to her father as they passed the nurses' station to let them know the cafeteria would be closing soon. "Your friend might be in surgery for hours. Why don't you go get something to eat? We'll page you down there if we need to."

"I don't think I could eat right now," Jocie said when her father looked at her.

Her father smiled at the nurse. "We'll go down and get something out of the vending machines later."

The nurse frowned a bit. "You should at least get something to drink. Here, wait a minute." She got up and disappeared into a room behind the nursing station. She came back with two paper cups full of a clear soft drink. "If you want coffee, we have that too."

"Thanks, but this is fine." Her father took both the cups and carried them down the hallway. He handed Jocie one of the cups after they settled back on the couch.

Jocie let the fizzy drink bubble against her lips for a second before she downed it all without taking a breath.

336

"You were thirsty." Her father poured half of his soda into her cup before he took a drink.

"I guess so. I hadn't really thought about it since I took a drink out of the creek. I know you say I shouldn't drink creek water." She peeked up at him and then looked back down at her cup. "But it looked clean, and I was really thirsty. But then it started raining and all, and I didn't think about anything but getting out of the storm."

"I'm glad the Lord kept you safe."

"But he didn't keep Wes safe," she said softly. "I wish Wes hadn't come hunting for me."

"He had to come hunting for you. He loves you."

"Yeah, I know, and because of that he got hurt. Dr. Markum said he might even die." Jocie studied the ice in her cup. "It's all my fault."

"Don't give up on Wes yet. We're praying, and the Lord's listening."

Jocie could feel her father's eyes on her, but she kept staring into her cup. She wanted to run back to the restroom just because she couldn't stand this strange feeling between them. That's why she'd run away in the first place. She couldn't bear the truth.

"I don't know what you're thinking, Jocie. You need to talk to me."

The questions she couldn't ask kept swelling up inside her until finally one of them burst out her mouth. "Is it true what Ronnie Martin told me?"

"What did he tell you?"

"That I'm a bastard," Jocie whispered.

Her father set his cup down on the floor, put his hand under her chin, and raised her face up to look at him. "You were born to my wife. You are my daughter legally and in every way that counts."

"But is what he said about his uncle true?"

337

Her father's eyes didn't waver from hers. "It could have been. Your mother was not always faithful to me, but what truly makes a father? A seed spilled out in a moment of passion or years of love and caring? I can't be positive that my seed formed you, but I know without any doubt that you are my daughter. I've loved you since I first knew you existed. I fought for you even before you were born, and after you were born, I fed you. I changed your diapers. I walked the floor with you when you cried. I wrapped my heart around you and made you mine. You are the daughter of my heart. No one can ever take you out of my heart."

Jocie had always believed him. There was no reason not to believe him now. "Wes told me that being your daughter that way was better than just being begatted."

"Begatted?" Her father smiled.

"That's not a word, is it? I told Wes it wasn't."

"I think it might be begotten."

"That doesn't sound much better. I was begatted. I was begotten," Jocie said.

"It sounds okay in John 3:16."

"Well, yeah, it fits there, doesn't it? 'For God so loved the world, that he gave his only *begotten* Son.' 'Only begatted son' just wouldn't work, would it?"

"You're one of a kind, Jocie. And however you were begotten, you are truly my daughter and I am truly your father. Are we straight on that?"

Jocie smiled at him and let herself be enfolded in his love. "Thank you for being my father. I guess the Lord was answering my prayers before I could even pray them, because if I'd ever said a daddy prayer, you would have been the best answer I could have ever gotten."

Tears filled her father's eyes, and he pulled her close. Up the hall, the elevator door opened. Jocie peeked over her father's arm to see Leigh coming down the hall toward them. "It's Leigh," she said.

"I see her," her father answered without turning her loose.

"I'll bet she has food."

"I wouldn't be surprised."

"I can start saying a stepmother prayer if you want me to," Jocie whispered.

"I've never been one to tell you what to pray. That's between you and the Lord."

"Maybe I should wait till we get Wes prayed better, but she is nice."

"Yes, she is."

43

Leigh stopped a few feet away from them. "Maybe I should come back later," she said.

Jocie pulled loose from her father and grabbed Leigh's hand. "No, no. This isn't a private hug. Of course, you might not want to hug us. We look pretty bad."

Leigh put her arms around Jocie. "I've never seen anybody who looked better to me. When that storm came up, we were all scared to death for you. Thank goodness you're all right." She looked at Jocie's father. "How's Wes?"

"We don't know. He's still in surgery," her father said.

"I'll have to go down and tell Zella."

"Zella's here?" her father asked.

"She's downstairs in the front lobby. She was beside herself with worry after Dr. Markum's wife called and said how bad Wes was hurt. But she wouldn't come up. Says elevators give her the willies and she'll just wait for news down there. I told her there would be steps somewhere, but to be honest, I think the whole hospital is giving her the willies."

"I can't believe she's worried about Wes," Jocie said.

"Zella's not heartless," Leigh said. "She and Wes have been working together for years. Of course she's worried about him. She called and got her prayer chain going before we left Hollyhill."

"He must owe her money or something," Jocie said.

"That's enough, Jocie," her father said.

"Sorry." Jocie ducked her head.

Leigh laughed. "Now that you mention it, she did say some-thing about a book she'd loaned him." She held out the sack she was carrying. "I hope you like peanut butter sandwiches. That's all I had that was fast."

"Peanut butter's good." Jocie sat the sack on the floor. "But first, you wouldn't happen to have a comb I could use, would you?"

Leigh rummaged in her purse. "You do look in need of one, but I guess you're lucky to have hair to comb after being in the middle of a tornado. Sandy Markum said that church out there—she said the name but I forget—that it was completely blown away."

Jocie's father stood up. "We'll need something to drink with our sandwiches. I'll go hunt up the vending machines downstairs and talk to Zella. I won't be gone long." He hesitated and looked at Jocie. "Will you be okay?"

Jocie met his eyes. "I won't run away again, Dad. Ever. I promise."

Leigh waited until the elevator door closed behind Jocie's father before she asked, "Everything okay between you two now?"

"He is my father," Jocie said.

"I know. I never doubted that."

"I shouldn't have either."

"No, you shouldn't have." Leigh handed Jocie the comb she'd finally pulled out of her purse.

"It doesn't matter what Ronnie Martin said." Jocie tugged the comb through her hair.

"No, it doesn't. Here, let me help." Leigh took the comb and carefully started working some of the tangles out of Jocie's hair.

Jocie felt funny letting Leigh comb her hair, but at the same time it felt good to just let somebody else handle the tangles. She couldn't remember the last time anybody but Jeanne at the beauty shop had combed her hair. At least not since she was a little girl and her father had made her stand still to comb her hair before church.

As if she'd been zapped back into time, she remembered one of those mornings. She didn't know whether it was before or after her mother left. It didn't really matter. Her father had always been the one who had helped her get ready for church.

"Stand still and let me get this rat's nest out of your hair, Jocie, so you'll look your best for God," he'd told her.

"But doesn't God see me all the time?" she had asked. "So he sees me when I just get up and my hair's all mussy. He loves me then too, doesn't he?"

"Of course he does. He'd love you if you didn't have any hair at all or if you had more hair than Rapunzel. And so do I. We love the whole package, every inch."

"Does God really know how many hairs I have? I tried to count just what was in my bangs once, but I kept losing count."

"The Bible says every hair on every head is numbered."

"On Wes's head too?"

"On his head too."

"I don't think Wes ever combs his hair."

"He doesn't spend much time in front of the mirror."

"But God loves him anyway, doesn't he? Just like he loves me?" Jocie had always tried to find ways to be sure that Wes was under God's love, since he didn't go to church or do the things her father was always saying a Christian should do.

"God loves everybody. God will never fail you, nor will he fail Wes. Just remember that, Jocie. God will never fail you or forsake you."

Jocie remembered the scent of lilacs again. God hadn't forsaken her. He'd pushed her out of the church building. He'd sent Wes to protect her from the tornado. He'd brought her father to help her and Wes. He'd kept Wes alive to get to the hospital. How could she doubt?

Leigh was still tugging on the tangles in the back of her hair, but so gently that Jocie hardly felt it. "I don't think I'll be able to stand it if Wes isn't okay," Jocie said after a moment.

"The Lord will help you stand whatever you have to stand," Leigh said.

"You sound like a preacher's wife already."

"Oh, that might not be good. Who'd want to kiss a preacher's wife?"

"A preacher?"

Leigh laughed. "I suppose that's true. And Wes will make it through. Zella's prayer chain will connect with another prayer chain and another until the whole town of Hollyhill will be praying for him. Along with all of us here, of course. I believe the Lord answers prayers, don't you?"

"I do, but what if he says no? Daddy says that's an answer too."

Leigh stopped combing Jocie's hair and tipped her face around until she was looking straight into her eyes. "If your Aunt Love were here, she could tell you the exact words and where in the Bible it is, but somewhere in the Bible, I think maybe in the Sermon on the Mount, Jesus asks what father would give his son a stone when he asks for bread, and if earthly fathers are that way, how much more loving is our heavenly Father who gives us the good things we ask for? Wes getting better is a good thing. I have faith the Lord won't say no."

And he didn't. Sometime after midnight, a doctor finally appeared in front of them and said Wes had made it through the surgery. Before the sun came up, Jocie and her father were standing by his bed. His face was pale and sunken looking, and some nurse must have combed his hair, which made him look even more unlike himself. Tubes were running medicine through IVs into his arm, and his leg was encased in a wire cage instead of a cast, with rods sticking through the bandages.

"Are you sure that's Wes?" Jocie whispered to her father.

One eye popped open and then the other as Wes looked straight at her. "And who were you expecting? Mr. Jupiter himself?"

343

"It's just that I've never seen you with your hair combed." Jocie grinned.

"I tell you. You let them put you out and they're liable to do anything to you. Can you fix it for me?"

Jocie tousled his hair. "There, that's more like it."

"Now fix my leg."

"I would if I could, Wes." Jocie's eyes filled with tears. "I'm sorry you got hurt. It's my fault."

"Ain't nobody's fault, Jo. Not unless you've been praying some kind of tornado prayer all summer."

"No, but I've been praying big time ever since the tornado hit. Everybody in Hollyhill has been praying."

"For me? You've got to be kidding."

"No. Zella started her prayer chain."

"Zella? Pinch me. I must be hallucinating," Wes said.

"No, it's true," Jocie said. "Isn't it, Dad?"

Jocie's father nodded. "Zella's camped out down in the lobby waiting to hear you're okay."

"That's scary," Wes said. "I can't believe she drove down here all by herself."

"No, she came with Leigh," Jocie said. "Leigh's out in the hall waiting on us. She said she'd come in to see you later."

"Ah, that explains it. What that woman won't do to do some matchmaking," Wes said. His eyes were drooping closed. "I don't know what they gave me, but I can't keep awake."

"The nurses said we couldn't stay but a minute, that you needed to rest," Jocie's father said. He started toward the door, but Jocie hung back.

"We'll be back in the morning as soon as the nurses let us," Jocie said. "I want to get your firsthand account of the storm before I write the story for the *Banner* next week."

"You have your own firsthand account," Wes said.

"Yeah, but I want the whole story. Not just a part of it," Jocie said.

Wes pushed his eyes open again and reached for Jocie's hand. "And do you have the whole story? From your dad?"

"It's not begatted. It's begotten."

"Well, I'm glad we got that straight," Wes said.

"And I got everything else straight too. He's my daddy, and you're my granddaddy."

"Granddaddy? Who said I was old enough to be a grand-daddy?"

"Me," Jocie said. "And you're mine, and I'm glad you missed your spaceship back to Jupiter. You know, I don't think it's ever coming back."

"You could be right, Jo. You could be right. Now let a poor old stranded Jupiterian get some Earth sleep."

Her father was waiting at the door to put his arm around her. "Let's go get some breakfast."

"That sounds great." She walked in the circle of his love toward where Leigh was waiting for them at the elevator. "Did I tell you about the lilacs, Dad? You're not going to believe about the lilacs."

Ann H. Gabhart and her husband live on a farm just over the hill from where she was born, in central Kentucky. Ann is the author of over a dozen novels for adults and young adults. She's active in her country church, and her husband sings bass in a southern gospel quartet.